The Bellagio Caper

The Bellagio Caper

Another police procedural thriller starring
Chief Investigator
Edward Augustus Fox
Now with the
Nevada State Gaming Control Board

Set in Las Vegas, Nevada

George H. Stollwerck

Copyright © 2008 by George H. Stollwerck.

First American Edition
Library of Congress Control Number: 2008905825
ISBN: Hardcover 978-1-4363-5023-5
Softcover 978-1-4363-5022-8

All rights reserved. Published in the United States by Xlibris, an imprint of Random House, Inc., New York. No part of this publication may be reproduced, stored in a retrieval system, or transmitted, in any form or by any means, electronic, mechanical, photocopying, recording, or otherwise, without the prior written permission of the author.

This is a work of fiction. While it is fact-based and contains references to historical events, organizations, public agencies, personages, organizations and locales, they have been included solely to lend historical context to the fiction.

Events, conversations, media product and sequence may have been created and/or modified to make the narrative flow of enhanced interest to the reader.

Characters in this book have no existence outside the imagination of the author, and have no relationship whatsoever to anyone bearing the same name, names, or titles. The characterizations were not inspired by any individual known to or by the author. The overall scenario has been interwoven with the documented history of Clark County, Nevada.

To order additional copies of this book, contact:
Xlibris Corporation
1-888-795-4274
www.Xlibris.com
Orders@Xlibris.com

SUGGESTED LIBRARY CROSS REFERENCING

[1. August 8, 2008 Olympic Summer Games—Fiction: 2. The People's Republic of China—Fiction: 3. History of Las Vegas—Fiction: 4. Las Vegas Casinos—Fiction: 5. Television Series Episode Taping—Fiction: 6. Nevada State Gaming Control Board—Fiction: 7. Clark County Detention Center—Fiction: 7. Las Vegas Metro Police—Fiction: 8. United States Marine Corps—Fiction: 9. Military weaponry—Fiction: 10. Forensic Science—Fiction: 11. CBS/CSI-Crime Scene Investigation—Fiction: 12. Federal Bureau of Investigation—Fiction: 13. Nellis Air Force Base—Fiction: 14. Mystery and Detective stories—Fiction.] Title.

PUBLISHED WORKS BY THE AUTHOR

FICTION NOVELS

The Bellagio Caper—2008
Angry Dragon—2007
Project 119—2006
Hongse Spider—2005
The Battlefields of Pax Americana!—2004
Terrorism: America's Incurable Disease!—2003
The Vanishing Hero!—2002
Nine lives Minus One!—2001

TRAVELOGUES OF ASIA—PUBLISHED BY THE PRINT MEDIA

Hong Kong
China
Macau
Singapore
Malaysia
Bangkok
Seoul, South Korea

IN APPRECIATION

This book couldn't have been written without the information and guidance provided by Nevada State Gaming Control Board's Special Agent-Investigations-Agency Liaison, Kathleen A. Faust. For being willing to take time away from her heavy case-load to assist me in keeping my facts straight, she has my undying gratitude.

I also would like to express my appreciation to those in the Las Vegas Metro Police department, the Clark Country Detention Center, and the Federal Bureau of Investigation who have provided the transparency into their respective operations, which has been critical in the researching for this book.

There are others that deserve a mention as their input and information provided has been critical to maintaining the level of factualism I strive for in my work.

Clark County Sheriff and Chief of Police
Douglas C. Gillespie

City of Las Vegas Mayor
Oscar Goodman

Former FBI Profiler, and now, Author
John Douglass

Director Of Surveillance—Rivera Hotel and Casino
Paul Halverson

Former Casino Manager, and now, Author
Bill Fieldman

Consultants

Business Advisor
Mrs. Eleanor Poppe

Computer Technology
Jeff McCormick, IT Consultant
Heather McCormick, Attorney-At-Law

Medical Consultant
Thomas J. Powers, M.D.

Optical Systems
Stuart B. Adams, O.D.

THOUGHTS

"I guess everything reminds me of something."

Ernest Hemingway, in 1952, after an argument with this son, Gregory, age 20.

"No matter how, a man alone ain't got no fucking chance."

From the character Harry Morgan, written by Ernest Hemingway, *To Have and Have Not,* in 1930, and again published in Cosmopolitan Magazine in 1934.

"How dreadful knowledge of the truth can be when there's no help in the truth."

Sophocles

"I not only use all the brains I have, but all the brains I can borrow."

Woodrow Wilson
Twenty-eighth President

"The flawed should be valued for their flaws because flaws are the conduits of humanity."

Unknown Author

CAST OF CHARCTERS

City of Las Vegas, State of Nevada:
  The Honorable Oscar Goodman: Mayor

Las Vegas Metro Police:
  Douglas C. Gillespie: Sheriff
  Izzy Petosa: Detective
  Barbara Houser: Patrolperson
  Billy Houser: Probationary Patrolperson
  Bethany Jones: Corporal, Sr. Patrolperson and Training Officer
  Linda La'Sard: Probationary Patrolperson
  Robert Shaw: Third-year Patrolperson
  Percy E. Smith III: Sr. Patrolperson and Training Officer

Nevada State Gaming Control Board:
  Maggie DuPont: Sr. Investigator
  Edward Augustus Fox: Chief Investigator
  Billy Frisbee: Special agent

Federal Bureau of Investigation-Las Vegas Field Office:
  Steffy Gardner: Supervising Special Agent, Task force SAC
  Freddie 'Fireball' Jefferson: HRT Commander, Team Two
  Thaddeus Holms: Probationary Special Agent

U.S. Marines-2/18 Military Police Battalion, Fallujah, Iraq
  Jeffrey 'Kick ass' Johnson: Lt. Colonel (Release from Obligation)
  Mary 'Ice Maiden' Levinson: Major (RFO)
  Leigh Copperfeld: Staff Sergeant, Recon (RFO)
  Robert 'Action' Jackson: Staff Sergeant, Recon (RF0)
  Maurice 'Preacher' Jones: Staff Sergeant, Recon (DD)
  David Shapiro: Staff Sergeant, Recon (RFO)
  Abraham Daniel: 2nd Lt, Bad Conduct Discharge (BCD)
  Robert Ho: Staff Sergeant, Dishonorable Discharge, (DD)
  Jose Martinez: Staff Sergeant, (DD)
  David Sturgis: Staff Sergeant, (BCD)

BOOK ONE

IRAQ
2006

ONE

September 9, 2006, 6:00 a.m.
First call to Muslim prayers
Town of Fallujah
An Bar Province, Iraq

A muffled Humvee had dropped him off two miles outside of town on this black, moonless night. It was getting towards dawn as he carefully made his way though the predawn darkness towards his objective.

His imagination began to play tricks with his mind. He halted his stealthy forward movement abruptly when he thought heard voices waffling in from across the sands of the desolate desert. Muted whispers, in Arabic, the voices of the men that he thought he could see crouched behind a small desert knoll, waiting for him, about a hundred-yards further down the nearly-invisible, dung covered, camel trail.

They shouldn't be here. In fact, he shouldn't be here. His common sense tried to convince him that the wispy figures he saw were just figments of his imagination. Maybe yes, maybe no. If they were not the product of his imagination, they might be a few conceivable reasons for their presence, and he didn't like any of them!

Later that morning
The town of Fallujah:

A tall, medium-built, dark-complected young man stood in the shadow of the Mosque next to the square where Muslim prayers were said five times daily. He had an unkempt beard and wore a traditional Arab robe called a *throbe,* topped off with an Arab headdress called a *gutra,* and a pair of thick Bedouin sandals made from cast off *GoodYear* tire treads.

Passersby on their way to morning prayers, those who bothered to give him a glimpse at all, didn't know if the man was Palestinian, Afghan, Bedouin, Saudi, Iranian, Kurd, or Iraqi. But the one thing they did know, and which each of them would have sworn comforted them, was that it was obvious that the man wasn't an accursed American, a hated *crusader.*

The white dome of Fallujah's main Mosque was eclipsed by the magnificence of the four, tall spires that occupied positions at the dome's four corners.

"*Hasten to Prayer! Hasten to Prayer!*" Repeated over and over, broadcast five times daily by the Muezzin.

Several hundred of Fallujah's residents stood waiting in the square with their prayer rugs, obeying the *Asr,* the call to prayer, waiting for the old Imam, the senior Muslim cleric, who, while never late, had in his old age, fine-tuned his habit of cutting his obligation to lead the masses in prayer *very closely.*

Many of the naysayers in the crowd eagerly waited the day he would show up late and the devoted would begin without him, which hopefully would pave the way for a younger, more enthusiastic Imam to take over the prayer duties.

Then the old man finally arrived. Without any explanation for his tardiness he went directly to his prayer position and knelt facing the East, immediately followed by the waiting believers. The prayer session droned on with the voices of the devoted repeating the *salat,* the required intonation of prayers, which is the obligation of every Muslim.

After the ten minutes required to finish their obligation, the old man stood, turned, raised his arms, and croaked, "*Allahu Akber,*" God is Great; followed by "*Salaam Aleikum,*" Peace be unto you. Which signaled to the gathered the end of the first prayer session of the day.

Throughout the ceremony the young man standing alone in the shadow of the Mosque, had never permitted his eyes to leave the old Imam, whose Coalition code name was *Yakhak Dubba,* the Red Locust.

A camouflaged Humvee, now more than ten miles out in the desert, had dropped the bearded man off earlier that morning. He was U.S. Marine Recon Staff Sergeant Leigh Copperfeld and his orders called for him to slip into town, locate, and follow the Imam.

Copperfeld's orders were to establish the location of the cleric's home, a fact that may be needed to support tomorrow's mission.

Red Locust outwardly was just another Muslim cleric, however he had been one of the Ba'ath party's closest advisors to Saddam before the war. Since Saddam's hanging, the old man had been declared a war criminal and was currently being sought by Coalition forces even though he wasn't considered important enough to have his face included in the infamous deck of playing cards.

The decrepit old man had been hiding in Fallujah, keeping his head down, hoping that Coalition forces would forget about their stated intention of bringing him to justice. He was known to have had a hand in the executions of numerous Shiite clerics who had refused to denounce their loyalty to the head Shiite cleric, Mohammad Al-Sadr.

But the wily old man had be unable to control the ego that drove his desire to be seen as a prime mover in what was left of the Ba'ath party, even though it put him at great risk as he was a fugitive.

If the old man had continued in his self-exile and kept his head down in Fallujah, Sergeant Copperfeld, at great personal risk to himself, would not be there now.

However, only the day before, Red Locust had impulsively ordered some of his younger, stupider followers to ambush the small road convoy of the American security contractor, Blackwater, about forty-miles-east of Fallujah. The insurgents had kidnapped six of the contractor's personnel and slaughtered the rest.

Copperfeld's assignment was gather information that would facilitate the early morning snatch of the Old Imam. Then CIA Intelligence personnel would extract the location of the kidnapped contractors from Red Locust using various interrogation techniques largely unknown nor approved by the average American citizen back in the States.

The young Marine sergeant shuddered as he remembered the insurgent interrogations that he had observed over the past year. He admitted to himself that he was sickened by the interrogations. And the Americans who participated in them. Not to mention the CIA's use of *waterboarding* to extract information.

But as he stood in the cool shadows of the Mosque, he acknowledged that orders were orders and he better get on the trail of the Imam, who was walking down a dusty street away from the Mosque. Hopefully the old man was heading back to his home.

Once Sergeant Copperfeld obtained the requested intelligence, and verified its authenticity by checking the mail found in the old man's mailbox, his orders were to send a burst transmission containing the information over his encrypted radio, back to the nearby Coalition's Forward Operating Base.

In case he was killed or captured by the insurgents on his way back into the desert to his pick-up point, the CIA wanted to be certain that the intelligence that Copperfeld had gathered would get through to the decision-makers even if the man, himself, didn't survive the mission.

Once he had done so and received the electronic acknowledgement that the intelligence had been received, he would carefully work his way back out into the desert and picked up at a pre-designated location by the same sand rail that had dropped him off, much earlier that morning.

TWO

September 10, 2006, 4:00 a.m.
The Town of Fallujah
An Bar Province
Iraq

At 4:00 a.m. on a dim, stagnant early morning pre-dawn, an old white French Milk truck looking to be in worse shape than its forty years of existence appeared to justify, having only one working headlight and no taillights at all, rattled as it turned south off State Highway 10 West, onto Ali Avenue, the south end of Fallujah's main thoroughfare. The north end of the avenue ran through the city center, which was situated on the far side of Iraq's Highway 10.

The dome light inside the cab was still working, albeit faintly, but well enough to see two, swarthy, dark-complected men wearing the traditional Arab garb of service personnel.

The driver struggled to guide the old truck that was equipped with manual steering around the street's decades-old potholes. His younger assistant, without the benefit of a seatbelt, bounced and ricocheted about the truck's cab on an old horsehair seat that had seen better days, holding on for dear life.

The assistant was attempting to concentrate on reading street addresses off to the driver, telling him where they were scheduled to deliver their products that morning. The delivery crew had to complete their dairy and bakery deliveries before sunrise, then return to Baghdad for their next assignment.

The truck they were driving had been stolen from a milk and bread delivery firm in Baghdad 90-minutes previously and had traveled some distance west on Iraq's Highway 10 to reach Fallujah City, as the truck normally did every morning, seven-days-a-week. The truck had the dairy's name stenciled on its sides,

The driver and his assistant were not locals or even Iraqis. Certainly not the regular crew who made the forty-mile trip from Baghdad trip to Fallujah, and whose physical appearance, over time, had become visually familiar to the Sunni's at the roadblocks along Highway 10. This morning's replacement crew had been expertly disguised, their skin and hair had been darkened, and they were wearing dark wigs and colored eye contacts, the total affect hopefully would pass for the regular crew from a distance.

As the rattletrap approached the main roadblock it didn't even need to slowdown as it was waved through under the upright red-and-white stripped gate arm by the sleepy guards. Which gave the occupants unfettered access to the City.

At each stop, the assistant carried the dairy products to the porch of the customer, removing any empty bottles from the plastic milk crate, and replaced it with the sweating bottles of goat's milk, plastic containers of goat's cheese, and fresh bread wrapped in newspaper, all of which the house's residents or the neighborhood dogs would eventually retrieve off the porch for a morning meal.

After the thirteenth delivery of the morning, the van headed for the commercial district, to the still-shuttered restaurants and small grocery stores that had survived the American bombings over the past four years.

Between 1979 and 2003, the residents of Fallujah had been employees and supporters of Saddam's government and the Ba'ath Party.

Coalition forces had been quick to designate Fallujah as part of the 'Sunni triangle' and apparently were doing their best to bomb the city back into the stone-age.

Hundreds of Fallujah's civilians had been killed during these attacks. Some of the bombing had been intentional, but most of it had been accidental or collateral damage. Such as when a British jet, that had been intending to bomb the bridge over the Euphrates River, instead dropped the laser-guided bomb 'short' into Fallujah's open-air market.

Fallujah is located in the east end of Al Anbar province, one of the places where Coalition Forces have yet to 'win the hearts and minds of the Iraqi people.' It is safe to say that the town's population hates the

Coalition, especially the Americans, and seethed when the U.S. Marines had the gall to establish a Forward Operation Base just thirty miles south of the city.

———

The old delivery truck pulled up to a wrought-iron gate in front of a walled-residence on Walid Street. The low-wattage light fixture atop the gate was not illuminated.

———

Walled residences are fairly a typical style of construction in the nicer areas of Iraq, enjoyed by middle-and-upper class residents as the wall helps keep out the dirt and debris that accumulate during the frequent sand storms that roll in, off the arid desert that encircles the town.

———

The assistant driver stepped out of the truck's open sliding door, pulled a small bag out from his coverall pocket, and began to fiddle with the gate's lock. After less than thirty seconds, he quietly pushed the two gate leaves open, permitting the truck to enter.

While occasionally a resident of Fallujah loaned a specific delivery firm a key to their gates so they would not have to be awakened to permit early morning dairy deliveries, this residence was not one of those. Normally a maid or relative would have been waiting at the gate to collect the morning delivery.

Opening the gate had required delicate racks, picks, and other locking-picking tools to defeat the gate's decades-old locking mechanism.

As soon as the truck had pulled inside the gate, it was driven behind some nearby sand shrubs. The assistant closed the gate carefully so that it would appear to the ordinary passerby to be locked.

Once inside the compound, the younger of the two men pulled an olive-drab-colored canvas Field Kit Medical Kit out of the back of the van, and again using the stunted desert landscaping for concealment, slipped a bit closer to the servant's entrance to the two-story stucco residence.

The black Mercedes driven by the Cleric's only daughter, normally parked in the residence's driveway at night, was absent this morning. Other agents had arranged for the vehicle to become disabled on the woman's return home from a day of shopping in the Baghdad market.

The daughter had called her father, as was expected, to assure him that she was staying with a girl friend and would be home as soon as her car was repaired the next morning.

To make the call, the young woman had used the illegal cell phone that her father had only recently given her. The average Iraqi is not permitted to have a cell phone. That is, unless the individual has a permit issued by the Iraqi police.

She had tried to get her father to agree to let her call a nurse in to care for him during her unplanned overnight absence. But, being a contrary argumentative old man, he had refused her offer.

As the old cleric was well aware, he wasn't respected by a significant percentage of devout Sunnis. So he lived with fear of being assassinated by members of his own staff. He had already sent the two bodyguards that he still trusted, home for the night. As a result, the old man was in the house alone.

At the servant's entrance, the assistant again used his lock picks to open the keyset in the heavy wooden door. The men paused to check the silenced handguns that were concealed under their coveralls, before stepping inside, and closing the door.

They pulled surgical cover-ups over their boots, latex gloves on their hands, and black cotton ski masks over their heads. Only then did they begin to ascend the house's interior back stairway to the master bedroom. Although they were making every effort to move as silently as mice, they weren't overly concerned about waking the old man.

Coalition agents had bribed a greedy druggist who lived with his parents in Fallujah. He had confided in them that the old cleric regularly took sleeping potions and morphine tablets to mask his pain, which enabled him to sleep.

Reaching the second floor landing, the men stood in the near darkness listening intently for any sound, any indication that the old man was either awake, or that there was someone in the house that they hadn't anticipated.

After five minutes, the older man tapped the younger on the back and they moved silently towards to the open bedroom door, from which came raucous snoring.

The young man cautiously poked his head around the doorframe exposing one eye to view the rumpled pile made-up of human, clothing and bed cloths, intermingled on the huge, mosquito-netted, four-poster bed.

As electricity was sporadic in Fallujah the room was slightly illuminated by a single flickering candle set on a table against the far wall.

Satisfying themselves that the loud rumble of the old man's snoring was continuing uninterrupted, the old man had sleep apnea according to the pharmacist, they moved to the near side of the bed, as the younger man removed the medical kit from his coveralls, and opened it.

He removed a paper-wrapped plastic syringe, a plastic rubber-stopped medicine vial, and a hermetically-sealed, plastic sleeve containing an 18-gauge surgical needle.

The man removed the syringe from the autoclaved paper, popped off the top of the needle sleeve, and pushed the needle into the vial. He handed the paper and sleeve debris to his partner who stuck it all in a Ziploc bag that he carried under his coverall.

The assistant drew an exacting amount of anesthesia from the vial, up into the syringe. The team doctor had carefully calculated the necessary amount. And he had been involved in planning this morning's operation from the start.

The bribed druggist had also volunteered the knowledge that the old man was a mouth-breather. Knowing this fact permitted the team doctor to zero in even further on the optimum dosage, which resulted in the cleric being injected with a ten additional ten cc's of Ketamine. Because his being a mouth-breather precluded them from the usual practice of taping his mouth closed.

The driver moved forward and aided his assistant by placed the bulk of his body weight on top of the sleeping man, making sure to clamp his strong hands over the snoring man's mouth to prevent the instinctive effort to cry out.

His partner located a vein in the old man's scrawny arm, used the strong fingers of his left hand as a tourniquet on the old man's wizened bicep, and injected the surgical anesthetic directly into his vein.

The young man knew he would have likely been unable to administer the injection without having to knock the man unconscious, had his partner not used his weight to hold the wiry old man down. Then both men put their entire weight on the struggling old man until the Ketamine took effect and the old man faded into unconsciousness.

The assistant plunged the syringe into the mattress, snapped off the needle, and handed it back to his partner, where it also went into the plastic bag. Once he had done so and zip-locked it shut, the driver stuffed it back into a large pocket in his overalls.

The old man was hefted up onto the shoulders of the younger man and the driver led them out of the bedroom and down the stairs, all the while fanning his semi-automatic pistol from side-to-side, anticipating the worst.

At the downstairs hall landing, the driver slowly eased the servant's door open a couple of inches to risk a sneak-and-peek. Seeing no one, he stood aside and waved his burden-carrying assistant out of the house.

While the man carrying the prisoner stood in the shadows, the driver snapped the auto-locking button on the inside of the house's door handle, pulled it toward him, locking it.

They and their burden the young man carried, hurried to the rear of the truck. The driver opened its bi-fold rear doors. The athletic young man and his seemingly weightless load, jumped into the back of the truck.

After the driver closed the van's rear doors, he got back in the truck, started it, and headed for the front gate. He carefully used the truck's bumper to push open the gate leafs open, drove through, then got out, closing the gate behind him. He would have loved to be able to relock it, but he lacked his partner's locksmith's skills required to do so.

Instead, he opted to toss the early morning edition of the Sunni daily newspaper over the gate and into the walled compound's yard, in hopes of confusing the first responders when they discovered the old man was missing.

He returned to the truck's cab and drove off to complete the delivery route as the sun began to peek over the eastern horizon, signaling the arrival of yet another blistering hot, unbelievably humid, day in Iraq.

———

The driver completed the remainder of the truck's scheduled deliveries, all of which were along Ali Avenue towards the city center. It required crossing Highway 10, this time northbound. He had to complete the deliveries himself as his young medically-trained assistant had to remain in the rear of the truck box monitoring the vital signs of the old man.

Just as the ferocious desert sun poked its orb up to the east, the truck completed the delivery route. The driver pulled off the road behind a two-story building in the process of falling down, to permit the assistant to return to the truck's cab. They both had to be in the cab at the Sunni roadblock because only having a single man in the cab of the truck would raise the guard's suspicions.

That was possible because the young man had medically stabilized the old man, who now slept the sleep of the dead.

The truck proceeded back southbound to Highway 10 once again, turned east towards Baghdad, and headed for the Sunni roadblock that was intended to protect Fallujah from the deadly but rare Coalition ground raids during the hours of darkness.

At the roadblock, the Sunni's were breaking down the temporary roadblock. Coalition forces did not permit it to remain in-place during daylight hours. The fatalistic Sunnis knew that ignoring the Coalition's edicts would only result in still more air strikes on their ravaged city.

Fallujah is under the rule of the Wahhabis branch of the Sunnis, the most fanatical. Coalition forces, having grown tired of the high-body counts of their forces anytime they attempted to enter the town's confines, have not declared Fallujah no-mans-land. But they still frequently made their presence known by shelling the village, and running an occasional covert patrol through the village during the darkest hours of darkness. The objective of the patrol was simply to make the insurgents aware that the Coalition forces could do so, at will.

Otherwise, the insurgents owned the town proper, night and day, despite the fact that State Highway 10 bisected the town and was traveled heavily by the Iraqi Army and members of the Coalition, throughout the day. The Coalition used the weapons of the Bradley Fighting Vehicles to keep Fallujah's Sunnis honest.

The delivery truck was once again waved through the roadblock by the Sunni guards, who were otherwise occupied dismantling their road block before the heavily-armed Coalition troops began their first patrol of the day.

Once out of sight of the roadblock, the young assistant returned to the rear of the vehicle to monitor the vital signs of their drugged prisoner. With the blinding rising sun to the east in the driver's eyes, the delivery truck continued north-east, past Highway 10's interchange with Saddam's Great Belt Interstate highway, until the driver spotted a red laser spot being projected onto his vehicle's windshield.

The driver yelled to warn his partner to 'hold on' for himself and the old man, before he wrestled the truck off the smooth macadam roadway onto a barely navigable unpaved mining road. As the truck bounced along the ruts, the desert dust poured into the cab and cargo box, causing even the heavily-sedated cleric to cough.

About three miles off Highway 10 the driver jammed on his brakes and slid the delivery truck to a stop. It was either that or crash into thirty-camouflaged-tons of U.S. Marine Bradley M2 Tracked Armored Fighting Vehicle parked alongside of a large mine opening, blocking the road.

The driver jumped out and ran around to the rear door to assist in lifting the unconscious prisoner out of the truck. As they accomplished that, six heavily-armed, MOS O-3 Recon Marines stepped out of the straggly brush and covered them with their M16s and M-206 dual-purpose weapons.

A Marine top sergeant stepped from the open rear hull of the Bradley and barked an order to his men. Two of them immediately handed over their long guns to the other assault team members and went to assist in moving the prisoner into the rear hull of the Fighting Vehicle. There a Fleet-Marine-attached Navy doctor relieved the two operatives of their responsibility for the man's medical care.

The bread truck occupants and the Bradley's assault force, except for the sergeant, stepped to the back of the Bradley and walked up into rear hull of the vehicle. The Bradley operator would wait for the top sergeant to climb aboard before he pushed the button permitting the metal ramp to raise and lock closed.

The Bradley maneuvered until it was able to push the delivery truck into the old mineshaft, out of sight of anyone but a dedicated ground search team. Then the rumbling beast rolled south on the dirt road for twenty feet and paused.

The sergeant, who had remained outside the Bradley, was tossed a broom and made quick work of erasing any evidence that either vehicle had been there. It would do until the afternoon when the desert's typical breeze came up. Any evidence of their presence would be soon be obliterated by desert sand.

The Sergeant hooked the broom back onto the hull of the Bradley and jogged up the rear hull ramp just as it was beginning to rise. The huge steel beast cranked up and headed out into the desert, enroute to the nearby Coalition's forward operating base. They had their high-value prisoner in custody but the men's mood would remain subdued until they reached the safety of the base.

If you wanted to live to return home at the end of your tour of duty in Iraq, you never, ever forgot that Iraq is a very dangerous place to be. Unless you want to have your name added to the list that had already exceeded 4,000, you'd better remember that and conduct yourself accordingly.

THREE

September 10, 2006, 10:15 a.m.
Road convoy to Baghdad's Green Zone
Highway #10, An Bar Province
Iraq.

The Coalition's forward operating base in An Bar Province was located thirty miles south of the town of Fallujah, off Iraq State Highway 10. The base had been placed on 'maximum alert' by the 2/18th Military police battalion's commanding officer, a Marine colonel, when a U.S. Marine Recon patrol brought the prisoner through the gate of the base, into his area of responsibility.

———

U.S. military and Coalition forward operating bases, or FOB's, are designated by sector as such as Alpha, Bravo, etc. An FBO is defined as *heavily-armed temporary encampments in close proximity to the enemy.*

The facility is surrounded by sixteen-foot-high, concrete tilt-up blast walls, which are topped with five-foot-in-diameter loops of concertina wire.

Buildings inside the compound did not have windows and were of single-story, standard construction, stucco over cinderblock, with steel girders for support frames, and were extensively sandbagged.

Directly outside the massive steel blast gates were five, oversized speed bumps and a series of steel drums filled with sand, arranged in a winding maze so you had to slow to a crawl to negotiate ten sharp-angle turns to gain access to the fortified facility.

Built into the wall adjacent to the entrance gate were two, heavily-reinforced, twenty-foot-high concrete towers with the protruding ugly snouts of heavy-duty, vehicle-killer, .50-caliber machine guns bristling like the hair on porcupine's back whose job it is to that track all vehicles coming into, and leaving the reinforced compound.

Inside, the forward operating base was further protected by shear steel bulk of three parked 18-wheel transporters, a handful of 70-ton M1A2 Abrams battle tanks, a dozen or so armored rubber-tracked Bradley M6 fighting vehicles, and stacks upon stacks of rusty Conex containers that the insurgents have thoughtfully decorated with bullet and RPG holes.

The idling battle tanks have skeleton crews on-board at all times. These enormous tanks all have their 120-mm long guns trained on the only entrance to the FOB, the heavily-fortified, main and only, gate. The gate's exterior thick steel facing has ten-foot-high block letters, painted in red, with the U.S. Marine motto, in Latin, *SEMPER FIDALIS*, Always Faithful!

The Iraqi cleric was deemed a high-value prisoner. Time was of the essence, especially if the Marines were going to rescue the six kidnapped American contractors. Fallujah was far too dangerous an area to surge an American Marine Infantry Company into, except during daylight hours, to do door-to-door searches, and otherwise kick butts and take names.

Especially since higher-authority has the well-earned reputation of developing highly unrealistic 'blue sky' expectations that some Iraqi resident will slip-up and just blurt out and volunteer where the kidnapped contractors were being held.

Normally, the base commander would of passed the football up-the-ladder by firing off a priority eyes-only text, over the encrypted U.S. military network to his boss, a brigadier general. The headquarters of that particular higher-authority was located in the secure Green Zone in Baghdad. Or, in the International Zone, which is the latest P.C. way to refer to the heavily-fortified zone, which also is home to the *current* Iraqi government.

The most common way that the Coalition handles the transfer of a high-value prisoner to headquarters was to dispatch in a Blackhawk helicopter from Baghdad, accompanied by a flight of deadly Apache gunships.

However, there were two things keeping the colonel from recommending that course of action to his boss, the brigadier.

The first being, that one of the listening posts inside Fallujah installed at great personal risk by one of the Americans of Iraqi's descent in the Marine contingent, was indicating that the insurgents had placed the city on maximum alert when the old Imam had not shown up for morning prayers that day.

Other electronically-monitored listening posts in the city indicated that a house-to-house search was being conducted by the insurgents in an attempt to locate the missing Imam.

Apparently some of the old man's detractors thought he was just tardy once again to tending to his appointed duties. Other, more politically-minded followers thought that while the Imam was contrary, he never would risk his life by failing to show to lead the first Muslim prayer session of the day.

The Marine communication room operators, eavesdropping as usual on the Iraqi insurgent's radio frequencies, thought they overheard that the Sunni insurgents had taken a merchant in for questioning after he had reported seeing two Arab-appearing men in a white dairy delivery van spending an inordinate amount of time at the Imam's home in that morning.

Secondly, and just as disturbing, the previous evening the colonel had received an Alert from the CIA Intelligence office in Baghdad. It warned base commanders that a senior insurgent in Fallujah had recently returned from a covert journey to Afghanistan, had come home bearing gifts, courtesy of the Taliban. Reportedly the booty consisted of a dozen, ground-to-air, shoulder-fired American Stinger rockets designed to down helicopters at-will.

The commanding colonel was convinced that the Sunni insurgents holed-up in Fallujah had the priceless rockets in their possession. And it was more than likely that the only thing preventing them from being used against Coalition forces was a black letter order from insurgent headquarters. It would state, that on the pain of death, the stingers were only to be used where they would render the biggest bang for the buck, or in the Iraqi's case, the biggest bang for the *dinar*.

The Coalition's forward operating base in An Bar province receives all their supplies and munitions via randomly-scheduled, well-protected, over-the-road convoys from Baghdad.

Therefore, the impromptu arrival of a Blackhawk helicopter with a hunter-killer team of Apaches in-escort, especially now the insurgents assumed the old Imam had been kidnapped, and most likely by the Americans, any inbound helicopter would suddenly be elevated to the top of the acceptable target list for the insurgent's use of the deadly Stinger missiles.

The colonel was unwilling to risk the Coalition's valuable helicopters to extract the prisoner, especially since the FOB was less than seventy-two-road-miles from the green zone in Baghdad.

A road convey from the FOB to the green zone was something that Coalition forces had successfully utilized without complications, countless times in the past. Although admittedly, not with such a high-value prisoner such as a senior Sunni Imam aboard. However, expediency was mandated by the need to extract the location where the kidnapped contractors were being held captive, from the old cleric, before the insurgents tortured and executed the American contractors.

A standard American military supply and munition replenishment road convoy consisted of a mix of heavy trucks loaded with green CONEX containers, flatbed trucks carrying replacement Bradley Fighting Vehicles, and, interspersed among those thin-skinned vehicles, an armored U.S. cavalry troop with Abrams M1A2 battle tanks, and the mounted weaponry of the Bradley's to keep the insurgent's heads down.

The subsistence convoys never reach speeds of much more than thirty-miles-per-hour because of what the American military calls the 'convoy effect,' and the inherent slowness of the tanks.

Convoy effect is a phenomenon where the individual convoy vehicles are constantly slowing down and speeding up, resulting in the commander's Humvee at the head of the procession, travels at a speed of up to ten-miles-per-hour less than the assistant commander's in the tail-end Charlie position at the rear of the convoy. That is a difficult aberration to accept but it is proven fact.

The convoy commander, Marine Lt. Colonel Jeffrey Johnson, the base commander's direct report, saw the mission as transporting the prisoner safely to Baghdad via the *most expedient* means possible.

His boss strongly recommended to Johnson that he use a standard convoy configuration using Abrams Battle tanks for fire support.

The convoy commander thought that a supply convoy configuration was too slow, and would make his men sitting ducks because the insurgents would be aware that any convoy leaving the FOB that morning could be transporting the cleric to Baghdad for interrogation.

The Lt. Colonel and his advisors urged the Colonel to allow them to use a *Slingshot convoy* concept, which could move faster, albeit with a reduced level of protection.

The colonel had once-again informed his subordinate, that higher-authority didn't believe that using the slingshot method of transporting the prisoner was advisable, considering the man's apparent importance to the insurgent's cause. And therefore the heightened priority the Sunni's would place on breaking the old man out of Coalition custody.

Lt. Colonel Johnson, and Marine Major Mary Levinson, his assistant, continued to argue that the strength of a slingshot road convoy was that it could travel as lightly-armed as was prudent, and at the top speed of its slowest equipment. Slingshots traveled at speeds twenty-to-thirty miles-per-hour faster than a routine heavy replenishment convoy.

The reason for that is the use of the heavy tanks. All personnel in the replenishment road convoys, outside CONUS, the continental United States in time of war, in addition to uniforms, weapons, and headgear, must carry at least six magazines for their assault rifles; first aid kits; two canteens; a flash light; at least one flash bang; a least one colored smoke grenade for use in signaling helicopters into a landing zone, fragmentation grenades; bullet-resistant vests; dust goggles, and night vision glasses. In a word, replenishment convoys travel heavy, and slow, very slow.

All convoys traveling highways in Iraq typically encounter ancient, battered, worn-out European vehicles, belching smoke and unburned low-grade gasoline, covered with Iraq's ever-present fine beige dust, some so riddled with bullet holes that they looked like sieves or very nasty Swiss cheese.

Along the convoy route, the convoys never see much roadside terrain that is not flat desert, palm trees, dead animals, broken down Japanese or European cars, demolished buildings, shabby huts, camels, ox carts, and in the distance, remote villages built around wells or an oasis.

Middle-and-working class Iraqis travel their country's roads on motorbikes, up to four-per-bike, or in decrepit thirty-year-old Russian cars, and antique buses and trucks loaded to the gunnels with goods and vegetables, which sometimes contain concealed weapons shipments for the insurgents.

Lt. Colonel Johnson and his fighting staff, that doubled as his advisors in times like this, knew that using the slower convoy method, that included the seventy-ton M1A2 Abrams main battle tanks going along to protect the mission, would, with reasonable traffic delays, take at least three-to-four hours. The heavy battle tank's top speed, which is mechanically governed, is only 41.5 miles-per-hour.

Not to mention, argued the convoy commander, the damage the tank's steel treads would do to the surface of State Highway 10. Battle tanks are normally kept off the paved surfaces of main roads in Iraqi, when possible. Still, this option was the preference of the commanding colonel. The Coalition couldn't afford to lose the Imam to hostile fire, or the convoy either, for that matter.

However, if the convoy commander was given a direct order by the colonel to use the Abrams tanks for backup, it would raise major logistical problem. First, some higher-up would have to obtain formal approval from the Iraqi regional political bureaucrat whose responsibility it is to keep the Iraqi State Highway grid in good repair.

Based on the Lt. Colonel's past experience, obtaining that approval could take up to 24-hours. The bureaucratic delay certainly wouldn't sit well with the brigadier general, neither would it do those kidnapped contractors any good.

The only other option, and the one being pushed by Marine Corps Lieutenant Colonel Jeffrey 'Kick Ass' Johnson and his subordinate, Major Mary 'Ice Maiden' Levinson, was to use a high-speed slingshot convoy with its only the protection being its speed, the cupola machine guns of the Humvees, and the heavy guns on the three Bradley Fighting Vehicles for backup.

Selecting the second option meant that the trip could be accomplished in a more timely manner as the convoy's speed would only be limited by the top-speed of the thirty-ton Bradley which was a hair over sixty miles-per-hour.

Using that mode of travel, the high-value prisoner could be delivered and safely ensconced in the Green Zone's stockade in less than two hours, even if the morning road traffic slowed the convey down some.

For that reason, the colonel decided to defer the decision to his subordinate, which in-fact would permit him to employ lightly-armed Humvees, backed up the heavier firepower of the rubber-wheeled Bradley fighting vehicles, which would not tear up the highway's pavement as the tanks would.

However, before deferring the decision to the convoy commander, the base commander went on-record as advising his subordinate that he didn't agree with the younger man's plan, thought it to be impetuous, unnecessarily risky, and perhaps too cowboy-like.

The base commander reminded Johnson for the record that if he persisted on using a slingshot convoy, and by doing so, the convoy failed to protect the prisoner from the anticipated attacks by insurgents who would be attempting to break the man out of Coalition custody, he would not stand behind him in the eventual official inquiry.

He reminded the headstrong convoy commander once again that his mission was to get the prisoner to the CIA Interrogation specialists in good condition. If the convoy failed to perform the mission as stated, the colonel told him that in all honesty that the younger man and members of his staff could be subject to severe disciplinary action, up to and including a general courts-martial.

The confident young man cockily told his boss that he was aware of the possible political ramifications of his decision to employ a radical concept to accomplish his mission.

By 11:10 a.m., September 10, 2006, the American slingshot convoy with the prisoner concealed inside a Humvee, which was set-up to transport wounded combatants, pulled out of the FOB and started east on State Highway 10 at a high-rate-of-speed.

The drivers used their horns to move other traffic off the road. If an Iraqi civilian vehicle refused to yield, they were forced off of the highway and onto the road's shoulders.

A slingshot road convoy, red lights flashing from the mounts on the vehicle's roofs, ran at the top-speed of its slowest vehicle, which in this case was the latest version of the Bradley Fighting Vehicle, the M6. It was able to maintain a cruising speed of 55-60 miles-per-hour.

That speed would permit them to motor-like-hell up Highway 10 to Baghdad, running over any insurgent opposition that happened to get in their way, and transport the high-value prisoner to the green zone for interrogation by the CIA intelligence pukes, in a little over ninety-minutes.

Everyone in the convoy knew that it was likely that the convoy would be attacked somewhere between the convoy's originating base and Baghdad, especially since the insurgents in Fallujah assumed that their Imam was in Coalition custody.

It was only a small step in insurgent logic that the old man would be transported to the green zone in Baghdad for interrogation, as that was standard operating procedure of American and Coalition forces.

Speed was the slingshot convoy's only ally. Therefore, a reasonable person could anticipate that any abundance of road courtesy would not be forthcoming from the convoy drivers this morning.

As the convoy ripped along the four-lane paved highway, the weapons in the cupolas atop of the armored Humvees and the Bradley fighting vehicles, traversed from side-to-side. With exception of those of the last Bradley in line, whose weapons were trained back along the route the convoy had traveled.

The heat off the concrete surface was intense. The air was laced with the scent of raw feces which villagers had been piled alongside the highway in a small but pungent message as to the perceived-occupation by Coalition troops.

Convoy drivers were warned to avoid dirt mounds, vehicle wrecks, piles of rubble, and especially the piles of excrement that the locals have piled beside the road to demonstrate their contempt for the Coalition, especially the Americans.

As the convoy continued to motor up Highway 10, which bisects the City of Fallujah, the convoy commander authorized his gunners to test-fire their machine guns to ensure they were operational and ready to rock-and-roll.

The convoy would be at the greatest risk where Highway 10 passed through Fallujah. Every soldier in the convoy, carrying a weapon, checked and rechecked to make sure his or her weapon was locked-and-loaded.

The convoy almost made it past the town of Fallujah without incident. The convoy had sped along until it reached Fallujah's eastside where Highway 10 passes over one of Saddam's magnificent six-lane Interstate highways, when everything went to hell.

Suddenly a huge explosion engulfed the lead vehicle. A mighty percussion wave filled with shrapnel hacked into the convoy. Drivers and passengers ducked behind the dashboards of their vehicles as the pressure wave rolled up and over the column.

The Marines heard nearby crashes and thumps as large pieces of metal rained down on the burning carcasses of what was left of the vehicles they had been driving.

As the sound of the massive explosion boomed and reverberated against the concrete block walls of the village, survivors of the maelstrom were heard whimpering, and calling out to wounded buddies and friends.

The horrible, wretched sounds the dying men and women were making, were those heard many times a day at the field hospitals across Iraq, when they were receiving Coalition casualties.

The insurgents jumped out of ditches where they had been hiding, ignoring the Marines of the patrol who were almost all walking-wounded, but still determined to return fire with their weapons.

The American troops were firing blind, hoping for a lucky hit or to drive the raiders off the convoy.

It was obvious that the insurgents were attempting to cherry-pick one particular vehicle out of the burning convoy. The one their spies inside the Coalition forward operating base, employed by civilian contractors as casual laborers to add diesel fuel and burn the contents of the honey pots, had gotten the word out of the FOB to their fellow insurgents telling them which vehicle contained the prisoner.

Once the Bradley fighting vehicle that served as the convoy's rolling medical dispensary had been identified by the insurgents, they began firing rocket-propelled-grenades at it, as well as the rest of the convoy's vehicles that had been untouched by the initial explosion.

The RPG rounds found their targets with maddening accuracy. Eventually the sound from the firing of weapons, exploding grenades, and RPG detonations, reduced in decibels to more like that coming from distance thunder. American dead lay everywhere.

Survivors that miraculously been spared from the in-coming fire began to check their comrades for a signs of life.

As they performed rudimentary triage on themselves and their buddies, they looked around in shock and awe, and saw the torn, ripped bodies through the black smoke, as flames engulfed one vehicle after another.

Secondary explosions sent showers of dancing orange sparks up through the smoke pall of the morning sky that was obscuring the heavens, over what had once been a well-organized, well-armed and well-led U.S. Marine combat convoy.

The surveillance camera mounted on top of the command Humvee had recorded the detonation of the IED, the improvised explosive device, as yellow, then orange. The flash jumped across the highway causing the asphalt to leap six-feet into the air, breaking the back of Humvee that had been crossing it.

The explosion created an ascending black cone of smoke, which would continue to hang over the ambush site throughout the day. From a distance the black column of smoke looked like a stalled tornado.

The roof-mounted camera on the command Humvee wasn't set-up to record sound. The blast wave had shattered the windows in Iraqi homes two blocks away from the highway. Shards of glass rained down onto the convoy and nearby homes.

What the camera *did see*, its computer brain converted to digits, ones and zeros. The encrypted signal was then transmitted to a WiFi transmitter antenna mounted atop a tall pole inside the forward operating base from which the convoy had just departed, fifteen minutes earlier.

From there, the electronic digits were transmitted through the air on radio frequency, 801.25, to another WiFi box on a second pole, inside the Coalition compound.

The signal flowed down the pole on fiber-optic cable, then to a router that was buried in a concrete vault under the FOB's gravel streets. Then the signal was transmitted 100-feet to the security-monitoring facility inside the forwarding operating base.

In the same instant, the signals from the attack scene were being duplicated and forwarded via repeater to the International Zone's main security command bunker in Baghdad.

The digits were routed to an intelligent surveillance server at both locations. The servers processed the signal and compared the image with a file copy of the exact section of highway where the ambush had occurred. High-end, high-speed military computer systems processed the information in less than a nanosecond against file images that depicted the way that section of road appeared normally.

Alarm bells started to clang at both locations when the computers first compared the two images, a second, then a third time, before informing its human operators that what it was seeing was not normal; indeed, it was not good, definitely not freaking good!

The specialized analytical software sent a signal to a large flat monitoring screen at both locations. The images on those screens immediately displayed a single large word in bright flashing red against a black background: ***ALERT!!*** Less than five seconds had elapsed since the IED had exploded.

A computerized voice calmly repeated the word *"Alert-Alert-Alert"* over speakers in the respective command posts, until an enlisted Marine in each punched the *Silence Alarm* button.

The large screens dissolved to show a feed of the scene depicting the explosion of the roadside bomb. The camera showed whitish dust and black explosive clouds billowing up from fires all over the convoy.

It also remotely panned images to security personnel of the subsequent explosions from a half-dozen RPGs. They were being launched by insurgents who initially had been hiding in scrub brush along the length of the convoy. Each new RPG explosion turned another vehicle into just so much scrap iron.

There were huge fires raging inside and outside each of the vehicles. The smoke from them combined to send a massive plume of the heat and smoke into the heavens where even godless Marines hoped their Savior was watching.

Deafened Marines, many with their uniforms and flesh on fire, were having to make the difficult choice to abandon their weapons, prohibit by the Marine Code-of-Conduct, when it became a choice of that, or be unable to use that theirs hands to extract themselves from the burning infernos. They staggered out of the burning vehicles, choking, bleeding, and coughing. A few had faces that were on fire.

The command Humvee had been partially shielded by one of the larger trucks, as it had been returning to its assigned slot at the head of the convoy after chastising a straggler. It had almost reached the head of the convoy when the IED had detonated.

Whoever had survived the explosion was now driving the Humvee as it used its massive front bumper to push the burning wreckage aside, stopping momentarily at each flaming hunk of metal, to check for survivors.

In the command Humvee, the driver in the front seat and the convoy commander's bodyguard in the rear seat, had been killed outright by shrapnel from the exploding IED. Miraculously, Lt. Colonel Johnson, sitting in the front seat, shoved the dead Marine driver out of the doorless Humvee and crawled over the center console and took control of the steering wheel of the still moving vehicle. His command sergeant in the rear seat, with exception of lacerations, broken limbs, burns, and deafness, was still alive. The wounded man's longevity would be short unless he received prompt medical attention.

Without stopping to assess his plan of action, the Lt. Colonel wrestled the Humvee back into gear, and tromped the gas pedal to the floor. He used the vehicle to push its way through the wreckage to the heads of the convoy.

Then Johnson systematically began to run over the insurgents, who were popping up out of hidey-holes in the nearby ditches and yelling some obscure Arab chant, were running towards the burning convoy, intent on killing any survivors.

The Lt. Colonel's vehicle ran over one, two, three, then two more insurgents. Then, out of the clouds bellowing over the bombing scene, a soldier's torsos fell from the sky and came crashing down on the command vehicle's roof-mounted camera, crushing it instantly, cutting off the convoy's visual lifeline with the base and the security bunker in the green zone.

Once he had rundown a number of charging insurgents in rage, concern for his men returned to forefront of the Lt. Colonel's mind. He spun the battered Humvee around and raced back into the carnage. There he hopped out and began pulling the troops that remained trapped under their vehicles, to relative safety.

Insurgents normally place IEDs to target the front or middle vehicles in convoys. Because in insurgent logic, an explosion creates a traffic jam, which in turn provides a lot of near-stationary targets, which provides the opportunity for them to use their RPGs.

Veteran Marines know that the rear of a convoy is the best and safest place to be in the column, despite the billowing dust. Those assigned to rear-end Charlie duty, typically wear goggles and a do-rag tied around the head cowboy-style. The saying among convoy troops is 'dust or shrapnel.'

The Marine manual for convoys, states something about vehicles are to maintain 100-feet separation between each other, depending on an assessment of risk.

However, in the real world, that almost never happens except on equipment moves on highways in the U.S. And it most certain doesn't apply in the real world of Iraq, on a slingshot convoy mission during wartime in hostile territory.

Major Levinson, who was the tail-end Humvee, had her head down digging around in her convoy kit looking for some Dramamine as she occasionally got car sick, when the improvised explosive device exploded at the front of the convoy, then secondly, when a RPG ricocheted off the lightly-armored contours of her vehicle.

The blast decapitated her driver. And wounded the bodyguard that sat behind her. However, he was able to crawl into the driver's seat and take control of the Humvee. Then things went to hell in a handbag as her mother used to say.

Ordering her replacement driver to hold position for a minute, she hopped out of the Humvee and ran thirty-feet through sporadic incoming fire to a nearby Humvee that was in flames.

The force from a RPG blast had flipped it onto its top, trapping the Marines inside the vehicle's cockpit.

While all this was going on, her mind was being assaulted by the bloodcurdling screams of the injured and soon-to-be-dead. The air stank of copper, carbon, and human waste that every body involuntarily excretes at the moment of death.

She saw a bloody hand reach out from beneath the smoldering, crushed steel side of the upside-down Bradley. She grabbed it and pulled with all her might. But she couldn't budge move the man, and eventually, his burning skin sloughed off in her gloved hands.

She turned to see another Marine, struggling in vain to escape from under another overturned Humvee.

The few troops that had survived that attack were attempting to pull lifeless bodies from the wreckage as other Marines searched for the missing.

Substantiating the fact that the insurgents had been ordered to make certain the old cleric never talked to CIA interrogators, the Bradley in which he had been riding, had been hit by no less than six RPGs. Nothing identifiable of the vehicle remained except for a smoldering pile of scorched metal and human body parts.

It was nearly forty minutes later that the Coalition's rescue force choppered into the ambush site.

The security personnel, always first out of the choppers, noted that the five or so Marines that had survived the attack without disabling injury, and those physically and mentally able to do so, had established a weak perimeter around the scrapyard. The troops continued to pop off an occasional rifle round to keep the insurgents at bay.

Scrap yard. That being the only word that came to mind for what remained of the slingshot convoy. Another five Marines, walking wounded actually, continued to provide emergency first-aid and a compassionate presence to Marines that were so badly wounded, they likely would only survive if they were transported to a field hospital inside of an hour, the proverbial golden hour.

Medevac helicopters and the larger air ambulances, only landing once the security personnel on the ground assured them that the landing zone was secure, proceeded to load the wounded on-board for transport to the 28th Combat Support Hospital in Baghdad.

Some of the wounded, continued to hold onto life, despite having exposed blackened skin, dark crimson blood spurting and flowing from hurriedly bandaged wounds, and ragged, unattended to, flaps of skins.

Emergency medical personnel were attempting to triage victims, their hands expertly flitting from body part to body part, searching for wounds, shouting instructions to the surviving troops acting as carrier bearers, with orders as to who got loaded onto which method of transport, the salvageable first, then later, those farther down the triage tree of required care. Some victims were silent because they were in shock, others attempted to scream, but their faces had melted and their lungs, seared.

After body hair, lips burn the easiest. Whatever a soldier's contortions, still gripping the steering wheel, sprawled on the hood, or thrown out of a vehicle entirely; whatever state of intactness or dismemberment, some bodies of the men and women who were mostly civilian reserve solders, were still smoking, body after body appearing to be manically *grinning*.

In the intense heat the bodies had already began to decompose. The smell of death rose above the odor of burning tires and diesel fumes, and the smell of cooked human flesh. The smell of blood, urine, and feces was overwhelming and so was the noise. Blood and urine flowed everywhere.

The flat-lined, those who had already began their journey into becoming worm farms, would be loaded on the air ambulances last, long after the living wounded had departed.

Most of the triage team's commands got ignored in the heat of the post-battle because survivors were still engaged in a pitched firefight with death. The insurgents were intent on not only overrunning the entire convoy, but also the medical emergency response team. That would be a huge public relations coup d' état for the insurgents.

The scrap yard was still absorbing occasional incoming sniper fire from the insurgents in hiding, and even from the nearby village. Deadly Cobra gunships, flying top cover, darted like humming birds overhead, here and there, daring the insurgents to show their cowardly heads even momentarily, to rain down hellfire and damnation up those who foolish enough to do so.

The decimated force of Marines running the slingshot convoy may have failed in their assignment to protect and deliver the prisoner to Baghdad for interrogation, but the security force that had just choppered into the ambush site, damn well were collecting the head tax for the atrocity.

BOOK TWO

LAS VEGAS

2008

ONE

June 1, 2008, Sunday, 6:15 a.m.
A residential condominium
Desert Willows Golf Course
Henderson, Nevada

A 47-year-old white male appearing to be in his late 30's, well-built, six-foot, four-inches-tall; dressed in a brilliant-white tee-shirt, starched tan rugby shorts, and leather-laced tan boat shoes, relaxed on the second floor lanai of his recently acquired condominium on the east side of the Desert Willows Golf Course.

He hadn't yet had the time or the inclination to stock his new condo with cooking utensils. The property had only closed escrow last week.

The new furniture he had selected and purchased during his first week in Las Vegas from the Milton Homer Fine Home Furnishings store had been delivered and set up this past Saturday.

He was living out of a suitcase until he could replace the clothes he'd been forced to leave behind in China when he had, without warning, been declared *persona non grata*, which in literal Latin means 'unwelcome person,' by the country's Communist Regime.

He had been evicted from China because of his refusal to be bullied into becoming an employee of the Peoples' Republic of China's domestic intelligence apparatus.

The man considered today, June 1st, to be the first day of the rest of his life. Tomorrow he would report for his first day at his new job, Chief Investigator, at a division of the regulatory agency that oversees and controls the gaming industry in the State of Nevada.

He had eaten a breakfast of glazed cinnamon sweet rolls, no-pulp Minute Maid orange juice, and washed it all down with several cups of Columbian coffee. The sun was rising over the condo's roof behind him as it began its ruthless ascent into the sky over Sin City. Soon street-level temperatures would sky rocket into the low 100's.

From where he sat, the smog hanging over Sin City reminded him of a dark cloak, heavily-adorned by the red pulsating aviation clearance lights flashing randomly from the Casino Hotel's roofs, which was being slowly drawn aside as the rays of the sun won their battle to display the less-than-flattering views of Las Vegas during daylight hours.

A crumb from one of the sweet rolls he was munching on dropped onto the lanai's indoor-outdoor carpet. His breeding showed when he reached over to pick it up and placed it back on his plate. Rather than his second option, which was just to use the tip of his shoe to kick it under the railing and over the edge where it would fall to the ground and eventually be swept up by a member of the Home Owners Association's grounds crew.

He stood up and walked back into the condo's generous designer kitchen to refill his coffee cup for the third time since purchasing the espresso machine that graced the granite counter. It sat on a marble counter alongside the huge stainless steel Sub-Zero refrigerator/freezer combination.

He turned the expensive coffee maker to the 'off' position, as three cups a day was his self-imposed caffeine limit when he wasn't working.

A couple days ago, the soon-to-be sworn law-enforcement officer for the State of Nevada had leased an ebony-colored, 2008 Chrysler 300 sedan. The vehicle was on the relative short list of approved personal vehicles that employees of the State Gaming Control Board, acronym GCB, were authorized to drive while on official business.

The agency didn't want their investigators cruising the streets of Las Vegas in the latest Corvettes or Porsches in the pursuit of gamblers that made their living by cheating Casinos out of gaming revenue, and the State of Nevada out of the income taxes levied on that revenue.

Before leasing the car, he had done the necessary calculations to ensure that the monthly lease payment, insurance cost, cost of operation, plus the mortgage payment on his condo, would not exceed 30% of his new salary.

The GCB had a small group of auditors that did nothing but keep an eye on the personal finances of the organization's employees. If a random audit revealed that a employee was getting him or herself into dangerous territory, financially, they were ordered to appear in front of a internal GCB's security officer to determine if the employee needed financial advice or counseling about his worsening money management situation.

In other words, to avoid any potential of embarrassment to the Board, the GCB had established, and put procedures in-place, to track potentially damaging behavior on the part of its employees.

If the employee refused to heed the GCB warning that he or she was financially getting in over their heads, the organization's Human Relation's Department would forthwith begin preliminary termination proceedings against the employee. The GCB would not tolerate any intentional or unintentional employee-generated situation that might bring a cloud of suspicion or corruption over the gaming regulatory agency.

The striking-looking man enjoying his continental breakfast on the sun-drenched lanai was former-Hong Kong Police Department Chief Inspector Edward Augustus Fox, a vibrant-looking man considered a clotheshorse by anyone who encountered him during their day-to-day activities.

Persons that didn't know him may have been surprised to learn that the man was a gourmet cook, and although obviously Caucasian, excelled in speaking and reading Cantonese, and spoke passable Mandarin.

He currently was single, although he had left a common-law wife and young son in Taiyunan, a city of three-million located in northwest China, southwest of the City of Beijing, the site of the future World's 2008 Olympic Summer Games.

In late 2007, Fox had been living with his young son and his mother in Taiyunan, recovering from wounds which he had incurred in the line-of-duty while in the employ of the Hong Kong Police Department.

He had been pensioned off and since moving from Hong Kong to China, had been living a mostly uneventful life taking care of their son while the child's mother maintained a thriving medical practice in the city.

He was still undergoing physical therapy as a result of his own injuries, and felt he was returning to acceptable physical condition considering his age, those injuries, and multiple corrective surgeries.

While still in China, Fox had been approached by a man from one of the Peoples Republic of China intelligence directorates. After the customary Chinese small talk, he had been surprised to be offered a job assisting China's law enforcement agencies in overseeing the security threats for the period when the Summer Olympics was being held in Beijing and at surrounding venues.

Citizen Fox knew the Chinese agent. The man had been one of his students when the Inspector had given a security seminar in Hong Kong a few years earlier.

The seminar had been presented by the Hong Kong Police Department under the orders of the HK special Economic Zone's chief executive who was generally acknowledged to report directly to the party headquarters in Beijing.

The seminar was intended to provide necessary training for various agents of the China's public and covert intelligence agencies to prepare them for the task of maintaining security, protecting athletes and tourists alike, while guarding China's national security, during the upcoming Summer Olympic Games.

However, in this instance, Fox had balked. He knew he would be working for the communists. And he would be expected to give his loyalty in all matters to the PRC and the agency he would be employed by, regardless of his American citizenship.

At the time, Fox and his family were financially comfortable, both from the earnings of his lover's clinic, and the generous pension that had been settled on him when he left the Hong Kong Police Department.

So, without discussing the matter with his son's birth mother, he had turned down the otherwise attractive job offer.

He realized that if he accepted the position, it would have required that he spend a great deal of time in Beijing away from home.

And Fox knew it was unrealistic to assume that he eventually wouldn't be placed in a sensitive situation where he would have to make a decision as to either being a loyal American citizen, or a lackey of the communist agency he would be working for.

So a week later, he had been totally unprepared for an early morning visit from agents from the intelligence organization that had made him the job offer.

They had informed him that his turning down the job had convinced their superiors that he was a significant risk to the PRC's national security.

The agents had informed him that he had seven days in which to leave the country, which the agents admitted they felt to be over-generous, or he would be arrested and put on trial as an American spy.

Fox was further shocked and felt betrayed when he learned that the Chinese intelligence agents had discussed his expulsion from China with the mother of his son, a week before.

Agents had informed her that she had two choices.

One was that she could leave her birth country and depart China with Fox and their son. However, they had emphasized to her, she was a valued Chinese citizen and she and her son were welcome to remain in the country without any sigma from being 'tricked' into living with the American spy.

After the PRC agents left, Fox made a quick call to the U.S. Consulate in Beijing. When he talked to the ambassador, he had been told that the Chinese had the power to evict him from China at any time by virtue of the fact that he did not possess the required foreigner's resident visa.

Additionally, Chinese officials always see themselves as being puritans, and he was not married to his son's mother. However, Chinese authorities considered she and their son as Chinese citizens in good standing.

Because of that fact, the Chinese government had labeled Fox's expulsion to be because he was a threat to China's national sovereignty. Therefore, he could not protest, or appeal the eviction order, and their decision was final.

The American Consulate also informed him of the fact that having been a fifteen-year NYPD detective, and then for the past ten years, a high-ranking administrator in the Hong Kong Police Department after the Chinese Communists took back control of the former British colony in June of 1997, and as a third strike, it was well-known that he once had been closely involved with the American FBI, all of which certainly didn't aid him in his current predicament.

Fox had turned to Alicia, his lover, and tried to convince her that since he had no other option than to leave the country, that she and their son had to drop everything and likewise accompany him back to America.

Fox thought he was being sensitive to her feelings when he told her to take twenty-four-hours to think the matter over before she made a decision for her and the boy.

However, the next day her response shocked him. She told him she and their son were Chinese. As such, both had a good life and bright future ahead of them and would never leave the People's Republic of China, which they considered to be their home.

Four days later, after drawing five-thousand American dollars out of his secret offshore rainy-day-fund-account, Fox packed a few changes of clothes in a carry-on bag, and Chinese intelligence agents escorted him to his gate at the international airport in Beijing, where he boarded a flight for San Francisco.

As Fox sat relaxing on his lanai enjoying his morning coffee, he looked off eleven miles in the distance to the northwest at the tall buildings of the Hotel Casinos on the Las Vegas strip.

Greetings readers. Please permit me to introduce myself. I am Edward Augustus Fox. This is my story. Those of you who have been following my adventures in the trilogy of novels set in Hong Kong since October of 2005, welcome back, and for those who have not, welcome aboard new friends.

Upon my flight from Beijing to San Francisco two weeks ago, I attempted to bury my sadness about losing my family. At least until I got a job, and after which, could take time to grieve.

After settling in at overly-priced hotel down by the San Francisco waterfront, I began making phone calls to friends in the FBI, former co-workers and administrative acquaintances in the NYPD, and to a close friend who was the head of the National Association of Police Chiefs.

Most of them told me that the only area that was going crazy with population growth at the current time was the State of Nevada.

Particularly, those agencies whose charter it is to monitor the State's Gaming industry.

I, of course, was familiar with the Las Vegas area, having taken several vacations there with my wife when she was alive and I had been a D-1 with the homicide unit of the NYPD.

When I got off the phone from my inquiries, I went out and had a delicious oyster lunch at Fisherman's Wharf. Due to the six-figure retirement pension settlement that had sitting in a legitimate offshore bank account earning interest over the past nine months, I wasn't in any immediate financial bind.

After lunch, I caught a cab to the San Francisco library, rented a computer terminal, and began a job search of Nevada State law enforcement agencies, specifically the State Gaming Commission, and the Gaming Control Board. And all the other leads my active law-enforcement friends had suggested to me.

Long story short, both the Board and the Commission had several open listings for investigative positions that were listed on their respective web sites, along with the experience requirements and the POST Standards for the positions.

The only other agency that friends had directed me to in Nevada was the Las Vegas Metropolitan Police Department. That agency apparently only had openings for lateral-transfer positions, mostly street detective jobs that at forty-seven-years-of-age were of zero interest to me, regardless of the salaries being offered.

I still was suffering from the physical injuries that I had received when a rogue Interpol agent, kidnapped, tortured, and generally kicked my ass from San Francisco to Macau while I was pursing a body-part harvesting ring while with the Hong Kong Police Department. It had taken four months of major surgeries, including both replacement of both knees, and painful physical therapy, before I was again capable of getting around without looking like I was physically handicapped or incapable of defending myself.

Anyway, I rented a car and drove to Carson City, Nevada that week, interviewed, took tests, managed to squeeze through the physical, and two weeks after returning to San Francisco to reclaim what belongings I did have, I received a formal offer of a job as Chief Inspector with the Board, and by proxy, the Commission.

———

Many members of the general public, and even some naïve law enforcement types, erroneously believe that the Board is solely chartered to be on the watch for the involvement of organized crime in the gaming industry in Nevada.

While that would be the case when and if such activity was uncovered, the truth is that most members of organized crime have long ago packed their bags and returned home to where ever they came.

Although Las Vegas was once referred to by the mob as an *open city,* back in its gangland days, the primary criminal organization with its fingers in the gaming industry, had been attached to the hands of the Chicago Mob, the Outfit, or the Mafia. Opps, sorry, apparently no one calls the Mafia, the Mafia, these days.

The casinos that were mobbed up back in those days, would have been well over twenty-years-old by this time, had they not all already been imploded. They and their allegedly mobbed-up bosses have no significant presence in Las Vegas today.

However, back in September of 2007, several of these old Chicago gangsters finally found their way into Federal Court in Chicago, charged with eighteen multiple counts of Murder One, and Conspiracy to Murder. The federal government referred to the case as *Operation Family Secrets.*

The indicted mob big shots were Frank Calabrese Sr., then age 70; Joseph "Joey the Clown" Lombardo, then age 78; and James Marcello, the age 65. Each of the men faced the maximum sentence of Life Without Parole.

One of the murders attributed to Marcello, for instance, and proof that organized crime has long ago worn out their welcome in Las Vegas, was the June 1986 murder of Tony "The Ant" Spilotro, the Chicago Mob's longtime man in Las Vegas and the inspiration for the Joe Pesci character in the movie *Casino.*

If you want further proof that the mob no longer controls things in Nevada, please review the GCB's Most Wanted List and you will find the members of the mob notoriously absent.

Out of the twenty-four undesirable elements on the Board's black list, three are males of East European heritage; four non-Italian Caucasian men; two non-Italian Caucasian women; four Latino males; one black female; eight Asian men; and two Asian women.

Today most of the Board's efforts are focused on protecting the integrity of Nevada gaming industry from cheats, internal and external. The board continues to track those criminals, and perform two-tier auditing of

Casino's gaming receipts and profits, to ensure the State of Nevada receives the tax revenues upon which the state is totally dependant.

Our function as a Special Investigative body is to ferret out any plans, hopefully before the fact, by criminal enterprises intending to cheat or rob the Casinos, subjugate their employees in any manner, or interfere in any manner with the financial revenue benefit the State of Nevada realizes from the gaming industry in the State.

As many of you know, in additional to the Board, there is another agency often mentioned in regards to Gaming in the State of Nevada, the Gaming Commission.

The Board was created by the Nevada legislature in 1955 within the existing Nevada Tax Commission. Its explicit charter was to inaugurate a policy to eliminate the undesirable element from Nevada gaming and to develop regulations for the licensing and the operation of the gambling industry.

In 1959, the Commission was created by the passage of the Gaming Control Act. The Commission acts as the final arbiter of all licensing matter by acting on the Board's recommendations for licensing. The Act is in response to a phenomenal growth of gaming in the State that laid the foundation for what has become modern gaming regulation.

The Nevada State Gaming Control Board acts as the facilitator and enforcement arm of the Commission, ensuring its rules and regulations are followed to the letter and that the State of Nevada receives all taxes on gaming revenue that are due it.

While I was looking forward to my new start on life with enthusiasm, I knew only too well of my past inabilities to logically deal with several incidents involving my personal grieving.

In 1996, when I was with NYPD, my beloved wife had unexpectedly been taken from me by cancer. As a result, I had nearly fallen to a level of non-recovery from self-induced alcoholism.

Then, in 2005, I lost another loved one in Hong Kong. My lover, Peng Lige, unbeknownst to me at the time, had been bearing our child. Our apartment had been broken into. Peng had been tortured and killed on the orders of a corrupt police official. This monster ordered this atrocity to be committed in an attempt to force me to end my investigations into numerous capital crimes this official had personally ordered against non-communist legislators in the former Queen's colony.

Now, in 2008, I been declared persona non-grata and forcibly exiled from China. Chinese officials told me I never would be permitted to return, leaving my eighteen-month-old son, Augustus Jr., and his Mother, Dr. Alicia Ho, behind.

The decision not to accompany me to the United States had been her decision based on what she believed would be the best long-range decision in the long run for she and our son.

———

To ensure that even with my full-time duties for the GCB, I wouldn't end up with a lot of time on my hands in which to brood, and after I received approval from the Human Relations Manager at the GCB, I applied, was accepted for, and given a rather lucrative one-year contract to be the Technical Script Advisor for the popular CBS television Series, *CSI: Crime Scene Investigation*, set in Las Vegas.

A former instructor friend of mine from the FBI academy, now working out of the Las Vegas FBI field office, had brought the opportunity to my attention. Federal employees are not permitted to moonlight. But he remembered that I had been cross-trained in forensics while with the NYPD, and had been fortunate to be accepted for certification in the ASCLD, the *American Society of Crime Lab Directors*, all of which would be considered a plus in my being considered for the script advisor position.

Besides being interviewed by the experts behind the camera—producers, directors, the manager of the episode writers, a director of scene management, and the head technical supervisor—I'd also had brief interviews with two of the show's principal stars: Mr. William Petersen who plays the character Gil Grissom; and Marg Helgenberger, who appears as Grissom's subordinate, but fellow lab supervisor, Catherine Willows, in the popular series.

My duties as a contract technical script advisor were to critique some of the show's twenty-two planned annual episodes, before the fact.

And if I wanted to take on additional responsibilities, and the pay that went with those tasks, I could make myself available to critique the show's locations, lab set-up, forensic procedures, advise cast members on how test procedures were done in a real operating crime lab, explain the likely police and court interface to writers and the producers, and meet with the series' property managers to advise them what forensic lab equipment they needed to rent for which scenes.

And, of course like all of our job descriptions, the personnel department added to my contract the term "And any other related task as may be assigned." Wow, I hope that didn't mean that I had to sweep the set or anything like that.

And that, my valued readers, brings you up to date on why I am sitting out on the lanai of my new golf course condo, and shaking my head at my disappointment that I feel when I look at the brown cloud of smog hovering over Las Vegas like a skullcap on that beautiful Sunday morning.

TWO

June 2, 2008, Monday, 6:15 a.m.
McCarran International Airport
Las Vegas, Nevada

Bright and early Monday morning I was at Las Vegas' McCarran International Airport to catch a regional commuter flight to the state capitol of Nevada, Carson City.

After orientation and the initial paperwork that plagues every new employee, I would be assigned to the Gaming Control of Board's office located at 555 E. Washington Street, Suite #2600 in Las Vegas, which reports to the Board's Deputy Chief, Patrick Wynn.

But orientation and the initial-hire main personnel functions were to take place at GCB headquarters, which is located at 1919 College Parkway in Carson City, and reports to the Board's Chief, James Martin.

I arrived in Carson City and was met by an attractive, middle-aged woman who had been waiting at the gate. She walked, talked, and smelled of cop. She introduced herself in a go-to-hell tone to me as Senior Board Investigator, Maggie Dupont.

After I retrieved my single piece of luggage, we walked to the front of the airport, which serves as both the Arrival and Departure entrance, where she had left her BuCar double-parked at the curb.

A *Police-Business* placard on its dashboard was all that was protecting the illegally-parked vehicle. The plain-wrap police car was a ubiquitous dark-green 2006 Crown Victoria, which after getting in and buckling up, I noted already had nearly 100,000 miles on the odometer. I assume that meant that DuPont spent a lot of time on the road handling cases, rather than sitting on her trim behind in the HQ shuffling paper.

She obviously was wearing a Glock semi-automatic firearm in a Safari holster under her left shoulder, covered by her suit jacket. She didn't have much to say to me on the way to the HQ other than "Welcome Aboard."

She *informed* me that she had reserved a local hotel room for me. That covered my lodging needs for the week. To make certain the new guy wasn't expecting her to provide portal-to-portal limo service all week, she told me I would have to call a taxi to get back and forth between the hotel and the Board's office.

―――

Monday and Tuesday were spent being fingerprinted, having blood drawn for DNA typing, being photographed, etc., etc.

Then I was sat down like an unruly elementary student in a small windowless beige office. An old bat of a personnel clerk harassed me as I completed ream-after-ream of forms that included background verification, my employment paperwork, a Nevada concealed weapons permit application, and surprisingly, a Bonding application.

She informed me that the boss, Chief Martin, would eventually meet with me mid-week to swear me in. After, I'm sure, he had been assured by his subordinates that I had completed the tons of employment paperwork correctly, selected one of the choices being offered me for State group insurance, selected my payroll deductions, and that I was on-schedule to complete my orientation, all which was programmed to be complete by the upcoming Friday, June 6th.

The only time I was permitted to leave the cramped little office was to go to the bathroom, and the basement firing range to meet with the Board's head Firearms Instructor, Dirk Duncan. It was his job to qualify me on various firearms, including the use of a Taser, which I had never touched in my life, and run a couple of clips through an AK and an Uzi.

Not surprising to me, nor unexpected by the Instructor I assume, in less than forty-five minutes, he interrupted my burning cartridges at the expense of the taxpayers. And brusquely instructed me to get the hell out of there, as you "obviously you are wasting my time. Go back up stairs. Return to the Personnel department's cave and continue to complete your hiring paperwork, Probie." I'm 47 years-of age, and he calls me a Probie?

I wasn't given any homework assignments for either Monday or Tuesday evenings. So I walked over to a nearby mall and rent a couple different versions of the movie *Elliot Ness*. I figuring that watching it would supplement my orientation into my new job.

On Wednesday morning, at 8:01 a.m., I met with Chief Martin for a grand total of five minutes for a swearing-in ceremony witnessed by a tough-looking male Administrative Assistant, who introduced himself to me, as Bart Bosco.

The AA, cum bodyguard, handed me my brand-new credentials and asked in a tongue-in-cheek manner if I had any questions? The intent of the question seemed spurious to me—after all, it only was my third day on the job.

Then Bart escorted me to the elevators for a one-floor-trip-down to the office shared by Chief Martin's seconds-in-command, Deputy Chief Scott Otterstrom, and Deputy Chief, Shawn Reid. The DCs were also the Board's most senior GCB's investigators. It fell to them to brief me on my initial assignment.

The first thing deputies Otterstrom and Reid handed me, was a bright *white* folder with red slashes along three of its four sides. From the way they had handled it, it appeared to be so hot that it figuratively had leapt from their hands into mine. It was stamped 'Open Case' in vivid blue, *Top Secret* in blood red, and along the spine it bore the case's code name, *Fire Bug*. Solving that case was to be my first assignment.

My initial thoughts, driven by how urgently the two men had transferred responsibility for the open case file from their hands into mine, made me understand that in their minds, they had just succeeded in dumping what they felt was a unsolvable crime on the new guy, and they really didn't give a tinker's damn if I failed. Survival instinct—better me than them—I guessed.

I was instructed to make the *Fire Bug* file my homework assignment for the evening. I was to familiarize myself thoroughly with all aspects of the case. Either Deputy Otterstrom or Deputy Reid would answer any questions I conceivably might come up, the following day, Thursday, the 5th.

As I would be flying back to Las Vegas late Friday afternoon, Thursday would be my last full day of welcome-aboard orientation at the Board's Carson City headquarters. Boy, I was totally devastated to learn that!

Then, Otterstrom's Administrative Assistant, a solid-looking Samoan woman who I had been introduced to as Ms. Marilyn Flag, took me to an adjoining office.

She said that she would answer any non-assignment questions for me at that time. And she provided me with an in-depth personnel briefing such as thumbnail sketches of the senior members of the Gaming Control Board and its relationship to the Gaming Commission.

She briefed me on the Las Vegas office's sworn personnel and their backgrounds. Then she made me sign for a copy of the GCB's explicit regulations regarding the carrying and use of firearms, and explained the permissibility of carrying personal firearms off-duty.

I was also handed me a six-inch-thick, three-hole blue manual that covered, among other things, the GCB policy on expense accounts, which explained exactly what constituted a conflict-of-interest, and thus was a violation of Board policy, and what did not.

The conflict-of-interest statutes covered such obvious things as having a meal with a casino employee, and permitting that employee to pay for it. Overtime policy? That was simple. There wasn't any overtime as I was considered to be an exempt-salaried employee.

The woman droned out endlessly about Board's absolute requirement that an investigator was required to report to their direct supervisor at least twice-a-week, unless said investigator was working an approved undercover operation. *She apparently was not aware that, by contract, I was an exception to that order.* Of course, that really wasn't applicable anymore as the Board now prohibited such operations as being too dangerous. Which in real speak probably meant that some finance Winnie had decided undercover operations exposed the board to excessive liability exposure. And, we couldn't have that, could we.

Wednesday evening after dinner I propped myself up in my hotel room's worn-out recliner and began to review the case folder that I had been given for homework. Frankly, I found it to be fascinating. It read like a Joseph Wambaugh police thriller. The case file chronicled an armed robbery of a casino in Laughlin, Nevada, that had occurred back on April 10, 2008.

Laughlin, Nevada, a town of 9,000 permanent residents, is best known as a smaller stepchild to Las Vegas and Reno. It is a town, like Las Vegas, which is totally dependent on revenues collected from Casino gaming and cash from free-spending tourists.

Several years ago, Harrah's Hotel Casino in Laughlin grabbed national Media attention when a melee between a couple of vicious motorcycle gangs, the Hells Angels and their rivals, the Mongols, erupted in the hotel's lobby in 2002. Several bikers had been killed and dozens of others, injured. And for a time, the town's appeal to tourists had suffered.

Despite the fact that Laughlin is 100-miles south of Las Vegas, the well-trained officers of Las Vegas Metro, police the city under-contract.

Laughlin, Nevada is a unique Stateline city separated from Arizona by the Colorado River. The town originally was established through the vision of its founder, Don Laughlin, who purchased an existing eight-room hotel there in 1966 and then proceeded to build the entire town from scratch.

By the 1980's Laughlin's Riverside Hotel-Casino was drawing gamblers and river rats from northwestern Arizona, southeastern California, and southern Nevada.

Today Don Laughlin's Riverside Hotel and Casino draws in over a million visitors annually.

Also during the late 1960's, an entrepreneur, former madam, named Barbara Anne Bush hit town and soon opened the Riverboat Hotel and Casino a couple hundred yards south of Don Laughlin's Riverside.

Both hotel/casinos have continued to enjoy immense popularity among gamers and non-gamblers, over the four decades since.

Current-day visitors to Laughlin find that the city is Nevada's third major resort area, and attracts slightly more than five-million tourists annually. There are ten hotel-casinos in Laughlin and an international airport located in Bullhead City, fifteen-minutes away, just across the Colorado River.

The *Firebug* case folder I opened provided a thumbnail sketch of the armed robbery that occurred at Lady Bush's Riverboat Hotel and Casino back on April 10, 2008, a Thursday.

I sped-read the GCB investigator's preliminary handwritten report, dated 11 April 2008: At approximately 4:00 a.m., three heavily-armed bandits, brandishing black-matte Uzi's, and 45-caliber semi-automatic handguns worn in shoulder holsters, robbed the Riverboat Casino's gaming floor's main cash room.

The robbers had been wearing military-style black jumpsuits, black jump boots, black bullet-resistance vests, and were wearing black balaclava facial coverings that concealed gas masks. Except for an eye holes and thin slits for the mouth, the facial covering served to fully obscure the robber's faces.

The three masked robbers that assaulted the Riverboat Hotel-Casino gaming floor were all of the members of the gang that staff and customers saw during the heist. All three bandits were wearing purple Nitrile medical gloves that investigators would later learn were only manufactured by UniRoyal Chemicals in Mexico.

The 1,000-room hotel-casino, owned and operated by Lady Bush, is located on the Colorado River just yards off Casino Drive, and somewhat south of that road's intersection with Laughlin Civic Drive.

As an apparent precursor to cause disruption for the robbery, at 3:50 a.m., five suspicious fires had been reported to be burning out-of-control inside the hotel proper, and two in the hotel's parking lot.

The first fire was in two of the upper-floor guest suites; the second was in the women's restroom at rear of the main floor Gourmet Room Restaurant; the third had been discovered by a customer on the main floor under several unoccupied cocktail tables in the Hotel's Racetrack Lounge; the fourth was detected inside of the cockpit of a priceless one-only Italian-designed Corvette concept car, among the expensive cars currently on display in the Riverboat Hotel-Casino's classic-car showroom.

The fifth fire, or fires, had been reported in the hotel-casino parking lot, and had involved two cars, parked apart. Before the fire department had arrived, it had been unknown if the fires were tied to the robbery.

If the fires were later determined to have been purposely set, it logically could point to the incidents being a part of the larger plan intended to promote confusion, the best friend of any armed robbery gang.

The Laughlin fire department had responded within minutes. Until the fire department arrived, it had not been known that the smoke from the fires inside the hotel-casino was unknowingly being re-circulated through the facility's forced-air HVAC system. There had been a lot of confusion and therefore, it was understandable that the hotel's maintenance people had been distracted by the shrilling and blaring of every fire alarm in the Hotel-Casino.

At exactly 4:00 a.m., thick smoke began to billow from behind shot machines on the Casino floor. And, in the confusion, aided by the multi-alarms that had split-up the Riverboat's normally implacable security force, three heavily-armed, uber-athletic-appearing, masked individuals, all wearing small white fireman's air tanks on their backs, strode purposely onto the gaming floor, acting as if they just bought it.

They began tossing smoke, flash bang, and pepper gas grenades to either side of their methodic approach to their apparent goal, the gaming floors main cashiers cage.

As the robbers approached the cage, it would be noted later, that the masked individuals had stopped using the military M-84 flash-bang grenades, and after that point, only disbursed smoke and pepper gas grenades into the crowd of patrons.

The resulting panic inside the cage caused the employees to break Casino procedures. They unlocked the cage's security doors to flee in an attempt to escape the blinding smoke, respiratory irritants, and the deafening noise made by the M-84 flash-bangs that had been deployed when the three men first had made their appearance onto the gaming floor.

The employees had already fled the cage when two of the three mask-wearing robbers had entered it, before the cage could lock behind staff as it was designed to do.

The third robber had been wearing military full body armor reminiscent of that national television had shown viewers back in February 28, 1997 during the Bank of America robbery in North Hollywood, California.

But in this case, the third gunman remained outside the cage sweeping his weapon menacingly left, right, left covering the customers and staff with an assault rifle.

The robbers had come well-prepared. They used wooden wedges they had brought with them to jam the cage's security door open, to ensure they wouldn't be trapped inside if some self-appointed hero slammed the self-locking partition closed behind them.

Both hurried about their business in the cash room, and began collecting stacks of bills, fifty-dollar denominations and larger, from the unlocked currency drawers under the expensive wrap-around marble counter.

The cash went into black rip-cloth bags, including everything from the portable cash cart, but only the fifties, and hundreds, that just had been loaded but not yet locked, preparatory to being taken by Security officers to a nearby elevator, and down one floor, to the Casino's fortified basement count room.

The robbers working in the cage made no effort to scoop up any of the valuable Casino chips, any currency under twenty-dollar denomination, nor the stacked rolls of dollar coins sitting in oak wooden cradles on the counter which Casino management routinely handed out as change, in hopes it would encourage customers will play the dollar slots. The safe in the cage didn't even draw a glance from the rapidly-moving, well-trained snatch team.

Following armed robber's first unbreakable maxim to elude capture, the three-minute rule, the heavily-armed robber outside the cage throughout the ordeal had loudly counted back from 180.

As soon as the gunman's count reached zero, the two bandits inside left everything they hadn't already bagged up, slipped out of the cage, easily handling their bulging black rip-cloth bags and made their way through the smoke towards access to the nearest exit.

Following behind them came their machine-gun wielding accomplice, finally done counting backwards, who had walked backwards behind the fleeing men to ensure no one followed them. He continued to deploy smoke and pepper gas grenades as the respiratory irritants and confusion aided them in making their escape.

Patrons would later describe the robbers as being broken-field-runners like Payton Manning or Walter Payton as they weaved their way through the crowd. The customers hadn't posed a threat to the robber's escape as most of them had fallen to their knees in an attempt to catch a whiff of fresh air off the Casino gaming floor.

As the two nimble bandits ducked, jived, and dodged, the full-body-armor-wearing individual plodded along behind them still walking backwards as if mechanical robot, still daring anyone to obstruct their flight.

The bandits successfully avoided any would-be heros through the well-timed use of athletic sidesteps that would have been envied by Dallas' number eighty-one, Terrill Owens, as the threesome vanished like nymphs into the lingering smoke.

By 4:08 a.m., all three apparently had left the premises with military-like precision, two of the three, toting the black rip-proof parachute cloth bags slung over their shoulders, leaving their hands free to use their weapons. The three had disappeared into the moonless April night.

Four minutes later, or by 4:12 a.m., the local fire department had arrived and immediately headed for the reported locations of the fires.

Two-dozen cops from Las Vegas' Metropolitan police department, a few of which had been transported to Laughlin only minutes before by police helicopter from Las Vegas, soon were on the scene directing their initial efforts towards calming frantic, scared, injured customers and staff, alike.

Fourteen customers and seven casino-hotel employees had complained of smoke inhalation, and subsequently were transported by rescue ambulances to area hospitals. A police officer accompanied each smoke inhalation victim to the hospital to obtain their statements before their memories began the natural human process of discarding information that their minds considered to be no longer relevant.

An addendum to the case file, five days later, revealed that the hearts of two elderly women customers hadn't been able to handle the stress. They had both died in the hospital emergency room from smoke inhalation, which led to massive heart attacks.

In the hours before dawn, Investigators from the Nevada State police, and Las Vegas Metro police, began to conduct interviews with customers and the hotel-casino staff that had been instructed to remain on the property.

The interviews continued to nearly to 6 p.m. that evening. No eyewitness, except the injured, regardless of self-proclaimed necessity, political influence, or social position, was permitted to leave before the cops had crossed their names off the incident's interview list.

Customer-relations-sensitive GCB protocol mandated that the customers be interviewed first. Once their interviews were finished, they would be permitted to go home or back to wherever they had been staying the previous evening.

Hotel-Casino staff had been offered a complimentary meal in one of the hotel's restaurants that had been opened to handle the previously unscheduled needs of customers, staff, and investigators.

Casino staff had each been permitted to occupy one of the hotel's empty rooms to sleep, until the front desk alerted them by telephone that their interviewer was waiting.

The establishment's security personnel, now that the cops were on the scene, placed a call to the Gaming Control Board's office in Las Vegas and to the Board's headquarters in Carson City, notifying them that the Casino had been hit, and begged the GCB to get a strike force of Board investigators on-scene, before the cops mucked up the crime scene.

Security personnel padlocked the door to the Casino's main cashier's cage and placed it under armed-guard until the arrival of Gaming Board investigators, some who had helicoptered in the four hundred-plus air miles from Carson City, and others, who were already on-scene, after driving the 100-miles from Las Vegas.

———

The follow-up report had been more formal, having been prepared using a laptop. The investigator had transmitted the file to the GCB headquarters in Carson City, and to an ink-jet printer in the Las Vegas field office. The report was dated 13 April 2008, two days following the robbery.

As expected, the follow-up case report was a thick document that contained copies of all the witness statements; a blurb on the medical condition of injured customers, casino or staff members; a comprehensive list of the hotel-casino's current and past employees going back five years, their tenure, copies of their bonding applications and Nevada police-issued State Work Card applications; any early forensic reports available, an preliminary estimate of the amount of the gang's take; and the investigator's initial shot at piecing together the anatomy of the crime.

In summary, the Board Investigator's armed robbery follow-up surmised the following:

1. That the take from the robbery, as verified by an preliminary audit of the basement counting room's receipts, both before and after the robbery, indicated that over $3,500,000 in United States Currency, $15,000 in now-being-accepted-at par Canadian currency, and the equivalent of $23,000 USD in large-denomination Mexican currency, had been taken.

No casino chips or dollar coins, or anything in the cash room's locked safe, had been touched.

2. The fires on the upper floors of the hotels, those in the restrooms on the gaming floor, and the fires in the classic car section, appeared to have been set using military-issue Phosphorous grenades, commonly called *Willy Peter*.

As many a soldier has learned, a phosphorous fire is almost impossible to put out without a huge supply of water to fight it. Completely stopping a Willy Peter fire requires massive amount of water, which must continuously be used to irrigate it. Then the burning phosphorous must be extracted with heat-resistant tongs and placed under the water inside a airtight container, that essentially robs the ignition source of the oxygen it requires to continue burning.

3. The fire setters had not yet been identified from the hotel's security tapes. But housekeeping staff did report that a maid's cart was missing. Several of the interviewed guests that had rooms on the floor where the rooms had been set ablaze, reported seeing an unusually large number of maids working on the floor, for so early in the morning.

The fact that an maid's cart was later found abandoned in the lounge outside the burned-out restroom, pretty well convinced the investigators that the same person or persons had been responsible for setting the guest room fires, the fire in the lounge's restroom, and the fires in the cars in the resort's exhibition hall.

4. Arson investigators determined that the ignition source of the cars, which had been torched in the parking lot, later discovered to have been stolen, only an hour before the crime, had been accomplished by using military-grade thermite grenades, which were capable of burning through steel.

The investigators felt the arsonists probably had no intention of causing incidental injury to passersby or other vehicles. However, they were familiar enough with the substance they were using to know that its use was over-kill. But they apparently had elected to use it anyway to ensure that they would not be seen loitering near the vehicles that they were torching. To reduce the probability that a roof-mounted security camera would electronically *alert* to the activity, and using its artificial intelligence, adjust itself to zoom in on the act the computer felt to be suspicious.

Law enforcement personnel went over the parking lot's security tapes for the four hours prior to the robbery. They were unable to isolate anyone walking near the parked vehicles, at least anyone who appeared more suspicious that the dozens of other persons in the immediate area of the target cars that morning.

5. The Nevada State Police crime scene investigators, referred to by other cops as *Staties,* reported that while their final report findings would not be available for several days, perhaps a week, criminalists had not reported finding any fingerprints or other preliminary forensics evidence that could be used to identify the bandits.

All that the head of the State Forensics team would share with the Board investigator, was that whoever the bandits were, they had been highly-organized, well-disciplined, well-equipped, and had followed the three-minute rule to the letter. The heist had been was superbly planned from concept through to its execution.

6. It is only possible at this preliminary stage of the investigation to estimate that a low figure of six, and a maximum figure of ten, most likely military-trained or former combat-experienced individuals, had been involved in the execution and support of the robbery.

In the confusion generated by the flash-bang explosions, pepper gas and smoke, no one reportedly saw how the assault team made its escape. No guest cars other than the two stolen vehicles that torched had been reported to be missing from the hotel's parking lot.

The black coverall and accoutrements the heist team wore really didn't provide much help to authorities in identifying the three bandits that attacked the gaming floor. The same basic outfits are worn by many organizations worldwide when on clandestine and covert operations. Just a few of those are:

- American Special Forces.
- The *FBI*, *DEA*, and *U.S.* Marshals.
- *Die Kommando Spezialkrääfte*: The German KSK.
- *Spetsnaz*: Russian elite Special Forces.
- *SAS:* England.
- *Legion etrangère:* French Foreign Legion.
- *Le premiere Rigiment de Parachutiestes d'Infmeric de Marine:* French Special Forces.

7. The preliminary report prepared by the GCB investigator promised that a follow-up report would be issued as soon as additional information became available. The Board investigator, like the other Law enforcement

personnel that had been rushed to Laughlin to deal with the robbery, had been offered complimentary rooms at the Riverboat until the investigation was completed.

And, like the other cops, the Board's investigator refused the offer of the complimentary room, but advised hotel management that she would accept its use if her employer could pay for the use of the room.

There was a brief addendum that had been added to the report a month later that stated that an armored-car robbery had taken place in Las Vegas on May 3, 2008. The senior investigator that had prepared the Riverboat heist reports, felt that perhaps there could be a tie-in with the April 10, 2008 Riverboat robbery, as she felt the tactics and manner of execution, appeared similar.

Both the Preliminary and follow-up reports were signed by the first GCB investigator to arrive on-scene at Laughlin, Ms. Maggie Dupont. Which I noted was the name of the investigator that had picked me up at the airport.

If the Powers-that-Be on the Gaming Board had brought me in to solve a strong-arm robbery that originally been her case, and had additionally portrayed me to Staff as a hot-shot, super-cop that could solve any case, I could understand her less-than-comradely demeanor towards me.

The next time I had the opportunity to see her, I'd make a genuine effort to make my sensitivity and awareness of the situation clear to her. I didn't want to make an enemy of one of the Board's investigators, right off the proverbial bat. Especially since she was such an attractive woman, which I admit was one of my many character flaws. Hell, *making up* might be enjoyable.

THREE

June 8, 2008, Friday, 6:15 a.m.
Dunking Donuts/Baskin Robins Shop
2800 Fremont Drive
Las Vegas, Nevada

About the same time that Inspector Fox was checking out of his Carson City hotel room, two Las Vegas Metro police officers were sitting in their black-and-white, in the parking lot of the newest Dunkin Donut/Baskin Robins franchise in the City of Las Vegas, drinking coffee and eating greasy pastries.

The junior of the two women, Probationary Patrolman Linda La'Sard, was in the report writer's seat while her training officer, Corporal Bethany Jones, drove. The squad was admittedly some distance outside the two officer's assigned patrol sector, but they had wanted to try out the new place's donuts which other officers had told them, *were to die fo*r.

The women were discussing an incident that had occurred the previous day when they had pulled over a black male driving a *pimp mobile,* intending only to inform him that his brake lights weren't working, a courtesy stop.

It had been Officer La'Sard's turn to approach the car and contact its driver. But just as the young rookie was within thirty feet of the rear of the vehicle, its six-foot, three-inch-tall driver opened his door and sprung from the car.

Seeing the five-foot, four-inch-tall rookie walking towards him, the driver screamed and began to walk towards her on his long legs, screaming unintelligible threats. He headed for the startled officer, in his right hand brandishing what, in the slang of Las Vegas Metropolitan Police Department, is referred to as a BFK, or a big fucking knife.

Fortunately for the rookie, a buffed-out, yellow-shirted, black-shorts-wearing Las Vegas bicycle cop by the name of Pete Wilson at the time was slowly pedaling down the sidewalk on the opposite side of the street.

The bike cop had been killing time by looking for jay-walking tourists to ticket when he had observed the dirt bag jump out of his ride and charge the young officer brandishing what appeared to be a twelve-inch-long butcher knife.

The experienced young bike cop saw that the startled young officer had frozen in-place. The woman's partner had been coming to the rookie's aid, but when half way out of the patrol unit, her progress was momentarily halted when her side-angled, black plastic baton caught in her seatbelt.

Patrol officers on bike patrol in Las Vegas are taught during their specialized training to use their bicycles as weapons if there isn't time to otherwise interdict or subdue a potentially dangerous individual.

The bicycle cop was only about five-foot-six and could see that the attacker was well over six-feet-tall. So he did as the training manual suggested, jumped his bike off the sidewalk into the street, frantically pedaled through light-traffic across the street and rammed his bike into the subject's groin.

The assailant fell to the concrete clutching his groin, screaming in pain. The bike cop was surprised at the damage his bike had caused, although knowing it was loaded down with equipment and weighed about seventy pounds.

The impact with the subject had also knocked Officer Wilson him off his bike and to the concrete. But the buff cop couldn't get over the fact that the training manual's maneuver had been so effective. He vaulted to his feet like an Olympic gymnast, dusted off his uniform, and using a kick that his college football coach would have raved about, kicked the suspect's weapon out of his hands and clear across the street to come to a stop against the far curb.

At essentially the same moment, Corporal Jones managed to extricate herself from the patrol car's seat belt, had ran over and pounced on the suspect's back with both her knees. That action served to cut off the assailant's screams as the Corporal's maneuver forcibly purged the man's lungs of air.

The bike cop, now realizing that everything was under control, walked over to check on shaken officer. She began to shake uncontrollably. Jones, her training officer, with perhaps a little more vigor than was required, moved her knee to the back of the gasping suspect's neck. She transferred all of her considerable weight to it as she pulled her handcuffs off her Sam Brown equipment belt and none too gently hooked the dude up.

As soon as assailant got his breath back, he began to rant, rave and threaten all the cops. He tried to howl at the top of his still under-inflated lungs, "My attorney is going to have all your badges. And after that, I'll sue the city. I'm going to own this freaking town, you pigs."

After making certain the rookie officer was okay and would recover as soon as she pulled herself together, the bike cop waited until there was an opening in traffic, then ran over to the opposite curb and retrieved the subject's weapon.

The weapon, now in the possession of the po-lice, sealed the deal. That would be all that was required to convict the subject for the 'attempted homicide on a police officer' that would send him to prison for a very long time.

The next day, at that point of the discussion in the donut shop parking lot, the MTD—Mobile Dispatch Terminal—in the squad car 'beeped.' Until the interruption, the training officer had been nibbling on her crème-filled donut while she counseled the young rookie. She'd just told her, "During the first week on the job the fact that you froze, could of happened to any new cop. You really ought to go a little easier on herself, sister."

"Cops must have short memories or they will always be living in the past, which could mean you could be a little slower in reacting to a life-threatening situation, the next time, in the future."

After the MDT beeped, Jones reached over and pushed a button acknowledging receipt of the transmission, then hit the 'en route' key. The cops hurriedly poured their coffee out the windows onto the pavement outside the car, stuffed the empty cups and what was left uneaten of their pastries under the front seat, and prepared to get underway.

The address they were being dispatched to was out near the city limits on the edge of the desert that surrounded Las Vegas.

The address appeared on the MDT's dashboard screen along with the dispatch: "*All units in the vicinity and Six-Adam-fourteen. See the woman regarding her husband that she claims has been bitten by a rattlesnake. The female complainant, a Ms. Lolly Johnson, will be standing in the street in front of that address to wave you down. She reports that street signs in the neighborhood are missing, having been torn down by gangs in retaliation for residents calling LVMPD with drug and weapons complaints. Primary unit, advise if you need Dispatch to direct you to the scene using GPS. Six-Adam-fourteen, your call is code three.*"

The rookie, who had herself back in control after a good night's sleep, told her training officer to advise Dispatch that they wouldn't require GPS directions. She had been raised in that neighborhood and knew right where the address was.

The training officer leaned over from the driver's seat and punched the MTD's keys to enter the message advising Dispatch that the unit was declining the GPS assist.

La'Sard reached under the monitor of the MDT to flip activate the emergency light bar and siren, as the squad squealed out of the donut shop parking lot and hurried to return to their AA, assigned area, and headed for the RP's—reporting parties—address.

As the squad sped through the quiet city streets enroute the address on the outskirts of the city, Jones slowed briefly at intersections until La'Sard advised her that they were either clear, or that traffic pulled to the curb in response to their flashing and blaring emergency equipment.

As she had been trained, La'Sard kept one eye on the traffic and the other on Jones' driving. Even experienced cops can get so caught up in an adrenaline moment that they find themselves getting in over their heads, skill-wise, when responding on code three calls. It only took a second of inattention to ruin your entire day.

Ten minutes later, as they entered the complainant's neighborhood, the cops slowed slightly for safety, and observed the colorful graffiti and gang signs that were liberally adorning every available surface. The street signs were missing, the street lamps were broken, and a homeowner attempting to defy the gangsters by installing a security fence, had it torn down. Both officers felt for the residents of the area who must feel that they lived in a combat zone.

The gang situation in Las Vegas and vicinity today is like that of other major cities in the country. It rapidly is getting out of control. Oh sure, the gangs knew better than to go anywhere near the Strip as the Metro cops protect that section of town that like they would the virginity of their sisters and daughters.

But here in the 'burbs' away from all the lights and glitter, gangs often have taken over entire neighborhoods. The *gangstas*, as they like to refer to themselves as, are fairly easy to identify them from a distance. They usually fall into a common description of being short, stocky, stupid-looking, with shaved heads, are heavily-tattooed, and are usually twelve-to-twenty-three-years of age.

In some gangs, the members wear do-rags or some other article of clothing that is either red or blue, depending on their gang affiliation.

Gang members and wannabe gang members wear low riders, baggy walking shorts hanging from their hips, and enormous sweatshirts, bulky and long enough to conceal any weapons they might be carrying.

At times it can be amusing. For when they attempt to run from the cops, they often trip on the baggy shorts and fall, which ends up not being much of a competition for the pursuing Po-lice.

Once a neighborhood is known to be occupied by one or more gangs, RAs, or rescue ambulances, often refuse to respond to some of the worst areas without a Metro police escort.

This delay in response, waiting for cops to escort the RAs to the address of the 911-callers requesting medical-assistance, often results in a number of unnecessary deaths of the several critically-injured-or-ill-citizens each month, due solely to the failure of patients being transported promptly to one of the emergency rooms in the area.

In Las Vegas, although deemed by some of the more naïve populace to be inexcusable cowardliness on the part of Metro, there were one or two extremely gang-dominated neighborhoods that RAs will not respond to at all once the sun had set.

In those areas, the responding squad often ends up transporting the victim to the ER.

Gangs have been able to establish a presence in Las Vegas primarily because law enforcement, at times, has been asleep at the switch, or tied up with one priority or another, when the gangs first began testing the waters back in the 1990's.

Current day, a list of the larger gangs represented in the greater Las Vegas include:

- The *Mexican Mafia,* the MM or '*El Eme*'. Most powerful gang of all. The MM is rumored to have up to 500 active members in Nevada alone. Their members wear a tattoo of a black hand with an M in the palm of it.
- African-American Gangs: The *Crips* and *Bloods*. Wear do-rags, a color-specific symbol of their gangs.
- Southeast Asian Gangsters: The *Tiny Oriental Crips, Oriental Boy Soldiers*, or TMC, The *Tiny Magicians Club*. (Oh, and please take note: Asians hate being referred to as Orientals.)

In Las Vegas, some of the gang's networking is so advanced that they are capable of continuing to conduct their illicit activities from jail. Gang slang that a person is "in the hat", or "green-lighted," means that a contract hit has been put out on that individual by an influential gang member, from inside prison walls.

―――

As Jones and La'Sard approached the address to which they had been dispatched, a large black lady standing in the middle of the potholed street waved them down. She was pointing to the driveway in front of a small white ranch-style house that was ten-years-past-due for a paint job.

A battered gunmetal gray 1956 Chevrolet quarter-ton pickup truck with primer paint was parked beside the house, protected from Las Vegas's burning sun by a simple four-post metal lean-to.

Jones turned the marked squad into the driveway, and parked behind the old pickup, La'Sard used the keyboard of the MDT to advise Dispatch that they had arrived on-scene.

The two officers had just gotten out of the car when the excited woman ran up to them, introduced herself as Lolly Johnson, and pointed to the house saying her husband was inside and in "bad shape."

Before entering the house, both officers took a moment to glance around the immediate neighborhood, a common practice of cops in an area heavily populated by gangs.

Seeing no immediate threat, they followed Mrs. Johnson into the house to find an older white man sitting in a recliner, in a surprisingly clean and orderly front room. He apparently had been watching a sports show on an expensive 50-inch plasma flat-screen television, an open, three-quarters-full fifth of expensive sipping whiskey sitting on a T.V. tray at his side.

Mrs. Johnson grabbed the remote, shutting the TV off, and ordered her husband, whose name she volunteered was Abraham, "Tell the Po-lice about your left hand." At the same time she gestured towards the hand that had already been wrapped in a iced towel, which he had been cradling in his lap as he watched TV, and sipped his whiskey.

Corporal Jones took the initiative. "Mr. Johnson, Abraham is it? I am Las Vegas Metro Police Officer Jones and this here is my partner, Officer La'Sard. We are responding to a citizen-needs-help call from Dispatch, from a woman at this address. Have you been bitten by a snake, Sir?"

Johnson glanced quickly at his wife as if asking her permission to speak before responding to the officer. "Yes, I believe I have been." Then he unwrapped the towel to reveal a pair of inflamed puncture wounds slightly less than one-inch-apart on the back of his swollen left wrist.

La'Sard, who had gone through training as a practical nurse several years before she took the big step and joined Metro, as locals refer to the Las Vegas Metropolitan Police Department, leaned over the man to get a better look at the hand and quietly asked, "How long ago did you get bitten, Mr. Johnson? And did you see what type of snake bit you? The type is very important if you happen to know what it was."

Johnson winced in pain from his injury, before responding. "Yeah, I know exactly what type of snake it was. You see, I was out in the back yard cleaning up a little. During the week we normally just stack garbage in plastic bags under the patio lean-to until the weekend when I can cart them to the dump."

"Well, tomorrow is dump day, so I was getting ready to put the trash bags into the rear of the old pickup. When I bent over to pickup one of the bags, I dropped my dime—store reading glasses out of my shirt pocket onto the ground. When I moved the bag aside and bent down again to pick them up, I felt something hit the back of my left hand."

"I must have jumped back about four feet before I looked for what had bit me. I was ready to run in the other direction if it turned out to be something like rabid coyote or a prairie dog that had been staying out of the sun by hiding in the crawl space under our house."

"Well, as first, I didn't see any damage to the back of my hand. So I stepped over and picked up a pointed-end, long-handled shovel and used the metal end to push the bag aside. And there was a coiled rattlesnake, tail-rattling, apparently just waiting for another shot at me."

"Mostly because I was scared, I guess, I started chopping at it with the sharp end of the shovel until I had cut it the sonofabitch in half. But it still was curling and uncurling, and moving around, jerking. So I gave it a few more whacks for good measure. I was pissed off."

Mr. Johnson reached over and took another sip of whiskey before continuing with his story. "Remembering a desert safety class I had gone to when I was working, I looked at my hand and then saw them two small holes on the back of my wrist. Remembering what the nurse had told us back in the class, I grabbed my left wrist, held it below my heart and yelled at Lolly to open the screen door so I could come into the house."

As a aside, he said, "She doesn't like me to do that, you know, yell at her and such. Anyway she let me into the house and I showed her the bite on my wrist. For the life of me, I initially couldn't remember what the nurse those years ago had told us to do next in case of a snake bite."

"But Lolly is pretty smart, except for when she married a no-count lazy honky like me. So she decided that it should be packed in ice until I could get to a hospital for medical treatment."

With a sheepish grin now on his face, Abraham went on. "It was beginning to hurt much more by then. We both thought that being bit by a snake was serious, but it wasn't too serious, if you know what I mean. Not like having a heart attack or some dang-fool thing like that, you know?"

"Then I remembers that the nurse saying those years ago, saying that anyone bit by a poisonous snake would need something called antivenom that is only available at a hospital."

"Anyway, I sat down in the recliner and turned on some re-telecasts of the UNLV basketball games that that are on TV now on Fridays. It's a sport show, you know."

Mr. Johnson helped himself to another sip of whiskey before proceeding. "And although she always bitches about me when I drink in the morning, she brought me a new bottle of whiskey over to sip on because she could see the pain that was in my eyes."

"Soon those tiny holes on my wrist had started to really smart, and my arm swelled up like a pillow. So to dull the pain, you know, while Lolly was on the phone calling 911, I had me a few good-sized swallows of this here sipping whiskey. That made the pain a little more bearable."

"And then," as he finished his story, "you ladies showed up. Anything else you want to know?" Then Abraham took another substantial swallow from what was now a half-empty whiskey bottle.

'Three things," La'Sard told him. "First, go easy on the whiskey. When you have been snake-bitten you are not supposed to drink alcohol. Second, how long ago were you bit? Third, you say you killed the snake. Where is it now?"

Abraham replied, "Going on an hour now, I suspect." He gestured to his wife who led the cops outside under the lean-to and pointed out the remains of a six-foot-long rattlesnake.

Then Mrs. Johnson returned to the house to check on her ailing husband.

"Shit," Jones said. "It's a goddamn Green Mohave—the venom from those is twice as dangerous as the Diamond Back rattlesnake—at least that is what my old man used to tell me when he managed to hold on to a job, believe it or not, for an entire year out at the Reptile Farm in the Las Vegas Dunes Recreational area, north of town."

Jones sent La'Sard out to the squad to retrieve two trash bags from the trunk of their patrol car. When La'Sard returned, Jones had her stuff one bag inside the other. Then she used the murder weapon to shovel the snake's remains into the jerry-rigged double-walled, plastic bag, and gave it back to the rookie to put in their trunk for transporting.

While La'Sard went out to the squad with the remains of the Mohave rattlesnake, Jones got on her rover, the portable radio all Metro officers wore on-duty. "Dispatch, please advise when we can expect the RA to arrive on-scene. The complainant's husband was bitten by a rattlesnake. Verified by RO, responding officers, on-scene, as being a Mohave rattlesnake. This guy needs to get to the emergency room, like *yesterday*. Carcass of deceased snake will accompany the victim to the ER to aid in the specification of the anti-venom."

After a brief pause, Dispatch came back up on Jones' rover to advise her that that as of yet, no RA had been rolled. Dispatch explained the delay by telling her, "The complaint's call only said that her husband needed assistance, and *may* have been bitten by a snake."

Jones was fully aware that Las Vegas Metro dispatch procedure is to roll a squad to ascertain the circumstances first, before dispatching one of the limited numbers of RAs that were available on the street on First Watch, Metro slang for dayshift.

As La'Sard returned from placing the body of the deceased rattlesnake in the squad's trunk Jones released the mike key of her Rover effectively disconnecting the radio transmission and said "Shit!" Then said it once again, just for good measure.

Now in order for them to save the victim's life the cops would have had to break one of many 'black letter law' rules of the Metro police department. This one read: *Never transport a non-custodial citizen in a marked squad car without first obtaining approval from higher-authority.*

La'Sard followed Jones back into the house to break the news to the Johnson family that they would be enjoying a ride in the rear seat of a Las Vegas Metro car running code three for the nearest hospital's emergency room.

By this time, Abraham's left arm had swelled all the way up to shoulder, until it was almost twice the size of his right, and the pain was starting to hit him in earnest. For that reason it took both Jones and Mrs. Johnson to wrestle the whiskey bottle out of his hands.

Then the women escorted him outside and bundled him into the rear seat of the squad. Mrs. Johnson followed her husband into the rear seat and put her large arm over his shoulder, attempting to console him in his pain.

While this was being accomplished, over Mr. Johnson's whining and cries of pain, La'Sard was raiding the couple's refrigerator and filled up some sandwich baggies with ice cubes. They would be used to replenish the ice bags that had already melted in the towel that Mrs. Johnson had previously wrapped around the man's snake-bit left wrist.

In less that two minutes, the squad was headed Code Three through the streets of the neighborhood, en-route the closest hospital. As La'Sard drove, Mrs. Johnson attempted to comfort her husband, while Jones had used her rover to contact the Metro Dispatcher again.

Jones requested that the Dispatcher contact the hospital's emergency room and make them aware that the squad would be arriving at the ER's doors in about twelve minutes.

She informed Dispatch that the passenger was accompanied by his wife. He was a critically ill, older Caucasian male who had been bitten by Green Mohave rattlesnake nearly two hours previously. Further, that the man was in extreme pain and the injured arm had swollen until it was more than twice the size of his uninjured arm.

Exactly eleven minutes later, the black-and-white pulled into the *No Parking—Loading Zone* of the ER to be met by two men and a woman in white hospital garb, pushing a wheelchair.

As the two orderlies gently assisted Mr. Johnson out of the squad's rear seat and into the wheelchair, Mrs. Johnson, now driven to tears out of concern for her husband, got out on her side of the squad and demanded to know why the ER staff hadn't brought a gurney out to the car to collect her husband?

The nurse attempted to explain to the upset wife over her shoulder as medical personnel rushed the ailing man through the sliding glass doors into the ER, that it was ER policy to keep the patient's injured extremity below his heart, hence the decision to use the wheelchair instead of a gurney.

The cops retrieved the green plastic trash bag that contained the body of the dead snake from their squad and followed the procession into the ER. They watched as Mr. Johnson was wheeled into a screened-off trauma room.

Mrs. Johnson was turned away when she attempted to follow her husband into the treatment area. The nurse, that refused the wife's entrance into the medical area, strongly suggested that she "take a seat" in the ER's waiting room.

She was told that someone would be out to get the necessary information required to admit her husband to the hospital.

That was all Mrs. Johnson needed to completely lose her self-control. She stood there, refusing to move, and yelled, accusing the nurse of what she felt was a lack of compassion.

Mrs. Johnson words were becoming mixed with spittle now as she yelled, "Fuck the paperwork, bitch. You do white women that way when they bring their loved ones in for emergency care?"

Mrs. Johnson then proceeded to call the African-American nurse, "an female Uncle Tom, a sell-out to the white community," and several other choice insults direct at the nurse for falling short of Mrs. Johnson's expectations.

But then, almost as abruptly, the wife suddenly shut her mouth when she realized that her blustering was delaying the treatment of her husband. Not to mention that her ranting, raving and stereotype racial epitaphs were getting her nowhere fast. She sighed and finally took the seat that the nurse had been pointed out to her previously.

While Mrs. Johnson sat, still simmering, a clerk cheerfully pulled up a chair and sat down across from the wife. She patiently asked for her husband's medical information, and began to fill out what only would be the first of many forms that must be completed to obtain medical care from any for-profit, current-day hospital.

While Mrs. Johnson fumed and gave short, abrupt, and rude answers to the clerk's questions, the two Metro officers, reasonably certain that a one-woman riot had been narrowly adverted, sought out a empty corner in the busy ER. Both officers began to write their incident reports. Mrs. Johnson may or may not have been comforted by knowing that the cops hated paperwork just as much as she did.

One of the interns hurried out and took the bag that contained the sliced-up snake from the cops. He carried it back into the treatment area, only pausing to explain that the attending doctor must verify the type of snake in order to know what type anti-venom to administer to the patient.

In about twenty minutes, the wife had completed the admissions paperwork for her husband, but the cops were still filling out their stacks of forms, which consisted of no less than four separate types of Metro incident report forms.

At that point, a doctor hurried out of the trauma room and cautiously approached the wife. He introduced himself as Dr. Raul Cisco. Then he gave Mrs. Johnson a brief verbal update report on the current condition of her husband.

"Mrs. Johnson, your husband is in very critical condition. We have taken his vital signs, drawn blood work, administered an EKG, and performed an abbreviated physical examination of his systemic responses to stimuli."

"The Metro officers fortunately had the forethought to bring the carcass of the dead snake in with them. Because of that, our poison expert has been able to confirm that it was a Mohave. This finding was critical in order to determine the correct type of antivenom that your husband will require."

"And, I'm very sorry, but the news isn't good at this point. The venom is attacking your husband's left arm. There is a possibility that even if his heart is strong enough to get him through this crisis, he may eventually lose all or a portion of the injured arm. We are fighting to prevent the debilitating effects of the venom from spreading throughout to the remainder of his body, especially to his nervous system, pulmonary system, and of course, his heart."

"Mrs. Johnson, I know you are very upset, but please try to keep faith in modern medical medicine. We intend to admit him to a private room and place him under around-the-clock observation. He is attached to machines that will monitor his vitals signs continuously. Blood work will be drawn every two hours, around the clock."

"We are not permitting visitors at this time. This frankly is because when we have permitted that practice in the past, often family will see horrendous physical manifestations that all snakebite patients go through, and misinterpret them to mean their loved one is terminal. Their assumption often proves to be unfounded."

"But when loved ones make those assumptions, even erroneously, it only serves to upset them even further. To the point where in the past, situations have gotten out of control and members of the family have assaulted the ER staff. That resulted in the interference with the critically-ill patient's trauma care. More than once, that disruption has resulted in the unnecessary death of the patient."

"I and the other doctors are aware that you are here. One of us will come back out to brief you as soon as we learn anything further about his condition or prognosis. Okay? Your husband appears to be an otherwise healthy person. We just have to hope that will bring him through this crisis. Now, please excuse me, I must get back to Mr. Johnson."

On the doctor's way back into the trauma room, the doctor detoured by the two cops that by now had completed their voluminous paperwork. He repeated to them the facts that he had shared with the wife. However, he added that he felt the victim would need to be administered at least twenty vials of the antivenom.

He reported that, Mr. Johnson's left arm had already swelled to at least three times normal size. And while the staff had him on a morphine drip, Mr. Johnson was still in such extreme pain that they'd had to further sedate him to prevent his disrupting the rest of the patients and families in the ER.

"Even then," he said to the officers, "there still is no assurance that the man will survive his wounds. Mainly due to the nearly two hours between the time he was bitten, the family decided to call 911 for assistance, and the overall time that unfortunately elapsed before Mr. Johnson was transported to the hospital so he could receive proper attention. Oh, and despite the fact that Johnson apparently chose to treat his pain with liquor before he arrived at the ER, which is the worse thing he could have done."

"Thank you both for having the presence of mind to bring the snake carcass in with him. The fact alone permitted the staff to know exactly which antivenom to start. That may be the one positive pivotal factor upon which, the patient's recovery may hinge. You have done an outstanding job. I will make certain the Chief of Service here calls your watch commander and makes that fact clear. You both should be awarded a *Bravo Zulu* for your work this morning. I have to run now. Again, good job."

As the doctor returned to the trauma room, the cops gathered up their completed paperwork and returned to their hastily-parked squad which luckily had not yet interfered with the unloading of any ambulances despite the extend length of time the cops had been inside the ER.

La'Sard noticed that as they got into the squad that Jones was shaking her head. "What is the matter, Bethany," she asked?

Still shaking her head, the T.O replied, "Wait until that poor woman gets the bill for twenty vials of antivenom. The antivenom is $2,000 per vial, you know. Even if they have insurance, added to the bill for his hospital stay here, they are going to be swamped paying their portion of the bill when it arrives at their home."

Jones picked up the squad's mike and notified Dispatch that they were clear of the hospital, available to handle calls, and headed back into their assigned patrol sector, the remains of their donuts forgotten under the front seat of the squad.

The good work the two officers had done that morning would soon reach the ears of the Honorable Oscar Goodman, Mayor, of Las Vegas.

FOUR

June 8, 2008, Sunday, 8:10 p.m.
Vicinity of Metro's Downtown Area Command
401—South 4th Street.
Las Vegas, Nevada

Seventeen-X-ray-thirty-two, an unmarked Ford Crown Victoria, rolled south on Las Vegas Blvd, better known as the Strip. This concentrated area of casinos was located in Metro's Downtown Command precinct. Both cops, experienced officers, paid close attention to what was going on the sidewalks to either side of their cruising slickback.

For the past five years, policing of the Las Vegas' Downtown Command had been performed under what the Media refers to as the Downtown Initiative. Basically it is a program established by downtown community leaders to reduce the amount of chronic crime occurring in Las Vegas' lucrative casino district.

What it meant to those with criminal records, was that if they were apprehended for committing a crime in the downtown area, a crime for which a citation was normally issued, they instead would be arrested and taken to the Clark County Detention Center, booked, and arraigned.

The Las Vegas Metro police department is huge, having 5,000 sworn police officers, primarily due to the fact that the combination city/county force also contracts police services to over a dozen other Nevada cities, such as Laughlin.

The senior officer in the squad tonight was driver by basis of seniority. His given name was Percy Edward Smith, the III. He was thirty-eight-years-of-age, a dark-skinned, substantial-looking African-American who was proud of his Harry Bellefonte good looks.

The cop was six-feet-tall and weighed a hefty two-hundred-and-five pounds, of which Smith would only admit to one-hundred-and-eighty-five pounds. Percy had graduated from UNLV, the University of Nevada-Las Vegas, where he played center on the University's championship basketball team in the mid-90s.

Smith's university degree was in Movie Directing and Producing, which he had mistakenly expected would guarantee him introductions to A-List Hollywood insiders as soon as he graduated.

When that didn't materialize, Percy had joined the cops and been on the job at Metro for five years. He was proud of the fact that he never had been required to fire his weapon during his brief career, although he had drawn it numerous times before.

As with cops in most law enforcement agencies, Officer Percy Edward Smith the III wasn't referred to by that name by other Las Vegas cops. The *nom de plume* or nickname his fellow cops had hung him with, was Hollywood.

Percy had acquired this moniker before graduating from the Nevada police academy.

Upon completing the academy, he moved to a small one-bedroom apartment inside the city limits of Laughlin, as was required by his new assignment.

While his single co-workers, the department-preferred marital state for any rookie assigned to Laughlin, spent their time off-duty prowling the casino's looking for a little action with the opposite sex, Hollywood instead spent his time getting to know the performers at the casinos.

Anytime Hollywood got word through his casino entertainment contacts that a movie or television series was going to be filmed in Laughlin, extras would be required, and he could work it into his real job's schedule, he made a point to be the first in-line to apply for the opportunity.

Soon he came to know the various television and movie talent agents who furnished extras to the movie industry on a first-name basis.

Among those many talent agents he kissed up to was one that had presented applicants for the cast for *Viva Laughlin*, then a new action show. Hollywood managed to secure a minor part on the show but soon after a couple episodes had aired, the network canceled it for having unacceptably low ratings.

After a couple months of keeping his nose clean on his real job, and continuing to ingratiate himself with these low-level show business functionaries, Hollywood suddenly he found that he no longer had to wait in-line to be hired like other potential extras. Instead he would receive calls on his cell phone offering him employment.

The agents all wanted to hire an extra who showed up on time, didn't expect special privileges as some cops had done before him, and never quibbled about the hourly rate paid.

Hollywood continued to work hard and gained the reputation for being a reliable and dependable contact for the agents. Not to mention that as an ambitious young Metro officer, he soon had a lot of equally young, ambitious, photogenic co-workers who thought Hollywood was their answer to getting in the movies in a big way. Based mostly on propaganda generated by the publicity-wise young cop.

When Hollywood's two years of paying penitence on Laughlin's streets finally gained him an opportunity to transfer back to Las Vegas Metro, he jumped at the chance.

He brought his moonlighting job along with him to his cushy new patrol assignment in Las Vegas' Downtown Area Command with him. He wanted to become known as a Joseph Wambaugh-caliber contact that could get things done.

His off-duty hours were spent working to enlarge his stable of influential contacts in Sin City's movie and television industry. He even managed to catch a few walk-on parts in some B-grade police procedural adventure flicks.

Ambitious, publicity-hungry cops in Las Vegas Metro soon came to learn that Hollywood was the man to see for an introduction to a hiring agent for one of the hundreds of 'extra' job opportunities that the movies and television brought to Vegas annually.

While Hollywood never took advantage of, or charged a finders fee, to introduce his co-workers to potential employers in the entertainment industry, talent agents specializing in hiring extras for productions frequently made sure he received either a bigger on-screen movie part, or some under-the-table cash remuneration as a consulting fee, for making their jobs easier.

Hollywood's partner, who was performing the right-seat job of Report Writer today, was Robert Shaw. He was five years younger and light-years more naïve than his senior partner. The young man was fair-haired and fair-skinned, and his face often sported a burn, a result of being out in Las Vegas' laser-like sun.

Shaw looked professorial, stood six-foot, three-inches in height, had a slightly elongated neck, was slim in build, and weighed in at little more than one-hundred, sixty-five pounds.

When he had been in the police academy his classmates had been christened him *Icabod*, after the character Icabod Crane who lost his head galloping his horse through the forest one night in some timeless nursery fable.

Shaw hated the nickname but knew it would normally take him at least a couple years on the job until an opportunity came along that would permit him to change it.

Year ago, Shaw had abruptly resigned from Harvard when he decided that he really didn't belong in a student body which mostly consisted of egocentric kids who cared nothing about the working man.

So, while he was sitting around wondering where he and his career had gone wrong, Shaw decided to apply to the Federal Bureau of Investigation.

After the requisite time in training, Shaw graduated from the FBI Academy with honors. However, he balked at accepting the only job that the Quantico instructors had offered him at the time. The hiring freeze that the Bureau was currently going through, was just another one of its periodic street-agent staffing 'reorganizations.'

Recognizing Shaw's qualifications, the FBI attempted to retain him in-house by offering him a management-training position in forensic accounting. But the offer was a disappointment for Shaw.

Quantico academy counselors frankly told him that the position was not, and never would, lead to employment as a street agent. It entailed sitting behind a desk working white-collar crime.

The position, while paying at a higher-pay-grade than that of a rookie FBI street agent, didn't meet Shaw's hankering to get into job where he would be tested both mentally and physically. So the young man turned down the position, resigned from the Bureau, and returned to mope about his apartment in Las Vegas.

One day, a friend of Shaw's suggested that his itch for action might best served working for a police department. On a whim, he applied for a job of patrolman on Las Vegas Metro.

When the police department's personnel recruiters completed a cursory background investigation, and verified his outstanding university credentials, they looked no further and moved Shaw up to the top of the hiring roster for the job he had applied for.

During training, Shaw breezed though any test or interview the department put in front of him. Department recruiters were stumbling over each other trying to lure the brilliant young man into accepting one of the professional support slots they were responsible for filling.

Since Metro's personnel department's had only rushed through an cursory background check in an effort to make certain they didn't lose such an ideal candidate, they hadn't learned nor had he had volunteered that he was had attended the FBI Academy and had graduated at the top of his class at Quantico.

Despite Metro's personnel recruiters wondering why he wanted to be a street cop, he was accepted, and again finished his training at the top of his class. Upon graduating Shaw followed the usual career path for a young cop in those days, that being serving as a patrol officer in the gaming City of Laughlin, which turned out to be about the same time that Hollywood had been promoted to a training officer slot back to Las Vegas.

Two years later when Shaw's time in Laughlin was up, and he'd been transferred back to patrol in Las Vegas, he ran into Hollywood at roll call, totally by coincidence.

The two single cops got together when they got off-duty that evening, stopping at a local cop hangout and had a few beers together. After a few hours of tipping more than a few and discussing each other's goals, experiences, and philosophy, the two wildly different officers grew to admit they understood each other's weaknesses, and respected their strengths.

So, after the next start-of-shift roll call, they walked in to see the watch commander, and submitted a personnel request to be partnered up with one another on patrol.

The only thing that Hollywood as senior man asked of Shaw was that he consider changing his nickname from Icabod to *Professor*. He felt the new nickname more scholarly and better befitting of Shaw's personality.

The two cops had just signed back on patrol after taking code seven at Fatburger, which is located across the street from the Monte Carlo casino.

Fatburger establishments can be found at a dozen other locations around Las Vegas, and all unashamedly use as their slogan, 'The last Great Hamburger Stand.' They specialize in toothsome charbroiled burgers, hefty chili dogs, and crispy 'fat fries.' All of which were extremely popular with street cops. The fact that, unofficially, Fatburger comps bottomless soft drinks for cops *may* of had something to do with the attraction.

With the typical routine of a subsequent burp or two to signify the cop's approval of the Fatburger high-caloric fare they had just consumed, and the insertion of a wooden tooth pick in their mouths, Seventeen-X-ray-thirty-two returned to their assignment for the evening. That was Pickpocket and Prostitution abatement on the Strip under the guidelines of the Downtown Initiative.

As visitors may or may not know, prostitution is not legal in the City of Las Vegas, or in Clark County, the political entity in which Las Vegas is located. Hooker and Pickpocket patrol, two of the most frequent crimes committed on the Strip, are the crimes that often drive otherwise fun-seeking tourists away, never to return to sin city.

If one of the often-clueless Metro bosses whose enjoyed offices in the Ivory Tower at 400 Stewart Street had asked either of these officers to sum up their assignment in three words, they would emphatically would state that it was *Protecting the Tourist*. Anything else invariably fell into a lower priority.

The cops rolled down the blvd in the unmarked squad. Both men were amazed by the number of tourists, con men, prostitutes, transsexuals, the homeless, and panhandlers that clogged the sidewalks and crosswalks along the Strip, even occasionally spilling out onto the street.

Panhandling was a misdemeanor transgression that Seventeen-X-ray-Thirty-two always dealt with by merely flipping the switch on their unmarked squad's siren on-and-off, which usually got the violators' attention and thus eliminated any need for the cops to stop and get out of their vehicle. Which would have resulted in the gridlock of Las Vegas' busiest thoroughfares.

As usual, the blinking, flashing, fluorescent lights emanating from the Casino signs on both sides of the busy tourist-clogged streets were beginning to give both officers headaches, one of the occupational hazards for those who drew the plum assignment of working the Strip.

As Hollywood stopped the squad for a stoplight at Las Vegas Blvd and Flamingo Road, Caesar's Palace on their right and the Barbary Coast on their left, both officer's attention was drawn to a gleaming white 1959 Cadillac convertible with its top down, sitting in the right-turn lane on Flamingo Road East.

The Professor, having the most recent Laughlin street experience, turned to his partner sitting in the driver's seat, and asked, "Percy, isn't that the good-for-nothing meth freak Mercado Chavez driving that primo old classic Cadillac convert?"

Hollywood shaded his eyes from the blinding light coming from Caesar's florescent signs, and replied, "By God, Professor, your peepers are in fine form tonight, my man. That certainly be that floor-flushing *tweeker* Chavez, who I've been told, claims he is related to the Governor of Puerto Rico. That Caribbean nigger never had two coins to rub together in all the time I knew him in Laughlin. Now how do you suppose he got enough scratch together to buy a fine ride like that?"

Just then, Chavez took a free right-hand-turn south off Flamingo Road onto Las Vegas Blvd. The Professor was unable to get the license number of the caddy because no plate was present in the car's rear license plate holder.

In its place was a white slip of official-looking paper taped where the license plate would normally be affixed. Apparently a temporary registration. Perhaps Chavez had just purchased the car and was waiting for license plates from Nevada' notoriously slow Department of Motor Vehicles.

When the squad's turn came for their light to turn green, Hollywood accelerated their car forward at a moderate place in order to not spook Chavez. However, he was able to pull within a couple of car lengths of the caddy which currently was being driven in the right hand lane. Chavez meandered along, appearing to be engaged in the same thing the two cops were, cruising and scoping out the crowd that filled the sidewalks on both sides of the blvd.

Then the caddy abruptly, without making the required lane change signal, pulled over to the curb in front of the Bellagio pool. The driver appeared to be engaging a young blond woman in earnest conversation. Based on both cop's experience and personal familiarity with the area, they knew that the woman was a prostitute who they had warned off the Strip several times in the past.

Apparently the negotiation didn't prove fruitful for Chavez because he gave the woman the finger and screeched the white caddy back into traffic, again without signaling.

The Professor spoke up, and said, "My, my, Percy. Did you observe that obvious traffic infraction? The boy and his vehicle are a safety hazard out here on the blvd, endangering the good tourists. What do you think we ought to do about that, partner, inasmuch as the man's reckless driving is endangering our future paychecks?"

"Yeah, partner, I think it's time we have a come-to-Jesus conversation with Mr. Chavez. But let's not reveal that that our probable cause for stopping him is based solely on his pulling back into traffic without signaling. One of those liberal judges in traffic court might see that action as petty," Hollywood chuckled.

He continued, "Professor, I'll tell him we've stopped him because of an equipment violation. Since it is just a fix-it ticket, perhaps our boy will be more forthcoming to us. I'm going to light the caddy up as he approaches Tropicana Avenue, and order him to turn right and pull into the rear parking lot of *New York, New York*. That way we'll have the for a meaningful conversation with the man, without blocking traffic."

"I don't think he will try to rabbit on us partner but stay alert once to get him pulled over. Stay hard on his right-hand car door. Have your weapon unholstered and down below the level of the top of the door as I approach him and request his documents. To the best of my knowledge, Chavez has never refused to comply before but there always is the first time. We don't know. The damn car could be stolen; he panics; goes off the deep end; and we end up with a firefight on our hands. That wouldn't be good, partner."

Shaw acknowledged his partner's instructions by a simple, soft-spoken concurrence, "Okay, Boss."

As the Squad passed the Monte Carlo Hotel on their right, Hollywood pulled directly up on the bumper of the convertible and lit-him-up with the emergency lights concealed behind the squad's grill.

Chavez apparently didn't see the lights in his rear view mirror at first, so Hollywood tickled the siren switch briefly which finally got the man's attention.

Now that he had Chavez's attention, Hollywood switched the radio over to outside loudspeaker and spoke into the mike that he had removed from the dashboard's retaining clip.

Annunciating clearly, he said, "*Sir, please turn your car westbound on Tropicana. Pull into the parking lot of the New York-New York so neither of us gets rear-ended in this traffic.*"

Chavez shook his head, obviously irritated, but he knew the drill. While he didn't think he had violated any traffic laws, he knew that ignoring lawful commands from the police could escalate a simple traffic stop into a major confrontation. That would most certainly end him up in serious trouble, he knew. He'd been there, done that, more times than he cared to remember.

He pulled the caddy into the parking lot, parking as close to the hotel's retaining wall as possible. Early evening was a busy time at the New York-New York Casino. Cars continued to pull past him into the parking lot, and he wanted to be far enough over to avoid getting any scratches on his new convertible.

Unfortunately, the four lines of Cocaine and the three shots of Tequila that Chavez had already consumed that evening would momentarily propel his mouth into a nasty confrontation with the two cops.

The squad pulled up directly behind the caddy, preventing Chavez from backing out of the lot. Both cops got out of their vehicle, inserting their riot batons into the Sam Brown belt ring holders. They had their heavy police-duty flashlights in their left hands, with their right hands cupped over the butts of their service weapons.

The nearby concrete retaining wall, and the way the mutt had stopped his car, forced Hollywood to squeeze his body into the narrow remaining space, causing him transfer the dust off the Cadillac onto the front of his uniform pants, and the dirt off the retaining wall, onto his butt.

As the senior Metro officer inched his way sideways up to the caddy's window, he was careful to not step in front of the 'B' post, the vehicle's lateral structural divider between the front and rear seats.

When he was just behind the drivers' door, Hollywood called out to the driver in a seemingly friendly, disarming voice, "Evening, Sir. You certainly got close to the wall, didn't you?" Jokingly he said, "Is it okay if I send you my uniform's dry-cleaning bill tomorrow? Wow, I shouldn't have eaten that last hamburger at lunch. I can barely fit through here."

He directed his flashlight's beam into the eyes of the Cadillac's driver while covertly removing his weapon from its holster with his right hand.

While Hollywood had been side-stepping up to contact Chavez, the Professor had moved up and was standing just behind the passenger's door, directing the beam of his flashlight onto the driver's lap. At the same time, he eased his weapon out of the holster and down along the rear of his right leg, out of the view of the caddy's driver.

Apparently the casual comment about the cleaning bill set Chavez off. He looked over his left shoulder at the cop, and barked, "Mother fucking, Hollywood. What's an Uncle Tom nigger doing stopping me anyway? Trying to come up with a script for another of your wasted attempts at hitting it big in the movies?"

"And I heard on the streets that you have been demoted and forced to partner-up in a salt-and-pepper team. With some failed ex-school teacher. Is that your speed now? Running around with a white cop who probably kisses your ass to get a part in a movie as one of your dog breath extras? What the hell did you stop me for, nigger?"

Hollywood took a deep breath, holding it for a couple of brief seconds before expelling it completely. Doing his best to remain calm, Hollywood leaned his head into the open window of the caddy violating the prohibition against doing exactly what he now was doing, solely to permit him to confront his tormentor eye-to-eye.

"Driver, I need to see your driver's license, proof-of-insurance, and the registration for this vehicle, please," Hollywood politely asked. All the while, he was biting his lip to keep from flying off the handle and slugging the man. That appeared to be what Chavez was trying to goad him into.

"Okay, okay, your motherfucker," Chavez said as he removed his seat belt and dug out his wallet to retrieve his drivers license and proof-of-insurance.

He told Hollywood, "Nigger, you'll have to slide your fat black ass back to the license plate rack at the rear of my ride if you want to get my registration."

By this time, catching an silent gesture from his partner indicating that the routine traffic stop was fast escalating into a physical confrontation, the Professor brought his weapon up and rested it on the sill of the windowless passenger door, pointing the barrel right at the driver's lap, and re-directing his flashlight directly into Chavez's eyes.

Hollywood, still maintaining his cool, took Chavez's license and proof-of-insurance in hand, and informed him, "You were stopped for an simple equipment violation, Mr. Chavez. You appear to have a broken taillight. If you hadn't gotten unruly, insulted me, my race, Las Vegas Metro, and through me, the fine citizens of Clark County, you possibly would have left here with a fix-it ticket."

Chavez's eye grew large and round, and he started sputtering. "What do you mean a broken taillight, nigger? I just got through hand-washing this ride a few hours ago and I can assure you that there ain't no damaged taillight, except in the bigoted minds of you and your homosexual partner."

The night air suddenly seemed to get darker and quieter, as if someone had shut off the constant noise of traffic rolling off Las Vegas blvd. Hollywood waved a hand at the Professor, silently telling him to chill. He knew the mope was trying to create an incident.

Hollywood continued in his efforts to give the man every opportunity to muzzle his mouth and avoid a session of roadside police justice, here in the darkened parking lot at the rear of the casino.

Taking another calming breath, Hollywood said, "Professor, I believe that I will take Mr. Chavez up on his helpful suggestion that I retrieve his vehicle registration off this fine car's rear license plate holder. Please be so good, Officer Shaw, to keep an eye on our friend from the mean streets of Laughlin here. We certainly don't want him to get injured, or suddenly fall ill during my brief trip to the rear of his automobile, do we?"

As Hollywood slid back the length of the classic Cadillac, Chavez turned his mouth on the Professor. "How does it feel to be Hollywood's asshole buddy, Professor? Bet when you have a quiet moment, and find a dark spot to park, he doesn't even use KY jelly does he?"

Suddenly the brittle sound of shattering plastic came from the rear of the car. Following which Hollywood shimmied his way back up the caddy's driver's door, and made a point of stuffing his flashlight back into its belt holder. Chavez began to get out of the car, but Hollywood blocked him, and began laughing.

The cop said, "Imagine that, Mr. Chavez. It turns out your car's left fin taillights—the two classic plastic taillight bullets—are broken. Pity you chose to not take my word for it at the time. Come on out of the car now, Mr. Chavez. Walk in front of me back to the rear of your car and I will show what I am talking about."

Hollywood stepped back and allowed Chavez to open the car door. Then the mutt got out and stepped in front of the cop as they both worked their way back to the rear of the caddy.

Hollywood, finally beginning to lose his cool, began to speak to the man in a condescending voice, "You have to be very careful when buying one of these restored old cars, Mr. Chavez. The plastic they used in taillight lens back in the late fifties was very brittle."

Chavez stood staring at the damaged tail light. Then he bent his knees slightly to glance at the red shards of the broken taillight lens that lay underneath the car, and turned his body to the left to look over at the holstered flashlight on Hollywood's Sam Brown belt.

Then a keening sound began to come from the driver's mouth as he cleared his throat, and then cleared his throat again, attempting to bring up some saliva.

Then Chavez launched himself at Hollywood while at the same time directing a huge glob of spit into his face.

The Professor made a valiant attempt to run around the car and grab the man before Chavez took his partner all the way down to the concrete. However, his lag in reaction time made him a nanosecond too late.

Failing in that, the Professor grabbed his can of pepper spray off his belt and holding Chavez's head back with a firm grip of the man's greasy hair, used his other to direct a three-second burst of chemical reeducation into the man's face.

Chavez began to scream and claw at his eyes while prudently electing to roll into a ball to avoid any further administration of any sort of attitude-modifying reeducation.

Driven by adrenaline, Hollywood bounded up onto his feet. It required both cops to wrestle Chavez's arms behind his back and hook him up. Then they dragged him to the rear of the squad, gave his pockets a brief shake to make certain he wasn't carrying anything that could be used as a weapon, opened the rear door, and threw him into the back seat.

After Chavez scrambled himself back up into a sitting position the cops locked him firmly in-place using the combination seat belt and shoulder harness.

Hollywood used his handkerchief rub the spit off his face and to dab at some of the cuts and abrasions he had received when he had been driven him down to the unforgiving pavement.

The Professor used the squad's MDT to call in a 10-13, a CODE RED, *"Officer Needs Immediate Assistance,"* and requested a rescue ambulance for Hollywood. While they waited for the ambulance, the Professor began to work on the pile of cover-your-ass paperwork that an incident like this always generates.

As the Professor worked on the reports in the squad's front passenger seat, Chavez continued to yell over the seat, insulting the cop's mother, heritage, sexual preference and anything else that came into his enraged drunken mind, while the tall cop ignored him and continued writing.

Hollywood had stopped most of the hemorrhaging from his mostly minor injuries using the squad's first-aid kit. He washed his face off and his mouth out with the sterile water the department provided to all patrol units in these days of AIDS and other STDs. Then he pulled on a pair of latex gloves.

Then the officer proceeded with the required inventory of the Cadillac which included the car's trunk, as was mandatory when any vehicle, abandoned or not, was impounded in the State of Nevada.

Hollywood inspected under the Cadillac's seats, in its ashtrays, inside its glove box, under the carpet, and into the little opening that exists behind most vehicle's ashtrays, before he gave up finding anything evidentiary inside the cockpit of the car.

So he slammed the doors closed and walked back to open the trunk with Chavez's keys. He flicked on his flashlight, tucked his head in and rooted around in there for a minute, until suddenly, he stopped digging.

The senior cop pulled his head out of the trunk smiling and yelled at his partner, "Professor, bring a few evidence bags over her, will ya?" As the Professor walked the bags over to the car, he was half expecting to see a live snake or scorpion loose in the caddy's voluminous trunk.

But Hollywood just shook his head, before grinning the biggest grin that the Professor had ever seen on his partner's face as he held up five pieces of white paper tape imprinted on one side with the script "Riverboat Casino-$100 denomination USD."

In Nevada casinos, currency bands by specific denomination are used to bind together bundles in like denominations, once the bills come off the gaming establishment's mechanical currency-counting machines.

However, when currency goes in the opposite direction, incoming cash deliveries from the Federal Reserve Bank are bound in 100-counts. In other words, one bundle of $100 bills would represent $10,000 in USD currency, commonly referred to as a 'brick' by street criminals and cops alike. Yes, Mr. Chavez was in deep kimche, all right.

FIVE

June 9, 2008, Monday, 9:30 a.m.
Las Vegas Metro Police Department HQ
400 Stewart Street
Las Vegas, Nevada

Senior Investigator Maggie DuPont and myself made our way through the revolving glass doors and into a lobby dominated by a large, well-equipped security cum reception desk to where two uniformed members of Metro's contract security contingent sat.

They were providing directions to visitors for various destinations throughout the immense building. Metro Headquarters is located in the same building that serves as Sin City's City Hall.

That morning, Maggie DuPont and I were anticipatory and on a bit of a natural high because a Metro detective thought he might have a tip for us on the open Laughlin Riverboat Casino-Hotel armed robbery case, back in April.

But here I go getting ahead of myself. Let me fill you in on the details.

I had flown back into Las Vegas from the orientation session at headquarters in Carson City late, Friday evening. I spent a lazy two days watching football on television and putting my few personal belongings away in the master bedroom.

I also had given some deep thought as to what I would say to Investigator DuPont the next time I saw her. It appeared that the Board, in its apparent wisdom, had elected to take the Laughlin case away from her, and assigned it to me, a new hire, apparently feeling that I could resolve the crime in a more timely manner than she would have. I'm certain that wasn't the way she saw the case transfer, and in her shoes, neither would I.

I had arrived for work at the Las Vegas office on Monday, the 9th, about 7:45 a.m. I was trying to make a good impression on my first real day on the job. You understand I'm sure.

I walked into the Gaming Control Board's suite 2600, which is located in a medium-security building at 555 E. Washington blvd. My arms were filled with my old beat-up maroon leather briefcase and a Bankers file box.

I set the box down on the reception counter, which freed up a hand permitting me to flip open my brand-new identification credentials, one-handed to display to the male administrative assistant apparently assigned to keep any unauthorized individuals from violating the sanctity of the GCB's Las Vegas regional office.

Then I picked up the Bankers box once again and was led by the AA down a wide-carpeted corridor to the corner office of Kathleen A. Faust, Special Agent, the Board's Liaison Officer, and I assume, official greeter of new-hires.

Although her office had glass floor-to-ceiling on two walls, it only gave her a view of the building's postage-stamp-sized rear parking lot.

Ms. Faust, a pleasant, attractive and business-like woman, exchanged banal greetings with me for a few minutes as she welcomed me to the Gaming Control Board, the Las Vegas office, and to my new on-the-job home.

Faust, smiling inwardly like she was privy to a secret that I was not, informed me that my first visitor was already waiting for me. And that said visitor had been patiently waiting for my arrival since 7:00 a.m. that morning.

It was obviously that I hadn't impressed Ms. Faust in the least by arriving at what I consider to be early for a Monday morning.

The Liaison Officer rose and escorted me further down the corridor that some tasteless maintenance individual years ago had painted a depressing shade of institutional gray. She stopped and gestured with the well-manicured fingers of her left hand, to what passes for the office as a Chief Investigator at the GCB.

It was a door-less, window-less room about ten-by-twelve in size. It was smaller than I had expected, and most certainly had grown used to over the past twenty years. Perhaps the undesirability of the accommodations was intended to keep me out on the street, working cases. Yeah, maybe.

I had to admit that its location could be considered to be desirable, depending on your gender, as it was located right across the hall from the ladies restroom whose door seemed to be constantly in motion.

Faust stopped just outside the 'cube-with-floor-to-ceiling walls,' wiggled her fingers goodbye, and told me, "Chief Investigator Fox, please not hesitate call on me if you have any questions or difficulty settling in." Then she vanished as if into a maritime fog, back to what is no doubt considered in the GCB to be an opulent corner office.

As I walked into the closet-sized office intent on setting the file box on the desk, tossing my briefcase into a visitor's chair, and having myself a good cry, the fickle finger of fate that seems to constantly to dog my life once again made an appearance.

Sitting at my desk, smoking a prohibited cigarette, was my old friend and no-doubt pissed off co-worker, Maggie DuPont. She made no effort to get up out of my chair as I stood there dumbfounded, my arms otherwise occupied.

She gave me a sarcastic lopsided grin, and said, "Why, good morning, Chief Investigator Cousteau. Finally stopped by to teach us hirelings how to solve all our open cases before noon?"

I sat the cardboard Bankers box on the corner of the battered laminated top of the gray-metal, Steelcase, double-pedestal desk, and motioned with two fingers to get out of my chair. She grinned evilly once again, butted her cigarette out in an empty Styrofoam cup, stood up and circled inside the narrow confines of the cube, rubbing her not insubstantial boobs along my back to enable us to exchange places.

Trying to get the thought of her firm body off my mind, I took the time to take my seat, opened the desk drawers and emptied the file box. Then I proceeded to empty my briefcase of inconsequential items such as a stapler, tape dispenser, box of pistol ammunition, an old lottery ticket, a four-pack of condoms, etc., all without saying a word to the brass-balled woman.

Then I stood up and walked around the desk, which necessitated us making body contact once again, *damn*, and walked down the hall until I found a coffee pot. When I located it, poured myself a Styrofoam cup, slipped in a couple Sweet-and-Lows, pointedly didn't get my office interloper a refill, and returned to the high-back armchair behind the desk in my new 'pretend' office.

I took a sip of scalding hot coffee before setting it down on the phony walnut laminate. Then I began, with what I had had mentally planned in my mind that weekend, to say to the woman the next time we ran into one another.

I had no more that opened my mouth and began my awkward apology-cum—explanation when she threw up her hands, palms out, and chuckled, "Forget it, Fox. It really doesn't matter. I was just screwing with you. Obviously the transfer of the Laughlin case wasn't your idea or your fault. We both just follow orders, regardless of how inane some of them are that come down from the Carson City headshed."

"No, the reason I was waiting for you, admittedly a little impatiently, was that a call was left on my business cell phone last night when I was out. It was from a Las Vegas Metro detective, Izzy Petosa.

" Now, Investigator Fox," DuPont continued, "I know you've never met the man, but you'll rapidly find that Izzy is a contradiction in appearance. He is short, not over five-foot-four I imagine, about one hundred-eighty pounds, and by all accounts a very hairy Italian."

"He must be Catholic because he and his wife have a dozen wonderful kids I'm told, all under the age of fourteen. He only has a high-school degree when the department these days only hires cops with college educations. However, he speaks fluent Italian and Spanish, and hands-down, I'm told, is one of the bravest and smartest dicks on Metro."

Dupont continued, "His case closure rate is absolutely unbelievable. Felons will open up to him before they will anyone else, even the dickless women on the P.D. that stoop to using their feminine wiles to get information from co-workers and other adults, even using it to get information for free from the informants in her snitch stable. And what impresses me most is that he never will steal someone else's case just to make a name for himself."

"Izzy left a long, detailed message on my phone asking I pass it along to your attention. He obviously has heard through the Metro grapevine that you have replaced me in having responsibility for solving the Laughlin case. And that, my friend, is why I have my reportedly cute ass sitting here in your office, yanking your chain."

Dryly, I asked, "What was Detective Petosa's message, Maggie?"

Reaching inside her superbly filled-out blazer jacket to access an inner pocket, Dupont pulled out a piece of scrap paper and slid it across the desk to me. I read it, and unconsciously said, "Sweet God almighty."

Grinning, DuPont said, "A little more proper than the words I would have chosen, but exactly my sentiments, Chief Investigator."

I glanced at the paper she had shoved over to me. All that was written on it were the words "Riverboat-April" and a phone number.

"Apparently a couple of beat cops on the Strip arrested a Mr. Mercado Chavez last night, Sunday, who is of Puerto Rican persuasion. He allegedly assaulted a Metro police officer during the performance of his duties."

"Long version short, after the cops got Chavez into custody, as required by Nevada Statute, the senior officer began to inventory the man's belongings in his vehicle as it was being hooked up and destined to be towed to one of Metro's impound lots."

"After tossing the interior of the car and finding nothing, the arresting officer popped the truck and began to search it. It was under the carpet, was under the spare tire, where the cop hit pay dirt that might connect Chavez to the Laughlin armed robbery."

DuPont continued, "Anyone even remotely connected to law enforcement in the Southwest has heard about the Riverboat Casino being knocked over in Laughlin in April of this year."

"So when Izzy stumbled across the Downtown Command's arrest reports in his in-box early this morning, and knowing it was still a open case, he thought that you would be very interested in following up on it."

"So this morning, I took the liberty of calling Izzy and telling him that you'd be down to Metro HQ as soon as you got into the office."

"Izzy says this loser is a tweeker and small-time opportunistic criminal. His yellow sheet shows a lot of nickel-and dime-arrests but no major scores."

I looked over at DuPont and saw she was fidgeting in the chair. Trying to calm her busy hands. Hoping against hope that I would ask her to go along with me to see Izzy.

I asked, "Investigator, why are you in Las Vegas this morning in the first place? I thought your office was in Carson City?"

"Yeah," she sheepishly replied, "but I had to be here anyway to investigate a couple of requests from the Bellagio to add some cheaters in the Nevada Black Book. You know, so they can the club can ban them from their gaming floors without having to justify evicting them from the premises."

"Finding this on my cell phone, I felt it was important enough to deliver Izzy's message to you personally before his lawyer bails him out of the CCDC, that's the Clark Country Detention Center."

"Okay," I said, "let's get over to the Detective's office. Your car or mine?"

She replied, "You mean you are asking little ole' me to go along? Even though I no longer am in-charge of the case? Is that what you are saying, hot-shot Chief Investigator Fox?"

I directed a much nicer grin at her than she had earlier used on me, and said, "Sure, why not? I can't find my way around this town on my own yet, anyway. So, if the agent with the most local logistical knowledge, even if no longer the assigned case manager, can drive, let's roll, partner."

On the way to the headquarters of the Las Vegas Metro Police, Investigator DuPont asked me why I left the NYPD? I explained briefly about my wife's untimely death from cancer, and the difficulty I had in accepting it.

She asked, "Do you mind if ask you something? I have a close friend who is pretty sick. Her doctor has told her to get her affairs in order. She has been asking me for advice on how she should be acting. Now that she knows she is dying."

"She wonders if she should direct all her mental effort towards getting herself ready, or does she owe it to close friends like me to make it easier on us. You know, joking around to the bitter end."

DuPont continued, "Making a joke of things like her incontinence which as you know is a common side effect of the pain medication. The smell of her body decaying, that only she can smell wafting from her body, no matter how many showers she takes or number of ounces of perfume she splashes on."

"Fox, I certain that you know what I mean. If you would just be willing to share what you and your wife went through in her last days, as rough as I'm sure it would be for you, you could really help another person in her last moments. Do you think I am overstepping our relationship by even asking you?"

"Maggie, you and I hardly even know each other. Perhaps someday I will feel comfortable enough to share my wife's final moments with you. But I really didn't feel comfortable discussing it at this time. I'm sorry."

The Las Vegas Metropolitan Police Department, known by locals as the LVMPD or Metro, is a joint city-county police force for Clark Country, Nevada. The Metro Police is currently run by Sheriff Douglas C. Gillespie. He is both the Police Chief of the City of Las Vegas and the Sheriff of Clark County, and must run for re-election every four years. The next time the office is up for grabs is 2010. Under Nevada law, the sheriff is the chief law enforcement officer in the county.

Metro has 5,000 commissioned officers, a police training academy located next to the Northwest Area Command, a custodial officer training facility located inside the CCDC, seven area commands, one airbase, the CCDC—the detention center, and seven helicopters.

Patrol functions are performed by bike patrols, motorcycle units and patrol cars assigned to one of the seven area commands, supported by police helicopters when available. The Commands are Bolden, Downtown, Northeast, Northwest, Southeast, Southwest, and South Central.

Metro also runs one of the only two crime labs in the state, the other being at the other end of the state in Reno, in Washoe County.

Once we arrived at Metro headquarters, you'd think we were a pair of suspected terrorists for all the hoops we had to jump through just to see the Detective Petosa.

After we had satisfied the rent-a-cops of our identity, and the reason we were standing in front of the reception desk like a couple of supplicants waiting to see the Pope, one of the Latino guards handed us Visitors Passes. Then they carefully watched to make certain that we attached them to our jackets.

Then we had to suffer though a two-minute-long lecture admonishing us to never, ever, remove the digital-coded badge or replace it with our official credentials while in the building.

The facility served multiple city tenants. And Mayor Oscar Goodman didn't want cops walking around the place with badges on their jackets, acting as if the city hall was under siege. We were also told not to remove our jackets while in the hallways or elevators as the mayor also didn't want the public visiting city offices to see cops walking around like a bunch of heavily-armed storm troopers.

As I was a new-hire, a person easily impressed by the authority vested in the rent-a-cops, I listened with rapt attention to every word of this important mini-lecture. I had to concentrate extra hard on the subject matter, so I could ignore the soft "Shit" word I heard from the lips of my temporary partner.

When the guard felt we were properly indoctrinated, he picked up the phone and buzzed Detective Izzy Petosa's office. Apparently Petosa ordered him to just send us up to his office on the third floor without any further bullshit.

Of course, we weren't going to get off that easy. The obviously-past-the-minimal-age-for-applying-for-Social Security-benefits guard said, "Yes, Sir, right away," into his Bluetooth headset, as he disconnected the call.

Then needing to show his importance was superior to that of a mere Detective third-grade, he gestured in the direction of a red-leather padded bench. There sat a gaggle of eager-looking, young administrative interns. Each one of them waiting for the opportunity to Be of Service to the Great City of Lost Wages.

A young, very attractive African-American woman ran over in response to the rent-a-cop's lordly summons. She tried to contain her nervous giggling as the guard, like he was talking to a idiot, carefully told her exactly what room on what floor to escort us to. He even repeated the instructions even though I was certain that the guard's I.Q. was at thirty percentage points lower than that of the intern he was addressing.

As the intern led us over to the main bank of elevators and we entered an Express car to the third floor, she, who said her name was Jasmine, whispered to Maggie, "Just ignore that dickhead. He thinks that I am highly-impressed by his permanent-press, drip-dry, no-iron uniform. And that oily old gun he carries on his belt like a pacifier. Not to mention the humongous wage of $12.00 an hour he has informed me that he earns. He has been trying to work up the nerve to ask me out, hoping that I subsequently will be suitably appreciative and sleep with him."

"I simply can't wait to see the look on his face when he gets enough nerve to ask me out, and I tell him, 'No, I don't date brown guys. And if I did, certainly not a grungy one old enough to be my grandfather!' "

We all got a chuckle out of that as the elevator slowed to stop at our floor. As the bronze-colored door slide open, we exited and followed the assertive young woman down the carpeted hallway to an open doorway that was located next to an emergency stairwell.

She stuck her head into a larger-than-normal-sized room which had three gray-metal-gray, double-pedestal desks with low-back chairs facing the three walls, and six gray five-drawer file cabinets equipped with stereotypical security locks attached, against the walls. In all that was left of the available space, sat three armchairs for visitors.

Only one desk was currently occupied, and that by a short man that fit Maggie's description of Izzy Petosa right down to the hairy hands. The detective stood up to welcome us, greeted Maggie first as he had apparently had worked with her in the past, and turned to shake my hand with a fairly bone-crushing grip. Realizing he was attempting what is referred to as a small-man's handshake, I didn't attempt to compete with his grasp.

After the introductions, he effusively welcomed us to his humble domain, especially Maggie who valiantly tried to pull her short skirt down to cover her knees as she bent over to drag over two of the office's three gray-fabric upholstered visitor chairs for us to sit down in.

He offered to get us a cop of coffee or a soft drink from the floor's kitchen, which we both politely declined. So he plopped down in his chair with a sigh and swung it around to face us.

"Okay," he said, "I think I may have something that will interest our friends over at the Gaming Control Board." He opened his middle desk drawer and pulled out a clear plastic evidence bag that was sealed at the top with a piece of red tape stamped in black letters with the words, "Evidence—Do not remove from the LVMPD Property room."

He tossed the bag to me and said, "You and Maggie are welcome to look at what the bag contains, Inspector Fox, but don't damage the seal if you please. I checked it out to myself, even though I am not the case manager, which is a procedural violation right there. If it gets lost, I will be tossed back in the Bag and demoted back to patrol, *tout de suite*."

I held the quart-sized plastic bag up to the light, turning it so Maggie could also view it, and asked, "Are those what I think they are?"

Izzy responded, "Yes, Investigators, I suspect they are. That is if you were thinking they are paper money straps used by the Federal Reserve."

He expanded on the statement. "The paper straps or bands are also used by Casino cash crib employees to wrap a bundle of like-denomination-bills together for ease of handling and accountability."

As Izzy droned on, obviously attempting to impress Maggie by using his deep voice, I remembered from my brief review of the Laughlin armed robbery case file during my orientation in Carson City last week, that one-hundred-dollar denomination U.S. currency from the Federal Reserve comes in bricks of 100, or $10,000.

Most casinos also band the hundred-dollar bills into $10,000 packets, secured by paper tape bands imprinted with the casino's name, when the funds are returned to the Federal Reserve Bank.

I forced my attention back to what Izzy was explaining to Maggie. "However, when arrested last night, the mutt was driving a primo classic 1959 Cadillac convertible that cost him $30,000 cash two weeks ago. He was wearing a couple thousand dollars of high-fashion threads and had a rent receipt in his glove box for a condo off Tropicana that rents 'furnished' for $2,500 per. Oh, and he had some white powder under his nose."

"Now this *moke* is a guy who has never had a pot to piss in, or a window to throw it out of. He only sets foot outside of Laughlin if someone else is footing the bill. But suddenly he has cash to buy a new-to-him car, has moved into a luxury condo here in Sin City, and acts like he has struck it rich for the first time in his miserable freaking life. You tell me."

"Before you two arrived, I made time to place a few calls to the FBI, the DEA, and the Mohave Sheriff's office to see if they had any information that would help us determine how this lowlife could have come into possession of the tape bands. And if anyone thought he had enough intelligence to have been directly involved in the Laughlin casino robbery."

"Without exception, no one felt Chavez has the smarts to be involved as a member in the well-disciplined team that would have been necessary to pull the job off."

Detective Petosa continued, "So we are left with the possibility that either Chavez was a very minor player, or he had something, access to something, that the robbery team needed badly enough to force them into taking a chance on trusting him."

Figuring the detective was long-winded and just was getting wound-up, I interrupted to announce Maggie and I have changed our minds.

"We'd love a cup of coffee. Black is okay for me. I know Investigator DuPont takes non-dairy creamer and three sugars."

When Izzy left the office to get our refreshments, Maggie leaned over and said, "Fox, thanks for including me, but I don't even drink coffee."

I answered, "Okay, Maggie, okay. But if it weren't for your short skirt and notable legs, this guy wouldn't be spending his valuable time to brief us. I think he is stringing it out piece-by-piece, just so he can admire the view a little bit longer."

"Why don't you step out of here," I suggested. "Go drop in on someone you know here in the office. When he returns and sees you gone, I'll betting he will finish this conversation quicker than a taxpayer cashes his Income Tax refund check."

"I'll meet you down in the lobby in ten minutes. Go ahead, Girl, time me. I know how lecherous men like Petosa think. In fact, I once was one of them myself, that is until I took a self-Improvement course."

When Izzy returned to the office, his hands full of a three Styrofoam cups of coffee, a handful of Sweet-and-Low, and non-dairy creamer packages for Maggie, he looked around and plaintively asked like a disappointed kid, "Where'd she go? I went to a lot of effort to get coffee for you guys. Now what am I supposed to do with her cup?"

"Detective," I answered, "Maggie has been having cramping problems this morning. You know, female stuff. She was embarrassed to excuse herself when you were here. But after you left to get coffee, she told me that she had to go pee immediately or she'd soil her panties. You and I are both men of the world, we know how these things go, right?"

Detective Petosa looked around his office once more before he answered. I guess making sure she wasn't hiding behind a file cabinet, preparing to jump out and scare him silly, and then replied, "Yeah, I guess so. Okay, here is the rest of the scoop."

"As I said, the law enforcement folks in Laughlin and Bullhead City know this lowlife as a smalltime petty-ante thief. He breaks into cars in Laughlin and Bullhead city to find something to sell to support his ice habit."

"Chavez also has been known to sell a teener or two of methamphetamine from time-to-time, mostly to college age kids who are in Laughlin to have a good time. Not so much, in Bullhead City."

Patosa, now glancing at his watch, continued. "If he has ever been known to specialize in any particular crime, it has been the theft of high-end boats to-order, up and down the Colorado River."

"The Feds think Chavez is stealing boats to-order for the Mexican Mafia, or the MM as we refer to them here. The MM Gang has gotten involved as silent owners in a number of high-end pleasure boat dealerships in Southern California."

"The more violent gangs had to diversify when the income from their murder-for-hire, extortion-for-hire, and protection rackets weren't bringing in enough revenue, forcing them to move on to more lucrative business endeavors."

"Those dealerships are successful, informants tell us, because they advertise in bars by word-of-mouth that they are able to locate and acquire any boat that a potential customer may desire. Providing he or she has the necessary do-ri-me, often half the amount being asked by less successful, but more honest, traditional dealerships."

"More often than not, in fact almost all of the time, the stolen boats are never recovered. Likely because as soon as they are stolen they are shoved into the enclosed cargo boxes of eighteen-wheelers and transported to one of the gang's body shops in Southern California"

"There, the engine and boat's VIN numbers will be replaced by ones taken from scrapped boats in junkyards. The hulls are repainted, upholstery switched between stolen boats of like types that are in the shop for rebirth at the same time, and re-titled using fake registration numbers."

Petosa, obviously tiring from the dog-and-pony, sighed, and said, "That leads us to an incident report that I dug out of the Coast Guard missing and stolen boat website. You may find this of interest. According to the report, a distinctive Baja-brand twenty-six-foot offshore racer was stolen from a marina below Bullhead City only a couple of hours before the robbery of the Riverboat casino."

The detective scratched his hairy head, before continuing. "Now, a stolen boat taken from one of the less-than-security-conscious marinas along the Colorado River ain't news. Happens nearly every week, in fact. But, what makes this theft notable, despite the time frame in which it was stolen, is that a boater later happened onto a partially sunken hull off the Fort Mohave Indian Reservation, less than ten miles south of Laughlin."

"Someone had attempted to sink the boat by removing the drain plug in its stern. But the river is fairly shallow there. And a boat like that has a cuddy cabin in the bow which can trap a lot of air if the boat is scuttled. So, long story short, the bow was left sticking about three feet above the surface of the river. The stern, which is where the big, heavy V-8 engine is mounted, apparently sunk to the bottom. That prevented the current from washing the hull down stream."

"And the question is?" I asked the Petosa.

"Fox, the question is why the thief stole a $100,000 boat only to scuttle it. A number of high-end boats are stolen in that area annually. But this is the first time, other than the few times we have we have been lucky enough to catch the thief in the act, that a pilfered boat has ever been seen again. Not just in our area, but that also holds true for Nevada and Arizona."

"You have to ask yourself. Was the expensive Baja offshore racer only required to commit a crime of a short duration? Was the intended use for the stolen boat, a one-time-only-deal? Or was the value of the boat low enough that it wasn't worth transporting the boat to Southern California to unload it? Or was disposing of it in some other, more successful manner, beyond the scope of the individuals who commissioned its theft in the first place?"

Petosa looked at the ceiling and signed. "Now, I am just a poor Las Vegas underpaid copper with twelve kids. I haven't received the fancy FBI training that you have, Chief Investigator Fox. And no FBI big shot has ever gone to bat for me in support of my getting one of the most sought-after jobs on Nevada's elite Gaming Control Board. As such, I would never try to tell you how to do your job, Investigator."

"And frankly," Izzy continued, "I don't really know if Chavez has enough stones to have been involved in your robbery or not."

"But, Fox, there is one thing I do know. The boat was abandoned and scuttled less than ten miles below where the Riverboat Casino's beach cuddles up against the Colorado River. And I know that up until last night, a known boat thief was running around Las Vegas with more money that he has ever seen in his life. And I know that the armed robbers of the Laughlin's Riverboat Casino haven't been apprehended. That's all I know."

"Now, Fox, get out of here and go to work. I enjoyed meeting you. Maybe you'll take me to lunch someday to compensate me for this tip. Or better, perhaps you can delegate that task to Maggie DuPont. No insult intended, but I'd really enjoy that a lot better that sitting across the table from you for an hour or so."

Petosa stood up, offered me once again his hand, and said, "Thanks for coming. It is against policy for anyone to interview a prisoner being held by Metro, without one of our detectives being present."

"But this time, this one time only, I have made an exception, just to do my humble bit to welcome you to Las Vegas, you might say. I left word at the CCDC that you are welcome to interview Chavez as long as there is a custodial officer in the room. Enjoy this one exception. Cause it ain't in my nature to grant a second one."

The detective reached over and tossed Maggie coffee into a metal trashcan before walking me back to the elevator. As the bronze elevator doors slide open to admit me, he took his parting shot.

"Good luck, Investigator. Evenings and weekends, the number of arrested and detained has forced the county to hold preliminary arraignments/bail hearings by video link every six hours. I checked and your boy's bail is set at $100,000."

"It's only that high because Chavez was stupid enough to spit on a cop who had stopped him on a routine traffic infraction. That means that anyone with $10,000 cash can go the fee of a bail bondsman and get him released."

"I suggest you and Maggie hustle your respective butts over there *tout de suite* before his partners in the robbery, assuming Chavez was even involved in the heist, bail him out to silence him. Once he gets in the wind you'll have only two chances of ever finding him again, slim and none."

With a big shit-eating grin on his puss, Izzy waved goodbye to me as the elevator polished brass doors closed.

When I arrived in the lobby, one of the rent-a-cops at the reception desk chewed me out for moving about in the facility unescorted. I hung my head and nodded like I was apologetic, then walked through the swing glass doors to meet Maggie who I located sitting on a concrete bench, enjoying a cancer stick.

I recognized the look in Maggie's blazing eyes as the urge to kill so I waited for her to reopen the conversation as I humbly followed her back into the city's parking garage to reclaim her car.

SIX

09 June 2008, Monday, 11:00 a.m.
Clark County Detention Center
330 Casino Center Drive
Las Vegas, Nevada

Maggie and I drove cross-town to the Clark County Detention Center that is located at 330 S. Casino Center Blvd in Las Vegas. During the ride over, Maggie had only communicated with me in business-like monosyllables, pointing out a number of gaming facilities along the way that had earned the current attention of the Control Board. For each that she pointed out, she gave me an abbreviated reason that the operation had achieved the dubious distinction of rating a heightened awareness on the part of the uber-powerful Nevada gaming control board.

The CCDC was built in 1984 to settle a Consent Decree. It was designed to hold 2,957 inmates, but its normal population today averages in excess of 3,100 detainees.

As official visitors to the Clark County Detention Center, with exception of Defense attorneys, apparently didn't rate high enough on the totem pole to rate free parking in the CCDC's parking garage, Maggie elected to park out front next to a fire hydrant, after flipping the BuCar's sun visor down that bore the stenciled placard, '*Official Business—Nevada Gaming Control Board.*'

I knew that in Hong Kong, or for that matter even New York City, underpaid, overworked parking enforcement officers would be impressed with that display of blatant official excess for about five seconds, the amount of time it would take them to write out a illegal parking summons. And if the car was still there on the meter maid's next circuit, it would be headed for the city impound lot on the back of a city-contracted flatbed tow truck.

But then, this was the city with the motto, 'What happens in Vegas, stays in Vegas.' So I suppose it was possible that her car would be safe from being towed where she had blatantly, illegally parked it. I have a bridge in Brooklyn available for sale, if you are naïve enough to believe that.

Unsolicited, readers, this is my personal opinion on jails and prisons in general. I believe jails are a waste of taxpayer's money, except for violent offenders, child rapists, and other persons who should have never seen the light of day in the first place. Jails and prisons down through history haven't been proven to be rehabilitative.

No one can point to a class of prisoner who can be redeemed and whose behavior acceptably modified by containment inside one of these monstrous facilities. Yet, the United States has the highest-per-capita incarceration rate of any country in the world; not just the free world.

Despite having a street address, a jail is not a physical location. It is a state of being. A condition. A jail or prison reverberates with the sounds of gates clanging; restraint chains rattling; toilets flushing; people screaming in anger, frustration or fear. Its corridors, cells, and occupied areas appear to have been overlooked when architects were busy designing in sound-deadening features to prevent ordinary citizens from overhearing the incarcerated, cry-out in fear, or in abject helplessness.

Inside every prison that I have ever visited, I have been able to smell the stink of palpable fear hanging in the air.

And it isn't just the inmates who contribute to the madness. The guards, albeit indirectly, add to the ambient noise level when they overreact to a prisoner spitting on their persons, or human feces is thrown through cell bars onto their uniforms, and into their faces.

Custodial personnel tend to treat everyone the same. From the normally mild-mannered bookkeeper who got arrested for having a few cocktails too many at a strip-joint-cum-titty-club on the Las Vegas Strip, to the crazed biker who is a tweeker, a *glass* or *ice* smoker, whose world totally revolves around his addiction, called a '*Jones*' on the street, to crystal methamphetamine.

The biker often will be larger than any of the members of the six custodial officer quick-response team, pronounced as QUIRT, restraining him. The violent hulk, who a couple of *not-on-my-beat* cops dropped onto the DC's intake staff, will be trussed up in chains, handcuffs, and plastic ties, and be drunk out of his mind on a combination of alcohol and meth.

The biker's body, breath, and clothes will stink. The apparel he was wearing when he was arrested is probably is lice-infested. He will not have taken a shower, washed his clothes, or his shoulder-length hair in a month. He may sport a tattoo of dog collar around neck, or perhaps he will be wearing a real dog collar.

His body likely will be covered in tattoos, many picked up during prior incarcerations. He'd be wearing shabby, dirty long pants, a long-sleeved shirt, and heavy socks to conceal the needle pop marks between his toes, inside his elbows, in his armpits, or between pubic hairs in his genital area.

If he is in the later stages of Methamphetamine addiction, he will likely have nasty weeping pustules on his face and a permanent twitch at the corner of one of his eyes.

The staff must remember that the detainee must be treated at all times like the danger he represents to custodial staff and other inmates. He, abruptly without notice, may suddenly morph into a raving manic when the booking staff speaks gently to him, attempting to get him to willingly comply with the facility's rules.

Escalating fear may have caused the shift intake supervisor to use a 50,000-volt Taser stun gun to control the large man. After a couple of jolts of juice large enough provide electricity to a dozen Las Vegas homes, he may be motionless and unconscious, curled into the fetal position, mewing like a kitten on the concrete floor of his cell, bleeding from his nose, ears, eyes, mouth, penis, and anus.

The man's heart may now be fibrillation, flirting dangerously with death, the electrical shock having forced him to unconsciously void and defecate in his trousers. His eyes may have rolled back in his head. Medical personnel will have been summoned, however they are none-too-quick to provide emergency care for the fearsome giant.

Half-a-dozen guards will then place the unruly inmate in a restraint chair. Although considered by uneducated to be a modern invention, the device is actually a throwback to ancient penal history where it was used to control unruly and violent prisoners.

A restraint chair's frame is fabricated out of quarter-inch-thick, welded square metal tubing, and fitted with a reinforced black vinyl seat. The seat will be recliner backward to about 30 degrees. The chair's restraints, augmenting those already being worn by the prisoner, will be attached to the prisoner's handcuffs, his waist chain, and the ankle shackles, by the use of black automotive-grade seatbelts, at the waist and in a cross-your-chest shoulder harness. For *spitters* or *biters*, a tan mesh mask called a spit hood will be secured over the prisoner's head.

The restraint chair came into use at the Clark Country Detention Center because of the inability of custodial officers to safely control tweekers stoned out of their minds, multiplied by an equal number of instances of self-destructive violent gang members who seek suicide-by-cop.

Maggie told me on the way over that device is reputedly used about six times on each of the CCDC's swing and midnight shifts on weekends and holidays when the number of persons being booked increases ten-fold.

Not matter how organized and rehabilitation-oriented, a jail is not based on rhythm or reason. Nor on humanity, concern for the individual, behavior modification, or on any proven policy's of penology.

Jails and prison, no matter what they are called, serve only as a warehouse for people, pure and simple. It is a short-term method of protecting the general public from the aberrant and undesirable individual who we fear may cause us injury.

If you feel superior and have a more enlightened vision of the necessity for these facilities, then perhaps you are the one who needs reintroduction into the real world.

Maggie and I presented our credentials at the visitor's desk. Maggie took care of the formalities by advising the clerk that we had been cleared by Las Vegas Metro Detective Izzy Petosa to talk with detainee Mercado Chavez.

The clerk, looking already tired out even though visiting hours hadn't even began yet, told us to take a seat and he'd pass the word to the shift sergeant to bring Chavez down to an Attorney meeting room.

We took seats in grimy molded plastic chairs that were bolted together to prevent them from being used by out-of-control family members as an impromptu weapon.

Investigator DuPont, who still was not talking with me anymore than was absolutely necessary—the woman certainly carries a grudge—picked up a discarded magazine off the linoleum floor to read. I, on the other hand, used the moment to admire the *beauty* of the Detention Center's visitors lobby.

Unknown to Maggie, I was fighting a battle within myself, forcing myself to not get up and flee the facility. Being here brought back some bad memories. It had been over a year since I had been physically confined. My ego foolishly had suckered me into placing myself into a position of jeopardy where I had been kidnapped and severely beaten while investigating a human body-part harvesting ring in Hong Kong, code named *Angry Dragon*.

Readers: That crime episode was covered in my 2007 Hong Kong novel that bears the same name.

In jail or prison, or any involuntary confinement, there are things that never change. Everything but the procedures are timeless. The authorities are always seeking to improve discipline, to protect both detainees and staff, to separate known gang members, and to prevent the in-flow of contraband.

Personnel who work in confinement facilities are quick to admit that detainees are expert scammers, and as a whole, are very believable. They invoke sympathy in their jailers, and are constantly trying to get little exceptions to every facility rule—such as keeping a prohibited cell phone, or to convince jail staff to not be too efficient when they do cavity searches for money, drugs, weapons and other contraband.

And the detainees are driven to continue to work the deception, as there always is another steel gate to go through, another opportunity to deceive jail staff during a search of their person, another cell to enter, and another cell mate to scam.

In a reactive effort, authorities supposedly develop a better method of control. And institute new procedure after new procedure. All aimed at increasing inmate discipline, protecting staff, preventing one-on-one inmate altercations, and eliminating detainee's constant attempts to smuggle contraband into the facility.

A person less intuitive may think that a job as a custodial officer would be a sweet assignment. After all, the walls and corridors are freshly-painted. The inmate either fears or hates the COs. Either way the CO enjoys a semblance of absolute control. The concrete floors have been polished to a shine from the efforts of the Trustees.

But the fact remains that a detention center will always be a detention center. People are unwillingly confined in extremely close quarters. Every cell has an open toilet. There is no provision for modesty in a jail. The fact that the toilet facilities are out in the open means that the ambient air reeks of the smell of passed gas, human waste, and vomit. It is impossible for inmate or staff to draw in a breath that is not contaminated by the overpowering smell of human waste.

The walls are painted institutional colors, except where the occasional reporter is occasionally permitted to shoot a couple of frames of film. Those areas are painted a blinding shade of white, as if the color denotes purity, cleanliness and safety.

The custodial procedures followed here at the 3,000-inmate Clark County Detention Center are similar to those followed in like facilities throughout the United States.

The CCDC has a police-only underground parking garage, accessed and egressed only through a pair of steel roll-up doors. Officers wishing entry, either must secure their weapons in the trunks of their locked patrol vehicles, or inside a bank of high security steel lockers provided specifically for that use.

The officers remove their weapons from their holsters, place them in the lockers, close the heavy-gauge steel doors, and pocket the unique key.

Detainees under custody of the police officers are led to the thick steel-and-glass entry door of the jail, which is guarded by one or more custodial officers sitting behind bulletproof glass with shotguns at hand.

The arresting officer completes endless booking paperwork, all the while bullshiting with other cops that are in the jail at that time.

If a prisoner is suspected of carrying drugs, the jailers will pull on latex gloves, escort him or her to an allegedly private bathroom, and conduct a potentially invasive strip search.

Which simply said, involves the unappealing process of ordering the prisoner to drop their pants, bend over, spread their cheeks, and cough several times so the custodial officer can look up the prisoner's anus for any sign of secreted drugs.

Then, while custody officers are standing by for her protection, a nurse will perform a quick medical examination of each prisoner. If any old hypodermic needle tracks are found during the cursory physical examination, the prisoner will have to submit to a blood test for HIV antibodies.

The total physical exam takes no more than six minutes. After which the prisoner is booked, strip-searched once again by jailers, and placed in a special isolation holding cell.

There the detainee will await booking pictures, prints and the results of the just-administered HIV/AIDS test to determine whether they will be placed in a cell with other prisoners, which is referenced to as the General Population, or the 'Main Line.' Or are to be segregated in a medical isolation cell, reserved for prisoners who are found to be AIDS positive, have other communicable diseases, or are a suicide risk.

In the last instance, the jump suits and underwear the detainee will be issued will be pink in color. The facility's name is printed in six-inch high letters printed across the shoulders of the jumpsuits.

Violent prisoners are incarcerated away from the general population in an Administrative Segregation unit, or *AdSeg*, such as here in the individual cells on 5C. 5C also houses prisoners who are waiting to be transferred to death row in a state prison.

The Clark County Detention Center, or as the locals refer to it, the CCDC, is a relatively modern facility although it was constructed twenty-four years ago. Each floor is made up of four-sections of pie-shaped facilities, known as pods.

The common areas of each of the inmate floors are of concrete block construction, divided into four, stand-alone pods. Each pod holds up to twenty-four prisoners housed in individual cells.

Each cell in each pod has a remotely-controlled steel door in a wall made of thick, heavy safety glass. There was no window in the door other than a lockable slot though which the detainees will receive mail, any medication that the jail doctor has ordered for him or her, and their meals.

In the pointy end of the pods is an elevated, glassed-in guard station that overlooks the entire floor. Anytime the inmates are permitted out of their cells for exercise or recreation, the activity takes place in the pod's common area.

The common area of all the pods are outfitted with six, five 4-man stainless tables bolted to the floor. The common-area serves as the inmate's dining area and recreation hall. In some cases, non-violent inmates may be permitted to go to the chow hall under strict guard.

The medical isolation floor has a small medical facility located outside the locked pod. Its windows are made of one-way glass which look out into the pods for observation purposes.

As mentioned before, even though the Clark County Detention Center is twenty-four-years-old, it has been updated and is considered to be relatively state-of-the-art. As such, it has been equipped with computerized suspect booking.

The photo taken of every inmate entering the facility will become part of a computerized system called BLACK CREEK. The security system is augmented by hundreds of color and black-and-white cameras. They all are controlled by the facility's touch-screen computer system.

The CCDC's custodial officers remotely-control all prisoner movement inside the facility. Depending on the size of the hard-drive, all images are saved. The intake booking office in a community wealthy such as Las Vegas have been equipped with over a dozen cameras suspended from the ceiling in the inmate intake room.

The intake room itself is large, clean, and brightly-lit by ceiling-hung fluorescent fixtures. There will be a foot-square white board card imprinted with a large red "X" hung in front of each camera, under which the inmates stand at the verbal direction of the intake officer.

The booking computer will enter a personalized booking number so the inmate does not have to hold a number sign against his chest. In larger cities, the I.D. boards went out of style along with black-and-white television sets years ago.

Each subject's fingerprints will be taken and processed through a computer system called CROSS-MATCH. The first print taken is the 'four-finger slap,' then the thumbs. Then each individual digit will be rolled across the glass, some more than once, when the computer is not satisfied with the print quality.

Then the palms of both hands will be scanned, then the 'writer blades' and wrists. No longer is there any need for moistened towelettes to remove fingerprint ink. It is all done by computer image.

Then another clerk will ask the inductee several questions such as name, address, age date of birth, Social Security number, basic medical information, whether you are or have ever contemplated committing suicide, and pulls other routine information off the arrest Warrant card.

The custodial officers who work under these stressful conditions have adopted a positive attitude to combat their fears. If not their own, then the fears of their family, friends, or loved ones.

Las Vegas Metro officers assigned to the Detention Center wear tan pants with a black stripe running down the seam. Males wear forest-green twill blouses with epaulets. Metro police patches, a gold 7-point badge on a green background, are sewn onto both shoulders.

Custodial officers regardless of gender are issued black-leather cushioned shoes, latex gloves, and Sam Brown belts with two handcuff cases, pepper spray, everything but a gun. Each CO wears a facility-wide rover radio with mike attached to the weak side epaulet of the uniform blouse. All officers wear a plastic-laminated ID badge clipped to a blouse pocket. A black turtleneck with LVMPD initial on the collars is optional and may be worn under the uniform blouse.

Women custodial officers wear the same basic uniform as their male counterparts, except their uniform blouses or shirts are bright-yellow in color, similar to those worn by the bike cops on the streets of Las Vegas.

However, it is impossible to get the two jobs mixed up. Bike cops know their job is far easier, less dangerous, and much less stressful than that of custodial officers.

I don't believe I've ever asked, nor anyone has ever told me, why the CCDC's male and female officers wear different-color shirts. Perhaps it is for ease of identification for the center's totally encompassing surveillance system. Or perhaps it is just a simple tool to assist intake supervisors in ensuring female detainees are being attended to by female officers.

After a half hour, any distraction that forces one's attention away from the gray concrete walls of the visitor's waiting room is desirable. So much so that Maggie had finally decided to forgive me for asking her to leave during our interview with Izzy.

I had assured her that my intentions had been good. I had simply asked her to take a break in order to get the lecherous Las Vegas detective's mind off her world class wheels, and back on the Chavez case.

So we were having a civil conversation once again when DC's reception clerk interrupted to motion us over to his desk with one hand, while pointing at a male detention officer standing at a loose approximation of parade rest with the other.

The clerk informed us that detainee Mercado Chavez (he hadn't been convicted yet. If he had, it would of referred to him as prisoner Chavez) had been transported down from 5C and placed in a interview room. He said that all the CCDC currently had available, was a defense counsel room and he hoped that would meet our needs.

The clerk informed us that the C.O. he was pointing out would be our escort, there and back, and would remain in the interview room, pursuant to instructions from Metro Detective Izzy Petosa, to monitor our conversation with the detained man. And prohibit us from exchanging anything with the detainee.

We followed the young C.O. down a couple of narrow but well-lighted hallways. We passed through a series of clanging metal gates, bullet-proof glass doors, and iron crossbars until we arrived at a standard-sized, steel, tan-colored walk door, which had a brass keyset but no handle. The door was identified by the placard '*For Defense Counsel use Only.*"

I knew that on the door into the detainee's side of interview room, a placard would be stenciled, '*Unsentenced Detainee*' to indicate that while detainees in the interview rooms in this area of the DC had been charged of a crime, but they hadn't yet been convicted or sentenced.

The C.O. unlocked the steel door with a large brass key that was on a heavy chain hooked to his belt, stood aside to permit Maggie and I to enter, then stepped in himself, and locked the door behind him.

Inside the metal door was a short, stark-white painted four-foot wide hallway off of which little rooms with eighteen-inch wide metal doors, branched. I suppose at first glance, you could assume the small rooms were study corrals like you find in libraries. That is if study rooms were partitioned off, waist-high-to-ceiling, by a sheet of two-inch-thick bullet-resistant Plexiglas.

On both sides of the glass was an 8-inch-wide, 42-inch-high plastic-laminated shelf. In one corner on each side of the thick glass, hung a gooseneck microphone and a single handset connected to the wall fixture by a curled, black, reinforced telephone cable.

Detective Third-grade Petosa had specifically instructed us that we would not be permitted to pass anything between the detainee and us. However, this room was specially designed for defense counsel. And as such, provisions had been built-in to facilitate the passage of legal forms between the detainee and his lawyer. It was a metal trough like those you find at drive-in windows at your neighborhood bank.

After a highly contentious lawsuit some years back that had made it way all the way to the land's highest court, it was obvious that the Clark County Detention Center has joined the precedent stampede of permitting a detention officer to remain posted, one step to the rear and another to the side, on the attorney's side of the glass to ensure that no prohibited items or contraband were passed through the slot to the detainee.

Sitting behind the window, looking at our official-if-bored escort standing at parade rest, was an individual with weasel-looking features, possibly of Hispanic or Puerto Rican heritage, wearing vivid orange-colored coveralls.

His wrists were manacled with a short length of chain to a steel ring screwed into the built-in shelf alongside the paperwork trough. As he was a detainee who was considered violent, for the protection of the custody personnel, Chavez's ankles had been chained together with a restraint chain fed through a chain belt, and then to his wrist and ankle cuffs.

Due to the restraint on his hands, he would be forced to use both hands to use the phone that permitted him to converse with visitors.

Based on experience, I knew stamped on the garment's shoulders in bold black letters was something to identify the wearer to detention personnel, and fellow inmates, as an episodic *VIOLENT DETAINEE*. The designation the result of the detainee's assault on two Metro cops the night before.

Behind the glass was detainee Mercado Chavez. His face was scarred by a series of moderately deep scratches and small puncture wounds. His dark eyes, which were constantly in motion like a feral cat's that constantly assess threats every day, and the skin around them, still bore the evidence of being pepper-sprayed.

The man, although sitting down, appeared to be stocky and of medium body weight. His hands were huge, and he obviously was not a frequent customer to local manicure salons.

As he sat in the chair on the detainee's side of the glass, he hung his head defiantly, avoiding eye contact, fatalistically figuring that nothing good could from making eye contact with the individuals on the other side of the partition.

Chavez, despite being a tweeker, appeared to be in fairly decent physical shape. At least, when compared to most of his fellow meth addicts walking the streets of Sin City.

Eventually, all tweekers end up looking like they are but one of a legion of identical human beings who have been stamped from a single mold.

Again, based on my experience, Chavez appeared to be one of the ever-increasing segment of America's population who feels disenfranchised and that they never get a break. They don't particularly care if they live or die, primarily because they have become terminally-disappointed with the hand that life has dealt them.

Due to the excessive number of non-violent crimes on his yellow sheet, and the fact that everytime he had chanced breaking the law, he had been apprehended, I'd venture that his IQ level was no more than eighty-five, which is the dividing line between what is euphemistically referred to as *normal*, and the socially-challenged.

Since he felt that no one had ever given him a hand up the achievement ladder of life, he would have felt that he must be his own advocate as he slid down the slippery slope into a life of crime. Hoping for the best, but cynically accepting the alternative, when his frequent incarcerations and attempts at rehabilitation turned out to be just another failure in a long line of many.

Chavez would be paranoid. But very experienced in cutting himself a deal that would win his freedom, no matter who he had to rat out to achieve that goal.

Because of that type of mindset, I felt that he might be receptive to helping us, if in fact he had came into possession of the five $100 currency wraps when committing an illegal act.

As Investigator DuPont had volunteered to be the 'bad cop' in today's interview, she introduced herself on the telephone headset that she and I would share.

But before she got into the interview, I took a quick look over my shoulder to ensure that our C.O. was daydreaming or not paying any attention to what was going on. I used that opportunity to slip a *Rights Waiver* through the slot for Chavez to sign, which he did without thinking, and stuffed it back through the tray where I snatched it up and jammed it into one my jacket's inside pockets.

I had to make certain there were no procedural mistakes on this case. No fruit-of-the-poison-tree appeal. No Blowback. The stakes were too high. The courts are notorious for being second-guessers. We had to get this right the first time.

Investigator DuPont began, using a no-bullshit, business-like tone of voice. "Good Morning, Mr. Chavez. You are detainee #706-134-08, a Mr. Mercado Chavez, are you not?"

Chavez didn't open his mouth, make eye contact, or move an inch to acknowledge Maggie's query.

I glanced over my shoulder to get the eye of the custodial officer, and nodded. Appearing relieved he was getting a chance to do something beside stand at parade rest and daydream, the CO pulled his baton from the retainer ring on his belt and rapped it on the glass.

Then, loudly enough to ensure his voice carried through the glass, he officiously informed the detainee, "Respond or you will be returned to your cell, detainee, and lose your opportunity to speak to your appointed counsel. Last chance!"

Maggie and I were only able to remain mute by biting our respective tongues. Apparently no one had briefed the CO as to who we were.

Neither of us had claimed to be an attorney. In fact, the only reason we had been assigned use of defense counsel's interview room was because no other interview room currently was available when we had appeared at the CCDC without a interview room reservation. Detective Petosa had smoothed over our oversight when he had called the CCDC to authorize our visit this morning.

If the CO didn't know who we were, then there a better-than-fair chance that Chavez wouldn't either.

Maggie quickly latched onto my unspoken line of thought, and once again introduced herself to the detainee.

This time Chavez raised his eyes, picked up the phone, and said, "Yeah, I'm Mercado Chavez. So what?"

Maggie continued, saying, "Mr. Chavez, we like to hear your side of what happened last night."

Making sure she didn't even *think* of saying the words, 'Attorney, representing, or appointed,' Maggie moved smoothly beyond our inadvertent, unintentional misrepresentation. She was trying to say lawyer-type things that hopefully would result in Chavez believing in our little farce long enough for him to tell us things that he should only tell his defense attorney.

"Mr. Chavez, from reading the officer's arrest report on my way down here, it appears that you may have initially only been guilty of a minor fix it traffic ticket offense, the broken taillight. Can you tell us a little about what happened?"

Chavez finally raised his eyes from his lap and stared at Maggie like she was a bag of garbage that needed to be kicked to the curb.

Then the detainee opened his mouth and popped off.

"Yo, lady, you almost got it right. Except that Caddy's taillight wasn't broken until that pig used his baton on it. I had just washed my ride an hour before I ran into those storm troopers. My car was primo at that time, you got that? Nothing was broken until the black pig decided that he didn't like my attitude, and needed to manufacture a reason to run me in."

Chavez, now warming to the denial, continued, "The Assault on an Officer, and Restricting Arrest charges, are bogus, bullshit, pure bullshit. Who wouldn't spit a goober on a cop that had seriously abused his ride, and for no reason, man? On top of that, there was also was no reason for that salt-and-pepper team to throw me to the ground, and proceed to pound on me, is there? I thought this was America? Ain't I got some rights, Lady?"

The detainee had his mouth in gear now, a head of steam built up, and he continued to speak in an insulting tone of voice to Investigator DuPont.

"I done heard on TV that Reverend Sharpton says all minority young males, be them black or brown, got to stand up to the Po-lice. Now those cops didn't have no grounds to act like that. Them two pigs beat me for no reason."

"Sure I spit on them, kicked at them, and I tried to bite that nigger cop, too. But that ain't no cause to treat me that a-way. And to damage the primo 1959 Cadillac I just paid $30,000 cash for. Which, incidentally, I bought when I came into a windfall, I guess that be what you honkies be calling it."

"Anyway, I earned every bit of that money. Just for helping out a friend. Except I can't tell you anymore about that, cause it's secret and I gave my word on the grave of sacred mother, God rest her soul."

Now Chavez was getting into the story he had created on the spur of the moment to explain his actions. "Besides, I might even get hurt if I rat. I used that money to finally move out of that dump I had been renting week-to-week in Laughlin for five years, bought some new threads worthy of my new status, and leased me a $2,000/month condo here in Las Vegas like any other person of respect."

"Lady," he asked, "won't the Courts stand behind me? What those cops did to my ride just wasn't right—wasn't American. Lady, you got to use that fancy DNA stuff I seen on TV to get me an acquittal. I am innocent as a newborn babe, I tell you Sister. I am thankful to My God in heaven that you two have come here to help poor Mercado Chavez out, make all this go away, and get me out of this piss hole," he said.

Now that Chavez had begun talking, there was no stopping him. "You both are obviously a cut above my usual court-appointed lawyers. Perhaps the Reverend Sharpton heard of this injustice, and sent me his A-Team. Now that you are here, how long do you think it going to take to get this misunderstanding straightened away? I won't put charges on the cops, either. But I might need you to sue the Po-lice for me if my new ride was damaged when it was towed to impound."

Now was about time for me to make my unscripted grand entrance. I reached across Maggie and retrieved the headset, holding it so both of us could still hear. Now it was time to bust Chavez's balloon, big time.

With a sincere apologetic look to the detainee that I have refined over the years, I spoke up forcibly.

"Er, Mr. Chavez. How did you get the impression we were your lawyers? I have been sitting here waiting for you to give us a break to tell you differently. But each time one of us tried to interrupt to inform you of your misconception, you just continued to trash talk over us."

Sensing rather than hearing the CO jump when he heard this information, knowing he was in deep kimche for not inspecting our credentials before letting us into the interview suite, I continued to speak rapidly into the headset.

"Now, Mr. Chavez, let's start this once again. At a slower pace so that neither of us misunderstands who is who, and what we are here for."

"I am Chief Investigator Augustus Fox and this is my colleague Senior Investigator Maggie DuPont. We both work for the Nevada Gaming Control Board. Neither of us is your court-appointed lawyer. Do you understand that?"

I could see Chavez's face turning red on the other side of the glass partition as he realized we hadn't properly identified ourselves, or our business. And we had let him rile himself up until he was out-of-control, spitting out his accusations about the two street cops who had arrested him last evening.

"You bastard. You bitch. You tricked me. I'll have your badges for this. Your badge also, you for-shit custody officer. I'll tell the freaking sheriff. I'll tell the freaking chief of police. I'll tell the freaking mayor. I'll tell the freaking Feds. You tricked me, you sons-of-a-bitches."

The CO, as surprised by the revelation as much as the detainee was, now began to realize that this was a situation where he had to quickly make up his mind. Either he was for us or against us. Supporting Chavez in his misrepresentation accusation would buy the CO nothing.

His other choice was to support our assertions, even though he probably now agreed to a certain extent with Chavez's assertion that we had purposely, or due to circumstances as a result of the detainee's tirade, misrepresented ourselves. He reasoned that if he took our side in the dispute, perhaps we would show our appreciation by putting a commendation in his personnel file. That would eventually enable the guard to transfer out of this sewer of a job at the CCDC and into the patrol slot, which he had put on his wish-list when he had graduated from the Academy.

For the CO, it really wasn't much of a choice. Spending every shift in this hell hole, getting spit on, or worse, bitten and having feces thrown on the clean, starched and pressed uniform he proudly put on at the beginning of every shift? Or being promoted to a patrol car where he could see the sun, ogle the female tourists strolling up and down the Strip. *Naw*, he thought. Actually, he had no choice at all.

So he spoke up. "Chavez, you are so full of bullshit. These two investigators would have identified themselves to you initially if you hadn't immediately interrupted the woman and been spewing that hate from your mouth about a pair of good cops that were only do their job."

Relived that the CO had chosen to support Maggie and I, I brought the conversation back around to Chavez's arrest the pervious evening.

"Mr. Chavez, Investigator DuPont and I are not here about your arrest of last night, at least not specifically. From reading the arrest report, it reveals that a number of currency bands used to gather together currency of a like denomination, in this case, U.S. $100 bills, was discovered by the arresting officer in the trunk of your car."

Pretending I was referring to my non-existent notes, I continued, "The same 1959 Cadillac convertible you admit to recently purchasing for $30,000 cash according to the copy of the temporary registration the officers found taped in place of the vehicle's rear license plate, issued by the classic car dealership here in Las Vegas."

"And, lo and behold," Maggie interrupted, "what else do you think was recovered from the vehicle's glove box in addition to the receipt for $30,000 is cash from the dealership?

"Of course, you already inadvertently admitted this to us a few minutes ago. But in case you've forgotten, the glove box contained a copy of your cash rent receipts in the exact amount you bragged about, $2,000 a month, and your receipts for thousands of dollars in high-end resort clothing, custom jewelry and shoes."

Chavez was now sputtering, trying to come up with a believable explanation for having all this cash money. Finally, he settled on a fabricated story, and blurted it out, his spittle striking the glass partition. After which he snapped his eyes downward and to his left, which every cop in the business knows to be an obvious body-english indicator that the person being questioned was being deceitful.

Chavez gamely tried his first ruse. "I won the money playing the tables at the MGM Grand last night before I was arrested by the two pigs. I won it fair and square. You can check."

Maggie, more knowledgeable of the gaming industry than I, laughed out loud. "Crap, Chavez, maybe I just got off the boat, but not *that* boat. You know that if you won that money at any casino in Nevada, your winnings would be accompanied by a cash receipt from the club, and a copy of the club's exception notice signed by you, directing the casino not to deduct the taxes from the gross amount of the winnings."

"If you, by a miracle of the first coming, had such a document, it could only be because you agreed to take full responsibility for paying the taxes on it, thereby releasing the casino from the State of Nevada statutory obligation to withhold twenty-percent of your winnings."

Now Maggie began her own rant at Chavez. "You know that copy of your signed exception request must be submitted along with your annual State income tax statement. Now, before you attempt to lie yourself out of that, Dude, I need to tell you that we have gone through that Caddy with a fine-tooth-comb. That included every imaginable hiding place known to civilized man. Not to mention tearing apart your wallet that is downstairs in property. Guess what? The copy of the exception form just ain't there."

"And, surprise, surprise. You aren't even permitted inside the MGM casino, because you know what, little man, this bitch took the time to checkout the Black Book, and your mug is in it. Now, what is you next fabrication, Chavez?"

As the Good Cop, this was the time for me to jump back into the questioning. But first, reader, the Black Book is Nevada's rogue's gallery of individuals, who, at the request of casino management, the Gaming Control Board has banned from all casinos for scamming, or cheating, or being a person of general ill-repute.

I knew Maggie hadn't checked it, nor had she torn up his wallet—she just was bullshiting her way along, like a lot of good cops and investigators do.

As a result of a past Supreme Court decision, cops are allowed to lie to suspects. It not only isn't a crime, it is permitted, and I can assure you, practiced aggressively as an investigatory tool by every law enforcement agency in the United States.

"Okay, Mr. Chavez," time for the good cop to intervene. "Ignore my partner for a minute. I think you must have a reasonable explanation for having all that cash. Perhaps if you could tell me what it is, we can smooth this out, and I will do what I can to get the Judge to P.R. you (release on his personal recognizance) and get you released before dinner." (Dear reader, another white lie, I'm afraid.)

Chavez just starred at me like I was an insect pinned to a corkboard. The man wasn't very smart. But he had paid his dues and spent a fair share of his life locked up with other cons. They would have taught him to keep his mouth closed unless he could get something for doing otherwise.

I locked my most earnest face on my mug and leaned towards the glass partition and proceed to tell him another white lie.

I continued to push. "Mr. Chavez, paper currency bands are marked by the institutions that use them for the express purpose of separating denominations of money, right? All five of the currency bands we have located so far, and there may be more when we get a search warrant for your condo, are from the Riverboat Casino in Laughlin."

Enough of the cat footing around, I thought. I have to set Chavez up for DuPont's bad cop routine. So I continued to converse in a sickeningly-sincere manner with the confused man sitting on the other side of the glass partition, who was trying his best to portray an attitude of disinterest.

"Mr. Chavez," (never hurts to treat a suspect respectfully), "as a former resident of Laughlin, I'm sure you are well aware of the armed robbery that occurred there on April 10th, 2008 at 4:00 a.m. Of course you are, because that is where the currency bands came from, am I correct?"

"You were personally involved in that robbery, weren't you. I think you may have been one of the three persons who assaulted the cashier's cage on the casino gaming floor. I'll bet a tough guy like you could handle that."

Now Chavez began to turn pale, and raise his hands, palms out in protest. "No, no, no! You've got it all wrong. I have never used a gun in any crime I have committed. You can ask the Laughlin cops. Just ask. They'll tell you that I am not a violent man. I'm just a down-and-out tweeker. I admit that I'll do almost anything to get money to buy meth. But nothing that had anything to do with guns."

Maggie lit the fuse on her bad cop routine again and jumped into the questioning. "Chavez, you say you are non-violent. Yet you injured two cops last night when they pulled you over on the Strip for a simple traffic citation—a fix-it ticket. So why should we believe that you aren't capable of being involved in the Riverboat heist?"

Chavez whiningly replied, "Investigators, you got to understand. I had been drinking. And besides being in my cups, I had socked down a couple *teeners*; you know, meth. And I snorted four lines of ass-kicking coke. So when the cops stopped me for no good reason, my mouth got ahead of my brain. I said stuff I never should of. And when the flashy nigger cop broke out my taillight lens with his baton, I lost it, I swear."

Chavez looked like he was ready to cry before he finally pulled himself together enough to continue with his convoluted, but likely at least partially true, explanation.

"That Caddy is the first real car that I have ever owned. Up to then, I'd heist cars, drive them for a day or so, them dump them in one of those big casino parking lots, and find another one. But that money made me somebody. It made it possible for me to move to Vegas, get some nice duds, rent a nice pad, and buy me a real car, for cash money," he said.

Chavez attempted to explain his violent actions, further. "I admit I lost it when that damn cop purposely damaged my new car to pay me back for trash talking him. The Caddy was new, or new-to-me, I mean. And that is what landed me here in this cell. But I never would be involved in a hold-up that involved guns. You got to believe me. Please believe me. I ain't that type of man."

Maggie inserted herself back into the conversation. "Chavez, you know that fourteen people had to be hospitalized due to burns, smoke inhalation, and cuts and bruises they suffered stumbling their way through the smoke from the fire the gang set, and from the smoke grenades they ignited. Right?"

The detainee responded quietly, "Yeah, I guess I do be knowing that, from the newspapers and all. Not first hand, you understand."

Maggie shoved her face right up to the glass partition, and nearly shouted, "Then you also know all about the two old women that died of heart attacks after they had been rushed to the hospital, don't you."

A con well-experienced with the penal code, Chavez's eyes suddenly got big and round and he began to shake his head so fast that at first I thought he was having a seizure and was going to up and die on us.

"No ma'am!" he insisted. "I certainly don't know knowing about anybody dying. I mean, no one told me."

He pleaded, "I thought the customers was just taken to the hospital, some were kept over night, then they all was discharged."

Standing up so she could figuratively tower over the man seated on the other side of the glass, DuPont laughed. "Chavez, you dumb fuck, didn't your partners tell you that two of the elderly women who had severe pulmonary disease were transported to the hospital where they suffered heart attacks and died as a direct result of all the smoke?"

She continued, "The smoke was so heavy and thick that they couldn't get their breath? Well, dickhead, they died in the emergency room. That's homicide, in fact, two homicides, you smart-ass prick."

Chavez just sat there, shaking his head back and forth, suddenly realizing that he was in deep shit. Because a street-smart con like him knew that those deaths would be categorized as homicides that occurred during the commission of a felony armed robbery.

He was well aware that prosecutors would charge everyone involved in the crime with first-degree homicide, no matter how minor each individual's involvement had been in it. Because first-degree homicide occurred in the commission of the crime, intentional or not, gets hung on everyone involved, end-of-story.

Maggie eyes shot daggers into Chavez's eyes that had began to tear up. She just stared at him until he opened his mouth and said, "You can't say that I am as guilty as the guys who actually did the crime. All I did was take fifty thousand large to assist them in their escape. You can't say that makes me as guilty as them, can you?"

Maggie didn't say anything but Chavez's grasp of felony law was correct. And he knew it, despite his prostrations.

Maggie sat back down, and spoke quietly but forcibly directly into the handset's mouthpiece. "What method of execution will you chose, Chavez?"

Playing straight man to her tough cop, and being a helpful person by nature, I leaned over until I could speak in the handset, and helpfully suggested, "I'd choose lethal injection if I were you, Mercado."

"That sounds like a real party, Chavez," DuPont yelled over the phone, continuing to press the trembling detainee. "They strap you onto a inclined gurney. The death room is painted nice and bright white—walls, ceiling, everything. You are tilted up about twenty-degrees so that a select group of invited, including both victim's families, all of whom are sitting in a dark room so you can't see them, will watch you suffer when you die."

Maggie continued her tirade. I almost began to believe it myself. "You'll be all alone, scared as hell, and about to meet Lucifer himself. They stick needles in your arms, and then load you with chemicals, the same way they put a monkey with syphilis down. "

Grinning an evil grin for Chavez's benefit, DuPont proceeded with her description of the grisly procedure. "Oh, I know. You've heard from the newspapers that death by injection is supposed to be painless. Are you really stupid enough to believe that crap, Chavez?"

DuPont chuckled to herself before continuing with her verbal torture. "I've asked a doctor once if that was true—you know, that it would be painless. He told me in confidence, after swearing me to silence, that lethal injection is the worst and most inhuman way for a person to die. Sure, the condemned is all doped up and therefore is incapable of demonstrating any perception of pain. But he or she feels it, big time."

The investigator shook her head as if in sorrow, before continuing. "The doc said the condemned just lays there paralyzed, helpless to give any indication of the hell their body and brain are going through. As soon as the potassium hits your veins, arteries, and heart, is it like molten lava is being force-fed into your body. Your brain feels like a blowtorch is being used to roast it. The doctor said it is the most painful way to die on earth, without exception."

"What choice of lethal injection will you choose, Chavez? Especially after you've have been sitting, sweating it out, day-after-day on death row for fifteen-years waiting for all your appeals to be turned down. And you know they will be denied. As far as the Court is concerned, you personally had a hand in killing two seniors citizens who had committed no crime other than wanting to spend a couple of hours of their short remaining lives, gambling away their social security checks at the Riverboat."

It was time I earned my salary, so I interjected myself momentarily into DuPont's conversation. "Chavez, there is zero hope that even a liberal lawyer could get your conviction set aside on the basis of faulty DNA, as you asked, because the criminalists found none at the crime scene."

DuPont turned to me, making certain she could be heard by Chavez over the dangling handset, "Let's get out of here, Fox. This guy doesn't want our help. Just leave him so he can begin imagining how pleasant those last few minutes on the gurney will be."

I shook my head in agreement and stood up as to leave. But suddenly Chavez shook his head as if making up his mind about something. He raised his hands, palm-out, and begged us to retake our seats.

To stay in character, I returned to my seat, but Maggie remained standing, starring with her patented 'killer' look at Chavez through the partition.

SEVEN

June 9, 2008, Monday, 3:00 p.m.
Clark County Detention Center
Defense Counsel's Interview Room
Las Vegas, Nevada

The man sitting hunched over behind the glass partition expelled a great sigh, mouthed the word "Please," and again motioned for Investigator DuPont to sit back down. Chavez looked over at me. He apparently believed that he had a more sympathetic listener in me; someone who would not judge him, or at least, not without giving him a chance to explain.

The detainee appeared to be resigned, looking down at his hands, which he compulsively washing, one against the other.

"Okay, Inspector Fox," he began, "it seems like you are willing to put in a good word with the Judge for me. And will see I am treated alright as long as I roll over and tell you the back story about my minor part in the Laughlin armed robbery."

"I'll only tell you what I know personally to be true. I won't speculate just to falsely implicate someone you may want to stick the robbery on, just so you can be a hero and the Gaming Control Board can get a conviction. If you agree to that, I'll tell you everything."

He continued, "I know I can't ask for a deal until I am charged, and the prosecuting attorney approves it, but I figure you got nothin' to lose by putting a good word in for me with the Court when that moment comes. I have to trust you to say something in my defense if I lay out everything I know, right?"

I nodded my head indicating 'Yes' to Chavez. Then Maggie rejoined me in the uncomfortable plastic jail chairs, and we both broke out our notepads.

We had agreed before we come into the Detention Center that if Chavez broke, I'd handle the interrogation. Most prisoners would sooner spill the beans to someone of his own sex, who he feels may be a little more compassionate towards him.

However, Maggie was free to jump in if she thought I was missing anything, or we needed a clarification to one of Chavez's admissions.

Chavez raised his head and reestablished eye contact with me. He was an experienced jailhouse con, trained by the unofficial inmate-continuing-education-program that exists in all penal facilities. So he was well aware that if he was to reap maximum possible benefit by agreeing to rat out the principals that had pulled off the armed robbery, he better get with the Program.

Chavez knew from listening to countless other inmates that the Po-lice never believe anything a con is telling them unless he or she maintains eye contact with the interviewer.

So he began to tell us his story, never taking his eyes away from my face except to glance over at Maggie occasionally. Just so she wouldn't get pissed, get in his face, or disregard out of hand anything he was telling us.

"First of all," Chavez said, "I ain't had much formal book learning so it will be easier for me to tell this as a story. Then after I have finished, you can ask your questions. Okay?"

When I nodded 'Yes' a second time, he began.

"I am what I guess you cops call a unsuccessful criminal. I do a little car theft, some car prowling, unoccupied residential burglary, and pick-pocketing if I need a fix bad enough and ain't got no funds, you know what I mean?"

"I have a pretty big *Jones* for Methamphetamine. Cops call addicts like me ice heads, crystal meth heads, tweekers, and several less polite names, I guess."

"My habit, or Jones, is currently a couple teeners a day."

A teener is 1/16th of an ounce. An eighth of an ounce of meth, called an 8-ball, maybe referred to as a teener, but you instantly know that the person that incorrectly used that terminology is either a tourist or a cop.

It takes sixteen teeners to make up an ounce. And there are sixteen ounces in a pound of methamphetamine. So a dealer can get 256 teeners out of a pound of meth without cutting the product. Currently, the street price for a teener is about $60. A pound of uncut crystal meth is worth $15,360 retail on the mean streets of Las Vegas.

Chavez continued, "I ain't never done no violent crime. You can check my record. I'm just a scammer. Something low-risk that will get me money to feed my habit. If it ain't tied down, it is fresh meat for me. And I got me a couple of girls who work the casinos that will let me to crash in their rooms once in a while. Especially if I share any meth that I am holding with them."

"Up to this casino robbery, my most profitable crime was stealing high-end boats to-order off the river. I mostly heist them from those marina docks that are too cheap to hire any security at night."

He proceeded, "Depending on whether the boat's engine is muffled or not, I either float them down river, or if muffled, start the engine and drive them down river to a specified recreational boat ramp on the Indian reservation."

"There I will be met by a representative of the guy who originally placed the order with me, to have the boat stolen."

"The guy who meets with me to take the boat off my hands, shows up at the pickup spot with a over-the-road rig, a boat trailer inside the rig, and a couple of punks to help him load up the booty. Like me, they all wear latex gloves to avoid leaving any fingerprints."

As it is O'-dark-thirty, the only light we have is from the flashlights the loading crew brings with them. Flashlights provide just enough illumination to get the job done. Still, their boss is on our ass all the time about being real careful not to flash the beams around in case the Tribal Po-lice see it bobbing around when they are making their patrols."

Continuing, Chavez said, "So the crew arrives in a eighteen-wheeler. They use the rig to back the trailer it into the water at the boat ramp."

"When they get the boat trailer submerged, I just power the boat up onto the trailer. It isn't as easy as it sounds. The boat ramp is only for daytime use. It doesn't have any pole lighting and without the flashlights, it would be dark as hell."

Chavez, apparently inexperienced in holding up his end of extended conversations, sighed, then went on. "When I first arrive at the boat ramp, before I do anything else, I wrestle my 90-cc dirt bike off the boat."

"The pickup crew brings a wide, light-weight, aluminum ramp with them. It provides a method by which to get the boat trailer out of and back into the cargo box on the over-the-road rig."

"Some of the boats we heist will weigh from 6,000 to 12,000 pounds. So they have to use an electric winch secured inside the metal box to pull the boat and trailer combination up the aluminum ramp and into the box."

Chavez paused briefly, before continuing with his story. "Once the cargo box's doors are closed and locked, the crew boss hands me the remainder of the regular fee owed me. I get a set amount for stealing boats, regardless of size or value."

"Once the boat/trailer combo is loaded, the punks pile into the tractor's cab and the eighteen-wheeler disappears into the night."

"Once they have gone, I kick-start my dirt bike and take one of several dirt paths back out to the highway. For my personal security, I never use the same trail twice."

"On my way back to my room in Laughlin, I always stop by my meth dealer in Bullhead City. In the four years I've been dealing with him, I've never once found him sleeping. I buy a handful of teeners from him and split."

"Since you are gaming cops, not the DEA or narcotic cops, I better explain something to you. This here lesson is absolutely free to you. My pleasure. You already know about teeners."

"Now a tweeker's average *hit* is roughly one-quarter of a gram. There are 28.3 grams in an ounce. And sixteen ounces in a pound. That makes 1,792 or *hits* to a pound. Sell a *hit* here, and a *hit* there, and pretty soon the low-level dealer that I buy from takes his money and go to *his* higher-level dealer, and replenishes his supply."

"Then the entire enterprise begins over. Supply and demand, Investigators. That's what makes America strong. So when cops bust the dealers, it is really un-American, right? They are interfering with free trade. And free trade is what makes America great, isn't it?"

Chavez resumed his narrative. "So as long as the money holds out, I enjoy myself for a week of so having cocktails, smoking ice, snorting up, riding the needle, and chasing women in the casinos. At least until I run out of money and am forced to go back to work."

DuPont verbally exploded at that point, scaring the hell out of Chavez. Her facial expression clearly told him that she believed that everything he was telling us was the evasive bragging and embellishment of a small-time con. He could see that her patience with him was fast running out.

"Look, Mercado," DuPont barked, "we aren't here to learn your life story, how you were abused by your father, that your Mother was a whore, or any of the usual tweeker behavioral excuses. Either get on with the story, or we are leaving."

Chavez cleared his throat, before replying, "Okay, Okay. I asked you at the beginning to let me tell this my own way. And I thought we agreed to that. So are you going to let me finish without jumping in my shit every few minutes, Chiquita?"

To maintain my facade of being the good cop, I raised my hands, palms out, patted the air in front of the glass partition and said, "Everyone calm down here. Go ahead and tell it the way you want, Chavez. But stick to the pertinent facts and don't go off on any wild-ass tangents. That is all Investigator DuPont is asking. *Stick to the point!*"

"Okay," Chavez resumed, "First of all, I have been working with the Southern California branch of the MM, or Mexican Mafia, for years. So our routine is based on a reasonable amount of trust, at least on my part. Any new order for the theft of a boat is just a repetition of many other heists that have turned out to be successful. The cops just are pissing into the wind if they think they ever are going to stop the boat thefts."

"Routinely, I get my orders no more than four days before the MM's eighteen-wheeler tractor-trailer arrives. The truck and crew will be scheduled to appear at a specific time and date, at night mind you, at the Fort Mohave Indian reservation to collect the stolen boat."

"I go to a pre-agreed pay phone in the parking lot of one of the casinos, on the same day and time, week-in and week-out. The phone location is changed monthly. The phone rings and a voice modified, I guess, with one of them new fangled voice modulators, tells me exactly what type and model boat is to be stolen, my absolute delivery drop-dead due date, and any special instructions for the heist."

"The heists are never scheduled for weekends because if it is good weather, the boat's owner may be out using it on the river."

"As I said," Chavez continued, "the voice on the phone gives me all the details. Such as the marina, the slip the boat currently is moored in, any special anti-theft alarm systems I need to bypass, if the marina has security lighting or a roving security service, and alike. Since recreational boats are almost always keyed to one of a dozen keysets, regardless of model or manufacturer, which I happen to have masters for, the ignition key isn't important."

"After I receive the phone call, I usually hot-wire a 1980 or older car that belongs to one of Laughlin's multitude of gambling-addicted senior citizens. They usually leave them unlocked, leaving the ignition key in the center console. I heist one out of a casino parking lots while the old folks are inside spending their monthly social security checks."

The detainee, which I noticed was capable of improving his use of the English language at will, apparently decided to embellished his tale on this subject. "Hell, most of the old farts stay for four-to-five hours in the casinos, drinking and playing the slots, until their mad money runs out. Then, after the casino finishes picking all the cash out of their pockets, gaming personnel suddenly inform them that they have had too much to drink, and must leave."

"The casino's floor bosses politely escort the old geezers out into blazing afternoon sun, thank them for coming, and invite them back the following month to try their luck. Most of them are so stumbling drunk from consuming complimentary cocktails that they couldn't find their cars even if I hadn't heisted them."

Chavez chuckled, the resumed his story. "Anyway, I drive these potential rent-a-wrecks across the Laughlin Bridge using the Bullhead Parkway which takes me from Nevada into Arizona. Then I turn north or south on Highway 95, to drive to the target marina, and hopefully, catch a look at the prize during daylight hours."

He explained, "I never keep the stolen cars more than ninety minutes if it has Nevada, Utah, or Arizona plates on it, but may keep it for up to two days if it has out of state plates other than those three. Everything having to do with recreational boating in this area, is pretty much within ten-to-fifteen miles above or below the bridge, even though the Colorado River is bisected by Nevada on one side and Arizona on the other."

"When I am finished with the car, I drop it off at one of the local gin miles along the Laughlin casino Strip. That way, when the likely inebriated car owner finally reports his car missing to the cops, the cops will recover it less than a mile away at one of these bars. Because a different car is reported 'missing' and found in the parking lots at local gin mill a couple times each month, cops tend to assume that these old guys have just been out drinking and have forgotten where they left their car."

"How do you get paid, Chavez?" I asked.

Shifting his eyes from the front of Maggie's blouse back to my face, he said, "Well, I told you that this theft has been debugged over time until it is as foolproof as we can get it. So we just keep on doing it the same way, time-after-time. Why fix something that ain't broken, right?"

"But keep one thing in mind. The MM *trusts no one*! Once you are stupid enough to think that you can fuck-over the Mexican Mafia, even one time, no matter how small the scam, you will end up a corpse."

"They'll torture you simply to send any wannabes the message. The body will be decapitated and de-limbed. The rumor is that the amputations are performed while the victim is still alive. The torso serves as a message to the foolish, and is put into the water where it will eventually float down the Colorado River until reaches a dam."

"It only took me seeing one of these floating logs once to permanently rid my mind of any and all thoughts of ever trying to put anything over on these guys."

"So," Chavez pulled himself reluctantly back to the point, "I am paid $2,500 cash for stealing the boat, and delivering it to boat ramp on the Indian reservation. A down payment of $500 will have been previously been slid under the door of my efficiency room when I am not at home. Which also tells you that the gang knows where I live and can get at me anytime if they even begin to suspect that I may be screwing with them."

Chavez went on, "Like I said, the collection date is usually scheduled to be within four days or less in the future. But it has to be on a night forecasted to be overcast so the moon won't give us away. If not, the gang will reschedule and advise me of the change in plans by leaving me a note tucked under the door of my room."

"I rip off the boat and deliver it to the collection crew down on the reservation at the agreed-upon time and place. As I said, once the boat and the trailer they brought with them are loaded back into the truck's enclosed cargo box, its rear doors are closed and locked. Then and only then does the crew boss hand me an envelope filled with twenty used $100 bills."

Then, I like jump on my bike, and head back for Laughlin a couple of thousand dollars richer. Sure, the boat may have cost the owner up to nearly half a million dollars. But us regular people can't afford that. So they should share the wealth, I say. No skin off my nose."

Dupont leaned forward in her chair, and interrupted, "Okay, Chavez, now we know more than we want about your life up *to* the Casino heist. Shit! Do you think we are interviewing you as a future actor for the soap opera *Days of our Lives*? Now, the only thing I want to hear out coming out of your mouth is exactly what was your part was in the Riverboat Casino heist. Nothing more. Nothing less. Do you get my meaning, dirt bag?"

Chavez looked over at me again, as if to say, *"How can you stand to work with this bitch?"*

"Okay," he sighed before resuming his story, "I was once a U.S. Marine. I served for eight months in Iraq before I got caught stealing money from the Quartermaster's safe. American Oil-for-Dollars receipts that our guys were collecting on the Q-tee from bomb-damaged Iraqi banks. The funds were unofficially ear-marked for use in paying indemnities to the families of Iraqi's that our troops had killed accidentally in firefights."

"Well, I watched the money-for-Iraqi-family payouts for months. I knew I could make a big score if I arranged everything in advance. So I got the Quartermaster drunk one night. We were playing poker together. He had been winning every hand, which of course was part of my plan. I was down to him well over four-hundred-dollars, U.S."

"Then I sheepishly admitted to him that I've had lost all my money. And that I was going back to my barracks unless he would loan me enough money to tied me over until payday. I knew he was greedy. He thought about it for about a nanosecond then asked me how much money I wanted to borrow? He said he would loan it to me if I promised him I'd stay and continue to pay cut-throat poker with him until lights out."

"When I agreed, as I had planned to, he asked me once again how much money I wanted to borrow. I told him a thousand, knowing he didn't have that kind of cash on him. And just as I thought he would, he got up, went over to the old cast iron safe, and spun the dials. Which I was watching closely over his shoulder, memorizing the combination."

"The QM yanked open the heavy safe and pulled out a banded bundle of bills. Then he counted out $1,000 of the blood money in twenty-dollar bills into my hands, and slammed the safe closed again, making certain to lock it by spinning both dials."

"Long story short, I purposely lost every dime of the borrowed money to him that night. But by the time that payday rolled around, I was already in the wind with every dollar of the cash that had been in that safe."

"I spent the next month AWOL in Baghdad until I had spent all the stolen money on drugs and whores. Then I got careless. Shot my mouth off about being a big shot into too many soldier's ears. And that is when the Military Police found me and dragged me back to the brig in the Green Zone," Chavez explained

"It didn't take them long to courts-martial me out of the crotch, which is military slang for the Marine Corps, and hang me with a Double D, a Dishonorable Discharge. Then I was shipped back to the states on the same airplane that was the last ride home for the occupants of twenty coffins."

Chavez asked if he could have a glass of water before continuing. The malicious glare from the guard and Investigator DuPont answered that question for him.

"When I got back to the states, I found out that no one would hire someone with a Dishonorable Discharge. Not even to drive a taxi, or shovel shit, whatever. And yes, it made me bitter. I was only able to scam together enough money together to support my meth habit."

I had to crash in shelters, or sleep on hot air vents in the sidewalks. It was bad, but not as bad as it sounds. You can get a couple squares a day at a soup kitchen shelter, so you won't starve to death.

Chavez continued, "A few months later I moved to Laughlin. There I worked pretty diligently to establish myself as a thief who was open to considering any opportunity that could led to big money. At the time I figured that with all that money flying around the casinos I might be able to get my hands on some of it."

"But, it turned out to be the same old hand-to-mouth existence. Then I fell into a sweet deal. All it required of me was to occasionally steal a specific upscale boat from one of the local marinas at night. All I had to do was deliver the booty, the boat to a prearranged location and the Mexican Mafia would pay me a set sum for it, no questions asked."

"Finally the deal with the MM developed into a more or less a steady income. A decent but illicitly earned income. But with my meth habit, I might have $2,000 one night, but within two days, I was broke. So I needed a way to make more money as my habit increased."

Chavez rolled his shoulders forward and back, getting a crick out of them before continuing on, "Then one of the local tweekers, an Section Eight mental case ex-Marine, I think, told me of a veteran's website which had been set-up by a bunch of veterans who felt that the military had screwed them over."

"I figured, why not, check it out. So I went down to the library, and rented a PC for an hour. Five-bucks or something like that. It took me less than an hour to get hooked up on-line with some very pissed-off Marines that eventually led me to this gig."

Chavez said, "It was really easy now that I think about it. I wrote a blog complaining about how I had been screwed, claiming the military was really responsible for not going after QM who had let me see the safe's combination in the first place. I ended my blog with the statement that I do *anything* to make some *real* money."

"When I stopped back by the library and paid my five-dollars-rent a couple days later, there was a reply waiting. It was very brief, simple, and to the point. It said that if I wanted to make a great deal of money in 'a single night' to call from a specific number at a given time and date."

Chavez shook his head, as if to clear his mind, and continued, "When I called the number, the guy on the other end asked me a bunch of questions about my military service."

"When he asked how I was supporting myself now, I was intentionally vague—I sensed that he knew all about my boat-theft gig with the Mexican Mafia. Fearing that the call was a trick by the MM to see if I would tell someone about our activities together, and remembering what a Mexican Mafia floating log looked like, I stopped being so open, especially since it so far the conversation had been one-way, information-wise."

Chavez took a breath and went on. "We arranged for a face-to-face meeting in Oatman. That's an old mining town now turned tourist trap that's off the beaten path. So I stole a car and we met at the bar in the old Oatman Hotel. It's really dark and caters mostly to tourists and the town's down-and-out alcoholics."

"It was mid-afternoon when we met. The guy appeared to ex-military. He was tall, and casually-dressed except that he was wearing spit-shined jump boots under the legs of his jeans. We moved off to a quiet corner as the tourist rush was having a monetarily lull. He introduced himself to me simply as the Colonel. He provided no more identification about himself other than that."

"The colonel didn't waste any time. He told me that he was planning an armed robbery of a casino during the early morning hours when the play was slow and it was still dark outside. He said he and his crew needed someone who could aid them in escaping from the crime scene, and who would see to a couple of minor chores."

"Then he captured my immediate interest by informing me that my portion of the take would be $50,000, regardless of how much the robbery netted. I asked him who I had to kill?"

Chavez kind of grinned lopsidedly at DuPont and said, "When the guy answered, 'No one,' I asked where could I sign up."

Investigator DuPont ignored Chavez's leer and interrupted once again, part of our strategy. "Okay, you say this guy who doesn't know you from Adam, and nothing about your dependability or track record, promises to pay to your worthless tweeker ass $50,000 for an hour or less of work. You may think that I just fell off the back of a farm truck filled with manure, but you are the shit, not us, dickhead. I want to you to tell us exactly what duties he expected you to provide for this grandiose fee."

"Well, this is specifically what he told me," Chavez said. "My boat, actually a stolen boat because it was up to me to acquire it without raising the suspicion of the cops, was to be nosed onto the beach at the rear of the Riverboat Casino/Hotel at exactly 4:00 a.m. on Thursday, April 10, 2008. No matter what, I had to be there exactly when and where stated, no excuses. Or, he promised me, I would be killed."

"When I arrive to pick them up for their escape, I was to leave the boat's engine running. And the Captain's Choice switch, you know, the one that controls the mufflers, was to be set on Silent."

Chavez continued to speak as if fondly remembering that night that had made him momentarily rich, $50,000 rich. "He said the boat had to be in excellent shape, capable of transporting up to four large men who would be carrying about fifty pounds each of swag. Oh, and I wasn't to say a single word to any of his crew."

"I only was permitted to speak to the colonel himself, and then, only when spoken to. He would issue orders and I would comply without question if wanted to get paid and survive the night."

Chavez, getting a little pale, finally realizing that he was now committing the exact transgression that the colonel had expressly warned against, said, "He threatened me that night at the bar that if I wasn't there for any reason, or told anyone, and it resulted in he and his crew being caught or killed, he'd come back someday and kill me in the worst manner I could imagine."

I interrupted the detainee, and confronted his account. "He must have given you more information than that, so you could plan the getaway from the casino. If for no other reason than because you wouldn't have much time to make the escape with all the cops swarming the grounds of the Casino."

"Yeah, you're right as rain about that, Chief Investigator. He told me that I was to transport them at the best speed I could safely navigate the river to the same spot on the Fort Mohave Indian Reservation where I previously had met the truck that picked up the boats I stole for the Mexican Mafia."

Chavez, continued, "I don't mind telling you that when he admitted to having firsthand knowledge of something covert I had been doing for the MM, I got real scared, real fast. I told him honestly that he was creeping me out. God Damn it, I told him, I don't want to become a Mexican Mafia log floating down the Colorado River."

With a deep sigh, Chavez went on. "Then the colonel grabbed my arm with fingers that felt like steel hooks, and told me not to be so paranoid."

"He claimed that he had bought that information from the MM in a business transaction when his crew was planning for their getaway. He assured me that everything was copasetic with the Mexican Mafia because they knew the information wouldn't go any further than his crew. My part-time job stealing high-end boats for the prison-run gang would go on, just like nothing had changed. His telling me that, made me feel better. After all, that was the real-world-way I made a living."

"Oh, then he gave me an envelope saying that was a down payment on what he would owe me if I performed flawlessly performed my part in the getaway. It had $5,000 in used $20 bills in it."

Chavez looked first at Maggie and then returned his eyes to me, and said, "Long story short, I did exactly as he instructed me to. I picked them up of the beach behind the Riverboat that morning a little after 4:00 a.m. They were very orderly. I guess you could call it disciplined. Like no one acted like they were frantic for me to push the boat off the beach. Despite the fire alarms ringing off the wall in the hotel. People were screaming, crying, and running everywhere."

"As they, only three, not the four I have been told to expect, jumped from the sandy beach into the boat, two of them were each carrying a large bag. By that time, I could smell and see a lot of smoke billowing out of the casino and hotel. I thought I heard some small explosions from first floor of the casino, but I didn't hear any gunfire. I got a occasional glimpse between the buildings of flames billowing from the casino's front parking lot."

"There were also flames visible behind the windows in some of the guest rooms on one of the upper floors. It was something like the hell, fire, and damnation movies that the networks haul out every Halloween. "

"About 4:20 a.m., I pushed off from the Riverboat's beach and headed south down the Colorado River with the boat's clearance lights extinguished. In a matter of fifteen minutes or less, I had offloaded them and my dirt bike at the Fort Mohave Indian Reservation's unlighted boat ramp."

Two of them, swag bags in hand, immediately vanished into dark night. They must have stashed a getaway car in the desert that probably had been camouflaged with tumbleweeds earlier in the evening."

Chavez, being a sexist, glanced briefly at impressive front of Investigator DuPont's blouse before resuming his convoluted tale. "Before the colonel followed his crew into the desert he paused to remind me once again of his promise of eventual retaliation if I messed up. He asked, if I believed him? All I could was stutter, 'Of course, Sir.' "

"The colonel did have one final order for me before departing. He ordered me to take the boat into the middle of the river and scuttle it. He said that would prevent the cops from finding any incriminating forensic clues off the boat's hull. Then he jammed a thick envelope in the pocket of the black jumpsuit I was wearing and jogged off into the darkness to meet up with his crew. He disappeared like a ship into the fog."

"At the time, I admit I thought he was being over cautious. All of us were doubled-gloved in latex."

"As soon as I heard the engine of their vehicle drive off far enough so I could no longer hear it, I realized I had to get my butt moving in case the cops were pursing us in boats, or more likely, helicopters."

Acting proud of himself, Chavez finished up his account. "But as you know, I didn't follow the colonel-of-the-urinal's order to take the boat out into the current in middle of the river to scuttle it. I rationalized that if I did as ordered, then I'd have to swim back to shore, and I'd be all wet for the ride on my dirt bike back to civilization. Naw, I might catch a cold from doing that. I wasn't about to do that. But I compromised by removing the boat's drain plug in its engine compartment before I shoved the hull back out into the river."

Chavez looked over at Maggie and I as if seeking our acceptance of either the deed, or the tale, he had just told us.

Maggie just shook her head in disgust before speaking again to the detainee. "Chavez, $50,000 is a lot of money for just stealing a boat and transporting some mokes away from a potential-death penalty crime scene. I cannot believe that is all you did. If you want me to believe anything that you have told us, and go to bat for you with the prosecutor, you are going to have to tell us everything. Now give it up, or we walk."

Chavez, a sheepish look crossing his dark face, replied, "Yeah, I might be holding something back, but it ain't no big thing."

I stuck my two bits into the conversation at that point, saying, "We'll be the judge of that. If you want us to put in a good word with the Court you better come clean. Remember that this is a death penalty case. Unless you want the needle along with the main actors, you better speak up now."

"Okay, okay, Man" Chavez said. "When I originally met with the colonel in the bar in the first week of April, he told me it was also my responsibility to recruit and pay a couple of my more reliable friends, square ones that I knew were not drug users, to set two vehicle fires in the Riverboat's parking lot at 3:59 a.m. the morning of the heist."

"The colonel gave me two devices for that use before we split up in the bar's parking lot that night. The two guys he forced me to hire, cost me $2,500 a piece, half up front and the other half four days after the robbery when the cop's investigations should normally have been cooling down."

Maggie had another question for the man, one that I should have remembered to ask. "Chavez, who besides us have you told this tale to? Any of your friends? Anyone at all. It is important, so think before your answer."

"Well," Chavez began, "when I was booked in the DC this morning I was pretty high. And I think that I might have mentioned some of the details to a con they had in the cell with me. Don't know his name, though."

"Chavez," Dupont said, jumping to her feet, "You are either are the stupidest shit or at least the most naïve street con I've ever run across. When you were booked last night, weren't you charged with a crime of violence against a police officer? And weren't you trussed up in handcuffs, ankle bracelets, and a waist chain?"

In an incredulous tone of voice, Maggie continued to berate Chavez. "And think back. After the medics looked you over and treated any injuries you may have suffered from the scuffle during the arrest, weren't you put in one of the cells in Administration Segregation on 5C? The individual cells that are reserved for detainees who have exhibited violence during their arrest?"

"Yeah, Investigator," Chavez replied, now thoughtful. "But so what? When the other dude was put into the cell with me, I just figured that the CCDC was filled to over capacity as usual, and they was just doubling-up on cells."

Maggie sighed, and said, "Do you know the definition of the word 'segregation' as it applies to Administrative Segregation, Chavez?"

"Well, I think," He answered, "it means to be by yourself—you know, alone."

"Then why in the hell," the female investigator pushed, "didn't you ask the guards why another inmate had been put into your cell when you knew your classification of prisoner meant you were supposed to be locked up by yourself?"

"Well, investigator," Chavez whined, "I didn't because I needed someone to talk to. You know, pass the time when I was coming down 'cold turkey' off my meth high. What harm is there in that?"

Maggie only had one suggestion for Chavez as we stood and indicated to the guard we were leaving. "Watch you ass in here, Chavez. You may have fucked up big time. In lockup, you never ever spill your guts to a new cellmate who just happens to be assigned to your cell. You better hope he was a undercover cop and not a friend of your armed robbery associates."

The guard had just unlocked the door of Defense Counsel interview room leading to the hallway, when Chavez directed a final statement at me. "Investigator Fox, I am pretty sure one of the three people I took down river was a woman. Or a man wearing perfume."

As the door to the interview room slam closed behind us, the guard led us down the hall, through the clanging doors again, to the non-secure side of the detention center. While Maggie and I mulled over Chavez's final revelation that would turn out to be a vital clue in the investigation.

I couldn't have known or anticipated that the end game from this investigation would be so violent and costly, in terms of human lives lost, or that it would go down in Las Vegas history as a crime that eclipsed even those of the bloody mob years, decades previously.

EIGHT

June 10, 2008, Tuesday, 9:00 a.m.
Gaming Control Board field office
555 E. Washington Avenue
Las Vegas, Nevada

The first thing I did, when I returned to the office the next day after Maggie dumped me off on her way back to McCarran to stuff her cardboard *Police Business* placard into her purse and turn in her rental car, was to call Detective Izzy Petosa. The Gaming Control Board owed him big time for the heads-up that turned us on to the possibility that Chavez may have been a player in the Riverboat Casino heist. In the interest of promoting the sharing of information between agencies, I gave him a brief overview covering what Chavez had admitted about his connection to our case.

I mentioned in passing that we were concerned because Mercado had told us that despite the fact that he had been assigned a one-man Administrative Segregation cell, a second inmate had been put in with him without explanation. Petosa said that surprised him as commingling AdSeg inmates was strictly against regulations. He'd promised to get on the phone to the CCDC and get the matter straightened out immediately.

Then we both uttered the normal goodbye niceties before hanging up and returning to our respective caseloads.

The remainder of the week I spent at my LANS terminal running every possible combination of keywords, such as *Military Background, Former-Service-Personnel-as-armed-robbers, Mixed-Gender Gangs*, and so on, through the various criminal data bases available to the GCB.

I was attempting to come up with a list of 'usual suspects.' But I didn't really know where to start looking. The possibilities were too diverse.

Apparently the gang that had hit the Riverboat back in April had displayed no fear. They had been excellent planners, and had demonstrated that they didn't shy away, when it proved necessary, from subjecting innocent citizens to the potential of grievous injury or death.

Adequate seed money was apparently available to the gang. As knowledgeable witnesses had later reported that the three men that had been observed, each appeared to be equipped with gear that costs thousands of dollars. And we now knew that the gang had at least a communication connection to the Mexican Mafia and possibly other Southern California gangs.

I had been assigned an administrative assistant, Billy Frisbee, to assist me with the computer searches. Frisbee was a fully-commissioned special agent and a decorated former Navy SEAL. However, he had only recently completed his specialized GCB training. Apparently some higher-ups in the Carson City headshed thought he might learn something from working with this old China hand, as some of the secretaries had began to refer to me, behind my back.

Maggie had wished me, "Goodbye and Good Luck" when she dropped me off in front of the office. She was enroute back to the headshed in Carson City to resume working her caseload.

So excluding my new inexperienced rookie partner, I really didn't have anyone of any experience to bounce ideas off. After all, I was still seen as the new Probie in the Las Vegas office.

Especially since it turned out that I had been brought on-board at a higher-starting salary than the *current* salary of some of the older agents who had been chasing gaming cheats for years. The resentment that caused could have been cut with a chain saw.

I guessed it would take a while until the veterans decided to give me a chance, the furor over my salary died out, and I was invited to join in the group's bullshit and brainstorming sessions.

Billy continued our search of law enforcement databases looking for potential candidates for our robbery gang. So I gave a friend in FBI/TTS, the FBI's Terrorist Threat Squad at Quantico a call, and requested any information that her squad might have on violence-prone, disgruntled, former-military types.

I told her I was specifically interested in anyone who, by self-admission, felt disgusted, traumatized, or abandoned by the U.S. military due to the perception, that they had been given inadequate or unfair treatment from Uncle Sam.

Any radical malcontents that may have decided to put his or her extensive combat training to work for the benefit of their wallets. Perhaps they believed that money, no matter how obtained, would provide salve to their wounded egos and a sense of retaliation for what they perceived to be unfair or undeserving treatment.

Of course, they wouldn't have been able to begin to execute this hypothetical payback scenario until after they had been discharged or released to inactive duty, upon their return the land of Uncle Sugar.

Billy eventually came up with a laundry list of possibilities. I had him add to that, the 50 or so names that FBI had provided, bringing the list to a total of about 150 names. The list we had assembled was long. All we could do was start at the top, and work down.

We'd first have to establish the current location of each of the individuals. Then working with the major credit card companies, we'd learn if any of them had been in Nevada or Arizona in April of this year. Any of that fell into that category, and were known to still be in the area, would be the ones we'd hit the street and interview first.

Any of the individuals who were currently out of state, but had used a credit card locally during the timeframe of the robbery, I'd ask out-of-state FBI field offices to invite the individuals in for a *substantive* interview.

Unfortunately, while Frisbee and I were sitting at our desks mining federal databases, someone on the other side was busy tying up loose ends.

June 13, 2008, Friday, 12:15 p.m.
Clark County Detention Center
Las Vegas, Nevada

It was a few minutes before the trustees would begin to bring the lunch meal around for prisoners housed in the CCDC's AdSeg cells. Meals for AdSeg inmates are timed so the serving of the trays was always performed *after* the General Population prisoners had been escorted to the chow hall for their meal.

Detainee Mercado Chavez was laying on the bunk of his one-man AdSeg cell in 5C with his eyes closed, very confused by his time in confinement. He hadn't heard from either of the two investigators. He assumed they were busy trying to identify of the members of the armed robbery gang.

Early evening, Monday, he had been returned to his fifth-tier AdSeg cell, who he was currently sharing even though it was against CCDC Policy, by guards following his interview with the two GCB investigators.

Then, less than an hour later, his impromptu room mate had been hustled out of the cell by guards that were looking a bit sheepish, like someone had just been given them an ass-chewing to top all ass-chewings.

Chavez was only permitted an-hour-a-day for a supervised shower and exercise in the detainment facility's yard. No one said anything to Chavez. He felt that the guards and fellow inmates alike were treating him like a non-person, like he didn't exist anymore. Much like the movies he had seen when a man on death row received the mantra chant, as he was escorted to and from his cell, "*Dead Man Walking!*"

Chavez knew he was becoming paranoid. After all, all he did was first steal, provide, and drive the getaway boat. He had convinced himself that he was not guilty of anything that could eventually send him to prison.

Suddenly he was startled out of his musing by the gong announcing the General Population lunch. It, as usual, hurt his ears. He could never figure out why the bulls thought they needed a gong loud enough to wake the dead.

And again as usual, he heard the clanging of dozens of doors in his pod being electronically unlocked. But then he was so shocked that he jumped to his feet when his own door clicked open.

Whoa! Chavez had been in Administrative Segregation since he arrived at the CCDC, except for one time when an apparent mistake by the bulls had resulted in an another inmate being shoved into his cell.

But now he was really confused. He knew as an AdSeg inmate, he wasn't permitted to be out of his cell except for his sixty-minutes-a-day of supervised personal time.

What should I do, thought Chavez? *Stay in the cell? Or leave since the door had been unlocked?*

Finally that question was answered for him when a guard he'd never seen before, strolled by his open cell door popping his night stick against the glass wall, and yelled, "Get you tweeker ass up off the cot and get to lunch, Chavez. Or are you waiting for an engraved invitation? Get going now, or I am going to take away your exercise and shower privileges away for a week!"

Chavez wasted no more time. He bolted from his cell and joined the long line of inmates who were lined up, shuffling past his cell.

The line started and stopped as the guards performed cursory searches of every inmate entering the lunchroom.

They would again be searched when they left the chow hall, before being permitted to return to their cells.

Chavez was concentrating on not bumping into the inmate in front of him, or stepping on the toes of the inmate following close behind him. Invasion of any inmate's personal space was one of the worst offenses you could commit in lock-up, and could result in you receiving a beating from the offended inmate.

So engrossed was he in not offending any of his fellow inmates that he almost didn't hear the commotion behind him. Before he could turn to see what was happening, he felt a searing, burning pain in his back, then another in his kidney, and a third to the rear of his exposed neck.

He could barely manage to glance over his shoulder and then only caught a brief glimpse of a tall, wizened old man, possibly a lifer, crouched behind him holding a shank, a homemade prison knife. The blade was bloody. Chavez couldn't figure out where the blood came from.

The pain in his back began to scream. *Or was that my voice screaming*, he wondered. It felt like he was pissing his pants and having an uncontrolled bowel movement at the same time. *How is that possible*, he thought, frantically?

Then he began to crumble to the concrete deck as his legs gave way. He desperately tried to catch himself by grabbing onto a nearby wall, but he discovered that his hands weren't working.

When he hit the concrete floor, he hit face first, and he hit hard. But even with the terrible pain in his head, he felt something very warm. Something very warm and very wet began to pool around him, as he lay curled up into the fetal position on the cold deck, beseeching someone, anyone, to "Please, please help me!"

He lay in ever-increasing pain as the pain-masking side effects of shock began to desert his body. The noise assaulting his ears once again got very, very loud, and then suddenly, died out all together.

It was about 5:30 p.m. that afternoon. I had been putting the list of the dozens of names remaining on our 'possibles' list into my drawer for a second look on Monday morning.

Just then I received a call from Detective Petosa, over at Metro. He reported that several hours ago, he had been called over to the CCDC. He'd been at the detainment center ever since, investigating the death of a prison inmate.

Turns out, our witness, Mercado Chavez, had gotten himself shanked. He'd been assassinated by a con that claimed he didn't even know his victim. Under questioning, the lifer had admitted to the murder, only saying that he had been forced to carry it because of a telephone threat he had received earlier that morning, concerning his teenage daughter who lived with his ex-wife in nearby Boulder City.

The lifer told Petosa he didn't think his knifing of Chavez was such a big deal. Especially since he was already waiting for transport to a maximum-security facility having been convicted of a wanton thrill-killing of a doctor and his entire family. The jury had sentenced him to life without parole. "In for a penny, in for a pound," is what the old con had told Petosa.

The killer maintained that he didn't know Chavez from George W. Bush. He claimed he had gotten a phone call earlier in the day from someone who told the guards that he was the lifer's lawyer.

The con said the voice on the telephone had sounded like an officer whose name he couldn't recall back when he had served a tour in Iraq. He said the voice told him in a no-bullshit manner exactly who he was to kill. Or that his young daughter would be kidnapped, raped, and disfigured.

The caller had provided the lifer with Chavez's cell number and the fact that an accommodation with a bent guard had been arranged to get the detainee out of his isolation cell for a few minutes at noon that day.

After the stabbing, and the subsequent interrogation, Petosa and a couple guards had been escorting the lifer down the stairs from the bloody fifth-floor-tier for further questioning. Suddenly, the lifer bolted and launched himself over the railing, breaking loose from the hold that the guard, following procedure, had been maintaining on the collar of the man's coveralls.

The lifer fell five-floors down to the concrete deck of the main-tier floor where he lay motionless in a bloody heap.

Petosa said he and the guards had run down the five staircases to reach the man's prostrate body, first called the facility's emergency medical team, and then attempted to administer first-aid.

However, likely as the lifer had intended, the five-story fall had broken his neck, severed his spinal cord, and caved in his skull making it look like an old carved pumpkin after Halloween festivities were over. The fall would have instantly killed the man.

Petosa assured me that his CSI technicians had already collected whatever crime scene evidence was available, and therefore there was no reason for me to join him at the facility.

Before hanging up, I thanked the detective for the notification. And thought, *There goes our only witness. The bosses are going to be pissed that we put off getting a written statement from Chavez until the next week. Damn the bureaucracy. All of the GCB transcriptionists were either on-vacation, or tied-up in court.*

The fact that Chavez had been killed before we had been able to obtain a signed, written statement from him, meant the verbal admissions he had made to Maggie and myself, could not be introduced as evidence in a Court of Law.

However, the man had told us enough to greatly aid in our investigation. We now knew that an individual who had introduced himself as 'the colonel' had been behind the heist. And we also now knew how the gang had made their escape.

And we had been told of Chavez's suspicion that one of the robbers that he transported from the crime scene had been wearing some type of heavy sweet perfume such as Jungle Gardenia. That individual could have been a woman, or a cross-dressing male. However, based on the fact that team appeared to be exclusively Marines, that appeared unlikely.

Even in death, Chavez had unwittingly become a strong arrow in the quiver of our investigation.

NINE

June 14, 2008, Saturday, 10:00 a.m.
CSI-Crime Scene Investigation. A TV series.
CBS Television Production Studio
A leased warehouse in North Las Vegas
Clark County, Nevada

I spent Friday night at home kicking my own butt for not immediately returning to interview Mercado Chavez in the Clark County Detention Center that Monday morning, even though a stenographer had not been available to accompany me.

That excuse may not hold much water anyway with the Clark County District Attorney's office, or my own bosses in Carson City.

I knew I hadn't violated any Gaming Control Board procedural guidelines by delaying the interview until I could find a transcriptionist. Even if I had, there hadn't been time to make arrangement for a steno because Dupont and I had driven straight from Izzy Petosa's Metro office to the Detention Center.

And no con in the whole-wide-world was going to open up to an interviewer during the first discussion with him or her, especially if a stenographer or even a electronic tape recorder, was present. That simply wasn't the way the complex criminal/cop relationship worked in the real world.

I had hoped to return to the Detention Center on Monday, June 16th, with a court-reporter-cum-stenographer, once I had a deal in-hand from the Nevada State Prosecutor's office in exchange for Chavez's testimony, to ensure his future cooperation.

However, Mr. Murphy had interceded at that time. Chavez had been brutally murdered, I was almost certain on the explicit orders of his former partners in the robbery of the Laughlin Riverboat.

Detective Izzy Petosa had called me at home the previous evening to report that none of the CCDC guards would admit to slipping a confidential informant or undercover cop into Chavez's cell soon after he had been booked by the cops on Sunday night, June 8th.

The reason that the powers-that-be would try an antiquated end-run like that would have been to learn what Chavez knew before his court-appointed attorney showed up and told him to keep his mouth shut.

So the failure of the CCDC's guards to admit to that transgression pointed one thing out to me. The person who had been slipped into Chavez's AdSeg cell had some connection to Chavez's partners. And it wouldn't have taken but a single bent guard to permit the illegal act, even though to do so, and be caught doing so, was a major violation of CCDC procedure.

The snitch had been permitted into the cell by a 'bent' guard for the express purpose of letting the inebriated Chavez cry on his shoulder, spilling all the details of the April 10th robbery.

After Chavez told us about his new cellmate, and I told Petosa, the detective had rattled some cages down at the CCDC. That probably made the guard that had prompted the prohibited incursion in the first place, to panic.

So the crooked guard and his buddies had immediately removed the plant from Chavez's AdSeg cell before their superiors came up to the 5C to check Petosa's claim out.

Afterward, the guard had obviously questioned the prisoner or other individual he had used to milk information from Chavez, and then called his paymaster in the armed robbery gang to report his findings. He probably even suggested the name of the lifer with nothing to lose, who would be willing to eliminate Chavez for the proper motivation.

It wasn't my job to root out crooked guards in the Clark County Detention Center. But I'll bet that Las Vegas Metro Detectives would be kicking asses and taking names in the CCDC until they got some answers that would led them to the guilty guard.

―――

This morning, Saturday, was another of Las Vegas' *to die for* beautiful mornings, after the prevailing winds swept through the valley overnight, carrying the brown smog away with it.

This morning was dedicated to being my first productive day on my part-time job. I would be attending a pre-production meeting to answer any questions that the producer, director, the various craft leads, and location personnel, might have on the episode script that had been messengered to my condo earlier in the week for review.

To double-check the changes I had subsequently suggested, I had read the revised paper galley once again last night before turning in. My job title on the part-time job was Contract Technical Script Advisor. My employer was CBS's very popular television series, *CSI: Crime Scene Investigation*.

According to what publicists put on the show's website, it was because of the several city-name CSI spin-offs that came on television after the original CSI debuted, that many have come to call the show *CSI: Las Vegas* rather than its real name.

The original cast featured William L. Peterson as Gil Grissom; Marg Helgenberger as Catherine Willows, Bad Boy Gary Dourdan as Warrick Brown; George Eads as Nick Stokes; Jorja Fox as Sara Sidle; Eric Szmanda as Greg Sanders; Robert David Hall as Dr. Al Robbins; and Paul Guilfoyle as Metro Police Captain, Jim Brass.

Again, according the hit show's website, a couple of its main actors apparently haven't been satisfied with their remuneration for the character roles they played, now that the show was highly successful. Two actors in particular had made a conscious decision to engage in a little brinkmanship, with the network instead of demonstrating their gratitude for the work, by keeping their respective noses to the proverbial grindstone.

In fact, before the 2004-5 season, actors George Eads and Jorja Fox had been fired. Eads for not showing up for a scheduled shoot, and Fox for not reporting to the show's producer that she was available for shooting, as clearly set forth in the language of her contract.

CBS reported they had felt that both of the actors were being disruptive by trying to upgrade the original contacts the actors had agreed to, now that the series had become exceptionally successful.

But then Mohammed had been forced to come to the Mountain. Despite Ead's claim that he had simply overslept, and Fox's explanation that she did not know about the requirement to submit a letter of interest, both were rehired at their original agreed-upon rate-of-pay, and neither received a new or upgraded contract.

In October of 2007, actor Jorja Fox explained to reporters that she was leaving the show "to pursue other opportunities." Her character on the popular show was not replaced, even though her character was supposed to be having a behind-the-scenes on-going sleep-over affair with character Gil Grissom.

The hit series turns out twenty-two episodes annually requiring the employment of twenty-seven producers.

The show's website also claims that besides being a hit series, CSI is behind the increase in student applications to colleges in the field of Forensic Science.

The term 'CSI effect' has also been coined to describe its affects on our Court System. Since the fictional CSI team finds proof of guilt in seemingly impossible situations, jurors often expect real-life forensic scientists (who don't have nearly the budget of the fictional CSI team, nor to mention that series writers are permitted to exercise some creative licenses) to be able to do the same.

That misconception places a tremendous burden on the Court System, on the offices of prosecutors and defense attorneys alike.

My qualifications for the part-time technical script advisor's job were two-fold: First, I was a qualified Crime Lab Director as certified by the ASCLD, the American Society of Crime Lab Directors. I'd been trained by the best, the FBI at Quantico. In short, I knew my stuff and had kept current on the latest in forensic science.

Secondly, due to my extensive law enforcement experience on the NYPD, and as the former head of the elite Crimes Against Citizens directorate of the Hong Kong Police department, I knew accepted law enforcement procedures, methods, record keeping, information management, typical case scenarios and how to solve them, probably better than all but a handful of persons employed in current day Nevada law enforcement.

A small part of my contract responsibility involved my filling in when a writer was out ill. However, my major responsibility was validating episode scripts, before the fact. This required I review the scripts, which are messengered to my home in Henderson.

I had to stay a couple weeks ahead of the show's taping, far enough in front of the producers that the episode's writers would have time to rewrite any obvious procedural errors or instances I discovered, that would have required methodology not yet available to real-life forensics scientists.

This task involved a lot more than me just sitting at home with my feet up, an episode's galley on one hand, and a glass of Merlot in the other.

Take, for instance, an episode where the storyline revolves around a completely skeletonized set of human remains found out in the desert. An event often documented to be fact over the past forty years in Las Vegas. More often than the Chamber of Commerce wants to admit, I imagine.

The finding of a body in the desert would require forensic anthropology scientists, or highly-trained forensic criminalists, to map, document, and photograph the crime scene. Enough data and evidence would have to be recovered and documented to support law enforcement and the corner's efforts to determine the COD, or the cause of death.

Forensic anthropologists would have to examine the skeletal remains, to both identify the body's identity, and hopefully work up a life history of that individual, so that investigators could work backward to determine how and why that person died. That is, if the autopsy revealed no obvious COD.

Medical Examiners also have the job of determining the victim's sex, approximate age, and race.

Most successful forensic shows, including the current trilogy of CSI; Las Vegas, Miami, and New York, keep people like me on the payroll. Our function is two-fold: First, we are expected to catch procedural errors in the script before the episode can be produced.

Secondly, it should be no great revelation to you that television is a notoriously unforgiving medium. Even less so, for series that are touted as being technically accurate, as it is for all of the three CSI series.

If the viewers catch a procedural error, especially if the mistake is major enough or repetitive enough to cause disbelief among the series' loyal fans, which after all keep the show on the air by aggressively buying the products advertised on the show, someone's head is going to roll.

The positive effect of the show's Neilson ratings, serves to drive up the advertisement rate that can be charged for a minute-long spot. Frankly, that is probably is the primary reason to justify the expense of hiring someone like me.

By accepting the technical script advisor position, we accept responsibility for ensuring the episodic storylines are functionally authentic. That gives directors, producers, and other assorted ivory castle riff-raff, a ready-made fall guy when things get screwed-up. In the words of modern television, it is our *'bad.'*

How do script writers, occasionally screw up the facts, you ask? Let me give you a couple of examples:

The first example would be, say, when the script calls for a Priest to be shot or stabbed, and down he goes, clutching his chest, taking his last dramatic breath. He is definitely dead, too bad, but very dead regardless.

The crux of the problem is that no one dies instantly and most intelligent viewers have been around this old world long enough to know that. Of course there are a few exceptions, like a homeless person who decides to take a seat on the rails just as the cowcatcher on the afternoon freight violates his personal space.

Instant death can occur from heart attacks, strokes, extremely abnormal heart rhythms, chemical poisoning, and so on and so forth.

However, gunshot and knife wounds rarely cause instant death, unless by coincidence, it happens to the individual that sat down to rest on the railroad tracks.

Another example would be when, say, the script calls for a death to be the direct result of ingesting a fast-acting poison. That would go something like this:

"Virginia took a deep drink of her scotch. Then suddenly a look of foreboding crossed her beautiful face, her heart sputtered to a halt, her eyes rolled back in her head, her half-full glass fell from her spasming fingers shattering itself on the kitchen floor, and she collapsed into my arms.

Okay, where is the problem you ask? First, poisons including that old Hollywood stand-by Arsenic do not kill that quickly. It can take days for a person who has acute arsenic poisoning to die. And it isn't a pretty death. The victim will first develop intense stomach pain. Then nausea, vomiting, and diarrhea, will eventually manifest themselves.

True, having a victim clutch their throat or chest does permit the producer to avoid having to show the viewers the victim's terrible death that eventually will ensue for the victim. But once again, a reasonably intelligent viewer will know the scene isn't even remotely how it is in the real world.

Here is a very brief thumbnail sketch of the episode script we were discussing in today's pre-production meetings.

Episode Title: *Things aren't always what they seem.*

The setting of this fictional crime drama was North Las Vegas, Nevada. Between 2007 and early 2008, a series of brutal sexual homicides swept that city which is known for its higher-than-normal rate of violent crimes. The victims basically more or less resembled each other. The victims all were male, wore buzz cuts, were Caucasian, about six-foot-tall, and weighed about one-hundred, eighty pounds.

The men were single, and had been well-dressed. The victim's family, friends and the bartenders at the venues where the men had been customers, had reported that the individuals liked to carry large amounts of cash on their persons. They hadn't been very circumspect in avoiding letting others know that, and the strip joints they frequented were known to condone drug use by employees and patrons alike.

Investigators who interviewed patrons and staff at the bawdy clubs learned that before their murders, each of the men had been seen in the presence of what was described as an attractive, possibly mixed-race, athletic-looking woman.

Several of strippers interviewed, who working at the various strip clubs, normally very observant as their livelihoods require them to make instant decisions such as which of their alleged admirers had money for table dances, and which are potential trouble makers, tended to provide better descriptions of the mystery woman.

Most of the dancers thought the woman to be about thirty-something, maybe five-feet-tall and one-hundred-pounds soaking wet. She had café au lait skin and thick, shoulder-length hair, the color of dark chocolate. Her face was broad, and her facial structure a mix of African and Asian features.

The woman's eyes reportedly were large, pitch-black and flashed with an impatient intelligence, despite the supposed enjoyment she should have been enjoying from the company of her escorts.

She was reported to have a square chin and dimpled jaw line marred by a small knot of muscle working to one side. Her full lips appeared to be chemically-enhanced.

Witness statements on her manner of dress had been less than helpful. Once she had been dressed casually in gray-wool pants and a black sweater, and at another club, she had been seen wearing a business suit.

One of the exotic dancers had noticed that the woman's only apparent jewelry was cheap black plastic watch, and she seemed anxious and impatient for some reason.

Her dark shoulder-length hair was described as being a somewhat mannish cut which seen to fit the first impression of most of the witnesses, who thought that the woman seemed to be very controlled, very disciplined, and was apparently used to being in-charge. They ventured the possibility that the woman could be a sexual dominatrix.

Police in the jurisdiction where the murders occurred, worked long hours attempting to identify the killer or killers. All of the interviewed witnesses had given slightly differing descriptions of the woman who had been accompanying each of the victims shortly before their deaths.

Investigators combed their databases time-after-time but couldn't come up with a woman fitting that description, who had a history of vicious sexual killings.

The only clue that the forensics people could give investigators, was that after the victims had their genitals bitten off, the killer had viciously bitten them about their faces, like a rat, until the men's features where no longer recognizable.

And in each of the homicides, the bite marks had left plenty of DNA for forensic typing. Of course, until the detectives could come up with a suspect, that definitive information, although probative, was useless.

North Las Vegas cops began pulling women with records of violence, in for questioning. In each case as applicable, the assigned investigator might choose not to strictly enforce their department's *No-Smoking* law in the interview rooms. Especially if the women appeared to have tobacco stains on the fingers, or the smell of burnt tobacco on their clothing.

Author's note: Interviewers rarely prevent a smoking suspect from lighting up, if he or she felt it may serve to build a kinship with the subject being interviewed, that could lead to eliciting information, at the least, or a confession, at the best.

If the person being questioned was wearing a business suit, bulky sweater, or other heavy clothing, before the detective went into the interview room to introduce himself or herself to the person being questioned, they'd jack up the room's thermostat to 84 degrees and keep the questioning going until the person sitting across the table from them began to show indications of being overheated.

In that case, the detective would continue the questioning for a couple of more minutes, then out of the blue, stand and exclaim, "Hell, it is too hot in here. Damn heating system is on the fritz. I've got to cool down. I'll be back in a minute. The vending machine is just down the hall. I'm going to get a diet coke. Can I get you anything? Treats on me."

Nine times out of ten, if the interviewer has been playing nice with the interviewee and timed his ploy correctly, the individual being questioned will respond in the affirmative, taking it as a hopeful indication that the detective is on their side.

Of course, back to the real world. Once the interviewee had finished with their cigarette, the detective finds a way to unobtrusively get the cigarette butt or empty soda can out of the interview room, into an evidence bag, and arranges for it to be hand-carried to the forensic crime lab for DNA sequencing and comparison.

All the above slight-of-hand accomplished, unfortunately, since none the covert samples subsequently matched the killer's, was adding a lot of female DNA markers into CODIS, the national DNA data bank.

The male sex murders went unsolved until they finally began cold cases. No one worked them on a regular basis. And sometimes the cases weren't being worked at all. Especially after budget-cutting reduced the number of full-time detectives working cold cases.

Then six-months later, a transvestite, or a *tranny* as they are known on the street, was arrested on the Vegas Strip for prostitution. Prostitution is illegal in Las Vegas, if not in several other locales in the State of Nevada.

The arresting officers had been attempting to handcuff the prostitute when the Methamphetamine running through the arrestee's veins brought the fight-or-flee syndrome to the forefront and both officers were severely bitten on the arms and faces. Like one would expect for a feral rat.

The cops called for backup and an aid car. The assailant was hauled off by the responding backup team but only after leg shackles had been clamped on the struggling *tranny*, and after a *spit mask* was secured over the prisoner's head.

The two severely injured cops were transported by the aid car to the nearest hospital for emergency treatment, and testing for HIV and other STD's.

The cop's injuries resulted in additional charges being added to those the prostitute already faced. As a matter of procedure, the attacker's saliva was sent to the Las Vegas crime lab for DNA typing. Then those results were submitted, again per procedure, to CODIS.

It turned out, through the combined efforts of persistent interviews during the investigational phase of the original sexual homicides cases, state-of-the-art improvements in DNA testing, and painstaking processing in the crime lab, the killer was identified and finally brought to justice.

No, despite the excellent descriptions the detectives had obtained from the employees of the North Las Vegas strip clubs, the killer had not been a woman, but a Mr. Larry Joe Smith, a transsexual who soon would admit that he regretted his earlier sex-change operations; hating it so much that he attempted to take his misfortune out on any virile man he came across in his chosen life of prostitution.

Following the CSI production meeting, I stopped by the Bellagio for dinner and a few cocktails before heading home to my condo in Henderson.

There was no way I could have known that the infamous armed robbery gang I was pursuing in my real job, was going to strike once again early the next morning as I lay in my bed at home experiencing a restless sleep brought on by eating too rich a meal.

TEN

June 15, 2008, Sunday, 3:00 a.m.
BRINKS Armored-Car facility
3200 E. Charleston Blvd.
Spectra Business Park
Las Vegas, Nevada.

Atypically for this time of year in Las Vegas, the pre-dawn sky was overcast, dark and dreary, and totally without any redeeming inspiration. As with most 24/7 destinations, vehicular traffic in Sin City was still evident, albeit sparse, even though sunrise was still hours away.

If a satellite had been watching, the eye-in-the-sky would have observed three vehicles, lights-extinguished, emerge from an abandoned warehouse. The building was located west of the Las Vegas Motor Speedway and south of Hollywood Road, which skirts the west perimeter boundary of the racetrack.

The building, one of many advertised 'for rent' in a local commercial real estate circular, had been rented by mail from its absentee landlord. The renter and the landlord had never come face-to-face. The first and last month's rent and the $2,500 damage deposit had been paid the owner, using a U.S. Postal Service money order.

It took less than two-minutes for the small caravan to reach Hollywood Road's bias intersection with Las Vegas Blvd North. At which time, they flipped on their headlights and merged into the sparse early morning traffic, headed into Las Vegas.

The caravan consisted of two freshly-painted, battleship-gray Ford one-ton Econovans. They were following a large 1998 dirt-brown Dodge Power Wagon equipped with eight-ply, heavy-duty truck tires, a commercial-grade crash bar and a military surplus cable winch. Everything an desert off-roader could hope for.

If any motorist, out and about at that ungodly hour, had bothered to take a close look at the sides of the vans, they would have noticed that gray newsprint was taped to both exterior surfaces of the vehicle's cargo boxes.

The three vehicles heading into Las Vegas religiously maintained a separation of one-hundred-yards. When they arrived at the intersection of Las Vegas Blvd and State Highway 612, they turned left and proceeded at slightly below the speed limit in a southerly direction, until they passed Bonanza and Stewart Streets.

A few moments later the small convoy reached Highway 612's intersection with Charleston Blvd, at which point the vehicles turned eastbound, after stopping for the flashing four-way, red-traffic light.

There they took a right and headed southbound once again, on Tree Line Road until all three reached the entrance to *Lewis Family Park*.

3:31 a.m.

The three trucks entered the park, backed into the sparse foliage until they were out-of-sight, and then extinguished their headlights. That maneuver left the trucks parked hood out, facing the park's front entrance.

The occupants of one of the vans and those in the Power Wagon stepped out of their vehicles and slipped into the second Econoline. The four men crawled in and took a knee in the back of the van, on its ridged metal floorboard. No tattletale courtesy lights revealed their presence. Before the vehicles had left the warehouse twenty minutes before, the vehicle's interior dome and courtesy lights had been removed.

The men were wearing brown BRINKS uniforms, right down to the Sam Brown gun belts, holstered pistols, and black ankle-high commando boots.

The man driving the Power Wagon laid out a Mylar map of their target on the floorboards. As the men continued to kneel uncomfortably on the floor, the Power Wagon driver took the time to individually inspect the faces of the five members of his crew, half the gang's total number, which would be participating in tonight's mission.

After achieving his intent to make his men nervous, he began to speak.

"Okay, we are good to go. Does anyone have any last-minute questions or concerns? I don't want us to go in there, possibly get in a gunfight, have someone screw-up, and later claim I hadn't preplanned this morning's heist well enough. If you have questions, now is the time to ask them, he said."

As the leader had previously arranged, Lt. Abraham Daniel, the Dodge truck's African-American passenger, spoke up as if skeptical, playing the devil's advocate as he had been assigned on the way over to the park.

"Boss, maybe we ought to have brought an eighteen-wheeler instead of these vans. That would be provided some real forcible entry power if the guards refuse to open the doors. And provide a lot more room for the money than in these one-ton vans."

Continuing, he went on, "Sure, as you say, there is a good chance that the real guards inside the building will see the BRINKS uniforms and livery on the Econolines, and be confused long enough that one of them will get curious and open a security door."

"But, you know those guards have it drummed into their heads before they ever participate in their first actual money pick-up, that you never make exceptions to BRINKS' time-tested procedures—never!"

Another one of the kneeling gang members, David Sturgis, who had once been a decorated Marine Recon Sergeant, spoke up to disagree with Lt. Daniel. "Lieutenant, how do you propose we get rid of the hypothetical tractor-trailer after the job? By using the vans, we can empty the money quickly from them into the big-box truck when we get back to the warehouse. Besides the Major says the facility's roll-up doors there aren't tall enough to accommodate an eighteen-wheeler."

Daniel verbally fired back at the sergeant. "Sarge, you know we aren't going to leave the vans just anywhere for the cops to find. As we've been briefed time and time again, they both get dumped after we transfer the money at the warehouse. The drivers from them get inside big box truck, along with the booty."

He continued, "I agree that it would be damn difficult to find a place to dump a tractor-trailer and still get the two-hour head start we need to get back to base camp. Especially because we have to get back there and get undercover before it gets daylight. As soon as it gets daylight, the cops and FBI will have their choppers in the air in an attempt to hunt us down."

The former recon Sergeant decided to ask another question, even though he was certain that he knew the answer without asking, "What happens to the Dodge truck?"

The colonel interrupted to answer that one. "Sturgis, we both know that old piece of junk will be disabled if we are forced to use it to crash through both the main gate and one of the roll-up doors at the rear of the BRINKS building to gain entry. We'll never get it running again. So it stays, and I pile into one of the vans on top of all those sweet money bags."

The lieutenant answered the ex-Marine's unstated question. "We'll toss a couple Willy Peter grenades into the Dodge before we head back to the warehouse. The colonel has seat-belted a couple of five-gallon gasoline cans into the backseat. Believe me, the rig will go up like a freaking Atlas rocket."

Now departing from his usual college-educated manner of speaking, the Lieutenant lapsed into ghetto parlance. "Ain't goin' to be no ev-i-dence left for the po-lice to find. Ain't goin' to be nothin' left but a lot of scorched metal and melted upholstery. When the Willy Pete gets burnin,' ain't no ev-i-dence remaining.'"

Another member of the gang, a Hispanic Recon corporal, turned to the leader, and asked, "Colonel, what has the Major reported about the size of the morning's security force that will be on-duty at the facility when we hit it?"

"We know that you told her to stay completely away from the rest of the us after she reported for her first day of work there, but she must have been getting status reports to you, somehow."

The leader sighed, and waved to prevent his subordinate from answering the question. "The Major reported to me at midnight last night using her cell when she went to the Ladies room to take a leak. She says that there is one dispatcher, herself, one supervisor, and six guards putting together the 9:00 a.m. money deliveries for the casinos."

Doing the arithmetic in his adrenaline-buzzed head, the corporal stated in jest, "Hell, that ain't too bad—Eight guards to the six of us, plus the Major, of course. Hell, we got them surrounded, I tell you. Let's go get 'em."

The two white men in the hijack gang continued to just kneel there, listening to the pre-game jitters being expressed by their comrades.

The older for the two, 45-years-of-age, who had been drummed out of the Marines after being caught selling American military bullet-proof vests out of the back of his warehouse to the Iraqi insurgents, asked,

"Okay, Colonel, one last thing, one last time. So we are up to date on the situation and to ensure there are no surprises."

"What has the Major reported regarding the BRINKS' physical security systems on the perimeter fence and in the building?"

"Okay, you guys," the colonel answered, anxious to get under way, "The Major's latest report to me was that there are motion detectors spaced every 100-feet along the perimeter fence, and swipe-card-operated internal locks on all the doors that have access to the cash room. The dispatch office isn't fortified. Which frankly seems stupid to me, but please bear in mind these people are civilians, albeit, armed, but still civilians."

Elaborating further, he said, "As you know, the gate guard usually is a ex-cop. The main gate is manned 24/7. With the number of people on-duty on the inside of the facility, every mother's son or daughter of them carrying, locked and loaded, that is all that BRINKS Security thinks it needs."

"BRINKS knows that there are people like us out there, just waiting for them to forget something or slip up. But don't worry about that tonight. We have planned this thing forward and backward for nearly a month. It is going to be a piece of cake. Way simpler than what you guys faced daily in Iraqi, I promise you."

The gang's other guy, Mohammed Mohammed, a skinny, owlish-looking guy, former Marine Intelligence Winnie, said "Eight guards."

"Yeh, eight guards. That is what the Major said would be on-duty this morning. She is very assertive and in-your-face as you all know. That attitude has served her well in gaining pretty much complete access to the entire facility, at least when the bosses are off-duty. Someday BRINKS is going to be kicking its own ass when it realizes how she manipulated them."

"Okay, then," mumbled the tobacco-chewing Staff Sergeant. "But perhaps you guys who have fooled yourself into thinking you are John Wayne, may have forgotten this? The eight of them are going to be barricaded inside that fortified building, as nice as you please. We, on the other hand, will be on the outside, unprotected, in a position of weakness. Despite what one of you said a minute ago, we definitely *do not* have them surrounded. They will be cut off from all communication with the outside world. At least for the three minutes that we will be inside the building, collecting the cash."

The colonel repeated for emphasis, "Three minutes, no more. That is all the time we have inside. No more, no less. We have talked about this many times. Gangs that stay inside a location beyond the three minutes, invariably get caught."

"Remember the bank robbery in North Hollywood at the B of A in Los Angeles back in February of 1997? The bank robbers purposely stayed at the facility beyond the three minutes, just to get their rocks off, killing citizens and cops. They fought a good withdrawal action, I have to admit. But in the end, hanging around solely for the macho reasons of putting a couple cop's scalps on their belt, still got them killed."

Once again, the slightly-built former intelligence Winnie spoke up, "But they are going to be comfortable barricaded inside a very serious fence. We, on the other hand, will be outside, looking in."

The Leader, growing tired of the last few minutes of *What ifs*, said, "You let me worry about the damn fence, Mohammed."

"But, Sir, it looks like BRINKS spent enough money on the main-gate to ensure it couldn't be breached. How do we get through it, using just that old truck?"

"Mohammad," the colonel now exasperated by the concerns the men were bringing up at this late stage in the operation, said, "we've gone over this time and time again, many times. There is a gate in the fenceline, in fact, two. The rear employee's gate is inaccessible after office hours. They use out-of-service, armored-cars to block the rear entrance on the inside of the fence."

"During business hours, which doesn't help us a tinker's damn, the back gate is open. But after hours, if someone on the property has a heart attack, whatever, the ambulance has to come and go through the main gate at the front of the compound."

The colonel reminded the man. "If you'll think back a couple of years, that gate has the same weaknesses as the one we had at the Forward Operating Base we worked out of in Iraqi. Right? Now don't you concern yourself about this, Mohammed. That old Dodge Power Wagon you are disrespecting will go through the front gate like shit through a goose."

"Now," the colonel asked, looking around at his men once more, "who in the hell else has stage jitters? Or can we just get this show on the goddamn road as we planned. At least, that is if you still want to be rich before dawn."

"You made me this gang's commanding officer. And I am telling you this plan will work, just like the combat operation we pulled at the Laughlin Riverboat back in April, and the armored-car hijacking on May 3rd."

The colonel was correct, of course. His people had studied the layout and role-played the responsibility each of them had in the assault, at least two-dozen times previously. The crew was highly-disciplined and excellence was expected. Failure was not an option.

Each member of the gang, without exception, had been relentlessly grilled over the past weeks concerning their assignments, and all contingency plans relative to those assignments.

If anyone of the men had raised a serious, deal-killing question or had voiced less than a positive attitude towards the plan's chance of success at this stage in the operation, the leader could have done one of two things. Either taken the highly unlikely action of canceling the night's mission, or more likely, have shot the less-than-enthusiastic troop dead and continued with the operation even though the gang would then be short-handed.

Too much time, front money and preparation had gone into planning the operation, starting two months earlier, to quit and abandon the mission.

The gang had five-weeks previously arranged to insert one of their team—the crew's female second-in-command, a battle-tested former Marine Major—into the target's operation as a Cash Room Count Verifier. The plant would be the key to this morning's operation. She would be vital to the operation's success.

Relative to the danger potential of the crew using this public park to stage in the pre-dawn hours of the morning, the Park Ranger who was responsible for the security of the park, whose duties included making hourly patrols after nightfall to make certain the main entrance gate was secured, had been bought off for $1,500.

However, the Ranger had been getting suspicious as of late. Possibly he'd begun to smell a big score. And he had grown ever more greedy by the day.

The colonel had decided that he couldn't afford to tempt fate by canceling the morning's operation, just to take time to renegotiate a deal with the Ranger. He'd kill the park cop first to ensure operational-security and to protect his crew.

3:45 a.m.

The men crawled out of the rear of the Econoline. Then used LED pin lights to inspect each other, making certain that their BRINKS uniforms and equipment were neat and pressed, and worn in a manner commensurate with that of real employees.

Being dressed in the same uniforms worn by the armored-car company's employees would provide the crew with a few additional seconds of confusion if they were forced to go to Plan B. In that case, if the seeing the imposters wearing BRINKS uniforms failed to bluff the interior guards into opening the security doors, the gang would be forced to resort to explosives to gain access to the building.

There was a possibility that the guards inside the facility couldn't be bluffed into opening the doors. Even though they would be observing what appeared to be company vans, driven by individuals wearing BRINKS uniforms, back into the loading dock in a routine manner.

In that case, and before the gang would resort to using noisy explosives, the gang planned to attempt to gain entry using the now-battered crash bar on the Dodge Power Wagon to crash through one of rollup doors, into the secure area of the building.

If the crew were forced to use explosives to break into the building, confusion would reign paramount. The threat environment would suddenly become even more deadly as the company's employees were all well-armed, and outnumbered the assault team.

Earlier in the week, the leader had failed in a cursory attempt to use a third party to bribe the gate guard in-control of the facility's main gate. At night, the main-gate guard was the employee who decided who entered the facility, and who didn't.

However, it soon became apparent that the armored-car company had prudently designed their security schedule to prevent that from happening.

They randomly rotating the security force that controlled access into the compound after working hours.

The gang has not been able to obtain the rotating gate activated electronic code that controlled the main gate, and hence access into the facility

That necessitated that the gang's first move would be to gain access to the facility, by force if necessary, circumventing the obstacle that the perimeter fencing represented. That would require they take the main gate guard out if he refused to open the gate on their demand. Then they would be forced to gain access to the facility by crashing the Power Wagon through the main gate.

After taking out the main gate, the Dodge would pull through and off to the side to permit the bogus BRINKS vans to enter onto the grounds.

The second priority, to be accomplished once the vans had pulled up to the loading dock in the rear of the facility, was for the men to attempt to bluff their way into the facility.

The third priority, if the second didn't work, was that the explosives expert riding in the Dodge with the colonel would use a remote ignition device to set off the shaped-charges the Major had placed earlier in the week.

When the facility's radio tower crashed to the ground, and the side of the concrete masonry building's wall blew in, putting the main telephone circuit box out of service, the Dodge would only attempt to crash through the building's truck bay doors, if the gang wasn't able to gain access in the facility in a less destructive violent manner.

If the original bluff failed to provide the gang access to building, it was unlikely that the armored-car company's guards inside the building could then be intimidated into willingly opening the doors.

The crew hoped that the commotion at the front gate wouldn't be heard or observed. The last thing they needed was for the employees to call the cops then lock down the facility in adherence to the excellent training that BRINKS gives their armed guard force.

The gang had contingency-planned for the use of alternative ways around that eventuality, but those options were noisy, dangerous, and excessively time-consuming. Not to mention that the necessity of going to the use of high explosives was extremely dangerous to both the robbery team and the company employees. No one wanted injure any of the employees, but now that they had killed the main gate guard, all bets were off.

But the later alternative would seal the fate of the employees inside the building, as they would then have to be considered armed defenders. And would have to be dealt with immediately and appropriately upon the gang's entry into the facility.

If the guards inside refused to open the loading dock doors, and the Power Wagon couldn't break through the roll-up doors, then the use of explosives would be necessary. It was entirely possible that the gang members forcing entry, and the guards inside the building, could have their eardrums injured or even could be momentarily blinded for up to twenty minutes.

And since the robbery crew intended to spend no more than three minutes inside the building, the time-tested and proven successful thief's mantra, forcible entry by explosive would be taken only as a last ditch necessity.

Fourth, when the gang finally gained access to the building, the robbers would immobilize all the armored-car company's employees, everyone inside the building. The crew was prepared to execute this action in whatever manner that the employee's chose. It would be the employee's call whether it was easy, without the loss of life, or the alternative.

———

As mentioned previously, a female gang member, the former USMC Major had managed to get a job in the facility's cash room there weeks earlier. By now she was considered by management to be a trusted employee.

After her first couple weeks on the job, she had gone to management and volunteered to work the unpopular graveyard shift.

Her motivation for requesting the shift was obvious. Working nights, long after management had gone home, she had enough freedom of movement to permit her to plant a couple powerful shape-charges to render the facility deaf and dumb on the morning of the assault.

During a prohibited cigarette break outside the building, she'd been able to place a concealed charge at the base of the exterior radio tower, and a second on the building's perimeter wall, opposite the location where the main terminal box for the facility's security telephone system was bolted to the wall inside the building.

The woman, a highly-competent marksman, would provide an additional gun to backup the assault team if the BRINKS guards decided to be heroic and start a firefight.

Assured that each member of the team knew his or her part of the assault forward and backward, as well as the various contingency plans for the operation, the leader gestured to the Econoline drivers. They ripped the gray newsprint that had been concealed the BRINKS decals mounted on both sides of the vans.

An ex-con Las Vegas print shop owner with a heavy meth *Jones* had been too desperate for cash to feed his habit, to risk asking the colonel any questions. He had whipped up the bogus BRINKS placards on his image printer. Then he had transferred the image onto thin adhesive backing. The crew had applied what essentially were decals to the sides of the Econoline vans after the fresh battleship-gray paint had dried.

The newsprint had been taped over the bogus BRINKS logos for the purpose of concealment, while the vehicles were driving to the park, prior to heading for armored-car facility.

Once the newsprint was removed, it would go into a green trash bag in one of the vans where everything that was even remotely traceable would be stored until the gang could burn it.

The crew had robbed the Riverboat Casino in Laughlin, Nevada, during the early morning of April 10th of this year.

Then they hijacked an armored-car from Loomis/Fargo on May 3rd. Only the fact that every member of the gang had checked and doubled-checked to ensure that no evidence was left behind, had the gang remained unidentified, out-of-jail, and their faces off the wanted posters.

3:55 a.m.

Each member of the robbery team was now running on pure adrenalin as they hopped back into their assigned vehicles. The leader once again was behind the wheel of the Dodge Power Wagon.

After the uniformed van drivers returned to their vehicles, the men who impersonating BRINKS guards, stepped back into the cargo box of the Econolines. The gang had learned through covert surveillance over the past weeks, that it was established procedure for the non-driving guard to remain locked in the back of the van, except when it was making pickups or deliveries to the casinos. The company had be forced by OSHA to install a truck seat with a seatbelt in back of the truck.

Then the gang's vehicles pulled out of the park, and headed for the armored-car facility, traveling at slightly below the posted speed limit.

Las Vegas' BRINKS armored-car facility is located inside the Spectra Business Park, off Charleston Blvd, east of State Highway 515, in a mixed commercial/residential area. It is poorly lit at night, and normally sees little traffic after normal buisness hours. And the tourists begin to hit the casinos in their relentless quest of a rare big win, complimentary drinks, or a ridiculously cheap meal.

The BRINKS facility is a reinforced, rectangle-shaped, concrete block, one-story building of 50,000 square feet, located in the center of a five-acre plot of land, surrounded by parking lot, and by a ten-foot-high electrified chain-link fence, which is topped with several rolls of interwoven concertina razor wire.

During office hours, the employee entrance at the rear of the compound can only be accessed through use of an employee security swipe cards. After hours, that entrance is totally inaccessible by virtue that security always arranged for several of the out-of-service armored cars to be parked up against, blocking it, on the inside of the locked gate, effectively denying all access and egress.

That left the front gate as the only available remaining entrance after-hours. But BRINKS considered the main-gate to be unassailable.

It was obvious that a regular car, normally weighing about three-thousand-pounds, would be unsuccessful if it attempted to breach the heavy, welded-steel gate that was made of 12-M galvanized nine-gauge chain-link fence fabric, its 4.1 pound-per-lineal-foot-steel-line-posts buried four-feet deep in a footing of 42-inch-in-diameter concrete.

But a heavy truck, if properly tricked out, might be able to do it. Even then, the coil strength of the chain-link material would bleed off a portion of the crash vehicle's energy.

The six-gauge, tension-wire woven into the 9-gauge chainlink mesh would make the fence stretch until it was as tight as a guitar string. But enough weight and momentum applied in certain manner, at a specific location, would eventually exceed its design-strength and cause it would rip apart.

Any effort to use a pair of bolt cutters to make an opening in the chainlink mesh was, at best, asinine. Anyone attempting to cut their way through the fabric of the fence would cut themselves badly on the rebounding sharp corners of the heavy wire as it was being sheared. Especially if the party attempted to use it on the razor-sharp rolls of concertina.

The fact that the fence was electrified and generously strung with active motion sensors every 100-feet, made it functionally impossible to scale.

With the armored car facility locked down after-office hours, the only entrance to the compound was through the main-gate entrance, which was guarded by a heavy-gauge rolling steel gate, and at least one guard armed with a 9mm semiautomatic pistol.

The gate guard manually operated the gate as the company's armored vehicles came and went. But none were scheduled to enter or leave the facility during the early morning hours. So the gang could expect the gate guard to refuse access when the bogus vans showed up demanding access to the facility.

The armored car company had provided the gate guard with a four-inch-in-diameter, red-mushroom panic button, which was connected to both the facility's dispatch center inside the building, and the dispatch office of the Metro police.

Anyone wanting to take down the facility off-hours had to reach the gate guard before he could push the panic button. That, of course, would be the assault team's first priority.

The early morning darkness and traditional lack of alertness on the part of most employees working the night shift would hopefully provide the gang with a few minutes of decreased attentiveness, permitting them to crash through the gate to enable them to get inside the perimeter fence.

4:17 a.m.

The leader tromped his foot down on the accelerator, accelerating the souped-up Power Wagon towards the gate at a speed approaching fifty-miles-per-hour. The truck only avoiding smashing into the gate by judicious use of the vehicle's heavy-duty brakes. The big rig slid to a halt just in front of the reinforced gate.

The guard was a big, heavy, old guy with long gray hair and a huge walrus mustache. He wore a wrinkled tan uniform like that worn by Metro Police. He was an ex-cop, taken with his minimal authority, the type guy that thinks he is bullet-proof. He was carrying a Glock 9-mm pistol in a ragged, old quick-draw holster that hung from a Sam Brown belt, that had seen better days.

The guard hearing the commotion, looked up from his evening paper. He knew that the old Dodge Power Wagon that had just slid up to the gate couldn't have any business here that couldn't more properly be taken care of during the facility's daytime business hours. So he ignored it and went back to reading the *Las Vegas Review-Journal*, the local newspaper.

After getting no response from the gate shack, the Dodge's driver laid on the horn, then flashed a replica Metro police badge out of his window to get the attention of the rent-a-cop.

The old man again adjusted his bifocals and peered a little harder out of the guard shack's window at the idling truck.

Finally hauling himself to his feet, the old man threw his newspaper down, spit on the floor, and stepped out into the cool morning air to find out what the hell the racket was about.

When neither of the men in the Dodge got out of the vehicle, the guard stomped up the open driver's window and demanded to see the badge that the driver had flashed.

The driver ignored the old man's demand, but he said, "You have one chance to save your life, Pops. Either put in the code to open gate right now or you won't live to see the end of your shift. Have you ever seen the game show on NBC, *Deal or No Deal?* Well, this is your one chance to make a life-*extending* decision."

In the driver's obtuse thinking, he was being charitable by even giving the guard a chance to quit being an asshole and save his life.

But the threat only made the guard more contrary. He was really getting fired up now. He began to pull the Glock out of its worn holster as he began backing away from the Dodge. The old man was so livid that he was spitting up phlegm as he yelled at the truck's driver.

"You back that piece of shit out of here, Sonny. Get the hell out of my sight before I call the cops. You drunks go find someone else to hassle. Now get going before I ventilate that piece of junk with my 'nine' and improve its looks."

The leader raised his right hand up from where it had been hidden behind the truck's door and double-tapped the obstinate old man to death with a silenced black Ruger .22 caliber semiautomatic target pistol.

ELEVEN

June 15, 2008, Sunday, 4:21 a.m.
BRINKS Armored-Car facility
3200 E. Charleston Blvd.
Spectra Business Park
Las Vegas, Nevada.

As the Power Wagon idled in front of the security gate the passenger riding shotgun hopped from the truck. He grabbed a handful of the old man's uniform collar and dragged the still-spasming body around to the rear of the guard shack which received very little light.

He turned the old man's pocket inside-out looking for keys or anything of value he could pilfer. Failing in that, he stripped the old man of his watch and gold wedding ring. Then he walked around front of the guard shack and peered inside to see if there were any keys or valuables hanging on hooks. Finding none, he cursed as he returned to the idling Dodge.

He hopped in and had barely closed his door before the colonel slammed the truck's heavy-duty manual transmission into reverse and screeched backed away from the security gate.

Then the driver paused as to roll down every window in the Power Wagon. This was necessary to bleed off of the percussive shock when the heavy vehicle impacted the gate, activating the airbags, which otherwise could rupture their eardrums.

Setting the hand brake, the driver used his left foot to push down on the foot brake before putting the transmission into granny gear. He pushed the accelerator pedal down to the floor with his right foot, feeding gas to the high-powered hemi-engine until it was wound up as tight as he dared without blowing a piston.

The colonel kept his right foot pressed to the floor. The truck's tires howled and smoked from the abuse they were being subjected to. The noise was deafening. The heavy tread on the recap tires began to melt.

Then both brakes on the big Dodge were released at once. He continued to keep his foot in the accelerator, which caused the Power Wagon to lunge for the gate like a cannon ball out of a howitzer. Both men had an arm up across their face, protecting their eyes against the airbag deployment.

The Dodge ate up the fifty feet like it hadn't been fed for a month. The truck's crash bar rammed into gate at a speed of fifty-miles-per-hour. The locking mechanism on the gate shattered, snapping open the gate's two chain-link leafs back against their respective fence lines.

The truck's airbags as expected deployed in a New York second. That being the reason both men had slipped on goggles before dumping the heavy truck's clutch. The goggles would protect them from the detonation of the poisonous dust that provided energy to explosively inflate the air bags.

Author's note: Using a poisonous substance to deploy a common day thing, used more often that we think by the consumer, seems like a lame way to do it, or am I the only one who thinks that?

The colonel steered with one-hand, while attempting to push the now-deflated air bag away from his face so he would see. The vehicle's open windows had permitted the momentarily increase in pressure inside the truck's cabin to disperse, and the poisonous dust to vent.

The colonel had researched the subject of airbag dispersal and knew that he and his passenger would monetarily be deafened. The sounds of the roaring engine he thought he was hearing were just products of his imagination. He knew he really wasn't hearing anything.

He pulled the heavy truck off to the side of the paved entrance road to permit the two bogus 'BRINKS' vans to pass them and head across the concrete parking lot towards the truck dock at the rear of the armored-car's building.

Once the vans reached the loading dock, they would pull in, and back-up to the doors. The gang was counting on the employees inside the building seeing the two vans bearing the company's paint scheme and BRINKS placards backing into the company dock, driven by men wearing BRINKS uniforms, acting casually as if they were expected, and did that everyday, to allay any suspicious the guards might have.

Hopefully, providing enough of a calming effect that one of the more curious anti-authority-types would open one of the facility's security doors to find out what was with up, the unscheduled arrival of what appeared to be a two BRINKS vans.

As soon as the two Econolines with headlights on, had driven past the Dodge, the colonel with his lights off, loosely followed them to the rear of the armored-car facility.

The Power Wagon slowed to remain out-of sight as the vans rounded the rear of the facility and backed up to the two of the four closed rollup-doors. Off to the side was a dock-high truck slot that was used to load and unload the eighteen-wheeler shipments to and from the Federal Reserve Bank.

The roll-up door to service over-the-road rigs was too low and too narrow to permit the rigs to back into the facility.

Normally, under BRINKS regular procedure, the 12-foot-wide-and-high rollup-vehicle doors would have already been raised to permit the company's vans, or one of its the larger International armored trucks, to back directly into the building.

4:36 a.m.

The Power Wagon rolled to a stop just outside the circle of illumination projecting from the building's security spots mounted high on the building's walls. Its two occupants watched as the charade being performed by the four occupants of the bogus Econolines, began. He was planning on it being a wonderfully successfully performance.

As soon as the fake Econolines had backed up to two of the closed roll-up doors, the drivers had hopped from the vans, schedule clipboards in-hand. The van drivers, without even a glance at the facility's security doors, knocked once on the van's rear double-leaf doors, supposedly a signal to the guards posted inside, that it was safe to unlatch and open the rear doors.

Only then did the shorter of the two drivers walk up to the facility's locked security doors, smile up at the camera mounted over the door, and knock loudly, requesting entry.

When there was no response, the driver knocked even harder.

In response, an audio mike mounted alongside the door broke squelch. A disembodied voice from inside the building asked the men to identify themselves, and provide the shift password. Additionally they were told to hold a copy of their routing sheets up so the supervising employee inside could view it through the lens of the security camera.

The van drivers could not answer as required, as the Major, their confederate on the inside hadn't been able to learn that morning's password, which is changed by the BRINKS security computer at the beginning of every shift.

Still hoping to bluff his way past the security safeguards, the driver waved his paper-filled clipboard in front of the door's viewing slot. An accomplished thief, he easily managed to put a look of irritation on his face, meant to display his agitation for the by-the-book hassle at this early hour.

The caper's other actors, the other driver and the two guards who had just gotten out of the van minutes before, did an excellent job of mirroring the pissed-off-look in support of their impatient spokesman.

Once again the voice coming from the speaker demanded that they state their business, and provide the shift password.

No one inside the facility recognized the men. So they knew that the men standing outside requesting entry weren't assigned to that BRINKS facility.

Once again, the disembodied voice ordered them to display their company picture identification cards, Las Vegas Metro work cards, bills of lading, and provide the shift password to prove they were authorized employees of the BRINKS Armored-Car Company.

It was then that then the larger of the two 'drivers' began to lose his cool and stepped up alongside the first man and yelled into the speaker, that was mounted chest-high alongside the door.

He said, "You numb nuts, we are a 'special detail' dispatched by the Laughlin dispatcher. We've been ordered to deliver a large shipment of possibly bogus $100 U.S. currency here. It apparently looked suspicious to a former IRS employee now employed in the cash room at Laughlin's Harrah's Hotel-Casino. He thinks the bills in question might be some of those North Korean-made *superbills*."

The man continued his rant, "IRS agents from the Las Vegas office have been called out from home to come to this location to meet with a member of the Secret Service."

"Your boss is also enroute from her home to grant them entry and assist the IRS agent in either validating or rejecting the bills. This all has to happen before the 8:00 a.m. scheduled pickup here this morning by the Federal Reserve Bank."

If the second driver had stopped right there, he might have sold the guards inside his bill of goods. But he had now totally lost control of his temper and began to bluster, over-playing his off-the-cuff script, "Now open the goddamn door before all of you are re-assigned to Omaha, Nebraska to count the proceeds of some one-horse Tribal Casino!"

When there was no reply from the overhead speaker, and the roll-up door hadn't opened, the large man turned and waved into the darkness to where the Dodge sat idling.

Then, hearing a gunshot echo from inside through the door, the bogus driver waved even more frantically.

4:38 a.m.

In the Dodge, the colonel nodded to his comrade. Who pulled a pre-armed remote detonator out of the glove box and pressed down on the detonation button.

Almost immediately, two explosions split the cool morning air. One blast signaled that the company's radio antenna, which was attached to the exterior perimeter concrete block wall on the north side of the building, was at the moment falling to the ground.

A second, separate somewhat more muffled explosion from a charge placed up against on the concrete block wall of the building, penetrated the wall, signally the destruction of the facility's telephone switchgear.

The explosions had effectively severed the BRINKS facility from all contact with the outside world.

The driver of the Dodge Power Wagon revved up the truck and dropped the transmission into granny gear once again. He aimed the reinforced front-end of the big truck for the center of the closest rollup door.

He was rolling at close to 45-miles-per-hour when the Dodge's front wheels bounced over the slight edge of the door's concrete apron and crashed into the coiled roll-up door, tearing it completely out of its frame.

When the truck's front tires rolled onto the sealed concrete floor inside, the driver stomped on the brakes to bring the truck to a sliding halt.

The steaming and smoking truck had suffered a number of fatal ills, as a result of the ramming. They included a ruptured radiator, a camshaft that had been driven into the bowels of the engine, and electricity was sparking from the shorted-out battery. Under the truck's collapsed front-end lay the bodies of two BRINKS guards that hadn't known or expected that they were in the intruding truck's way.

The colonel assumed the guards under truck were dead, because once they had stopped spasming, neither one of them moved or made a sound.

The major who had gotten herself a job inside the company, lay on the cold concrete floor of the counting area using both of her hands, trying to stem the flow of blood that was spurting almost five-feet in the air from a severed femoral artery in her left inner groin area.

Somehow, she was managing her pain enough to keep her Glock trained on the surviving employees, who by now had their hands raised, clawing for the ceiling. The smell of fresh urine was prevalent.

The second of the member of the gang to enter through the breached door, took one look at their wounded comrade, turned and raced back to retrieve a combat first-aid kit from one of the Econolines. He returned to the building and went directly to the woman, set down and opened the kit, and asked if she had been hit anywhere else besides her inner thigh.

She gritted her teeth and muttered, "No." The man immediately applied a tourniquet after using his knife to cut off the woman clothes including her black silk panties. The position at where the tourniquet had to be applied because of the magnitude of her wound was not one that usually proved to be effective. Her blood flow had only been reduced from a five-foot-high arterial spurt, to a slightly less profound stream of bright red blood.

While the man attempted to tend to her grievous wound, the woman reported in a factual, emotionless voice, despite obviously being in unbearable pain, telling the colonel who stood nearby that one of her BRINKS co-workers, who was now under her pistol with the other five co-workers, must have seen her moving to open the roll-up doors, when the other driver of the bogus vans outside had demanded entry a second time.

The co-worker, who she said had been harassing her for a date every night since she first came to work at BRINKS, had shot her from behind and to add insult to injury, had then kicked her as she lay bleeding on the floor.

According to the injured woman, the man then profaned her as she lay on the concrete floor, saying, "Well, I guess you ain't too good for me now, are you, you uppity cunt?"

That emergency first-aid being rendered the woman only served to reduce the amount of blood coming from the wound from a wild spurt, to a more sedate stream, but she still was experiencing far too much hemorrhaging. The man attempting to attend her did administer two military one-eighth-grain surettes of morphine to help deaden her pain.

The wounded woman would of had to be on operating table at that exact moment, tended to by a team of expert combat-trained medical professionals, to have even had a remote chance of saving her life, let alone the leg.

With full knowledge of the impossibility of the woman's change of survival, the solder, only trained in basic first-aid, assisted the colonel in carrying her to the closest van.

In the meantime, on the colonel's order, four out of the five BRINKS employees were manhandled into a maintenance closet. There they were placed face down on the cold concrete floor, and their hands and their feet wired together behind their backs. Then the ends of the wires were wrapped around a nearby plumbing standpipe.

Duct tape was roughly applied across their mouths without a lot of concern being shown in making sure they would still be able to breath.

4:39 a.m.

Back inside the facility everything and everybody was moving at a feverish pitch because gang members were aware that the maximum three-minute time they had been allotted inside the facility, was rapidly counting down.

The members of the gang were all gloved-up with latex. They were in the cash room area with handcarts, and loading up banded bundles of fifty-dollar denomination bills and larger. It was obvious from the colonel's cursory glance at the over-burdened shelves that were lagged to the CMU walls, that there were well over four-hundred-fifty, eighteen-inch square, shrink-wrapped Federal Reserve-sized $10,000 bundles, plus dozens more additional bundles of fifty-dollar bills.

The colonel hoped that they could be able to fit it all into the two one-ton vans they had brought with them. The Dodge was out as a conveyance, and certainly would never spend another minute on the road.

He knew there were 100-count of like denomination bills in every Federal Reserve Bank bundle, which normally is ten-times the volume of a Casino bundle. But he know from what the major has previously told him, that including the $100 denomination bills, there was over fourteen million U.S. dollars sitting on the over-burdened shelves.

The leader then turned his attention to the cowering employee who had shot the woman. Although trembling from the loss of blood, she had pointed out the shooter before being carried out to one of the idling vans.

Everyone on the gang was ex-military and therefore had seen enough wounds in combat to know that the major had zero chance of surviving her injuries. They knew she'd never survive, even if they forgot the money and instead, immediately transported her to the closest hospital that had a trauma unit.

4:40 a.m.

Incensed, the leader strode over the man who had shot the woman who served with him in Iraq, and then hung with him as his second-in-command in the gang after they both resigned their commissions from the Marine Corps in disgust.

The trembling man had his hands raised over his face when the colonel pulled out his Glock and shot the man right in the forehead. He didn't even wait to see the man fall to the floor.

Then the colonel returned to the cash room to assist his men in transferring as much cash as they could, before either the three minutes expired, or both Econolines were filled to capacity.

When the carts were wheeled out to the vans, at the woman's insistence, they had stacked bundles all around her as she lay fighting for consciousness.

4:42 a.m.

As the second hand on the colonel's blue bezel Rolex Submariner watch swung past 3:42 a.m., he yelled, "STOP! Time is up! No arguments! Drop what you are doing and get back to the vans. One of you take the Lieutenant Daniel in the van with you, and the other van will wait until I make sure the Dodge won't provide them with any evidence."

The men in both vans had been forced to stuff bundles of cold, hard cash into any available crevice to make room for the colonel and major in the rear cargo areas. The van's driver and the single guard per each vehicle rode up front, and rest of them stuffed themselves in where ever they could find room in the back of heavily-laden vans.

One of the more compassionate men, as he turned and to begin his sprint for the vans, yelled back over his departing shoulder, "Colonel, are we making a stop at a hospital to drop the major off?"

Mostly to himself, the Colonel muttered, "Too damn late for that. Too damn late! She knew that she was effectively dead from blood loss the moment that bastard shot her."

Tossing two phosphorous grenades into the pool of gasoline from the two ruptured cans inside the truck, that had leaked out and was now pooling under the shattered Power Wagon, he ran for the open back doors of the last van waiting, vaulted in, and struggled to pulled the doors closed behind him.

Nanoseconds later, the Dodge truck exploded. Less than two seconds later, phosphorous-fed flames ignited the truck's gas tank and the fire became fully-involved as the flames first washed, then caught the supposedly fire-proof insulation in the ceiling on fire, and began to race its way across the underside of building's roof.

The fire extinguisher sprinkler heads located in the warehouse ceiling had been intentionally set to a slightly-higher bulb-burst level than in other areas in the building. The intent being to protect the bulbs from the higher heat generated by idling truck exhaust. But soon the heat in the warehouse ceiling was so hot that all the activation bulbs melted simultaneously and a great gush of water began to inundate everything. Soaking everything that remained with cool, stagnant, rank-smelling city water.

Crouched in the rear of a van that was speeding for what remained of the main gate, the colonel was temporarily mesmerized at the sight of the body of his real-world partner and lover for four-years who had died only moments before.

Soldiers live only for today. Because circumstances may dictate they die tomorrow. Therefore they can't afford to be emotional when in battle or while on a mission. Keeping that in mind, their deceased comrade's body had been stacked high with bundles of United States currency.

The colonel returned his concentration to present day. He yelled up to the driver of the van, "Let's get the hell out of here and back to the warehouse. We need to transfer this stuff into the cargo truck and get out of Dodge before the cops set up roadblocks on all the major highways and State routes around here."

The bogus vans passed through the demolished front gate, out of the business park, and headed back to the old warehouse alongside the speedway. There the loot and the woman's body would quickly be transferred to the large white official-looking Ford 450 cargo box truck waiting there. It had been stolen only hours before from a hazardous materials transporters yard. It already had been placarded, announcing that the vehicle was carrying deadly Level-4 biological hazards.

The gang only spent minutes at the warehouse once they arrived. They had policed-up, or cleaned up, the building the evening before. A successful, incident-free escape back to their base was their one and only mission now.

Each of them, including the colonel, wondered anxiously if they would make it back their hideout? Or run into the cops and have to shoot their way out of ambush, like Bonnie and Clyde, but hopefully with better results?

TWELVE

June 15, 2008, Sunday, 7:00 a.m.
Las Vegas Motor Speedway
7000 Las Vegas Blvd North
Las Vegas, Nevada.

A chance discovery provides cops with the location of the warehouse that the gang used as a staging, setup, and transfer point. And in a related stroke of luck, the current location of the two Econolines that were used in the BRINKS robbery are also discovered.

The Las Vegas Speedway, which hosts at least one NASCAR race annually, employs a private security service to patrol and protect its multi-million dollar property after-hours and when an event isn't scheduled. Among the duties of the private security force is preventing trespassing, vandalism, and unauthorized use of the facility, which could expose the racetrack to liability and fire insurance claims.

The security firm's guards are commissioned as Special Officers by the Metro police, which give them limited-police powers. The guards are authorized to carry weapons while on-duty, and detain any unauthorized individual who they discover *on the property*. That is a large caveat, as it also includes those properties that surround the facility's massive graveled parking lots, which the speedway leases out to tenants.

Trespassers on speedway property most often turn out to be teenagers or other illegal street racers who mistakenly figured that no one was around to interrupt their activities.

The guards take the trespassers into custody, notify Metro police dispatch, and detain them until Metro responds to arrest and take the subjects into official custody.

Metro then transports the detainees to the Clark County Detainment Center for booking and arraignment. As Nevada State law permits the confiscation of detainee's vehicles in some cases, Metro may also dispatch a tow truck to impound the often expensive conveyance being driven and raced by the trespassers.

65-year-old rent-a-cop, Mr. Jody Johnson, no relation to Junior Johnson the NASCAR driver, employed in the capacity of a security guard by Speedway Security, had been on patrol since midnight.

It was now a little before 6:00 a.m. The sun was peeking above the eastern desert and it was rapidly getting light announcing the arrival of another blisteringly hot Las Vegas summer day.

Officer Johnson had just pulled off the speedway's oblong track and onto a frontage road. Being a careful driver, he checked both ways for oncoming traffic before proceeding on his rounds to another section of the huge facility.

As he turned his aging hand-me-down patrol car left to go southbound, he noticed a large cargo van about 100-yards in front of him placarded for the transport of biohazard materials. It was followed in-trail by two, battleship-gray Econolines.

The three vehicles had pulled out of one of the many abandoned warehouses that encircle the massive parking areas of the racetrack complex.

Johnson wasn't surprised to see the early morning traffic. *Hells Bells*, he thought, *wasn't Las Vegas known as the City That Never Sleeps?*

The only other thought that crossed Johnson's mind, at least that the only one that he would remembered later, was thinking that the guys in the trucks were just more working stiffs getting the shaft from their boss who apparently was forcing them to work on Sunday, the traditional day of rest.

Most of the businesses that occupy the little rundown shops and warehouses around the speedway, are so unprofitable that the buildings there were probably the only place in Vegas where they could afford the cheap rent being asked during the current recession.

In his personal opinion, formed mostly from watching the evening television news on FOX, he thought the shops looked a lot like residences of refuges on the Gaza Strip.

Johnson reminded himself that his wife was always on him to mind his own business. He wondered what he ought to do about what he had just witnessed. Call it in? Or ignore it? He decided to do the later.

He took comfort in his decision by thinking, *Hell. I'll let sleeping dogs lie.* Therefore he'd made a conscious decision to ignore company policy and not call the early morning parade of three vehicles leaving an abandoned warehouse that they had no business occupying, into Metro dispatch.

It wasn't as if he didn't see that type of activity on his early morning rounds from time-to-time. But rarely, he had to admit. Most of those he assumed were major-weight drug deals. He didn't want to get anywhere close to dangerous situations such as that.

As he thought back, he remembered observing something similar over the past five years he had been employed as a guard for the track. Something that was just coincidence and in the end, it didn't add up to a tinker's damn.

Stupid is as stupid does, was the way the legendary Forrest Gump would have put it. It would only be an hour or so later that something happened that would cause Security Officer Johnson to rue his decision to not pass the sighting along to the Metro police.

Despite it being against company regulations, Johnson carried a small transistor radio in the patrol car at night to keep him awake. He liked country western music and one of the Vegas all-night AM stations flooded the airwaves with it between Midnight and 6:00 a.m.

So his prior decision to overlook the early morning mysterious caravan of vehicles was abruptly reversed when the station broke into scheduled programming to report the BRINKS robbery that had occurred only a couple of hours before.

Johnson pulled the Crown Vic over to the side of the road and turned up the volume on the little radio. He sat transfixed, listening to the news of the robbery that had happened earlier at the BRINKS facility on Charleston Street.

According to the radio announcer, the armored-car facility had been knocked over by a heavily-armed gang, and had left the bodies of four

BRINKS employees behind at the scene, before making what the disk jockey was calling a "clean escape."

The part of the crime report that jarred Johnson the most, was when the DJ revealed that the gang had made its getaway in two late-model battleship gray Econolines.

Shortly after calling in his belated observation to the Metro police, Johnson returned to his patrol duties. He amused himself by thinking that Metro may not even respond to his report, depending on their current call load, and whether they were able to get into and out of their neighborhood Dunkin' Donut stores quickly.

He reasoned that even if Metro did respond, it would take at least a half-hour for them to arrive. If they arrived much later, he might not even be around to talk with the cops as he was off-shift at 8:00 a.m.

He continued to patrol around the properties that the speedway owned. Periodically his duties required him to drive the fence lines around the small businesses that leased the buildings, all located up against the perimeter fence of the track's vast parking lots, whether the buildings were currently rented or not.

While the news of the BRINKS armed robbery was fresh in his mind, he was shocked when drove around the corner of a building and almost plowed into two-gray Econolines.

The vans didn't have any exterior signage. Despite that fact, Johnson had the premonition that these two vans might be the same ones he had seen following the hazardous materials box-truck earlier that morning.

The Econolines had been stashed under a rotting canvas canopy at the rear of a defunct wrecking yard.

Thrilled with the possibility that his name might get into the newspaper in the capacity of working a case with Metro, adrenaline began to course through his veins. Johnson rationalized that Metro would have to pass on that information to the Media that he had assisted in the recovery of the potential getaway vehicles. They couldn't deny his fifteen seconds of fame, could they? Isn't there supposed to be transparency in police work?

He might just be a rent-a-cop to some. But if it became known that he had even a marginal involvement in bringing the robbers to justice, he knew he could be considered a hero in his neighborhood bar.

It was at that time that Security Officer Johnson permitted the possibility of his shot at future fame, to override his common good sense. And the law-abiding manner he generally conducted himself in, and advised others to do the same.

The old man parked his black-and-white recycled patrol unit behind the two vans to prevent them from leaving should they still be occupied. Then he undertook an action that not even a rookie cop would have attempted.

He didn't take time to consider the possible consequences. All he knew was these two vans may have been used in the robbery. The radio indicated that a lot of money had been taken.

And he knew that when he got around to reporting his latest find, with rush hour starting up, it could take an hour before the Metro police arrived on-scene.

Until they arrive, he thought, *I'm on my own. My actions here will be dictated by what is best for me, and my family.*

His mind raced with the possibilities. His wife needed money for the medical treatments and pain medication. Money he didn't have. For years they had been forced to live in near-slum-like conditions. Just to be able to pay for her treatments and keep her living a few weeks longer.

The government had told him that they didn't qualify for financial aid. His minimum wage earnings from the security company, plus both of their social security checks, supposedly exceeded the poverty limits that were required in-order to qualify for benefits.

But he may have just stumbled on to a windfall. And he wasn't going to make the call to Metro to report finding the vans until he had first searched them both. The vans may contain some overlooked money. And no one was here to observe or criticize any action he took, including that, should he decide to 'take into custody' any money he found in the vehicles.

So with that muddled thinking clouding his mind, he unhooked his seat belt, forced the thought of the potential future consequences out of his mind, and stepped out of his patrol car.

Johnson knew he was risking his livelihood. If he stole some money and he was found out, arrested, and convicted, that as a former cop, and a Metro-licensed security guard, he likely would end up in state prison, sentenced to Natural Life.

Quietly closing the squeaky door of his patrol car, and after taking a deep breath to call up his long-dormant courage, Johnson drew the old Ruger .44 Magnum out of his Safariland hip holster. He crouched down and began to stealthily creep towards the two vans.

From outward appearances the vans appeared to be unoccupied. And Johnson noted that the ubiquitous dust from the speedway's unpaved parking lots had yet to settle on the vans, indicating that the Econolines had been dropped off there in the last hour or so. That timing coincidently dovetailed with his previous sighting of the two vans.

As the adrenaline coursed through the old man's plaque-clogged arteries, he already had convinced himself that the two vans in front of him were the ones he has observed departing the abandoned warehouse a mile or so away, earlier that morning.

He reasoned that it was damn lucky he had finally called the cops to report the initial sighting. Reports of his attention-to-detail would ensure that his name would find its way into the local newspaper.

Maybe I should call the paper myself, the old man thought. *Well, maybe not. Metro is pretty hardnosed about sharing the credit. They could get pissed at me and complain to my boss. And I need the miserable pay this job provides me to pay for my wife's cancer medicine.*

When Johnson observed no movement or sounds coming from the vehicles, and envisioning the possibility that a great fortune awaited him, he took another deep breath and resumed inching himself forward as silently as he could to get a closer look.

The old man cautiously worked his way up to the B-post on the driver's side of the closest van. Then he craned his long neck around and snuck a peek into the driver's compartment. He was surprised. It appeared to be in showroom condition as if it had just been detailed.

His fear was over-ridden by his excitement and the possibility of sudden wealth. He forced himself to slide up closer to driver's window. He struck his weapon down into the front of his Sam Brown gunbelt to permit quick access if he needed it, and placed both of his cupped palms up against the side window, to shield his eyes from the glare.

He rested his forehead against the glass straining to see if there was anything of value in the van's cab of the rising sun.

Then Johnson tried the driver's door. He was surprised to find it unlocked. The keys were in the ignition. He knew that joy riders often did that in hopes that someone would come along and rip-off the stolen vehicle before the cops were able to recover them. That practice drove the insurance companies wild, and agitated the cops, not just a little.

Seeing nothing of value in the cab, he retraced his steps to the rear of the vehicle. He twisted the cargo area door lever to find that it was also unlocked. Drawing in another breath to keep his fear under control, he eased one of the rear cargo compartment doors open.

Its painted interior appeared to be spotless which frankly amazed an alcoholic like himself. The cleanliness of his personal vehicle, fully twenty-years-old, had never been a priority for him.

Just to be certain there was nothing inside of value, he took a pair of latex gloves from his pocket and worked them onto his hands. Then he crawled on hands and knees into the back of the van. He forced his arthritic fingers to poke and prod into every crease and crevasse where he thought the prior occupants may have overlooked some loot.

Finding nothing, he began to wonder if the cargo box had also been recently detailed.

When Johnson discovered nothing in the first van, his bad knees and back forced him to use his hands to brace himself against the inner wall surface of the cargo box, to assist him in getting his old body out of the van.

Discouraged at finding nothing, Johnson walked over to the second van and repeated his search. Again, the painful expenditure of effort necessitated by the need to crawl into the cargo box, revealed nothing of value.

However, as he worked himself out of the cargo box of the second van, he noticed that whoever had cleaned that van had missed some brown spots, down inside the ribs of its metal floor. But that was of no value to him.

The sum of his efforts revealed that there was nothing of value that he could 'take into custody' before calling in his discovery to Vegas' glory-hunting cops. You'd think they got enough publicity from being seen a couple times a week on the Fox Channel television show, *Cops*.

Disgustedly, Johnson pulled off the latex gloves and crammed them down into a uniform trouser pocket. Then, without giving any thought to his actions, he used his ungloved hands to slam the rear cargo doors shut on both vans.

He returned to his idling patrol car and covered his ass by belatedly calling his discovery of the two vans into the Las Vegas Metro dispatcher.

June 15, 2008, Sunday.

The first cops arrived at the BRINKS crime scene before 5:00 a.m. Before passing through the demolished gate and preceding any further into facility, they stopped to look for the missing gate guard. When they found him, he was long dead.

They notified Metro dispatch by radio to send a couple of aid cars, a patrol supervisor, the crime lab, and a lot of armed backup.

The Metro dispatcher acted immediately on cop's priority requests. Per established procedure, she also notified the local FBI office. The federal bureau is designated as the primary investigative agency for all bank and armored-car robberies.

―――

Five minutes later, two additional two-man *David* units, running code-two without siren as to not attract attention from nosey bystanders or the Media, quietly rolled up behind the primary unit which had been parked to prohibit all access into the facility.

A third *David* unit had been dispatched to assume responsibility for blocking the public entrance off Charleston Blvd, into Spectra Business Park. A fourth unit was dispatched to close off the business park's rear entrance, off North Pecos Road.

This brought the Metro presence on the scene to six armed officers, plus the blocking units that had been dispatched to protecting the integrity of the crime scene. Their assignment was to permit no one but authorized police personnel to enter the business park. A patrol supervisor, the aid cars, and Metro's CSI team, was en-route.

The senior officers in the primary patrol units made the decision that the likelihood of there being injured BRINKS employees inside the facility outweighed normal procedure that mandated that the street cops wait for a shift supervisor, to arrive on-scene.

Therefore, leaving a marked unit to secure the gate entrance, the primary car and the backup unit proceeded across the huge parking lot to the warehouse.

The two marked units pulled up 50-yards away from the front of the building in an attempt to ascertain whether the gang had left shooters behind to ambush them. Or, God Forbid, the killers were still on the property.

That was when one of the cops in the backup unit next to them, called over through the open window and advised the primary that they were observing dark smoke billowing from the rear of the building.

Both units then rolled around the building to reach the loading dock area. The first thing they noticed was a demolished metal roll-up door. Wedged into the doorway, was what appeared to be the smoking wreckage of an older, dirt-brown, SUV.

Not knowing what that portended, both units again hesitated and pulled up alongside one another to further discuss the situation, before proceeding.

But the Metro cops knew they couldn't delay any longer. It was possible that there were BRINKS employees inside that requiring urgent medical-aid or their protection.

After the senior man made that decision, both black-and-whites quietly rolled up to the two of the three remaining undamaged roll-up doors and blocked them. The four cops stepped out of their units using care to not slam the doors.

The senior officers in both teams had their fifteen-round 9 mm locked-and-loaded Glock in-hand. Their partners were sweeping the barrels side-to-side, covering their advance, with pistol grip Remington model 870 MCS shotgun loaded with five rounds of 12-gauge buckshot.

The four officers continued to cautiously advance towards the damaged doorway.

One of the senior officers hesitated to warily play a quick game of sneak-and-peek, around the damaged door mullion. His brief glimpse revealed two bloody uniformed bodies wedged under the front-end of the smoldering Dodge.

In accordance with Las Vegas Metro procedure, all four officers now entered the crime scene as two-man assault teams, each covering the other's movements, all at maximum vigilance should a ambush be waiting for them. They certainly had zero desire to become part of the crime's death toll.

THIRTEEN

June 15, 2008, Sunday, 10:00 a.m.
Edward Augustus Fox's residence
Desert Willows Golf Course
2020 W. Horizon Ridge Parkway
Henderson, Nevada

Edward Augustus Fox was home relaxing on a brilliantly-bright Sunday morning when he received a call, alerting him to the fact that the local BRINKS armored-car facility had been hit nearly six hours earlier that morning. The notification came courtesy of the Las Vegas FBI office.

News of the crime had trickled slowly down the bureaucratic phone ladder. The FBI was not yet aware that there could be a related connection out near at the speedway. That was because the Metro police hadn't yet established the linkage between the BRINKS robbery and the report by a security guard in the same general timeframe, who had chanced upon a couple of similar vans stashed behind a defunct wrecking yard.

The FBI is always the primary investigative agency on any crime that involves even indirectly, a bank. As the BRINKS Armored-Car service is a contractor to the Federal Reserve Bank, any robbery or major theft involving the company fell under FBI jurisdiction.

As soon as the cops arrived at the armored-car facility and reported their arrival, the Metro police dispatcher notified the duty FBI agent, who in-turn began to call down his agency's telephone notification tree.

It was early on a balmy Sunday morning. I was slouched down in my new lanai lounge chair, bare feet up on the wrought iron railing, enjoying a leisurely continental breakfast of pastries and freshly-brewed Columbian coffee.

On the same morning, but twelve miles further north, Thaddeus Holms, a bored rookie Special Agent who was paying his dues by pulling weekend duty at the FBI's 700 E. Charleston Blvd office in Las Vegas, reluctantly took his shoes off the desk. He moved his coffee cup aside and punched the Return key on his computer keyboard in response to the loud *ping* it had just generated.

The *ping* was an audio indicator programmed into the FBI's hardwired *Trilogy* database. Its purpose is to alert the duty agent that the Las Vegas Metro dispatcher had just electronically transmitted the Bureau, a *headsup* alert requiring Bureau action.

Almost instantly, the computer notified Special Agent Holms by way of a second *ping* that it had run a search of the *Trilogy* database. In doing so, it had located an electronic CN, or Command Notice, that was programmed into the FBI's *Rapid-Start* case management system.

The notice's affectivity, as Holms learned from speed-reading it on his screen, told the agent that the CN applied to any major crime that was posted on the bureau's electronic Major Crimes Alert Log.

Holms, a little excited now, tapped a few more keys on his computer keyboard to pull the CN up on his 24-inch double screen monitor, so it was displayed alongside the BRINKS robbery notice that had just been received from Metro.

A CN is an inner-office-only FBI directive that informs agents and senior support staff of the existence of a mandatory standing order. This particular CN instructed that the duty FBI Special Agent was notify the duty Special Agent of the Nevada State Gaming Control Board office, in the event of a crime that falls within the bureau's purview of interest.

This phone call, documented into the Bureau's Alert log, was to be made anytime a major robbery, directly or indirectly involving a major amount of currency, was committed inside the boundaries of Nevada's Clark County.

A follow-up proviso in the CN emphasized that the order was valid and in-effect, whether or not preliminary investigative information indicated that the crime had been committed at a Nevada casino. Of course, the GCB wouldn't respond unless the crime was somehow connected to Nevada's gaming casinos.

As I had the duty that Sunday for the GCB, the individual that the FBI agent notified was me.

But before rushing off to respond to the robbery alert, I decided to review a hunch I have just recently developed. Admittedly, I based this flash of intuition on the sparse details the FBI agent had provided me. Therefore, I thought it prudent to run it by a more experienced GCB agent.

Being Sunday, I was fortunate that my phone call caught Maggie DuPont at home in her Carson City apartment. After the initial polite chitchat, I got around to explaining my hunch to Maggie, inviting her to play devil's advocate to my theory.

I reviewed the brief incident summary with her that I had just gotten from the FBI Special Agent, who had gotten it from Metro Dispatch, who had gotten it from the radio reports of the first cops that had been first to arrived on-scene.

My first thought was that this heist's M.O., or modus operandi, labeled *shock-and-awe*, at first blush matched that employed by the perps that had pulled the Laughlin Riverboat heist back in April, and the armored-car hijacking in May.

According to what the FBI agent had told me, the BRINKS employees claimed the perps appeared to be working from a disciplined, military-like plan. That would have been necessary if the gang was to circumvent the company's rigid internal security safeguards. Breaching of those called for stealth, a pair of brass cojones, and at least the appearance of over-powering firepower and the willingness to use it.

Although the primary unit that had arrived on-scene had yet to report back to Dispatch as to what they had discovered inside the building, the pressure on the gang to escape after pulling off the heist, would be immense.

The police response time to the silent electronic cash room alarm would have been significantly less than ten minutes. More than likely not more than six to eight minutes if a Metro patrol unit or sector car had been within a couple miles response distance.

That limited window of time would have given the robbers only minutes to establish custodial control of the BRINKS employees, locate and retrieve the money, and then only after locating and short circuiting any time-delay alarms. Say, not less than two minutes, nor more than three.

When the three minutes was up, the gang would be forced to leave anything behind that they already hadn't loaded up. Get back into their rigs, and attempt to make a successful escape. I couldn't think of any civilians that had that type of discipline, but I knew of a lot of ex-military types that did.

If it was the same gang that pulled the Riverboat heist in April, and the armored-car hijacking in May, they didn't appear to kill wantonly once they had establish control over the situation. But if the perps were military veterans, I had no doubt that they wouldn't hesitate to kill anyone who interfered with their mission.

I had given Maggie DuPont a brief summary of my thinking and was pleasantly surprised when she agreed with my hunch.

She said, "Fox, this appears to have been a heist made by a tight, cohesive group, so it may well be they are same doers of the heists that were pulled in April and May."

She asked that I hold on the line while she called the GCB Director at home on her cell phone to inform him of this morning's robbery of BRINKS. She'd bring him up to speed on the obvious fact that this incident created an opportunity for GCB to have another go at identifying and arresting the doers of the Riverboat Casino heist.

We were less concerned about who pulled the armored-car heist in May, because at the time, we mistakenly didn't think that the GCB had a dog in that fight.

When Maggie came back on the phone, she told me that the Director had agreed to let her come to Las Vegas to assist on the investigation.

The unsolved heist of the Laughlin Riverboat Casino had become such a thorn in the department's side that he had even authorized Maggie to use one of the State's executive jets, that were currently sitting idle in a hanger at Carson City, with their pilots were on 30-minute call, which would get her to get to Sin City as soon as possible.

Of course, there was no doubt that the Director's motivation for granting this unusual dispensation was based solely on political considerations. But from an investigative standpoint, the need-for-speed was very practical. There is an institutional concept, validated many times by everyone in law enforcement, that if an investigator hasn't solved a felony crime in 48-hours, his or her chances of doing so logarithmically decrease with each passing hour.

Maggie estimated that she would be touching down at McCarran Field here in Las Vegas, no later than 2:00 P.M. this afternoon. She would grab a rental car and meet me at the BRINKS crime scene by 3:00 p.m., unless my friend Mr. Murphy decided to stick his oar into the situation.

In the meantime, Maggie suggested that I go to the BRINKS crime scene and hang around while the combination task force of Metro detectives and FBI agents, and their combined teams of criminalists, processed the scene. Just to make certain that the *experts* didn't overlook a piece of potential evidence.

She said she'd meet me at BRINKS a little after 3:00 p.m. Then we'd go wherever the case led us from there.

12:30 p.m.

I left for the BRINKS facility about half-an-hour past noon. On the way there, I planned on using the in-grill emergency lights but not push the big 300 Chrysler hemi-engine. Nor would I use the car's wobbler, which in the United States is more commonly known as the siren.

It is my experience that when a citizen driver sees a unmarked vehicle using flashing lights and siren roar up behind them, their first reaction is to stomp on the brakes, would could result in a major injury accident or even a fatality.

Of course my intentions to drive safe-and-sane only lasted until I had accelerated up the ramp from the condominium's basement garage, flipped on my emergency behind-the-grill blinkers, and tightened my seat belt.

But then I was forced to come to a complete stop just inside the complex's main security gate, which I forgot was closed when not in-use.

The rent-a-cop on-duty took his time to activate the mechanized, twenty-four-foot wrought-iron sliding gate. As soon as it was open enough that I could pass through without gouging both sides of my new car, I roared through. I rolled up to the arterial stop sign and made my usual *California pause* before entering Horizon Parkway westbound.

After my sloppy stop at the sign, I pulled out into the intersection before turning left onto the Parkway, and tromped down on the big car's accelerator after instinctively glancing in my rear view mirror to make certain no passing Las Vegas sector car had taken umbrage at my abbreviated stop at the traffic sign.

Failing to discover any pissed-off cop in my rear-view mirror however did not mean that I was pleased to notice that there was a light-colored car, illegally-parked in a No Parking Zone, a few cars lengths down from my security gate.

I saw a puff of white smoke as the car pulled away from the curb, squealing its tires as it accelerated to catch up with me. Apparently to ensure I didn't get too much of a lead on him. This chase had yet to graduate to NASCAR bumper tag status. But I could only wonder as to their intent.

I forced myself to pull my attention off my tail and concentrate on my own driving. I headed west on Horizon Ridge Parkway before taking a right onto South Green Valley Parkway.

Behind me, the late-1990's Honda Accord with heavily-tinted windows, dinged up left front fender, broken right headlight, a silver sedan, pulled up until it was no more that six car-lengths back. The driver made no attempt to conceal his presence from me.

When I merged with the Bruce Woodbury Beltway, the Accord pulled up even closer until it there was only four car-lengths between us. He struck there like glue until I merged onto I-515 North and recklessly swerved across four-lanes of traffic, ignoring the blaring horns, until I got in the fast lane. I increased my speed a little more as I headed for downtown Las Vegas.

My paranoia had been telling me for the past several weeks that someone had been following me everywhere I went. I had picked up the tail soon after reporting to the Las Vegas field office in early June.

A week or so back, the *Las Vegas Sun* and the *Journal-Review* had erroneously reported that the powers-that-be on Nevada Gaming Control

Board had brought me aboard, specifically to catch the criminals that had been hitting casinos and other cash-rich Clark County enterprises at-will.

Glancing again in my rear-view, I knew that some hood's mother would be overjoyed to know that her son was reading the newspaper, and better yet, believing the sensational bull-crap that passes for responsible journalism these days.

In reality, the GCB, with the Nevada State governor's concurrence, had brought me on-board to provide another set of experienced eyes to aid in the investigations into any major crimes, associated directly and indirectly with the gaming industry.

Gaming is Nevada's largest employer and tax base. It was just coincidence that my tenure at GCB began a couple months after a gang knocked over the Laughlin-Riverboat in April.

Although the mutts following me had used at least three different vehicles in their on-going surveillance of me over the past weeks, this time they had screwed up. Because the Honda behind me certainly was the same car that had followed me home, thirty-six hours before, on Friday evening.

As I sped north on Highway 93/95, heading the sixteen miles to the BRINKS facility, I began to switch lanes frequently. Then at the Tropicana exit, I tempted fate by cutting back across four lanes of fast-moving traffic from the fast lane to the slow lane, and taking the off-ramp off the highway and down onto surface streets in a attempt to lose the car that was shadowing me.

However, I quickly discovered that little slight-of-hand presented a new problem. I had to get back on 93/95 in order to take the Charleston Blvd off-ramp, turn under I-515 North, and onto Charleston Blvd westbound. So I took a deep breath, sucked it up, and re-entered the freeway at the Flamingo Road on-ramp.

1:00 p.m.

I arrived at the crime scene in one piece, surprisingly unencumbered by a tail. I doubted that the absence of the tail was an indication of my expert driving abilities. The disappearance of the tail could be explained as the Accord having first-hand knowledge of, and already knowing exactly where, I was headed.

The Spectra Business Park is located in the northwest corner of E. Charleston Blvd and North Pecos Road. I pulled into the business park using the public entrance off E. Charleston blvd. There was a black-and-white partially blocking the entrance so I badged him and he waved me through. Then I drove a couple blocks back into the complex until I arrived outside the gated entrance onto of Las Vegas' BRINKS Armored-Car facility.

Another Las Vegas Metro black-and-white was parked at the curb just outside what was left of the main gate. There, two young cops preened in all their uniformed finery, which to me only sent the message that they were fresh out of the police academy, as certain as death and taxes. They were feeling very important at the moment and displaying their academy-taught and self-bestowed officialdom. A couple of slick-back BuCars were waiting in-line for entrance into the facility, ahead of me.

One of the rookie cops was standing at parade rest with a clipboard at his left side, his right hand hovering over the handle of his holstered weapon, prepared to demand the credentials of anyone and everyone who dared seek admittance. If anyone seeking entrance into the facility was unwilling or unable to provide the credentials, it appeared obvious that the two rookies were prepared to shoot-to-kill.

The other rookie stood off to the side, shotgun in his right hand, barrel pointed at the ground, leaving no doubt that he intended to back-up his partner to the maximus, a Latin word meaning the greatest or largest.

The young cop standing in the middle of the road had anointed himself Big Dog, leaving no doubt he was in complete control of his little piece of the World. Any vehicles that approached his checkpoint, and I assume none but official vehicles had attempted to do so yet, would find themselves placed in the position of being a supplicant and thus subject to the young man's righteous scrutiny.

I watched as the self-important young cop would write down the supplicant's name off his or her proffered credential, then pointedly turn his back on the person requesting admittance. Hunched over as to prevent the not-so-patiently-waiting requestor from overhearing, the kid would act like he was having a brief conversation with someone on the other end of his personal radio communicator, perhaps pretending he was talking with his good friend, Mayor Oscar Goodman.

The rookie went through his inane song-and-dance each time, before he would pass anyone beyond the checkpoint. Regardless of enforcement agency, uniform or rank. The kid was a real *alpha hotel*, if you get my meaning. No doubt he'd be in front of a review board under charges of being an armed, egotistic, uniformed zealot before the end of the year. He was the type of kid that likely had a picture of the *Duke* over his bathroom mirror, and saluted it before leaving for work each day.

As I waited my turn to be passed through, I noted that something had converted the front gate into scrap metal. A heavy car or truck must have been used to blast the metal gate to smithereens.

The twisted gate leafs were draped in crime scene tape. That told me that the perpetrators had probably had killed the security guard, and forced their way into the facility, probably after the guard had advised the mutts that the finesse they had learned in charm school didn't automatically grant them entrance into the complex.

1:09 p.m.

After finally being passed through the gate by the self-important rookie, I found a parking spot near the rear of the large single-floor building, away from all the draped crime scene tape. I got out, opened my truck and pulled out a vacuum-sealed, freshly—autoclaved, crime scene garment bag.

Removing and placing my Sunday-best yellow cashmere sweater in the trunk, I shrugged myself into the white, impervious micro-fiber coveralls, surgical mask, cotton cap, booties, and pulled on a pair of new surgical-quality purple latex gloves.

Clipping on my Nevada State GCB identification credential, I worked my way around to the rear of the facility and located the senior on-scene FBI Special Agent standing just inside the count room. According to the FBI identify card, which she wore on a chain around her neck like back stage pass to a *Grateful Dead* concert, she was FBI Supervising Special Agent Steffy Gardner.

When I spotted her, she was standing inside the count room just inside the damaged doorway, which contained the remains of a smoldering truck. I noticed that she had a cigarette cupped into her left hand. Smoking is forbidden at any crime scene. No exceptions. She apparently had been attempting to drop it on the concrete apron and covertly step on it so she could claim that it didn't belong to her when I walked up to her. Nice try, Lady. Like, years ago when I still smoked, I hadn't used that old trick myself?

Smoking-addicted crime scene technicians, cops, and now I noted, even FBI Special Agents, have been using that old trick for decades. Or at least ever since some bright-eyed FBI forensic scientist had realized that smoking at crime scenes contaminates all evidence collected during the investigation. But some diehards still try to cover up their addiction by playing childish games like this.

If a defense attorney found out that anyone with access to the crime scene had been smoking anywhere in or around the facility, it could effectively negate all the fine work the team had done in collecting probative evidence, as the attorney would petition the Court to toss it all out.

Case in point—remember the double-murder trail of O. J. Simpson? O.J. walked away from that proceeding due to mistakes made by a rookie Criminalist and over-zealous detectives. What about the expertise of the defendant's expensive *Dream team*, you ask? Not so much!

Special Agent Gardner hadn't been too difficult to identify because she was only agent who looked like he or she had a broom up their ass. And if that didn't do it for you, she was wearing *freshly-pressed* puke-green crime scene garb, carrying a clipboard with what must have been at least a half ream of paper forms clamped to it, all the while, working very hard to appear officious and aggressively intense.

The agent was a woman whose unblemished complexion told everyone who came in contact with her that she was a descendant of Western European parents. She appeared to be on the fair side of thirty in a jock-kind of way, nearly six-feet-one inches in her booties, with a severely-cut short blond do, was wearing blood-red lipstick, was very well-proportioned, and undoubtedly could beat me in arm wrestling and the fifty-yard dash.

After exchanging introductions and other pleasantries, *not*, she agreed to give me her abbreviated, preliminary status-report verbally as she "hadn't yet had the opportunity to input the material from her PDA into *Rapid-Start*."

She began by informing me of something I already knew, that the Las Vegas Metro cops had responded to a remote alarm from the BRINKS facility earlier that morning.

She explained, "As of yet, the FBI and Metro investigators have not been able to determine what activated the alarm. However, we are assuming it was one of the delay-response devices that BRINKS uses to alert the cops after the perps have left the property."

―――

To explain that, let's take a brief pause here: If the electronic remote alarm activated while the preps were still on-scene—professional heist teams always monitor the police bands using an inexpensive Radio Shack police scanners—and as the robbers would still have the employees in the facility under the gun, the ill-timing of such an alarm could result in their deaths."

Gardner referred to her notes before continuing, "The Metro cops, who controlled the crime scene prior to my FBI team taking over, discovered four dead bodies on-scene. They all appeared to be employees rather than members of the robbery gang."

"Two of the corpses were male BRINKS employees. Apparently they were run over when the Power Wagon crashed through the closed roll-up door."

"The Gang resorted to crashing the truck through the roll-up door, after their demands for immediate admittance into the facility were ignored."

"The third body was that of a male employee who the gang executed for shooting a female that may have been masquerading as a employee up to the actual moment of the robbery. The survivors claim that the woman had been working in the cash room of the facility for weeks."

"As you may know, we found the body of the fourth employee out at the main entrance gate. The mutts executed the old guard, who was a retired cop."

Gardner expanded on her report. "When the cops arrived on-scene, they gained access to the facility through the damaged roll-up door. It was then that they discovered the surviving employees that the gang had left behind. They all were scared to death, in shock, and in need of immediate medical attention."

"Paramedics arrived and were passed into the facility by the cops guarding the gate, less than nine minutes later. I think that is excellent emergency response for a Sunday morning," she said.

"Fortunately, a bored young intern in the ER had a hunch and managed to hop into one of the responding aid cars."

Referring once again to her hand-written notes, she continued, "The employees that survived are mainly suffering from cuts, bruises, being scared out of their wits, and were very thirsty. Fear does that to a person you know," she explained as if I was some rookie cop.

"Their wrists and ankles were tied together using wire ties before they were dragged into a closet in the cash room and wired to plumbing.

Before the perps left, they kicked the self-locking door to the cash room closed, which effectively imprisoned the survivors inside with no means of summoning help. Some of the employees had soiled their trousers out of terror and were forced to lay in their filth until the cops showed up and rescued them."

I interrupted her to ask, "Were you able to question any of the survivors?" Gardner continued on as if she hadn't heard me.

"The employees who were fortunate enough to live through the assault, reported that the hold-up crew took the gunshot female employee with them. The employees said they didn't know why the gang had only taken just one of the guards with them, when they took the money and escaped."

"According to the doctor, which one of my people interviewed at his hospital earlier this morning, the surviving employees are in a mild state of shock and therefore hadn't yet come to the realization that the wounded female was a plant who infiltrated into the BRINKS operation to aid the thieves before and during the robbery."

"All that my agents and the cops could get out of the employees was that a minute before the thieves breached the roll-up door, the woman was shot by a fellow employee. Once the gang learned who had shot the woman, that individual was executed by the gang's leader."

"Apparently sexual harassment is still alive and well in the workplace. One of the surviving females said she remembered that the co-worker who had shot the female had been making unwelcome advances to her, ever since she had been hired weeks earlier."

"Fox," she said, "before the male chauvinist pig was executed by the gang leader, he explained to his co-workers that he had shot the female employee because she was acting suspiciously."

"He claimed, which eventually turned out to be a correct assumption on his part, that the woman who he had shot, had been running across the floor at the time to activate the electric motors that opens the overhead doors. The employee shooter told his co-workers that he had assumed that her intent was to permit the four men wearing BRINKS uniforms to enter the building, where they could rob the cash room."

"Employees are prohibited from permitting access to any unknown individual into the facility after-hours. Even if the individual demanding entry are wearing BRINKS uniforms," she explained.

"Then procedure requires that the senior BRINKS employee on-duty place an immediate telephone call via landline to the BRINKS facility that allegedly had dispatched the unknown party to their location. That call was not made. According to the survivors we talked to, the senior employee charged with that responsibility forgot to make the call in all the confusion."

Gardner, continued, "All the employees know for certain is that the leader of the gang summarily executed the male employee who had shot the woman. And that the gang took the severely-wounded woman with them. This, despite the fact that a BRINKS employee, who once trained to be a Paramedic, feels the woman could not have survived her wounds. Based on his medical training, he is reasonable certain that she must have died shortly after being loaded into one of the gang's vans."

"But," Gardner reminded me, "None of the employees could be certain. They were in a traumatized state and the wounded woman had been out of their sight once they had been locked down in the cash room, and the gang made their escape with the woman and loot."

Gardner paused briefly as if she wished she could take a quick draw on the cigarette she continued to conceal in her palm. I assumed the butt had long ago gone out, unless she was immune to pain.

"One of the surviving employees did tell the cops that the woman who had been shot was 'okay as a worker.' But she didn't interact socially with her co-workers, turned down all offers to have lunch with them, and had politely refused when one of her co-workers asked her along for their nightly beer at a local bar after shift change."

"One of the male employees said he thought he recognized the woman's perfume as *Jungle Gardenia*, a heavy scent that his ex-wife allegedly wore to excess."

Gardner, still attempting to create a diversion so she could pocket the cigarette butt, sought to distract me momentarily by moving a couple of additional steps away from the smoking metal door. It was almost as if she didn't completely trust her fellow investigators working inside.

However, more likely, it was yet another example of an over-ambitious woman willing to keep things from her co-workers so that she would be able to reap all the glory for herself.

Frankly, I really didn't give a damn either way. Then she began to click off the items of evidence her forensics peoples had collected thus far, on her fingers.

1. "A sample of wounded woman's blood." *Still thought by her co-workers to be a very unlucky employee who had been shot by a gun-happy co-worker, attempting to be seen as a hero.*

2. "The wounded woman's fingerprints and DNA." *It would turn out that someone had removed the woman's personnel folder from the company files, perhaps herself, prior to the robbery. She apparently had not brought any personal things into the facility when she reported for work that that day, such as ID, a wallet, purse, keys, pocket trash, etc. And since she took a taxi to and from work, there was no vehicle for investigators to search in the company parking lot*
3. "The woman had used a phony name on her employment application. However, she had to supply her real fingerprints when she went down to Metro to be fingerprinted for her Nevada Gaming Work Card." *Surprise, surprise. Most Armored-car companies are so desperate for reasonably acceptable personnel, due to the low pay and lousy hours, that they often permit an outwardly clean applicant to start work before their background check has been completed. This lag in completing non-gaming applications is due to the pending backlog of applications for those whose jobs do require a State of Nevada gaming work permit.*
4. "The bullets in the heads of the gate guard and male employee, who had been executed, will be recovered at autopsy, hopefully identified, and compared to those in the federal NIBIN database."
5. "The smoldering remains of the Dodge Power Wagon that the gang had left behind, will be torn apart by the forensic team in an attempt to determine ownership and chain of registration."
6. "None of the gang appears to have left any fingerprints or DNA behind. The perps wore latex gloves, bloused their boots and taped them closed with the same duct tape they later used to gag the employees, and on hairnets taped to their heads, as soon as they broke into the facility. Therefore, realistically there is a good chance that whatever hair and fiber the criminalists turn up will be those of the employees."
7. "Electrical wire ties were used to bind the employees hand and foot, and then to the pipes in closet of the cash room. For whatever worth they are, the ties have been recovered."

Agent Gardner told me that her ERT, Evidence Response Team, would be unable to finish up collecting evidence collection until the following day, due to the size of the crime scene. However, the FBI had arranged with Metro to post a guard at the main gate to keep the media out, and another inside the building to protect against anyone crawling over the perimeter fence and contaminating the scene that was still waiting completion of the Criminalist's forensic processing.

Each FBI office supports an ERT, which specializes in recovery of physical evidence and the execution of search warrants. The ERTs are called out in cases with complicated or multiple crime scenes, in multi-jurisdictional cases, and in cases requiring the most sophisticated forensic analyses. Seventeen ERTs from across the country participated in evidence recovery at the bombing of the Oklahoma City federal building.

Earlier, BRINKS management and a hot-shot crew accompanied by an armored-car representative had visited the facility, and went into those areas not the subject of the investigation. With permission of Agent Gardner and forensic personnel, they had retrieved files and other items critical to their daily operations.

Their hot-shot team had transferred their entire operation over to the BRINKS Home Security office, which is located at 2325 Western Avenue in Las Vegas, a little less than four miles from the crime scene at the Spectra Business Park.

The BRINKS bosses had assured FBI Agent Gardner they were "Okay with having to operate out of the remote location but would greatly appreciate her notifying them as soon as she could release the facility back into their hands, permitting them to resume normal operations.

No one had bothered to ask my opinion, so I decided to let it slide until I talked with my manager at the office on Monday morning.

I was getting the feeling the woman was dismissing me. I glanced at my watch and saw it was 3:00 p.m. GCB Investigator Maggie DuPont ought to be making an appearance here any minute.

Before Special Agent Garner could turn her condescending back on me, and return to the supervision of her investigative team, a young FBI agent fast-walked up to her. He pulled a couple crumpled hand-written notes out of his pocket and handed them to her.

I assume they contained late-breaking news or new information that must have come to light while she had been briefing me.

She sped-read both before glancing into the young agent's face and caught him rolling his eyes and shrugging his shoulders. Apparently personnel relations were not all wine-and-roses on FBI Agent Gardner's team.

She hesitated a few moments, keeping her eyes boring into her subordinate's eyes, before turning back to face me.

She said, "Fox, the dispatcher at Metro has reported that the security company that patrols the Las Vegas Motor Speedway has passed on information that may or may not be relevant to this robbery."

"As you know, it was reported that in addition to the Dodge truck that was left at the scene, the gang were driving two battleship-gray Econolines outfitted in BRINKS livery. Those were the vehicles that the gang used to escape with the money and the wounded woman."

"Well, this report indicates that a speedway security guard working the graveyard shift this morning came across a couple of similar gray vans, but they are slick-sided with no livery on them. If these vehicles turn out to be those the gang used, they must have dumped them. The guard found them in the rear of an old wrecking yard off North Hollywood Road on the track's southern perimeter."

She continued, "The cops have already visited to the apparent dumpsite. Neither van had a license plate. So Metro ran the vehicle's VIN numbers against Nevada State Metro stolen vehicle database. Both were on the hit sheet. That's no big surprise, right?"

"Since both the vans came back as being reported stolen, Metro had them flat-bedded to their crime lab in the complex at the Clark County Medical Examiners office. Everyone, from the two tow truck drivers to the cops involved, have been duly-warned against touching either of them without being gloved up."

She ventured an optimistic hope. "Maybe they can raise some prints. But if these guys are the pros that robbed the Riverboat in April—and hijacked the armored-car in May—maybe not. As soon as Metro obtains a search warrant, the Crime Lab will began going over them both with the proverbial fine-tooth comb."

"In an apparent stoke of good luck, if you can believe a minimum-wage earning security guard, he claims that earlier this morning he saw two gray Econoline vans like those he found dumped, following a newer ten-wheel white hazardous materials box cargo truck leaving an abandoned warehouse about two miles from the dump scene. The address of the warehouse is 30303 North Hollywood Street, which is adjacent to the speedway."

"Fox, I know you are chaffing to get involved in this. You are welcome to go out and check that warehouse out. The vans are long gone and under security lockdown in the Medical Examiner's lot at 1704 Pinto Lane in Vegas. I'll have Mr. Comedy here call the Federal Attorney at home and obtain an immediate telephone warrant to search the premises of that warehouse."

"Additionally, he'll arrange for the supervisor of the security company to meet you at the warehouse to hand-deliver a copy of his guard's report."

"I am okay with you asking the supervisor to accompany you during your search of the warehouse. You'll have a telephone search warrant by then, so you can gain access to the building in whatever expeditious manner you choose."

Take a deep breath that had the effect of puffing out her impressive chest, she went on. "But Investigator Fox, listen to what I am going to say very carefully so we do not have any misunderstanding. If you find anything, anything at all, you are to call me on my cell phone immediately. Do *not* attempt to collect any evidence."

"Your job is to search and inform my Criminalist if you see anything that might turn out to be probative. She has been instructed to accompany you and will handle the collection of any evidence you come across."

"I've heard you consider yourself a hotshot forensic investigator. Training courtesy of the FBI at Quantico, I've heard."

"I've also heard the scuttlebutt that you have gotten a sweetheart contract as a technical consultant to *CSI-Crime Scene Investigation*."

"But hear this,' she threatened. "You touch one piece of evidence or screw up my crime scene in any manner and I personally will have your ass regardless of who your Rabbi in the FBI is, got that? The forensic specialist is accompanying you is to make certain you follow my orders to the letter. You won't have to wait for her. I'll have Mr. Comedy here give her the warehouse address so she can meet you there."

"Now go away and let the professionals finish our work here. You can get started for the warehouse."

You ask, how did I respond to her tirade? Well I just favored her with one of my humble grins. I held out my hand for the warehouse address, the number of the security company, and her cell phone number.

She scribbled it all out on the back of one of her business cards, flipped it through the air at me, gave me a shot at her game face, and walked back inside the crime scene followed closely by the now-properly chastised junior agent.

As I pocketed the information Gardner had tossed at me, I had just turned to return to my car when I saw Maggie DuPont come barreling through the main gate in a white 2008 Ford Edge crossover SUV. She must have run over the Mutt and Jeff team at the main gate because she was moving the rental along at a pretty good clip.

She pulled up alongside my car and hopped out. Her face was flushed and I could tell she was all stoked to get her head into the robbery. She was wearing a purple blouse, her Glock, cuff case, extra ammo holder, and a pair of very, very tight, stone-washed jeans.

I briefed her on what the FBI supervising Special Agent had told me, and that I was headed for an abandoned warehouse about twelve miles away at the Las Vegas Motor Speedway, that could figure in the BRINKS caper at this location.

Deciding not to spook her by telling her of my possible paranoia that I was being followed since the erroneous newspaper article had aired, I decided that we'd convoy out there. She looked the warehouse address up in the Thomas Guide we all carry in our cars, and headed off with me following her about six car lengths behind. I wanted to see if I still had a tail.

After a couple of miles I'd decided that we either didn't have a tail or that my tail already knew where I was headed.

I knew that we could be heading for trouble. We could be running headlong into an ingeniously-prepared ambush, and thus be on the way to our deaths.

FOURTEEN

June 15, 2008, Sunday, 4:00 p.m.
The abandoned warehouse
30303 North Hollywood Street
Las Vegas Motor Speedway
Las Vegas, Nevada

It was getting to be mid-afternoon when Maggie and I pulled up to the address that Agent Gardner had give me. It was an old, faded, yellow, 30,000-square-foot, single-story, clear-span Butler-type metal building that had seen better days, multi-decades earlier.

A white concrete block structure on the front of the building apparently was an office that had been added after the original construction.

Somehow the agent, a member of the Las Vegas FBI office's ERT unit, sitting in her blue Tahoe looking bored from having to wait on us, had beat us to the address. When we introduced ourselves, we learned her name was Susan Olson.

The Security company supervisor was also waiting for us. He was sitting in a black-and-white marked patrol unit, which looked like a hand-me-down from Las Vegas Metro. He had his feet outside the driver's door smoking a cigarette. Probably had a lot more important things to do than baby-sit a couple of investigators, each who made about two-and-a half times his monthly salary.

Maggie and I got out of our cars. She walked over to the evidence technician, while I walked over to speak to the security supervisor.

I introduced myself to the supervisor, whose name was Bill Wallis, and thanked him for taking time out of his busy day to hand-carry his subordinate's report to me.

Bill handed the report to me. I took a minute to speed-read it. It had been handwritten which considering the source that generated it, was no surprise to me. Nor was finding that it was filled with misspelled words. Or words that didn't even exist in the English language. Over all, the report was just barely understandable.

The supervisor, probably some retired Las Vegas Metro sergeant who needed a little extra money to augment his retirement pay, obviously knew how crappy the reports written by his employee would appear to a trained investigator. He obviously was embarrassed by the lack of professionalism conveyed by the report.

He had waited patiently for me to finish reading the report, then said to me, "This is the warehouse that Johnson claims to have observed the three vehicles leaving shortly before 6:00 a.m. this morning."

Bill informed us that he had walked the property before we'd arrived and checked each of the doors and windows. He'd found nothing unlocked. Nor had any of the walk doors yet become so warped by time and normal abuse that you can slip their locksets with a credit card.

"How do you plan on gaining entry," he asked?

I just smiled, patted him on the shoulder like an old Dutch uncle, and leaned over like I was telling him something in confidence. "Just you leave that to me, Sir. I was a real juvenile delinquent when I was young. I think I may still have some of my old lock-picking skills."

"And Supervisor Wallis, if you aren't too busy, I'd appreciate it greatly if you would accompany us when we enter the building."

I continued, "In case anyone is still in there who takes exception to our visit, having a well-experienced trained Metro officer such as yourself backing us up, would make me feel much more comfortable."

Bill, of course, had to know that both Maggie and I were armed. As was the ERT technician, as she was a fully-sworn FBI special agent. But there is nothing that ever prevents me from telling a little white lie to make a retired cop feel a little important once again, even if it is just for a few minutes.

The man puffed out his chest a little bit, agreed, then said, "Of course, if it would make you and the ladies feel safer. Some of these mutts have no respect for authority—I'll be glad to back to you up, Investigator Fox."

My ego-building complete, we walked over to where Maggie was talking with the ERT technician who still hadn't gotten out of her Tahoe.

Maggie turned to Bill and I, and said, "Susan Olson," gesturing towards the FBI evidence tech, "just verified over her cell phone that the

Federal U.S. Attorney has gotten a Judge to issue us a telephone warrant to search this place. The warrant includes forcible entry, if required."

That was what I was waiting to hear. I grabbed a crow bar out of my trunk. That was my low-tech, lock-picking set. I also grabbed a three-cell police flashlight and rejoined the others who now also carried multi-cell flashlights.

I was assuming that even if the robbery gang had occupied this building, they would not have drawn unnecessary attention to themselves by having the utilities reconnected. After all, it was an abandoned building, according to the security supervisor, and had been so for sometime.

Just having the utility service hooked up, even if it is not in-use, costs the building owner what is called a 'customer fee.' The gang would have used a portable generator to power any equipment they had.

The four of us, the ERT technician hauling a large brushed-aluminum Halliburton-type evidence-collection case on wheels that she refused any help with, walked around to the rear of the building. In the very back was a metal walk door that obviously had seen better days. It didn't take but one pry with the hardened steel bar to snap it open.

Maggie, myself, and the security supervisor drew our weapons and entered the facility individually, one going left-one going right-one going left; you get the idea. It was deathly quiet inside the warehouse building. No walls or dividers. No equipment, fixtures, tools, brooms, no anything. Totally clear-span and totally empty.

More importantly, no one confronted us, shot at us, or acted in a manner the least bit hostile, which was exceptionally good news.

Flicking on our flashlights, the three of us, except for the evidence tech who was peering around hoping to find a trove of evidence just sitting there, with her name on it, just waiting for her, headed for the two restrooms and the break room. We verified they were empty before we began our search. The restroom and break room were as spotlessly clean as the shiny warehouse floor.

Similar to the level cleanliness you'd expect in the latrines of an active military facility. Which reportedly are so clean that you could eat off the floor.

The abandoned facility appeared to be deserted. But clean. Very, very clean. Actually it was too clean for a vacant commercial building. Even the trash had been removed. I hadn't seen any debris out back by the dumpsters, either. So the former occupants had taken their trash with them.

The building was deserted. Very, very deserted. The place had an eerie silence to it, as if someone had just died here. And thinking back to the BRINKS employees' report of a wounded woman being taken away by the gang, perhaps that wasn't too far out of the realm of possibility.

The evidence tech had located the warehouse's master electrical cabinet and the ceiling light switch. She was flipped it up and down, expecting it to be dead, but wishing otherwise. All wishing aside, it was evident that the power has been turned off at the electrical pole outside, ages ago.

The floors had obviously recently been swept and wet-mopped. Light from our high luminosity flashlights reflected off the clean floor surface.

Finally the ERT tech, looking for miracles set her kit down on the floor, opened it, and began to set out her equipment.

As she did that, Maggie and Bill, the security guy, began to walk the warehouse floor in a grid pattern. They moved at an orderly pace, keeping their eyes mostly glued to the floor, prepared to stop to take notes and set out a multi-colored flag marker if they happened to discover anything notable, which I doubted would happen. Someone had gone to a lot of extra effort to sanitize the warehouse.

While Inspector DuPont and Bill surveyed the floor, I walked over and kicked open the door leading into the small office area. It had been sloppily nailed shut but my size-fourteen easily accomplished the mission. Once inside, I'd stopped to play the flashlight beam around the area. I noticed that there was good half-inch of undisturbed dust, coating all the surfaces. No one had been in this area for years. Including the prior occupants.

There weren't even any rat tracks or evidence of any insect infestation in the dust. The window air-conditioning units had long ago been removed and the empty windows boarded up. This meant the office area was not air-conditioned and with the hot tar roof, it must get close to 140 degrees in here during Las Vegas's notorious sweltering summers. Even inspects and rodents had better sense than to hang around this hot box.

I returned to the warehouse and began to assist with searching the floor for evidence along with Maggie and Bill Willis. In a half hour, we had effectively covered the entire floor, except for under an old battered gas-fired furnace sitting in a corner, resting on a metal catwalk, which was about ten-inches off the concrete warehouse floor.

Maggie decided we ought to check under that. So we had a diplomatic vote, and Maggie being the most trim was elected to the job of getting down on her butt and shimming underneath the cat walk.

A moment later, we heard a shout of triumph.

She shimmied back out from under the furnace with a handful of discarded cardboard packets and packing debris.

"What is that, Maggie?" I asked.

"Shit, Fox, weren't you ever in the military?" she asked.

"Nope, But does graduating from College and the FBI's National Academy at Quantico count?"

"Jesus, Fox," Maggie said, "For an international cop, you really have lived a sheltered life. This is a MRE, a military ration, more properly known as a Meal-Ready-to-Eat."

My comeback, you ask? "Maggie, it's nearly 5:00 p.m. in the damn afternoon. We both got called out from our homes on a Sunday, a day that I assume you also planned to be a day of rest and relaxation."

"Dear Agent Gardner dispatched me up here to see if this place has any relevance to the Brinks crime scene. You were directed by the boss to get yourself to Las Vegas, like yesterday. And I, for one, am a little too sleep-deprived and dirty to be hungry."

"Fox," Dupont said, shaking her head, "you, kind Sir, apparently do not realize the importance of what I have found behind this old furnace. We have been through this warehouse from stem-to-stern, whatever that oxy-moron means, and up until now, all we've found is some paper-backing off adhesive film, that '*someone*' may have used to stick a couple placards onto '*something*.'"

She continued, "Susan here claims that the local crime lab can trace the backing off those decals back to whoever made them. Perhaps it was some local print shop. But the packing materials from this partially-eaten MRE are fresh. That alone is pretty indicative that we are dealing with current or ex-military people here."

DuPont had intrigued my interest, so I asked, "Those MRE's as you call them, aren't they available to civilians? How do you think the gang came into possession of them? The left over paper and containers look pretty fresh to me."

"That's my point, Fox. As a general rule these days, especially with the war in Iraq still dragging its way along, MRE's are most likely only available to a National Guard unit, one which has either deployed to Iraq, or is scheduled to."

"Maggie, you seem to be convinced that this hijack crew is ex-military?"

"What I am saying Fox is that there is a high likelihood that someone in this crew is either military with access to National Guard stores, or an actual guard member. The latter, I tend to doubt, because with *Stop-Loss*, the guard units are too busy coming and going from multiple tours in Iraq."

"According to the stenciling on the two MRE cartons I found, I think Susan will find these particular Meal-Ready-To-Eat rations were recently distributed to one of the Nevada Guard units."

I thought, *Maybe I ought to pick Maggie's mind to learn a little more about MRE's in case her find proves to be probative evidence.*

So I admitted, "Maggie, I don't know much about MRE's. I thought U. S. military emergency rations were call K-RATs."

"They were, Fox, back during the Korean conflict. But they have been improved considerably since then and are now called MRE's. For instance, these particular cardboard boxes contained the entrée Lima Beans, not one of the more popular choices, I understand."

She continued, "The fact that the MRE was only partially-eaten indicates to me that the person who began eating it, decided that he or she couldn't stomach it, and tossed it behind the old furnace, hoping that their leader wouldn't notice. Trouble is, the thrower forgot that a partially-eaten MRE could provide us with DNA. And fingerprints, unless that individual was wearing gloves."

I gave that some thought, before asking, "If the person didn't eat the Lima Beans, would he or she had to go hungry?"

"No, Fox, that is what is makes a MRE an excellent field ration. If you don't like the entrée, then you can fill up on the side dishes.

"Look," she said putting the carton on a steel table, removed a sealed MRE, and tore it open. "There is a lot of nutritious stuff here, especially if you are a little nervous about having to put your life on the line. Such as robbing a well-armed security facility? You need to pile a lot of sugar on-board, for energy."

DuPont tore the package open revealing a bunch of small camouflage-wrapped packets. She held each up like a proud mother. "What we have here, Fox, is your basic Wheat Snack Bread, Beverage Base-lemonade, Mixed Fruit, Cheese spread, Cocoa Beverage Powder, Vegetable Crackers, Marmalade Jam, and what they call the Accessory Pack."

"Here," she held up one of the packets, "we have here MRE crackers. Yum-yum." She popped all eight of them out of the vacuum-packed container, smeared lumpy peanut butter from a packet and offered one to me to taste.

When I held up hands rejecting her kind offer, she laughed deep down in her gut at my hesitation to try even a small bite. Then she reached into the open carton once again and began to pick out little one-person-serving snack packs of salt, nondairy creamer, ketchup, mustard, and pack containing two tiny pieces of gun, and for a grand finale, she ripped open a tiny compressed packet of single-ply toilet paper.

I asked her, "How do they heat the MRE?"

She delved a bit deeper into the carton and extracted what she explained was called a heater pack.

"This is how you heat the entrée," she demonstrated. "All you have to do is rip the top of this little bag open and pour in a small amount of water."

DuPont asked Susan, the evidence technician, for a bottle of water. She removed the cap and dribbled a small amount of the liquid into the pouch. Then she continued with her demonstration.

"There is a chemical in there that mixes with the water. It produces hydrogen and an unbelievable amount of focused heat. Just rest the entrée container against the heat pouch, which is fuming now, as you can see. Inside of five minutes, you have a warm Meal, and you didn't even have to put on a pair of clean cammies and go to a restaurant to get it."

"And, Fox, that is a MRE."

Perhaps Maggie was right. There could be prints and DNA all over the MRE packets.

I turned and called for the ERT agent Gardner had sent along to shadow my every move. She was bent over in a hopeless attempt to vacuum up hairs and fiber off the spotless concrete floor, even though she knew it was obvious that the gang had swept and mopped up behind themselves before they abandoning the warehouse, to deny law enforcement any trace evidence.

Having a senior moment, I had to glance at the technician's nametag to tickle my memory before making my request. "Ms. Olson, Susan, please bag this MRE packing along with the paper decal backing you already have, and transport them to the Metro crime lab right away. And please ask the lab manager real nicely to put a high-priority on it."

"These are the only things that the last persons using this warehouse, left behind. They are our only hope for coming out of here with some trace evidence."

Without another word, Susan pulled a large evidence bag from one of the voluminous pockets in her jumpsuit, bagged the new piece of possible evidence, carefully marking her name, the case number, time, date, and place found, on the top of the bag using an black indelible ink Sharpie.

She packed up her evidence collection kit, left the building without saying goodbye, and I assume got back into her midnight blue Tahoe. Heck, I didn't blame her for her eagerness to leave and let the old folks deal with the 100+ temperature in this damn place.

Once in the Tahoe, Susan started up her rig, put on her seat belt, turned her air conditioning selector up on *Auto re-circ MAX*, and only then did she pulled out her cell phone and call the crime lab manager and Special Agent Gardner, to inform both she was enroute back to the Metro crime lab with some potential evidence.

Moments later all that remained of her presence at the warehouse would have been the momentary glimpse of the dust thrown up by her SUV's tires as she raced south on North Hollywood Blvd.

As we left the building, Bill and I worked to force closed the walk door through which we had entered. He said he would send one of his people later in the evening to properly secure the door closed.

We were finished with the old warehouse for the time being. But as we returned to our cars, I could tell Maggie was still pumped by the discovery of evidence she had found under the furnace.

Before I got into the Chrysler, I thanked Bill Willis for his help. I told him that I would be in touch with him personally to let him know what we had been able to recover, once the Las Vegas crime lab told us.

He shook Maggie's and my hands, told us that we were welcome, that he had enjoyed it, as he walked back to his car with a cocky-cop-swagger I'll bet he hadn't used in a long time. He tossed his flashlight into the rear seat of his patrol car before getting in and starting up the big-block Crown Victoria. He burned rubber out of the parking lot like a teenager, no doubt prepared to explain, if asked, that he was driving that way to permit him to get back to his supervising of the speedway guards under his command in the shortest amount of time.

He was one of those typically overlooked individuals who accepted his place without complaining on the merry-go-round of life. He reasoned that everyone had to be somewhere, sometime. People like him made the world go round.

I liked ole' Bill, but sincerely hoped that I wouldn't end up wearing his shoes someday. After an interesting life chasing down bad guys, to being assigned to riding around in a decades old patrol car, earning only slightly better than minimum wage.

5:05 p.m.

As we stowed our flashlights in our vehicles, I asked which hotel she was staying at tonight?

"Hell, Fox," she replied, "I hadn't had any time from the moment you interrupted my weekend when you called this morning, I landed at McCarran Field and grabbed a rental and met you at the BRINKS location, but didn't have time to call and make bunking arrangements. I'm certain I can find a room somewhere. Don't worry about it. I'm a big girl, you know."

"Dupont, that isn't necessary. Look, we both are dirty and sweaty from crawling around this damn warehouse. So I have a suggestion," I said.

"My condo had two master bedrooms, complete with individual bathrooms, lanais, etc. Why don't you borrow my spare bedroom tonight? We'll keep it from the rest of the GCB office, of course. Don't want to sully your stellar reputation, do we? That way we can head over there, both of us wash up, and go out and get a decent restaurant meal—my treat—before we retire from a long day of investigating this *whodoneit?* How about it? Take a walk on the wild side? No strings attached."

Maggie appeared to give the matter some deep thought. For about fifteen seconds, I venture. Then she said, "Okay, Fox, no hanky-panky. But I buy dinner. That is my counter offer."

"Done deal, Investigator DuPont," I grinned. "Now just follow me back to my place in Henderson. Oh, I hope this doesn't shake you up, but I believe that I have been tailed fairly regularly, as of late. Ever since the *Las Vegas Sun* and *Review-Journal* published that less-than-factual article about the Board bringing me on-board as a trouble shooter after this last spate of casino-related robberies."

"So, please keep your eye on your rear view mirror to see if our little two-car caravan is attracting an audience. This noon, on my way to the BRINKS facility from my condo, it was a battered, gray, four-door Honda."

Continuing, I said, "But unless I am losing my mind completely, or have an overactive case of paranoia, which I sincerely hope that's all it is, they have used several vehicles to follow me over the past week. They pick me up at my home, at the local GCB office, wherever I happen to be."

"They haven't tried anything physical yet. They always break off the tail when I surprise them by throwing in a couple of evasive action techniques. But they seem to know where I am, when I am leaving or going somewhere, which I admit makes me a more than a little edgy."

"Twice, I've asked the Nevada State Patrol, the *Staties,* to put a loose tail on me. But when the subject's car following me noticed a marked patrol car tailing them, and as soon as the troopers radioed their dispatcher to advise they would be making a traffic stop on a suspicious vehicle tailing a State Gaming Agent, the mutts suddenly take the first off-ramp and disappear into traffic. They must be using a scanner to monitor both Metro and the State police dispatch channels."

Realizing that DuPont was taking my story in with an amused look on her face, I decided to put it off further discussion of the subject until later. As she appeared to be very amused, it would be *very* much later.

"See you at my place, Maggie," I said, handing her one of the business cards I especially had printed up when I infrequently interact face-to-face with CBS, and cast members and supporting staff of the popular *CSI: Crime Scene Investigation* television series. I didn't, and I assumed that CBS didn't, feel that those individuals needed to be reminded that one of their script consultants was a sworn Chief Investigator for Nevada State Gaming Control Board. "Here's my home address in case we get separated, Maggie," I said. "Which could happen in this late weekend afternoon traffic."

We piled into our respective vehicles and headed south on North Hollywood Road. At the intersection of Hollywood and Las Vegas Blvd, we turned right, arriving at Highway 93/95, which we got on and headed east for the City of Henderson.

5:59 p.m.

I pulled up to the entrance gate into my condo complex with Maggie right on my tail about 6:00 p.m. As we were passed through the security gate, I used my left hand to point out to her the guest spots where she could park her rental overnight, before I pulled under the building to park the Chrysler.

We met outside in the parking lot, she with a cop's war bag over her shoulder, and took the elevator up to my floor. Once inside the condo, Maggie dropped her war bag on the carpet, as I pulled a couple of cold Becks out of the refrigerator, handed one to her, and we walked out onto the lanai to enjoy the final rays of the late afternoon sun.

"Well, Maggie, did we pick up any company on the way here?"

"Tell you the truth, Augustus, *this was the first time she had ever used my given middle name*, I think there was a late-model, dark-blue, Ford Explorer that changed lanes several times until he had pulled to within a couple of car lengths behind me."

"I thought it was the same car that was parked on the shoulder of Las Vegas Blvd, that had pulled out and followed us when we headed downtown. I was maintaining a separation of a half dozen of car lengths behind your black muscle car."

"Frankly, Augustus"—*she used one of my given names once again*, "I was too tired and sweaty from crawling under that furnace to really give a shit. If they were tailing us, they would have being doing so at their own risk. I haven't shot anyone in a couple years. If provoked, I'm about ready to break that streak, if you know what I mean," she said.

Laughing, I said, "Yeah, I been there—felt that way too. So why don't we take our beers and go get cleaned up. Clean towels are in the guest bathroom's linen cabinet. The bed is made up with clean sheets. But it is with manly reluctance that I admit that you are my first overnight visitor since I bought the place."

Then quickly changing the subject, I asked, "Is forty-five minutes long enough for you?"

Maggie laughed and responded, "Hell, I'm hungry. Thirty minutes is all I need. I will see you back out here on the lanai, hopefully with couple more bottles of Becks in your hand, in a *half hour*. Give some thought to where you want to eat. Some place with a lax dress code that will let me in because all I have to put on is a slightly-wrinkled blazer and a fresh pair of perma-press slacks."

As Maggie headed off for her shower, I said to her retreating back, "Maggie, this is Las Vegas—there are *no* dress codes. Even the Bellagio doesn't have a dress code beyond wearing a casual jacket with lapels."

We joined up on my lanai again, as I thought, closer to forty-five minutes than a half hour. Maggie asked for my suggestion on where we could get a decent meal without her feeling underdressed. Somewhere that was relatively close.

"Why not try the Sunset Station Hotel and Casino over on West Sunset Drive?" I responded"

"The hotel has ten restaurants and is located right down the road from here, in Henderson. We won't have to go downtown to get some decent food. They even have a pool if you are in the mood for a drip," I teased.

"Forget the pool for now, Romeo," She replied. "I am famished. I'll try not to fall asleep on you during dinner. These early morning Sunday call-outs really aren't my cup of tea, Fox."

Then, seemingly as if she had just thought of it, she suggested, "How about we take my rental? Being stalked reminds me too much of my ex-husband. Perhaps the dummies will spend the rest of the night looking for your car."

"I don't think the Explorer following me was aware that I was following you. He was just trying to maintain separation and I happened to be a six-pack of cars behind you. With traffic being so hectic that time of day, he probably didn't want to chance pulling around me and narrowing his comfort zone behind your Chrysler."

6:50 p.m.

As we prepared to leave for dinner, I suddenly inexplicably experienced a flashback to a physical attack on my person that occurred a little more that a week before.

Because I barely knew the woman, I decided not to tell her that I had received a beat-down here at the condo complex only a week before. It may or may not have been ordered by the gang we were investigating. But they easily could have put out a contract on me, which only would cost them $500 a head to hire a couple some street punks for muscle. Or, hopefully, which is more logical, it simply was a mindless assault unrelated to my work.

Under-employed and unemployed punks, still yearning for the old mob days of Sin City, are plentiful and available-for-hire rather inexpensively.

The punk's motivation wouldn't be any different from that of one of Las Vegas' ubiquitous hard-working Hispanic day laborers. Both will accept unchallenging work from well-heeled Norto Americanos to earn enough money to support themselves or their families.

But these punks belong to a much lower social stratum than the hard-working day laborer, which most likely was an undocumented alien. Like say the difference between a cockroach and an orchard-pollinating, honey bee.

A week before, I had taken my new car to the garage for its first recommended service. The service department told me to plan on it taking two days, so I had been forced to take a van-type taxi home from the office about 8:30 p.m. that night. It had gotten dark while I had been inside working late at my desk.

It was an unusual summer evening for Las Vegas. A low-pressure front had blown in from the Pacific Northwest and brought with it blowing rain and the threat of a thunderstorm.

The cab was driven by a Turban-wearing Punjab. Perhaps an exchange-student, I thought. The cab reeked of garlic. After nearly a half-hour in heavy traffic we finally arrived inside the city limits of Henderson and eventually drove up to the security gate of my condo complex.

For some unknown reason, the gate guard wasn't in his red-and-white shack at the moment.

Perhaps, I mused, *the guard had been forced to briefly abandon his post to answer the call of nature.* I assumed our wait for his return would be five minutes at the most.

However, the taxi driver instantly began to wave his hands and jabber at me in a language I didn't understand. These were prime money-making hours for a Las Vegas cabbie, considering the weather, and my driver was indicating he was not *okay* with having to wait for the security guard to return and let us into the complex.

Sighing over the realization that most Las Vegas hacks had long ago given up any semblance of civility or interest in customer satisfaction, I tossed a couple twenties to him over front seat and without any offer from the driver to assist me, slid the van's side door open, enabling me to step out of the van.

The sliding door was nearly ripped from my grasp by the howling wind as I got out into the rain, dragging my briefcase behind me. Now that I think about it, maybe I did slid the cab door closed a little more *forcibly* than was necessary.

Without a simple "Thank You," the cabbie sped off into the darkness. I immediately was inundated with rain. Then I noticed that the lights inside the guard shack were out. As was all other illumination in the immediate vicinity.

Funny, I thought, *even the lights mounted on the two poles at either side of the approaches of the manually-operated, electrically-powered sliding gate were out—what a hell of a night for that to happen.*

I stuck my briefcase under my left arm and turned to unlock the small walk gate that was set into the fenceline, off to the side of the sliding gate. I had to squint in the near darkness to fit my key into the gate.

Just as I got the gate open and began to walk through it, someone exiting the complex flew through, bouncing a substantial shoulder off my torso.

Thinking the collision had been my fault, I paused and began to apologize. After all, it was dark and I admittedly had been occupied trying to get my key into the lockset. I guess I must not have seen him approaching the gate from inside the complex.

But then a couple things instantly made me realize that I had not been the guilty party. Was it just I, or just the fact the individual was wearing a ski mask, or the blackjack he was swinging at my head with his right hand?

The guy was white, not a tall as I, but still about six-feet tall and built like a swapper at a warehouse. Stocky. All shoulders and muscle. Enormous hands and a lot of muscle. It was hard for me to make a better assessment than that in a microsecond. And, of course, the gate guard had not yet reappeared.

As I managed to dodge his first swing, I thought, *Crap, here I am in town less than a month and some mutt is trying to mug me.* My rain-soaked coat was making it near impossible for me to reach the gun I wore in a high-rise holster in the small of my back.

The crime of mugging, despite the fiction touted by the Las Vegas Chamber of Commerce, is not all that uncommon in Las Vegas. Caulk it up to too much money flowing out of and into intoxicated tourist's pockets from the gaming tables and the slots, and a lot of those same tourists treating their winnings with no more regard as to their personal security, than if it was Monopoly play money.

Of course, the first thing I did was ditch the briefcase, and put my left arm up in an attempt to deflect his second attempt at bouncing his sap off my skull with his right hand. Then, during his back swing, my hand dove for my weapon. But he swung the sap at my noggin once again and I was forced to yank my right hand out from underneath my coat without the weapon in-hand, in order to protect the left side of my skull.

The rain was coming down even harder now, pelting our heads, the concrete, and other surfaces with a sound not unlike a machine gun firing.

Then to make things more interesting, another ski mask-wearing individual sprinted out of the darkness towards us. He was a short, mixed-race Filipino, who was in the process of flipping open a balisong. And there was no question in my mind that he knew how to use it.

A balisong is a Filipino butterfly knife. It has a four-inch steel blade, which normally is concealed between the two halves of the handle. With a few flicks of the wrist, the handles separate and the blade comes out, and handles rejoin. An experienced knife fighter can open the blade in less than a second.

As the new entrant to our dance reached us, I spit into the taller assailant's face shocking him, while I twisted my torso and narrowly avoided being eviscerated by the blade of the knife the newcomer had swung at my gut.

Fleetingly, I began to wonder if the fact that the gate guard was absent from his duty station, was accidental or the result of cash passing between hands.

The assailants' slashes and swings were rapidly forcing me back further into the darkness of the parking lot. There was really no other choice. I knew from my experience the damage a blade can do, if slipped between the ribs into the aorta, or used to cut the spinal cord at the base of the skull. And I wasn't about to go there.

My mind raced to consider the few options I had. For one, I knew both assailants wouldn't attack me at once. These guys were experienced, not just some street thugs. They knew as well as I did, that in the darkness, there was too much chance that one of them might accidentally put the other out of commission.

As I finally managed to rip my gun from its holster, the big guy apparently decided that this had gone on long enough. He spun in the air and using a karate swing kick, slammed his heavy shoe against my head. The gun flew out of my hand and sailed away into the darkness.

Then, as I stumbled and began to lose my balance, he followed through with a with a karate knife strike with the side of his hand to the soft spot in my abdomen under the sternum, which finished taking me the rest of the way down to the pavement. It effectively purged my lungs of air. I lay struggling to gulp in a breath of lifesaving air.

Then he and his companion abandoned any pretense of civility. They began to viciously kick me in the head and ribs. I tried to catch their repeated kicks on my arms and elbows, but they were alternately coming for me, from two separate directions. I attempted to twist and turn to avoid or deflect their kicks, but man, my chest was really starting to hurt.

My vision was rapidly getting darker, narrowing into a tunnel. I knew I was slipping in unconsciousness.

I had gotten to the point in my lack of consciousness where I began to fantasize that I was holding my dearly-departed wife in my arms and my born out-of-wedlock son was sitting at our feet. Of course, nothing of the sort was really happening. I was just hallucinating, usually a precursor to slipping into a deep unconsciousness state.

Suddenly, the lights of a car approaching the security gate surprised the thugs that were intent on finishing the job they had started. Their eyes reflected the look found in the eyes of a wild deer, when illuminated by a poacher's hand-held one-million-candle power spotlight.

Both thugs struggled to their feet only to slip on the wet non-porous concrete and fall again. Then they got organized and leaned against one another, which assisted them in regaining their footing. Then they vanished into the night like the wisp of a bad dream.

They left me lying bloody and beaten on my back, now illuminated by the unintentional Good Samaritan's headlights.

A large, middle-aged, African-American woman stepped from her car. With some hesitation she edged her way over to where I was lying, and asked me if she should call an ambulance.

Realizing that I had no idea what had brought on this beat-down. But knew I better get to my condo and patch myself up before I decided on a course of action to take.

Between the woman and myself, we managed to get me back up on my feet. She loaned me a strong shoulder for support, as I awkwardly stumbled over to the passenger side of her car. She opened the car door, and apparently being a pragmatic person who at the moment wasn't worried about the damage my blood would do to her upholstery, pushed on my back to assist me to getting my gluteus into the car.

The gate guard chose then to return to his assigned duty station, apparently oblivious to what had happened during his absence. He punched the button that permitted the gate to slide open to admit the woman's car. That told me she was a resident.

As we drove through the opening I glanced in my side view mirror and watched the guard nonchalantly turned his back and fire up a cigarette before walking back into the guard shack to avoid the pummeling rain.

As we pulled up in front of the elevator up to my condo, the woman asked if I needed help getting out of the car and up to my condo.

I could tell she was getting more nervous by the minute, only now beginning to wonder what type of man had she found laying in the rain, beaten-down to a fair-thee-well. She reasonably was beginning to fear for her own safety.

I thanked her for helping me and politely declined her offer. Which I could tell had the effect of visibly reducing her fear level enough that she managed to give me a little smile of compassion.

I gritted my teeth and managed to get out of her car, into the elevator, and up to my warm, dry, safe condo without further complications.

I fell into bed not even bothering to administer any first-aid to my injuries, or take off the bloody, ripped and torn clothing that I was wearing.

I slept fitfully, getting up once to take a handful of Excedrin, and as usual, four times to urinate. Never let anyone tell you that having HBD, or benign hyperplasia disease of the prostrate, is no big thing.

I woke at about 5:00 a.m. deciding that nothing was broken. My entire body was very sore. I bandaged up my cuts and gashes with a dozen butterfly bandages, and six extra-large Tough-strips. Then I crawled painful back into bed to replay last night's incident in my mind.

I decided that I had absolutely no idea if the attack was related to my work. Oh, I was certain that they had intended to do me great bodily harm. But until I was able to puzzle out the incident further, I figured I was better off not reporting the attack to the GCB for a couple of days. Hopefully, with help from Neosporin, my cuts and other superficial stuff would be well on their way to recovery over the weekend.

If anything surfaced over the next several days that illuminated the reason behind the attack, then I could, hat-in-hand, belatedly report it to my supervisor in the Las Vegas GCB office, on Monday, three days hence.

If the attack proved out to be job-related, it would be his call anyway as to how the GCB elected to deal with the matter, not mine.

Shrugging the incident from my mind, and returning to present day, I told Maggie I was looking forward to our dinner meal.

Both of us were ravenous. Anyone attempting to disrupt our dinner would result in my ripping off the arm of the perpetrator, and jamming it up into him where the sun didn't shine, and Maggie would have applied the toe of her shoe into his crotch.

Neither of us was omniscient and knew that someone was going to attempt to kill us, pre-dawn, early the next morning,

FIFTEEN

April 15, 2008, Sunday, 8:00 p.m.
Desert Willows Golf and Country Club
2020 W. Horizon Ridge Parkway
Henderson, Nevada.

It was well past dusk when we piled into Maggie's rental and drove out of my condo complex. I found that the hair on the top of my head brushed the crossover SUV's ceiling. Probably wasn't intended for someone well over six-feet-tall like myself.

There was no apparent tail waiting for us when cleared the Complex's security gate and headed towards Sunset Drive.

As we drove, Maggie asked, "What possible motivation could those mutts have for tailing you, Augustus?"

I held my hand up indicating I would have to give her question some thought. I had been mulling that question over the past week. Searching my memory, I remembered something that the mob had occasionally attempted years, ago when I had been a D-1 on NYPD's elite Homicide squad.

In those bygone days, say back in the mid-1970's, my team was regularly being assigned homicides that the hotshots in the head shed were convinced had been perpetrated, or at least green-lighted, by the New York Mob.

Back in those halcyon days, the mob had been pretty quiet because it was under intense scrutiny by the Feds. So much so, that New York's five Mafia families were losing their Dons and high-ranking soldiers regularly to successful prosecutions by the FBI, IRS, and ATF.

However, all the mob could do was bite the bullet. The top echelon in the five families and their Commission was too-seasoned and too-smart to attempt to intimidate a federal agent or his family. The few mobsters that had stupidly tried it, ended up in Attica upstate, with Life-Without-Parole sentences.

But the mutts were occasionally were willing to attempt to intimidate one of the task force investigators, if he or she was NYPD, not a fed. The mob's attempt to coerce New York detectives did not only apply to homicides, but the investigation of any major crime that could put the doers away in the gray bar hotel for five years or longer, especially if the *person of interest* in the commission of the crime, was a mob boss.

Cops had a name for it, *disruption*. And I could think of no valid reason that Maggie didn't deserve to learn of it, even though the practice had supposedly ceased years ago.

The Mob had learned through painful experience that cops and federal agents tend to get pissed when they or their families are harassed. Then law enforcement accidentally began to overlook the niceties and safeguards built into the criminal's constitutional rights. That is, if the mokes were stupid enough to attempt to mess with anyone in the *thin blue line*.

"Maggie," I remarked, "this gang may be inexperienced enough to be attempting to bring back a practice that both the cops and the five New York Mafia families called *disruption*."

"Today," I said, "the practice can't work anymore. History is against its success."

"While I was in the NYPD, I only knew of a single attempt that was successful, but then only temporarily. It was rumored later that some rogue cops extracted their revenge by setting up the favorite son of one of the mob family's Dons, a kid who wasn't even in the business, for loan sharking, transporting a minor across the state lines for immoral purposes, and for dealing in hardcore porn where the kid went to school at New York University."

"The innocent kid was convicted, sent up for a Fifteen-Years-To-Life term in Attica. A month later the kid he was *shanked* by a Mexican Mafia inmate who just wanted to crowd into the chow line ahead of him. Prison officials claimed they never were able to identify the killer. Some thought they didn't try very hard "

"Sometime later, one of Organized Crime Unit's wiretaps recorded a mysterious call coming into that particular mob family's social club, coincidently at the exact time that NYPD's graveyard shift reports for night duty."

"According to what I later heard, the Mafia Don who answered the unlisted phone number, claimed to have overheard the blare of a police radio in the background."

"The informant told the cops that a muffled voice had said, *Guido, See what happens when you fuck over a cop, your fucking Italian cocksucker? If it happens again, we'll make sure what happened to your son, happens to one of your daughters. I leave you with that thought.* And the caller hung up. Back into those days there was no access to Caller I.D."

I continued, "After that call, the Mob abandoned trying to run any type of a *disruption* attack on law enforcement officers. Especially territory controlled by New York's Five Mafia Families. According to informants inside the mob the New York Mafia Commission formally banned the practice in 1979."

"The Mob lawyers been warning the heads of New York's five Mafia families for years that the tentacles of law enforcement had grown to be too far-reaching to have that crap work anymore. Even back in those days, there was too much backup, too many databases, too much repetitive data stored in the multiple police investigative systems."

"In retrospect, I have to agree that maybe in the case of a five-man police department, a small ego-centric organization, tightly-compartmentalized, then maybe. But as a general rule, a crude attempt like that only ends up earning the defendant a much longer prison sentence."

Maggie broke into my explanation, saying, "But what was the purpose of the criminals trying that, Augustus? Surely they had to know from long experience that cops close ranks regardless of what agency is being threatened."

"Well, Maggie," I explained, "the criminal's motivation of what we called *disruption* in those days, was to cause as much chaos as possible within a particular agency. There were many reasons why it as employed: To cover up something that was happening, to cover up something that was about to happen, to foul up an ongoing investigation, to get rid of an annoying competitor, or simply to take down another bothersome family or organization just for the hell of it."

"Augustus, do you think is why you are being tailed most everywhere you go? Do you think that crap is making a comeback? "

As we pulled into the parking lot and parked in the casino/hotel's rear parking lot, I concluded by saying, "Well, Maggie, I've been giving that a lot of thought. I am almost certain that anyone affiliated with the Mob wouldn't try it. The Commission's edict is still in force to the best of my knowledge."

"But an independent, non-aligned criminal organization in Sin City, now? Yeah, that is something else. Maybe they don't know better, or perhaps they have so much to gain from their criminal activities, they just don't give a good goddamn. In their estimation, they may figure that risk is less than the value of their potential monetary reward."

As I opened the passenger door, I glanced back at her as I got out of the car. Her forehead was wrinkled in deep thought. Breaking her concentration, I said, "Now. How about us dropping this unpleasant discussion and getting some dinner? Okay with you?

Little did I know that subject matter behind Maggie's question would raise its ugly head later that evening.

The Sonoma Cellar steakhouse is located off Sunset on Stephanie Street in Henderson. Their public relations flacks tout the restaurant style as Open Table-Home, whatever that means. Even though it is an older restaurant, a lot of locals patronize it because of its reasonably-priced, if unimaginative, fare of steaks, prime rib, chicken, and veal.

Some tourists have claimed that the wait staff is abrupt. However, I've been in the place twice and have never observed that. But then I'm not a budget-seeking tourist who demands the World but expects their bill for a full-service dinner to be less than $15 a person.

Sunday isn't normally a busy night for restaurants in Las Vegas. For that reason we found ourselves being seated as soon as we walked in. The first thing that Maggie said, after taking a seat, stashing her purse under the table, and opening her starched white cloth napkin—it was her first visit to the Sunset Station Hotel and Casino—was that she loved the traditional decorative scheme.

Most Las Vegas eateries strive to outshine their competition through never-ending renovations of their establishments to make them more glitzy and flashy, hoping the gullible tourists will equate the superficial *flash* with a restaurant that offers great food at budget prices.

The Sonoma Cellar Steakhouse oozes traditional Las Vegas style. It is a relatively large place seating one-hundred-fifty guests at a time.

There is a bar running along one wall for those diners wishing to enjoy a cocktail while waiting for a table. The bar has a couple dozen old Vegas-type bar stools made of highly-polished dark woods.

Most of the lighting in the lounge comes from under the surface of the red leather-covered bar, and from inside the three tall, built-in liquor display cabinets. The middle such cabinet is topped by a heavy, maritime, eight-inch brass clock hanging on the dark-paneled wall behind the bartender's position.

The sturdy bar stools are handmade, wrapped in red leather, and inset with dark woods. Each has a highly-polished brass handle on the seat back, with a bright-metal pedestal ashtray standing alongside each of the seating positions.

Over the access portal, provided so the head bartender has serving access to the two bartenders who are responsible for keeping the dining room guests satisfied, are shelves of extra-large elaborately decorated glasses, which assumedly are for the restaurant's celebrated jumbo margaritas.

Individually-lighted portraits of long deceased notables of the old seedy Las Vegas days, adorn the dark-panel walls: Among them, Benjamin "Bugsy" Seagel; Virginia Hill; "Tony the Ant" Spilotro; Frank Calabrase Sr.; "Joey the Clown" Lombardo; James Marcello; and more recently, the current Las Vegas mayor, Oscar Goodman, who reportedly has proposed legalizing prostitution in Las Vegas and Clark County. The mood in the bar is softened through the use of small discrete spotlights, recessed in the high, dark-paneled ceiling.

The Sonoma Cellars steakhouse is also a favorite rendezvous of the local business community for the finest of traditional fare served in salubrious surroundings, be it for lunch or dinner.

The high-ceilinged dining area has 24-inch-thick, light wood panel-wrapped columns. The tables rest on a raised dais against carved and inlayed wooden walls, surrounded by huge windows that have a view of some of the glitter of Las Vegas. Thrown in to polish the presentation is indirect lighting, large potted plants, and during dinner hours, the romantic subdued atmosphere of a piano bar.

We both were famished and ordered the 12-ounce king's cut of the prime rib, cooked medium-rare, a huge ocean shrimp salad, soup, cheese-covered onion soup, a baked potato with all the trimmings, and a bottomless basket of delicious hand-baked country butter rolls.

We were both tired from the rigorous day we'd put in. Maggie provided the dinner conversation by telling me about her disabled Mother who also lives in Carson City. The woman had struggled most her life to raise Maggie on the limited resources of a single mother. I could tell she worshiped her mom. It really bothered Maggie when she had to go out of town on bureau business, as her Mother was restricted to a wheelchair and had to carry an oxygen bottle around with her because she had some form of untreatable COPD.

After dinner and after consuming a single after-dinner liquor, Maggie paid the bill. The food had been excellent. We left the restaurant and walked out to her car in the parking lot.

We were in her car headed back to my place, when out of nowhere Maggie asked me what I thought about O.J. Simpson's problems. I could tell she was tired and trying to keep herself awake by babbling.

We discussed O.J. and his misadventures at the Palace Station Hotel and Casino on West Sahara in Las Vegas last year. He was being charged with kidnapping and armed robbery. That meant he would face a jury once again, this time charged with at least two, perhaps up to twelve, very serious felonies. Trial was scheduled for September 9th, 2008.

I remember reading in the newspaper back on May 23rd that the Judge had ordered the screening of over 400 prospective jurors for the trial.

Maggie said, "I don't think that O.J. can't get a fair trial in Las Vegas. Too many of the persons that will be called for jury duty, have it in for him. The main stream of America still resents that his expensive *Dream Team* won his acquittal for his wife's murder in Los Angeles a few years back."

"I didn't disagree with you, Maggie. But I figure that O.J. has gotten a lot of free passes in his celebrity career. Sooner or later he was going to have to take responsibility for his precipitous wrong-time, wrong-place, actions."

As Maggie sped through the light evening traffic, she raised another matter; one I thought we had previously had decided was off-limits as it was my personal business. She was back on the '*Proper actions towards close friends by a person in their final days dying from a fatal disease*' subject.

"Augustus, I know you didn't want to talk about this when I asked you about it last time. But is it possible that you may have you changed your mind? It really would make a difference to my friend if I was able to share with her, what someone in the same situation had experienced during their loved one's final days."

"Maggie, I'll meet you halfway on this. I won't share our personal feelings in those terrible last days, but I will share a small bit more about my wife's illness with you. But that will be it. No more. Will that be enough to get you off this subject?"

"Yes, Fox, you know I hate asking you. But will you please, this one time?"

Somewhat dramatically, I began. "The Beginning." I said. "She had stage-four pancreatic cancer. The worst type, we were told. It had spread from her pancreas all over the place. Into the lymph nodes, stomach, bowels, reproductive organs, almost everywhere."

"Doctor told us it was inoperable. Said chemotherapy wouldn't do any good at this stage. Said six months was about the typical live expectancy at this stage of the disease, give or take. Maybe a few days more. The doctor said all this to us as if he was expecting a thank you, from us. *Well, thank you fucking much, kind doctor.*"

"Her last days were hell. Pain so bad that the oncology ward nurses couldn't give her enough morphine is offset it. They said the additional painkiller would stop her heart. Even addict her, maybe."

"Maggie, I couldn't help but wonder. What difference would it make? Dying then with dignity, or screaming in pain and cursing everything in sight, including me for failing her when I was unable to make the pain stop."

I took a deep breath before continuing to explain what it had been like at the end. It was very unsetting to me that Maggie was asking me to relive those dark times.

"She peed and moved her bowels constantly. She drooled. She was so embarrassed about her incontinency, that she finally stopped asking the nurses to bath her, change her bed linen and nightgown."

"After that, I made up her bed and bathed her hourly, in last days. Otherwise, she would have just laid there crying, in the stink and waste from her urine and feces."

"Now, I mean it, Maggie. Never, ever ask me about this again. I don't know your friend. Certainly don't even know you well enough to permit you to force me to relive the terrible memories I've had locked up in the back of my mind all these years. You are a real bitch for opening that door."

"I am very disappointed that you persist in asking me to dredge this back up, Maggie."

Just then she turned into the drive of the Desert Willows Golf and Condo complex, and the guard let us through the security gate. She parked, locked the rental car, and we took the elevator up to the condo.

When Maggie and I got inside my condo, shucked our outerwear, and poured ourselves a nightcap, I was trying to control an impulse to yell at her for once again asking me about such a personal matter.

On the other hand, I realized that she seemed sincere if not been needy in her desire to know how my wife and I had dealt with the worst life can throw at you.

Perhaps it was no more, no less, than what she had said. The first-hand information she gleaned from me was innocently intended as advice for someone that soon would be going down this same section of bad road. For a friend of hers, she claimed. So I decided to show a little maturity and move on past it. Going to bed mad, even in separate bedrooms, was as counter-productive as it gets.

Delta sleep, at least according to those in the medical field associated with learning what the brain sub-consciously does while we are rejuvenating our minds and bodies, claim our brains often seize on a particular issue, like a dog on a bone, and worry it to death.

The result being that when we do wake up, we often have tossed the issue around in our minds all night long, magnifying its importance and context many times beyond its original scope. So we come out ready to do battle instead of attempting to seek compromise to deal with the issue in a manner more appropriate to its actual importance.

Then I changed the subject completely. We discussed what evidence we hoped would be recovered from the BRINKS crime scene. Also, from the crime scene we found out at the abandoned warehouse.

From the BRINKS scene, I figured we'd recover DNA, ballistics, and supplement information relating to the alleged woman imposter. The man who had later claimed to a co-worker that she had been working as a plant inside the BRINKS operation for the gang.

That didn't seem too far-fetched from what Agent Gardner had reported finding at the scene. The fact that the gang leader had executed the employee who shot the woman, lent some credence to the dead man's allegation.

The usual forensics evidence was be recovered from the BRINKS scene: fingerprints, and the ballistics on the bullets that killed the gate guard and the employee shooter. But some of those tests, such as the DNA, and if the medical examiner's office requested toxicology screens, didn't happen overnight. We were weeks away from obtaining probative reports from those tests, alone.

BRINKS hadn't yet been able to give authorities a rough count on how much money had been taken. At the FBI's request, the company had temporarily moved their day-to-day operations to one of the corporation's subordinate locations.

However, management of the armored-car company was in disagreement with the FBI, demanding that the company and its insurer's own investigative personnel be given full access to the crime scene.

Per usual, the historically uncooperative Bureau, at least for the present time, was refusing all requests from BRINKS and their insurance carrier for access. The bureau was claiming the FBI/ERT, its Evidence Response Team, had to maintain absolute control over the crime scene until they had recovered every bit of probable evidence on the property.

Eventually, the FBI would give in. But only after BRINKS and their insurance company agreed that their investigators would be willing to work under the watchful eye of the FBI/ERT unit which would remain on-site throughout the entire process.

Maggie and I agreed that her findings at the warehouse could have real promise.

No one cleans up that thoroughly unless they have been specifically trained to do so. Such as those trained as a Special Forces, behind-the-lines, scene-sanitation units. Of course that served to greatly reduce our suspect list. To tens-of-thousands of active duty and former Marine Rangers, Army Green Berets, Air Force Special Operators, and Navy Seals, and not excluding a rather new occupation, that of Restoration of Crime Scene Technician—they allegedly return everything to its original condition.

Both of us doubted that we'd discover any stray fingerprints if men from one of those elite military organizations had been involved. But the MRE's packages that Maggie had discovered under the warehouse furnace could prove to be invaluable. Perhaps even provide some DNA markers and partial fingerprint lifts.

Our theory was that whoever had tossed the stuff under the furnace had reacted as most of us typically would. They were just being lazy. They didn't want to take the time to bag the debris along with all the probative stuff that the gang had carted off from their past crime scenes. Or if caught discarding MRE packaging, they would get an ass chewing or worse from the gang's leader for breaking the leave-no-evidence-that-we-were-ever-here prohibition that is drummed into top-drawer soldiers from the first day they report for training that is designed to wash them out of the elite programs.

Maggie reminded me of one additional fact that had momentarily escaped my assessment of the overall BRINKS robbery—the abandoned vans. The Las Vegas crime lab was currently pouring over them with a fine toothcomb.

If the gang had been sloppy and left any blood or fingerprints behind on or in the vans, the Las Vegas Criminalists would find it. It may take a few days, but forensic crime busting is not an overnight activity, despite what you see on American television.

I can't remember a single crime where obvious evidence at the crime scene resulted in the case being solved and the perpetrators being arrested in thirty-minutes, or even an hour. Not even the assassination of President Lincoln at the Ford Theater, where multiple witnesses had observed John Wilkes Booth committing the heinous act.

By now, neither of us could contain our yawns. It had been an action-filled, stressful day. Now we needed to rest our bodies and our minds. So the aperitif glasses went into the sink and we headed off to our separate bedrooms to recharge our mental and physical batteries. Tomorrow was Monday, and wouldn't you know it, a scheduled day of labor.

As we parted company I said over my shoulder, "Try to get some sleep, Maggie. We'll leave for the office at eight a.m."

2:30 a.m.

I was dead to the world, sleeping, when I subconsciously felt what appeared to be a minor earthquake tremor shaking me. Now, back in late April of this year, they had experienced earthquakes in Reno, but we hadn't felt any in Las Vegas, at least, not yet.

By the time I began to stir and swim up and out of the heavy mist that was obscuring my consciousness, I realized it wasn't a tremor at all, unless earthquakes had recently acquired the ability to whisper.

Opening my eyes slowly, I glimpsed a figure bending over me, shaking my shoulder with one hand and covering my mouth with the other. The nocturnal manifestation was whispering, "Fox! Augustus! Something is wrong. You have to wakeup, now!"

Pushing her hand away from my mouth, I propped myself up on my right elbow and muttered, "What?"

By this time my eyes had started to acclimate to the gloom of my bedroom. Which permitted me to identify the shape leaning over my bed as Maggie DuPont, who was wearing a white cotton T-Shirt, that left nothing to the imagination. She'd been shaking me after laying her Glock and a spare clip of ammunition on the bed so she could use both hands.

"What?" I muttered again. "This better be good. What time is it?"

Maggie responded in a soft but excited whisper, "About two-thirty in the god damn morning, Chief Investigator, Fox. And keep your voice down," she whispered tersely. "Your security alarm tripped a few moments ago. I was awake, heard it faintly, and then heard what I thought was someone on the lanai attempting to lift the sliding glass door out of its track."

She was whispering in an under-control, terse tone of voice. Her tone told me that if I thought this woman was afraid of anything, I was an extremely poor judge of character. She was excited and anxious to confront the problem.

"When the noise stopped, I crawled out of bed and crept up the hall on my hands and knees to your room to awake you. Then the same type of noise started once again, but now it was coming from the front door."

That got my attention. I gently pushed her away, leaned over and slid open the drawer of my nightstand. I'd had a backup panel for the condo's new alarm system installed inside it in the my bedroom bedside drawer the moment I'd moved into the condo.

As soon as I slid the drawer open, I saw that the monitor unit underneath my personal weapon, a .45 caliber Colt ACP semiautomatic, was frantically blinking *red*, not the normal flashing 'system-armed' color of yellow. The unit was making a chirping sound, which the closed drawer had deadened it, somewhat, plus the mental exhaustion from yesterday's stressful activities had buried my normally alert consciousness under layers of fatigue.

I'd been in such a deep state of sleep that I hadn't heard the alarm. Or at least hadn't heard it loud enough that I had been awakened. *Thank god that Maggie had been awake and had excellent hearing*, I thought briefly.

I put upgrading the master bedroom's alarm monitor to a louder audio chirper on my mental to-do list.

"Maggie," I whispered, "do you think that the noise coming from the front room could have been the wind?"

Her soft reply hinted at sarcasm, "Not unless the wind is strong enough to lift and shake the lanai's 100-pound, triple-pane, sliding glass door. And we both know that there is no way for this imaginary wind of yours to get into the hallway leading to your front door!"

I acknowledged she was right by nodding my head before I whispered back, "Yeah, Maggie, I was afraid that you were going to say that."

I rolled out of bed. Since I slept in the nude, I slipped into a pair of gray UNLV workout sweats I taken off this morning before I had dressed and headed out to the BRINKS crime scene. Next, I toed a pair of expensive calf-leather Ferragamo loafers out from under the bed, and slipped my feet into them. If Ferragamo loafers were good enough for O.J., they were good enough for me, right?

I lifted the phone receiver to my ear but wasn't surprised to find the line dead. Maggie bent her head over indicating she wanted to listen. The dead phone didn't seem surprise her either. Whoever was outside had cut the line, which, by fate, had been our only access that night to call for backup.

Our friends lurking outside would have no way of knowing that cutting my landline had severed all our contact with the outside world. You see, both of our cell phones had been in heavy-use all day long, and we hadn't had an opportunity to recharge them.

When we headed off to bed a couple of hours earlier, we left them both dead as the proverbial doornail, sitting on the kitchen counter, intending to recharge them once we got into the office Monday morning.

I grabbed my .45 automatic and the extra magazine of ammo I never left home without, and we quietly heel-and-toed it towards my open bedroom door. We stopped in the open doorway and listened once again, this time for a good five minutes.

My condo layout is single-level, and large by today's Las Vegas standards. Between two large master bedrooms with full baths, a dining room large enough to seat eight, a full-living room also referred to as a viewing room these days, the library I planned to eventually use as an office, and a full-service kitchen, it was easily over 2,400 square feet not counting the west-facing lanai.

Maggie and I only had each other to backup one another up and defend the condo to protect our lives. We had no idea how many of them were out there, what their objective was, or how dearly they were willing to pay to achieve their goals, whatever they may be.

The only positive thought I had in my head at the moment was that they may have expected me to be home alone on a Sunday night. Having an extra gun in the hands of a trained marksperson leveled the playing field quite substantially. Perhaps that was enough, but maybe not. We'd just have to give it our best shot and see.

I worked my way over to the sliding door leading out onto the lanai, carefully picking my way by feel through the yet unfamiliar arrangement of living room furniture. I leaned up against the weight-bearing wall adjacent to the sliding lanai door, and peeked out between the vertical slats of the blinds.

I saw a single intruder kneeling, stethoscope on his ears, its microphone held against the glass, and some type of night-vision goggles on his head. Near his left hand was what appeared to be a ball-peen hammer. Near his right lay a large automatic pistol. He was intently listening, crouching at the glass door.

As the lanai only received minimal illumination from the reflected glow from the security lights in the parking lot, I was going off a mental picture I perceived, rather than a hard-wired observation. However, the ability to perceive that I had been taught me at the FBI academy years ago, had served me well before in other life-threatening situations. If it had not, frankly, I wouldn't be here now dealing with this dilemma.

In the meantime, Maggie had used the heavy carpet to muffle her footsteps as she slid over to the front door. She had her forehead cocked against it, listening intently to something I was unable to hear from where I was, thirty-feet-away.

I started to crawl across the carpet towards her with the intent of sharing intelligence when she noticed my advance. She held up a hand indicting that I should stop and hold my position.

After a few maddening moments she crept over to me and whispered, "My guy is using one of this computerized, locking-picking guns you can buy on Ebay. I can faintly hear it electronically running through the various combination permutations of the lockset."

She continued, "It ain't fast, but it is sure. I've tried one out at an in-service ATF training class a couple of months ago. The GCB director was pissed when the instructor used it to defeat the high-priced security locks on our office 'long and automatic weapons locker,' something that is outfitted with a bank vault-like lock and is supposed to be impregnable."

"Okay, here is what I know about our friend who has temporarily set up housekeep out on the lanai," I told her. "First, he is armed. But he apparently has given up on the stealthy removal of the sliding door from its track. I saw what appears to be a ball-peen hammer near his hand that is capable of shattering the windows glass layers, turning it all into little granules of round glass like the safety-glass in a windshield."

"Once he busts it out using the hammer, he will be able to step through the then-glassless frame, and not even cut himself in the process. Right now he is listening at the glass door using a medical stethoscope. And he is wearing night-vision goggles," I whispered.

"These guys ain't amateurs, DuPont," I said. "You have the time-in-agency seniority here, time-in-grade, if not the benefit of the salary grade. Have any inspirational ideas you'd like to share with me?"

"Yeah, Fox, I do," she murmured under her breath. "Especially, since you so diplomatically have asked for my subordinate agent opinion, and all that PC crap. Any thoughts of the chances that we could simply get the drop on these mutts, and put them on their faces on the carpet?"

Then reconsidering, she continued, "Probably too dangerous to try to get them into handcuffs. Besides, if there are more than two of them, we'll be shit out of luck. Because if there is more than two of them, we'll be unable to immobilize them with our pitiful supply of two sets of cuffs, between us."

DuPont kept up her standup comedy act going as I politely listened. "Meanwhile, we get them on the floor, hopefully scared out of their ever-loving minds, hoping that you aren't some James Bronson vigilante asshole standing over them with that cannon."

"Then, while you have them scared to death, I go out to your car and use the radio to call in the cavalry. Now how does that plan fancy your palette? What do you think, Chief Investigator, Fox?"

"Well, DuPont, first of all quit calling me Chief Investigator. Also that plan isn't going to work here. These guys were sent here to take me out, or perhaps both of us, assuming they know you are in here. Rolling over and giving up when they are faced with a little adversity, probably isn't in their job description. So, what is Plan B?"

"Fox," she cautioned, holding up her hand to get my attention, "I think the guy at the front door has just removed the lock pick from the lockset. I think I also heard a voice quietly speaking over a hand communicator. If I had to make a bet, it would be that these assholes are both coming through the doors at the same time, about now!"

She softly said, "They either don't know or don't care that you are no longer in the master bedroom. Really makes no difference to them. I suspect their orders are to waste anyone here, and then get the hell out of Dodge."

Before turning back to face the front door, she uttered a single statement, then repeated it one more time to make certain I heard her, "Center-of-mass, Fox. *Center-of-mass.*"

If she said anything further, I didn't hear it because at that moment the front door slammed open and a huge brute of a man holding a shotgun stepped through it. At the same time, the glass in the lanai's sliding door shattered inward and a smaller but no less threatening figure, automatic pistol in-hand, stepped through the opening, his boots crunching the beaded glass that now lay at his feet.

As soon as we heard the first sound of the doors were breached, Maggie and myself had darted for the closest walls, took up the stylized Weaver stance, and proceeded to empty our weapons into the chests of the two intruders.

Luckily, these mutts were traveling light. No bullet-resistant vests. Each of our bullets penetrated their chests with a mushy *slap, slap, slap, slap, slap, slap, slap* sound. The air in the condo was thick with smoke and gunpowder, and the coppery smell of blood, guts, intestinal gore, urine and feces. Somewhere a fire alarm was going off and sirens could be heard in the distance headed our way.

Even though both of the trespassers lay motionless as their blood continued pumping out onto my new carpet, we followed procedure, punched out our empty magazines and butt-pounded in fresh ones.

Only then did we cautiously advance to where they lay bleeding-out, and administered a few kicks to make ensure they just weren't lying doggo, playing possum.

We glanced at one another before bending over and barfing up our rich evening meals onto my now blood-soaked new carpet.

SIXTEEN

June 16, 2008, Monday, 3:16 a.m.
Desert Willows Golf and Country Club
2020 W. Horizon Ridge Parkway
Henderson, Nevada

The firemen arrived, found no fire, and figured the alarm must have been pulled by a resident who had been woken up by the shooting. The paramedics made a cursory check on the two dead mutts, decided they were beyond help this side of heaven, and asked if Maggie or I had any wounds before they called in the cops.

When the cops arrived, they put both of us face down on the floor. The senior officer issued orders to the follow-up units to lock the complex down in hopes of snagging the shooter's getaway transportation. Most experienced hitters don't take the chance that the car they arrived in will start when they need it for the getaway. So as a rule, they make arrangements for a getaway driver, whether they are pros or just casual labor hired for the job.

When the detectives finally arrived on-scene, they began to poke and prod the deceased even though we could have told them it was a waste of time. But then, no one asked us. We remained sprawled in a undignified manner on our faces alongside our own vomit with our wrists tightly hand-cuffed behind us.

When the Henderson cops sent a rookie out for coffee and donuts, I figured it was safe enough for us now to identify ourselves. Then I planned on explaining exactly what our part has been in the shoot-out.

Still uncomfortably on our bellies, I attempted to explain what had just transpired. At first my explanation appeared to be falling on deaf ears until a Henderson Homicide lieutenant named Rivers was summoned to the scene.

Rivers ordered the cops to assist us to getting to our feet, but only one at a time.

Then they escorted back into our respective bedrooms to retrieve our GCB credential wallets.

Once the Lieutenant had glanced at our identification, he motioned cops to remove our handcuffs. After he heard my account of what had gone down, he *invited* us both to return with him to police headquarters at 223 Lead Street in Henderson.

After Maggie and I agreed to an arrangement that temporarily placed us in his custody, the Lieutenant called his direct supervisor, then the Henderson chief of police. The chief called the FBI. The FBI called the GCB Director at his home in Carson City. I knew that no one would suggest calling the Media. Those jackals would find out about the homicides within hours anyway. Every damn reporter on the planet owns a police-band scanner.

The Henderson cops confiscated the shooter's weapons which be taken to the Forensic lab for Ballistics testing

Our weapons also were taken into evidence. They would not be returned to us until the investigation into the shooting incident was closed.

I still retained my agency-issued Glock, which had played no part in the shooting. Maggie would be issued a replacement weapon by the GCB so that she wasn't walking around like an unarmed clay pidgin, especially since there had been at least one documented attempt on her life, and two on mine.

I'd been forced to belatedly make my GCB supervisor aware of the incident that had occurred outside my complex's security gate, when I returned home in a taxi from a late evening in the office on Wednesday, June 11, 2008.

Needless to say, the GCB Agent in-charge of the Las Vegas office wasn't very supporting when he learned that I have concealed the incident from him, and from the Gaming Bureau's Professional Standards, read *Internal Affairs*, unit.

My lame explanation initially had been that I hadn't necessarily connected the 'beat-down' with the various instances of harassment by unknown individuals who had been following me hither and yon, ever since the local newspapers reported my involvement in the casino robberies. That didn't hold much water with them, and if the shoe had been on the other foot, it wouldn't have done much for me either.

At one point, while I was being interviewed after the shooting at my condo, I'd been politely asked if I was really dumb enough to think that the confrontation on Wednesday, June 11th could be a unrelated coincidence?

So now GCB higher-authority might begin to wonder if I was a loose cannon, just hoping for a chance to extract retribution at some point in the future. And basically being a realist, I'd had to admit that sub-consciously, perhaps that had been my motivation for not promptly informing management of the incidents.

The intruders would later be identified as a couple Las Vegas ex-cons that were known to sell their services as guns-for-hire. Unfortunately, I guess we had cut their careers short.

Monday was a long morning and afternoon for all involved. I think Maggie and I were questioned at-length by every law enforcement agency listed in the red-cover Las Vegas phone book. Finally, about 7:00 p.m. that evening, the rats came to the conclusion that we had told them everything of substance that there was to tell. And try as they might, no one had discovered any holes in our statements. Much to the disappointment of the Professional Standards winnies.

Since my condo was a crime scene, my boss had made room reservations for us at the Golden Nugget Hotel. Maggie's for Monday night only, and mine an open reservation for a week. We were told to feel free to charge anything we needed, including meals, except gambling, to our *respective room's* charge account.

Note that I emphasize the word *rooms*—as in more than one. My boss might personally be willing to give us the benefit of the doubt, relative to the fact that DuPont and I had been attacked in the early morning hours of a Monday morning. Albeit it, while apparently occupying the same domicile.

However, my boss wasn't going to put his pension on the line by having his fingerprints on any action that could be misinterpreted by the higher-ups in Carson City, as condoning a situation that was specifically prohibited by the Bureau's written P&P, Policies and Procedures.

We both had been placed on *paid administrative leave* per GCB established procedure. I knew that the matter of Maggie staying the night at my place, no matter how innocent, would rear its ugly head again, at sometime in the near future.

We could be disciplined, which conceivably could include suspension or even termination. Or if the powers-that-be accepted our explanation, we might get off with just having a letter placed in our personnel files, documenting what would be referred to as a *lapse in judgment*.

Investigator DuPont had been ordered to be on a flight out of Las Vegas Tuesday morning, and back to her Carson City office no later than Wednesday morning, June 18th.

GCB higher-ups had been obviously been told to expect that the Professional Standards rats would release her for return to full-duty, prior to that time.

Maggie's supervisor had flown in from Carson City and had met with her at Golden Nugget Hotel room at 9:00 p.m. Monday evening to make certain that DuPont was clear as to the Bureau's future expectations of her.

She was told that when she returned to work on Wednesday morning, she would direct all of her many talents to working own caseload. She no longer would be permitted to assist me on the casino robbery, the armored-car hijacking, or and the BRINKS armed-robbery cases.

Investigator DuPont was informed that her involvements in those open cases was no longer required as I had been assigned a new partner who had only recently been assigned to the Las Vegas GCB office.

When she called my room to give me the news, I found myself to be sincerely disappointed. I'd miss her intelligence, guts, shooting skills, and disrespect for authority.

However, I didn't get off that easy. Once my supervisor learned I had knowingly concealed the June 11th beat-down from him, he was less than supportive of continuing to permit me to run my cases unsupervised.

The Agency Personnel Director had then reminded him that *being permitted to work without the requirement to keep supervision daily informed of my progress* had be one of the stipulations in my employment agreement. The higher-ups had accepted that proviso, as they knew the agency had chosen to make an exception and bring in a highly-experienced investigator on-board, over the heads of others who had been with the organization for many years.

And the appointed Director of the GCB, who knew from experience, and from checking my references before extending the offer of a extremely generous employment package to me, that investigators of my experience tend to be more productive when not encumbered by a lot of bureaucratic crapola.

On the other hand, the rats in the board's Professional Standards unit continued to harp on the fact "while acting without day-to-day supervision, Chief Investigator Fox, chose, after only a couple of weeks on the job, to conceal pertinent information from my direct supervisor concerning several threats on my life."

Frankly, if I was honest with myself, I would have to admit that that both positions had some merit.

As a result of the incident, I was ordered to remain a guest of the Golden Nugget Hotel until such time as the office made arrangements for a contractor to replace the broken doors at my condo, replace the blood-soaked living room carpet, and patch the through-and-through bullet holes in the walls.

It was obvious to my bosses and myself that the danger represented by the holdup gang hadn't been eliminated, but rather had been exacerbated when Maggie and I had killed the two hired-guns.

Therefore, management strongly recommended that I contract with a good security firm, at Gaming Bureau expense of course, to upgrade the intrusion alarm system that had failed to wake me, that early morning, past.

Once the repairs and modifications to my condo were complete, I was told I could return home.

However, there was a further proviso added to my revised mission orders. One that I can't help but think was intended to give higher-ups some wiggle room. For instance, when the Media eventually learned that a public employee who had gunned down a hired assassin hadn't taken adequate downtime to contemplate his actions. Time that the average bleeding heart citizen believed may have given said employee the opportunity of discovering a method that would have accomplished the same goal, without employing lethal force. *I'm certain that you readers don't want to hear my response to that.*

These brilliant minds I work for, in their profound wisdom, decided while the Professional Standards rats had ruled that the shooting was justified, I would not be permitted to return to until 8:00 a.m., Monday morning, June 23, 2008, a week hence.

The contractors paid by the Bureau to upgrade the alarm system and repair my condo, finished their work on Wednesday night, June 18, 2008.

I packed-up my belongings early Thursday morning, checked out of my hotel, and was overjoyed to be returning to my home, even though it smelled of new paint and carpet. The repairs had been accomplished expertly. I couldn't even find where the bullet holes had been repaired. The glass sliding door and metal front door, looked like they had come with the place when it was new. An excellent artisan job all the way around. I'd have to thank my boss at GCB for popping for that.

I hadn't heard from Maggie. I could only assume that she had buried herself in her caseload and was keeping a low profile. A good survival move when you consider how petty some public bureaucrats can be. And you'd be on the wrong planet if you believe that Nevada Gaming Control Board is immune to that type of foolishness.

But I had not had anything to occupy my inquisitive mind for the past three days. So I decided to drop a dime to my part-time job, and see what was shaking.

We've discussed in previous chapters how my employment contract with CBS for the *CSI-Crime Scene Investigation* television show was structured.

Basically, I was considered a part-time, episode consultant. I review episode scripts that are created months in advance. Each script is created by a single writer or teams of writers that the producer had selected based on their proven track record of writing scenes, dealing with that particular proposed story line.

The story lines behind the episodic storylines that will be aired annually were chosen by other senior writers or possibly even directors, three months before the current shooting season in Las Vegas began.

In the case of this television series, the cast was more or less set. Occasionally there were cast changes, resulting from artistic differences of opinion, or ego battles between the production staff and individual actors.

With an occasional exception, the same actors appear in most every episode of the highly successful television series.

My job was hardwired. I reviewed each episode script that the production staff couriered to me, to review. Generally, I only needed to suggest a few minor technical corrections in the script's forensic process. Then I promptly couriered the script back to the show's creative staff director.

Seldom did I find that a proposed scenario was totally outside the realm of possibility even for a fictional television script.

The few that needed a complete rewrite were extremely rare. In fact, most of the show's writers have demonstrated such expertise in creating bulletproof scripts matching their assigned storyline, that they could have finessed their way into a mid-level job in any crime lab in the country.

I currently had no scripts waiting for my attention. So I called and left a message for the CSI Production Director, asking where the company scenes were being taped the following day, Friday, and asking for her permission for me to drive out the *shoot* and observe the moving-making process, first-hand.

She returned my call late that afternoon, gave me the shoot location which was out in the desert, north of Las Vegas. I was invited me to come out and learn the physical side of the business.

I thanked her and hung up. I assumed she had been referring to the production process versus the creative side of the business, for which I was being paid excellent money to facilitate.

I couldn't imagine that the Gaming Control Board would having any objection to my driving out to the shoot location during in my *mandated* downtime. After all, they had approved my accepting the part-time job with CBS in the first place, the only proviso being that it didn't interfere with my full-time employment.

The bureau reasoned that my having a professional role on the successful television production could conceivably provide some positive public relations value for the bureau, when and if the Media ever got wind of it.

June 19, 2008, Friday, 9:00 a.m.
CBS television CSI series desert *shoot* location
Twenty-three miles north of Nellis Air Force Base
State Highway 167 East, two miles east of Las Vegas Blvd.

I stopped at the Hertz Car Rental office at 9:00 a.m. to exchange my Chrysler Sedan for a low-mileage, 2008, white, four-wheel-drive Ford Expedition. The production company planner had told me that the physical shoot location was off highway 169E, on a gravel road, which she assured me was freshly-graded.

The question whether I would take my own vehicle to the shoot site or rent a 4-wheel stand-in never entered my mind. After all, I was a contract consultant to the CBS show and therefore my expenses were tax-deducible. Where the cost of having to get my car repaired in the event of road damage, was not.

About 9:30 a.m., I reached the place where I had been instructed to turn off Las Vegas Blvd onto eastbound State Highway 169. I gave a sigh of relief over my decision to rent an appropriate vehicle. The planner had been correct. The road had been graded, *back when Jimmy Carter was President.*

Having to slow down to avoid potholes, held my speed down to barely fifteen m.p.h. It was that or break my neck when the SUV's heavy-duty shocks slammed my head up against the unpadded headliner.

I hate the Nevada desert. In fact, I hate all deserts. After working in New York City, then Hong Kong, and now Las Vegas, I guess I am city boy at heart.

Deserts are either hot or cold. The constant wind abrades the dirt and sand that stretches in all directions until in places it is as hard-packed as a concrete floor.

During the summer months, and those in Las Vegas are particularly torrid, the godless dry heat sucks moisture from the bodies of all creatures. A person who died two weeks previously in the desert will have skin and tissue the texture of beef jerky.

Even before the body had taken its final breath, the mummification process would have begun.

During the winter months the wind will pierce your outer clothing regardless of its thickness or the number of layers you are wearing.

Wind-blown sand invades everything: Your clothing, shoes, and *every* crevice of your body.

Everywhere I looked, Desert Hawks were lazily floating on-patrol, riding thermals through the blistering-bright daytime sky, searching for morsels of food that the vultures may have overlooked.

When it gets to be nighttime in the desert, you can hear the mournful yips and yodels from gangs of coyotes trotting through the scrub hoping to score a rabbit, rattlesnake, or scorpion that hasn't hid itself well enough, or a CBS script consultant who couldn't run fast enough.

As I looked to the south, looking for the production troupe's vehicles that I had been assured would to serve as a visual landmark for me, all I could see were rock outcroppings here and rock outcroppings there. And trash that the lazy had dumped out here rather than pay the monthly fee for garbage collection. And abandoned old shacks that I suppose would all have a storied past to tell, if they could only talk.

―――

I knew from listening to gossip around the water cooler in the GCB office that the desert around Las Vegas is rich in the wealth of buried human body remains. Back in old Las Vegas, during the mob days, only the foolish cheated, stole, or otherwise incurred the wrath of Casino owners.

Within a few hours of the mob or a casino owner becoming aware of your dastardly transgression, you were invited to accompanying your new BFF's, best friends forever, on a little nighttime ride in a black limousine away from the glare and glitter of Sin City.

Once the car arrived at a pre-determined location in the inky darkness of the desert, and before anyone got out, a brief discussion would take place in the car between you and trusted employees of the very important man you have offended.

The errors of your ways would be carefully explained to you. And it was explained to you why such grievous conduct couldn't be permitted to continue. "No", you were told, "your actions just this one time *can't be* overlooked, even if you *do* promise on your mother's grave to never, ever, commit such an infraction again. Surely you can understand that," they would ask?

When the hopelessness of your situation became obvious to you, and you began beg for forgiveness, you are told to get out of the car. A brand new oak-handled shovel was placed in your hands.

Then you were ordered to dig a grave. "Dig it deep," you are told. "you don't want to have the coyotes digging you up, do you?"

Of course the mob era in Las Vegas has come and gone. Private and public corporations now own all of Nevada's casinos. And a more enlightened pubic demands more sophistication in the disciplining of a miscreant.

Today, should you be caught cheating, you will be escorted down to a sound-proof room called the *Box* which is located in one of the casino's sub-basements.

The room's expensive sound-proofing is strictly for the purpose of intimidation, not to blunt the sounds of any beating you might deserve.

No one will have touched you up to that point, other than a rather large security guard who has guided you by an arm 'so you wouldn't lose your way.'

You will be offered a seat in a nice, heavily-padded, black leather armchair, your choice of a soft drink, and be told that it is "Okay to smoke."

Then you will be shown videotapes of your indiscretions courtesy of the casino's ubiquitous Eyes-In-The-Sky.

After viewing of your indiscretion several times, the monitor will be shut off, and a well-dressed man, a management official of the Casino, probably a floor boss, will join you in the box and pleasantly ask you what you have to say for yourself.

Here is where it can get tricky. If you have won a lot of money off the casino through your misguided actions, you could try denying everything.

Or you could admit to everything, offer to give the casino its money back, apologize, and respectfully ask the floor manager for forgiveness. You might try promising never to come to the casino again, but of course, you are already destined to become an entry into Nevada's Casino List of Excluded Persons, called the Black Book, so your attempt to gain a dispensation in this manner is a total waste of time.

If this was your first transgression, at least in that particular casino, you could elect to empty your pockets of all the money you have, even that which you have not stolen from the casino, then standup and walk out of the Box.

Remember though, either way, you will never walk out of the Box while still in possession of any of their money. Casinos are given reasonable latitude to recover what is theirs before permitting you to leave the premises.

But don't be too surprised to find two of Metro's finest sitting in a pair of very comfortable chairs just outside the room, drinking cups of excellent Columbian coffee provided them by the casino, patiently waiting to *hook you up*.

Of course, it is often rumored that there are a few small casinos *off-strip*, which still live in the past.

In those shadowy establishments, your first indiscretion at that club will be dealt with by a trip down to the Box. Any money you have illicitly won will be removed from your person. Then you will be given a stern warning about what will happen should you ever be caught cheating in their casino again, or in any casino in Las Vegas, for that matter. The inner-communications between casinos is very, very tight.

The casino's security personnel will then physically escort you back up on the gaming floor, to a side door where you will accidentally stumble while stepping out into the parking lot. Again, a couple Metro's finest will patiently be sitting in their car waiting for you, just 'another drunk' in their eyes, to make your appearance.

Your second offense in the same casino probably will result in you once again being escorted down to the Box. Everything but your personal identification will be taken away from you. However, this time you will not have to sit through a second warning.

Instead, one of the large security individuals will break one or more of your fingers, or beat your face into a barely recognizable pulp.

The thugs, democratically, will give you the option of which you'd prefer, before they start your reeducation.

Should you be foolish enough to chance a third indiscretion, again bet on being caught by the Casino's surveillance systems. Your face will already have been programmed into their facial recognition system.

This time you won't have to make an appearance in the box.

You once again will find yourself none-too-gently hurried through a side door and shoved out onto the parking lot concrete. You momentarily may feel relieved that there isn't a police car waiting to hook you up.

Rumor has it that at this point you will be ordered leave town immediately. And told to not bother to take the time to call anyone or stop to pack your belongings.

If you elect to *not* take advantage of this opportunity, things from that point will get a little unpleasant. Someday, when you least expect it, you will find yourself picked up off the street by a couple of thugs, which are paid-by-the-job, and should you care to ask, their combined intelligence quotients, I.Q., the total won't be over 150.

They won't say a thing. Or answer your questions. It is strictly a job to them. You'll be handcuffed and gagged. Then you'll be taken out some distance away from town to the darkest areas of desert they can find.

First, you'll be removed from the car. You will be forced to stand motionless while one of the thugs places a rubber hospital incontinence sheet on the car's carpet and upholstery of its rear seat. By now, you will have soiled your trousers in fear.

You'll be injected with a half-grain of Morphine. Then after the painkiller has taken effect, someone obviously well-skilled in the procedure will amputate your strong-arm hand. It will be thrown out in the desert as food for the coyotes that have silently been circling your small party since the car arrived.

While you are still unconscious from the shock, one of your assailants will professionally apply a tourniquet to the stump.

Then while you are still groggy, and under the soothing effects of the pain killer, you'll be led back to the car and forced to lie on the rubber sheet, which is protecting the carpet and upholstery as you are driven to a nearby hospital where you will unceremoniously be kicked out and left at the entrance to the emergency room.

Back to present day, I finally spotted what appeared to be a number of old mining shacks and an quasi-orderly row of vehicles parked far to the south, at the base of 5,400-foot Muddy Peak.

I turned right down an access road, again thanking myself for being so omniscient to rent the four-wheel Drive SUV. I bumped along for about a mile until I come upon the shoot location. With difficulty, I select a place to park, along what had become a linear parking lot, making certain that I would not be blocked-in when I decided to leave.

What the average citizen doesn't know, or probably to be more truthful, doesn't care to ever know, is that shooting scenes in field locations require a lot amount of work and even more expense.

While it is true that filming exterior screens for the small screen is far less costly than those for the silver-screen, both require a vast amount of planning and coordination.

The average public perception is that silver screen productions require dozens of motor homes, both pre-and post-production facilities, exotic lighting equipment, kitchens, dispensaries, a communication center, a small self-contained mobile emergency care center, and several hundred technicians, not counting the stars, extras, cooks, administrative assistants, directors, producers, special effects personnel, lightning engineers, stunt men, security guards—oh, well you get the idea.

While a shoot for a television series is definitely small potatoes as compared to that for a silver screen project, the basic functions that must be provided for are similar in complexity, and critical to the professionalism of the finished product.

I knew from the script the production planner had faxed me, that this segment of the episode called for a prospector to stumble onto what he feels may be number of buried bodies at the site of the former ranch of a serial killer now serving a life sentence in a federal Penitentiary.

Today's shoot is only budgeted for eight-hours of time-on-location. That allocates less than sixty-minutes for each and every scene that is required to dovetail with the 'insides lab scenes' of the show that are already in the can.

That requires dozens of people coordinating their efforts and subverting, albeit temporarily, their egos to permit this to happen before darkness shuts the shoot down. Fortunately, nightfall comes about 8:15 p.m. out here in the desert during the summer months.

No one, except possibly myself, would be permitted to head for home until the shoot is complete, even if it means working overtime. Missing a shoot is a career killer, and highly-frowned on, in the business of professional film or tape production.

Episodic budgets are strict. If one scene or a number of scenes unavoidably run over budget, the shooting of other portions of the episode will have to be reduced in-scope to compensate for lack of available funds, remaining.

The amount of equipment required to support a taping shoot, such as is planned for today, would amaze the average citizen, and frankly, myself included.

For instance, like an army parked at the roadside waiting to advance upon an enemy battlefield, I count over a dozen vehicles intended for variously specific purposes.

There are two, forty-foot, diesel-pusher motor homes. One will be used as a lounge for the performing stars when the script allows them to be off-screen. The other is to be used as the shoot's production office.

There is a twenty-foot trailer being pulled by a huge Ford pickup. On the flat bed of the trailer there are ten port-a-potties, five placed back-to-back, each accessible by a wooden stairway with handrails.

Then there are two kneeling, lowboy trailers, each pulled by diesel-powered, cab-over tractor. On the trailer of each, rests most of the major equipment required for today's shoot.

Everything on the trailers has been chained-down. The shoot location is too far out of town to risk something critical falling off a truck, and having a gofer drive the twenty-three plus miles back to Las Vegas to obtain a replacement, even if one was available on such short notice.

One of the trailers carries such operational equipment as klieg lights, props, scenery, scaffolding, ladders, light reflectors, and other equipment required to physically make the shoot possible.

The other lowboy is stacked end-to-end with chained-down green John Deere four-wheel *Gators,* which will be used to transport personnel back-and-forth between the road and the shooting locating.

Then there are pickups towing industrial-size generators that will provide the electrical power for the shoot's needs, such the cameras, lighting, and sound equipment, and much more.

The contract Security force and emergency first-aid personnel have arrived in self-contained vehicles, specifically designed for their intended use. The medical crew is certified and equipped to handle broken bones, heat exhaustion, cuts and bruises, snake bites, and twisted ankles. The medical providers always have a med-evac helicopter standing-by on-call at the North Las Vegas airport.

Then there are the two, refrigerated ten-wheel trucks of the caterers, each towing a powerful electric-generator that provide juice for the soft drink dispensers, ice machines, misters, and so on. They will set-up a large tent to provide sunshade during meals and breaks from shooting, and furnish it with rough furniture, collapsible tables and chairs.

Last, but certainly not least, are three modern Trailways air-conditioned passenger buses that had been contracted to transport the crew to-and-from the shoot.

Personal vehicles are not permitted at a shoot unless the driver has obtained prior permission, as I had.

I parked my rental. Then retrieved a canteen filled with partially frozen water and a campy, floppy, desert hat from the back seat before locking it.

I hiked over to a *Gator* whose driver was sitting there with a bored look on his face, and asked for a ride down to the location where today's scenes were being shot.

Today's shoot was about a mile from the gravel access road where all the vehicles were parked. The location was a typical desert scene, a bunch of old fallen down prospector cabins.

There also was an old pole corral in the middle of the set that I assume had held burros at one time.

The set crew had put in a fair amount of work to make the dwellings and corral appear to have been inhabitable in the not too distant past. The scene was supposedly a close approximation of the serial killer's Barker

Ranch farm that actually exists in California. It is located in Death Valley, 150-miles west of Las Vegas in Inyo County, California.

The killer's cult of hippie followers have been dubbed by the Media as 'The Family.' They lived communally at the ranch up until most of them went into prison in 1970 for killing of a prominent actress and her friends at her California home in August of 1969.

One of the larger Gators had dragged the ten-plex, port-a-potty rig as close to the shoot location scene as possible. The trailer has to remain out of view of the cameras that were taping the scenes. It had been leveled and made operational and was only a short walk down and behind a convenient outcropping of rock.

I had arrived during a brief recess when one scene had been put to bed and another was being set up for filming. Anyone not assisting in setting up the scene had gathered under a caterer's tent that had been erected a hundred feet away from the action. Refrigerators were running on auxiliary generators. Its canvas roof and self-contained misters provides actors and crew alike with a brief respite from the blazing desert sun and the opportunity to enjoy a cold beverage.

Medical personnel were circulating in the tent, asking questions and checking pulses to ensure that no one was getting dehydrated.

When I stepped out of the Gator, the driver jumped out, shut it off, engaged its handbrake, before hoofing it over to the tent apparently to hydrate himself until another customer going the other way came along requiring his services.

I was walking towards the tent when a tall burly black man and short Hispanic woman stepped out from under the awning and walked over to me, intending to more-or-less interdict my forward progress.

I didn't know who the man was. But I did know he wasn't one of the show's stars as I had met most of them previously.

I assumed the woman was Shoot location Planner Barbara Johnson with whom I had coordinated today's visit.

"I'm Davis Jones, this episode's Director," the man said. "Now who pray tell are you?"

"Augustus Fox. I'm one of your technical advisors," I replied.

"Mr. Fox is one of our script critics," Johnson explained nervously.

Turning to the woman who was at least a foot-shorter than him, Jones asked her, "Does this man come with a working mouth, Barbara?"

"Yes, Sir," she said, "I imagine he does. I invited him out here today to give him the opportunity to see how we dovetail the script with the physical scenes."

Looking back at me, he asked, "Fox, could you have told me all that yourself without the help from this ventriloquist?"

"Yes, Mr. Jones, I probably could. But she says it so much nicer than I could."

"Oh," Jones said. "In addition to being a know-it-all script expert, you also are a ladies man I see. Well, hell, come over and sit with me a spell, and have a cold $5.00 bottle of CBS over-priced chilled water."

I followed Jones back into the shade of the tent while Barbara headed off to take care of other responsibilities, hopefully working with individuals who were more polite than this egomaniac.

Within a heartbeat of sitting down in a couple of directors' chairs, we had received chilled bottles of water in our hands, courtesy of an administrative assistant, read *gofer*. Jones insisted on introducing me to those sitting at the portable tables nearby.

He referred to each person by their job titles: Producer, lighting specialists, chief grip, assistant director, cinematographer, construction coordinator, transportation captain—pointing over to the glum man who had driven me to the shoot location—transportation chief, set decorator, costume manager, and the unit production manager who looked exasperated at having to be sitting here in the tent wasting valuable time bullshitting, just to please the egocentric director.

"I understand you are a policeman,' Jones said. "I supposed this is pretty tame for you. I imagine you always are in the middle of a gunfight or some other emergency to uphold the law of the land."

"Actually, Mr. Jones, I have been involved in a little action lately. Frankly, that is one of the reasons I decided to come out and see how the professionals like you and your crew here would handle it. Maybe pickup a couple pointers, you know. Never hurts to learn from real professionals, I always say, " as I attempted to not break into a belly laugh.

Chuckles begin to bubble up from those seated at the surrounding tables, which of course, both Jones and I studiously ignored. I, because I might not be able to keep a straight face, and he, because he honestly seem to believe the bullshit I had just spun him.

"Always willing to help the police, Fox, " He said. "Stop by anytime. We'll be glad to give you some pointers based on our experience."

Changing the subject, I turned away from observing his crew's attempts to not laugh out loud at Jones' buffoonery, and asked him a disarming question to change the subject.

"Sir, if you have a moment free right now, could you please explain to how the script you are using will dovetail into the actual filming of the various scenes? As you know, I am only one of several consultants that CBS has under contract to review scripts."

I humbly continued, " Unfortunately, this script isn't one of mine so I am a little in the dark about what today's shoot is hoping to accomplish."

Looking at me with a hint of a new regard, he asked, "I assume that the dearly departed Ms. Johnson faxed you a copy of the screenplay when she invited you to attend today's taping?"

"Yes, Sir, she most certainly did. It is my understanding that this episode, to some extent, is based on Charlie Manson's Barker Ranch back in the late 1960's. He lived on a farm with his cult of hippie followers before he dispatched some of them to commit the atrocities in California in August 1969."

Searching my memory for facts, I continued, "This location is supposed to mimic that of his California's Death Valley ranch in those days. It has always been assumed that Charlie killed a number of his followers who had stood up to him to and refused to follow out his orders before the 1969 massacre of Sharon Tate and her friends. Some think the ranch was the final resting place for those rebels who defied him and risked all, rather than kill innocent people."

I went on, "Those rumors have gained more credence over the years when authors who have researched investigative materials discovered that eight of the closest members of what is called "his family" have never been located. Nor are they believed to be in hiding."

"The premise behind today's shoot is that an old prospector was digging around in the desert here, and happened to stumble upon a fleshless pair of foot bones sticking out of the hard-packed earth that surrounds the sets you have created here."

I continued, "The storyline as I understand it, is that the old prospector called the Metro Police to report it that night when he returned to Las Vegas to pick up some supplies."

"The old man's story was initially taken by authorities with a grain of salt. Typically these old prospectors are homeless old boozers who spend their time in the desert, looking for that one big score that is going to put them over-the-top, forever," I said.

"But with the serial killer, supposedly patterned off Manson, coming up for parole next year, the cops figured they better not leave the proverbial stone unturned because members of the California Parole Board have told the press they will be facing a major legal challenge if they deny his constitutional right to parole once again. That is unless the authorities can come up with some new capital crimes to charge him with."

Authors' Note: In May of 2008, the search of Manson's ranch resulted in a finding of negative results. As such Manson is expected to win his battle for parole at its next session.

"So," I expanded, "It is my understanding the actors are portraying the CSI team that the Metro Police have dispatched to this location in hopes of locating and digging up the bodies of the cult followers who vanished back here at the farm back in the July of 1969."

"Look, Fox," Jones said. "You obviously came out here knowing your stuff. But now the production crew has to get back to filming. Wonder around where you want. But two rules. Stay out of the crew's way. And stay out of the camera shots. Got it?"

I nodded that I did, and watched as the man marched off to direct the next scene. Then I walked over to where the Unit Product Manager, who first name was Ned, who was supervising the preparation of fake burial mounds a couple of hundred feet away from the main farm structures.

I'd learned that all television scenes must be taped under the direct supervision of a producer. For the 2008 season filming season, as previously noted, CBS had employed twenty-seven producers to support the 2008 season for the hit show.

According to what I overheard Ned discussing with his assistant, the script called for two teams of criminalists (the television show only has two teams of CSI's) to arrive at the farm in unmarked dark-blue Chevrolet Tahoe SUV's.

Television actors playing a part must stick to wearing clothing appropriate to that worn by professional Criminalists in the real world.

Acknowledging that premise lends believability to the show. The actors, when shown in lab scenes, wear navy-blue cargo trousers, matching pull-over shirts, and the ubiquitous CSI baseball cap.

In the real world, CSI's keep jump-out bags and crime scene kits at strategic locations, such as residences and their vehicles.

Police department Forensic evidence gatherers will tell you that it is amazing what they manage to get away by the virtue of garbing themselves in ankle-high black leather boots, black-polo shirts, black-cargo pants, dark windbreakers with 'Forensics' on the back in bold yellow letters, the usual camera slung around their neck, and other basic equipment that television has taught the viewing public to expect.

Television writers have taken creative license and added navy-blue jump suits for those actors at crime scenes. Individual actors have pushed the envelope of propriety and donned the blackest of black sunglasses, I suppose meant to create a deliberate, menacing mixture of a message to match their make-believe uniforms.

Authors note: As a rule, criminologists do not carry weapons. And as with every rule, there are some exceptions to this.

In the coming scene, the actor portraying the old prospector would lead the CSIs across to bleak desert landscape to the fake farm scene, accompanied by LVPD *Captain Jim Brass*, portrayed by character actor Paul Gilfoyle.

After they had stopped to inspect and photograph the rickety old buildings, the script has the actors proceeding further out into the desert to where prospector had stumbled upon the foot bones. Of course they weren't using real human bones. Just forensic facsimiles or props. Which by now had been carefully planted in the ground by show's scene preparation technicians.

Upon inspecting the fake bones sticking out of the ground, one of the team supervisors, *Gil Grissom*, played by actor William L. Petersen;

dispatched the Criminalist *Warrick Brown*, played by actor Gary Dourdan; and *Nick Stokes*, portrayed by actor George Eads, back to the trailer that one of the CSI's SUVs had towed to the location.

Characters *Brown* and *Stokes* would wrestle a machine known as the GPR, or Ground Penetrating Radar, out of the trailer and manhandled it over to the *pretend* grave. The team's other supervisor, *Catherine Willows*, portrayed by veteran actor Marg Helgenberger, would be kneeling down next to the grave and using an ordinary paint brush to brush away the dirt from around the bones.

Criminalists *Brown* and *Stokes*, assisted by *Greg Sanders* who is portrayed by actor Eric Szmanda, and other individuals on the CSI team, in the meantime had staked out a 50-yard square grid using yellow crime scene tape, while characters Brown and Stokes set up the GPR unit on the rough ground.

Then *Brown* was scripted to push the device back and forth up and down the 50-yard long rows, closely following the stakes that previously had been placed to define the grid that was to be searched.

Now for those of you who haven't watched enough of the zillion CSI shows on television yet to recognize the term GPR, I will provide a brief explanation.

Despite the fictional plots created by television writers regarding locating buried bodies, the science behind the forensic tool of Ground Penetrating Radar is really nothing that isn't used regularly in other fields, such as the airplane you are probably going to take when you go on vacation this year.

It is a fairly simplistic system like most radar systems currently in-use today. The first radar system, incidentally, was developed by the British as a way to give their flyers early warning of in-coming German bombers during World War Two. The English developed the system, and as they say, the rest is history. Radar is even used to find fish today.

A ground radar system consists of a powerful radio transmitter and receiver. They are coupled to a pair of antennae that scan the ground surface. A signal is sent into the soil. A subsurface object, a large rock or other obstruction, reflects the signal.

Every subsurface object has electrical properties that differ from those of the surrounding dirt.

Depending on what the object is, the signal will bounce back to the receiver in slightly different periods for time, each of which produces a different length wave pattern on the monitor. Which is differentiated and enhanced by the use of variations of the colors of red, green and blue.

The subsurface object itself will appear only as a pale gray lump of matter. But the radar system and its signals are able to determine the depth of the item, and expert operators of the equipment sometimes can tell if it is remains of an animal, or garbage that has been buried in the past.

The script called for the GPR to locate five buried bodies in a very short time, which of course it did, this all being theater.

Then the script called for time to be foreshortened, permitting the bodies to be carefully extracted and any available evidence collected.

Regrettably, again according to the script, not much probative evidence was recovered that would enable the actors to solve the mystery in allocated thirty-minutes or less.

The script called for all the bodies to have been burned before burial. This meant the props had to support the condition.

The skulls *props* appeared to be nothing but charred fragments, which were collected in brown evidence bags. The torso was an amorphous black mass with upper arms and legs raised due to the contraction of the flexor muscles. The lower limbs were shriveled stumps. The killer had cut off the hands and feet before setting the bodies on fire, and had taken the extremities with him. Now even real CSIs would have had a problem identifying what remained of the corpses.

The script called for the five bodies to have been shot before they were burned and buried. Guess the serial killer really wanted to make certain they were really dead.

And the script called for the bodies to have been sprinkled with lime before the graves were closed over them.

Actually, the concept of using lime in an attempt to conceal a dead body is mostly an old wives tale, despite what generations of television writers have claimed. They have convinced the general public to believe that by sprinkling quick lime over a body before an illicit burial in an impromptu grave, accelerates decomposition. Not so. Calcium oxide (quick lime) only masks the odor of decay and helps keep scavengers away from the gravesite.

A homicide victim whose been shot to death before being burned in a cover-up fire, will appear to be somewhat relaxed. But if a victim is burned alive, the body writhes, and is generally found in a fetal position.

Of course, these television bodies according to the episode's script had been buried back in 1969. In reality, due to the harsh environment of the desert, there would be nothing but bones remaining. The ferocious heat of the desert would have long ago turned any tissue into jerky.

As soon as the evidence had been collected and the television bodies had been properly dug up—which would of taken two, eight-hour days, not the ten minutes the script allotted—and after crime scene personnel recovered any probative evidence from the dead bodies, two coroners, garbed head-to-toe white Tyvek biohazard suits, heavy-duty body-handling Nitrile gloves, special masks and booties, appeared, seeming to have magically materialized out of the desert.

I hadn't seen where the actors portraying the coroners had come from. However, the answer to my question could be as simple as some of the CSI actors pulling double duty portraying the coroner duo, since the actor's faces were obscured because they were wearing HEPA masks.

The coroners put a tag on each victim's left big toe bone. Then they slipped the various bones that had been collected into individually body bags. To maintain the appearance of factualism, each body bag had a C-shaped zipper running around the three sides of the bag.

I'd had enough. The sun was hotter than Hades. And I was on-leave supposedly to recover from the beat down I suffered a week or so ago, not to mention the '*mental anguish*' that I had suffered from shooting the mokes that had been trying to kill me, early Monday morning.

So I hiked back to the caterer's tent, located Barbara Johnson, and asked her to convey my appreciation for the field day to Director Davis Jones.

Johnson rolled her eyes telling me she recognized bullshit when she heard it. But she politely used her walkie-talkie to summon up a green monster to transport me back to my car.

I must admit to you my readers that I wantonly broke the posted speed limit on Las Vegas Blvd on the way home to the *real world* for what I planned to be a extended hot shower to wash away the desert grit.

Soon I would return to work on the stickup cases, which I would discover that during my absence had turned even more elusive, violent, and deadly. A note had been clipped to the case file, I assume by the Bureau's case manager, indicating that a prompt resolution of the cases was expected from me, *not* excuses, *not* shootouts and *no* car chases.

Gee, I guess that only left me with the option of using my Star Trek Ray Gun to vaporize the bad guys.

SEVENTEEN

June 21, 2008, Saturday, 11:30 a.m.
Red Rock Canyon Recreation area
Off Highway 167
20 miles NW of Las Vegas, NV.

It was noon. The desert surrounding Red Rock Canyon kept the temperature up during the day, and not much lower at night. Today, the air was exceptionally dry. As usual there was a light wind whipping up particles of sand and dust.

Bill and Barbara Houser, a young, recently married couple were both diehard off-road enthusiasts. They'd met a year ago in the Mohave Desert when Barbara's ATV had gotten a vapor lock. Fortunately Bill had come along to give her assistance.

It was love at first sight. Both were in their late twenties, both divorced, neither had children, and somehow it just seemed right that they would become a couple.

Both worked stressful jobs in Las Vegas. Barbara was a Metro police officer. Bill had recently had completed the Metro police academy, and like about half of the graduating rookies, had been assigned to the Clark County Detention Center.

They had planned for months to get this weekend off together and they weren't going to let a little blowing sand ruin their day.

When they tied the knot, both had decided against having children right away. That left them some discretionary income that they decided to splurge on their hobby, off-roading.

Like most county employees, they had elected to apply for a loan from the Clark County Employee Credit Union rather than pay the usurious financing rates charged by the ATV dealerships. When their loan was approved, they both had taken their first sick day, ever, off work and headed for a nearby ATV dealership to spend the money.

After taking a couple test rides on the ATVs that the dealer had in stock, they settled on two, electric-blue Yamaha Grizzly 600 models that had 595cc 4-stroke engines. They selected the 2008 models over the slightly cheaper 2007 models that also were sitting on the dealer's showroom floor.

Due to their enthusiasm for the off-road experience, they expected outstanding performance out of whichever ATV they purchased. They made their selection based on the fact that the new 2008 Grizzly with its independent rear suspension with dual shocks, was the way to go.

It was time for them to stop for the brown bag lunch they always carried with them. At the time, both were urging their Yamahas up a steep slope, clawing their way up to the top of a small butte.

While they were competitive towards each other, Bill generally tried to keep his ATV a little behind Barbara's in case an unforeseen problem materialized that could put her in jeopardy.

They had just come to a stop on top of the Butte when Bill abruptly jammed on his ATV's brakes and held his right hand up, signaling Barbara to stop.

Holding his hand to his forehead to shield his eyes from the blinding sun, he pointed with the index finger of his left hand indicating a wash about a half-mile-away over which a couple of buzzards were circling and making a racket.

Bill felt that the two birds of prey were debating the rights of possession, relative to something that was lying in the wash. Perhaps it was a snake-bit coyote, or a dehydrated small animal.

"What do you think it is, Bill?" Barbara asked. She reached back into the Emergency bag they always brought along whenever they went off-road. She dug out a pair of expensive binoculars that her family had given them for a wedding present, and put them to her forehead.

Now she see what was going on better than her husband. "Bill," she said. "It might be something other than a small animal. There are at least four buzzards trying to drive each other off to determine which them will stake its claim to whatever is down there. They must think it is worth fighting over. I want to go down there. We can stop for lunch later."

Bill looked around until he located a reasonably direct route down to the wash and pointed it out to her. They revved-up their ATVs and took off in-trail, one behind the other, with Bill in the lead, and cautiously made their way off the butte, down to the wash.

A few minutes later, still in-trail, they entered the wash. Bill abruptly jammed on his brakes when he caught a whiff of a gut-wrenching putrid smell. Instinctively he swerved his ATV violently to avoid running over the macabre sight in front of him.

Perched on a partially-uncovered body that was no longer on the wrong side of the dirt, screaming at the two off-roaders who had interrupted their meal, were two huge buzzards that each appeared to be a hundred-years-old.

First thing that popped into Bill's head, was *Ah, ha. These must be the patriarch and matriarch buzzards. I'll bet the kids won't get a single bite of this grisly morsel.*

To the uninitiated, the first time the rank smell of death assaults your nostrils, you think you have died and gone to hell.

It was obvious that what was left of the body in front of them had once been buried in a shallow grave. The buzzards must have been working diligently for god knows how long to dig the corpse up.

At first glance, it was obvious that the body's hands and head have been amputated. As cops, they knew the extremities could have been disposed of anywhere, presumably to conceal the victim's identify. There was no clothing so it was obvious the corpse had been buried nude, and fairly recently. The stage of the body's decomposition and mummification indicated the body hadn't been dead more than a few days.

The couple observed that the corpse had a stain of dried blood in the area of the victim's left groin. Perhaps it is a gunshot wound. There is a pucker of an entry hole that was purple and blue, and the stippling of gunshot residue surrounded the wound.

From their training at the academy, they knew that factor indicated that the body had been shot from a distance of about five feet. Not exactly close range but not across the room either.

Barbara's job had exposed her to a dead body before, but Bill's as of yet, had not.

The smell of a decomposing corpse, dead flesh, rotting, supplemented by the rank smell of old urine and excrement, the putrid fluids and gasses splitting the victim's skin to find a away to get out of the body, is the worst thing that law enforcement officers must get used to.

Although the body had been buried out in the desert, the smell of decomposition had attracted the presence of big, blue, shiny flies; buzzing, bouncing off the red rocks that surround the body. The noise this activity creates is a gentle, papery sound.

Barbara pulled out the satellite phone that most experienced and prudent off-roaders carry in their emergency kits, and called the Las Vegas Metro dispatcher to report finding an apparent homicide victim.

During training, budding Criminalists and police officers are taught to use burned fingernail clippings to approximate the smell of death, so they aren't blindsided by it at their first homicide crime scene.

It is necessary for anyone who regularly comes into the presence of a dead body, or has any contact with death, that they accept the reality that the smell of death is a physical mechanism that *only* is possible because minute pieces of dead flesh have come to rest on their nasal lining. These fragments are actual pieces of the dead body they have smelled.

June 23, 1008, Monday, 9:00 a.m.
GCB Southern District Office
555 E. Washington Blvd
Las Vegas, Nevada

Chief Investigator Fox returns to his GCB office eager to resume working the hijack robbery case, which had been monitored during his week-long mandatory administrative leave by his new partner, Special Agent Billy Frisbee.

I walked up to the security keypad on the main entrance door to our office, at 555 East Washington Avenue, Suite 2600, at exactly 9:01 a.m. I tried to convince myself that I hadn't timed my arrival for exactly that time, thinking my supervisor might be so petty as to have the office's security system reject my identification card until the exact minute that his formal letter of notification had informed me that I would be permitted to return to work.

Once inside, I grabbed a cup of typically lousy public servant coffee on my way back to my office. As I passed by the offices and cubicles of the other agents, I noticed that to a person, they all seemed to have their heads buried in their work.

I rationalized that no one wants to acts overly-friendly to an agent just coming off mandatory administrative leave. Even if the reason for the time off was the result of bureaucratic paranoia. It nauseates me that it is just part of the cover-your-ass corporate culture that has unfortunately washed over into a field where men and women are asked to willingly put their lives on the line for the public good, everyday.

I noticed that my new partner wasn't in his bullpen cubicle. Therefore, I wasn't surprised to find him in my office, patiently waiting in the visitor's chair in front of my desk that was stacked high with files and reports.

Billy had a big grin on his face. Either the young eager agent was glad to see me, or he had enjoyed the brief respite my absence created, permitting him to work on his own without me looking over his shoulder, or both.

I put down my briefcase down on what little available room was left on my desk, removed my suit coat, and as usual, made an effort to toss it onto a hook of the coat rack. Of course, and also per usual, I missed and had to walk over to retrieve it off the carpet and hang it up like a grown man would.

I sank down in my desk chair musing how much I had missed its comfort even though I'd only been on-board for three weeks. Briefly, the thought crossed my mind wondering if I was the first GCB agent in department history to be put on mandatory Administrative leave less than two weeks after being sworn in?

I decided to ask one of the old-timers in the office that question in the near future.

Then I asked, "Hey! Well, Billy, you got the case solved yet? Whatsup?" He grinned back, indicating with his hand the pile on my desk.

"Boss, I think you are going to be happy about what has come in since you decided to take your paid vacation last week."

Looking away from the stack of paper on my desk, I gave Billy one of my more sour looks, then asked, "And what exactly would that be? Do I have to read through this six-inch thick stack of reports, or are you going to quit playing *Stump the Boss*, and give me an overview?"

Flipping open his agent's black spiral notebook, he began. "Okay, Boss, I'm going to give you a summary and a compilation of the results we've obtained so far. This work product is courtesy of the FBI crime lab in Virginia, Metro's crime lab, and the Nevada State Police lab in Reno, up in Washoe County."

Billy continued enthusiastically, "While the techs were processing the evidence, I was attempting to second-source, validate or expand on each of their findings."

"Let's start first with the Laughlin caper back on April 10, 2008. With Chavez dead, we've almost run out of leads to follow up on. There was no meaningful forensic evidence recovered from that scene that proved to be probative. These guys were slick. They followed a routine, double-checked each other to make certain no evidence was left behind, and acted with military-like precision."

"It appears the deaths of the two elderly persons who were overcome by smoke and suffered heart attacks wasn't part of their game plan. But of course they should know that when they are captured they'll soon find themselves in the docket charged for the deaths anyway. They are legally liable for the homicides as the deaths occurred relative to the commission of a crime."

Glancing at his notebook, once again, the young agent shifted gears. "Now, on to the May 3, 2008 armored-card hijacking. Actually, I'm not sure how the FBI is classifying this crime since it involved the indirect theft of funds from five businesses, not to mention that the armored-car company is on the hook, because they contracted to protect the money. Long story short, it obviously was an inside job."

Frisbee continued. "Loomis/Fargo's missing armored-car was discovered by a roaming section car outside an area junkyard, within a day. As of this date, none of the money has been recovered. The truck was part of Loomis/Fargo's ATM cash delivery operation."

I interrupted, "Billy, this is ringing a bell in back of my head. Hasn't this type thing happened before in Las Vegas? Years ago?"

"Yeah, Boss. Some of the GCB old-timers around here say the perps appear to have been working from a successful blueprint established by a Heather Tallchief and a Roberto Solis in an almost identical hijacking of an armored-car back in 1993."

"Apparently, on the basis of her looks or smarts, or both, Tallchief worked her way into a job as a driver for one of the armored-car companies that were under contact to make large deliveries of cash to ATM machines located in casinos and hotels."

"Then one day, Tallchief dropped off the two guards that always accompany a delivery of cash to the ATM machines in the casino's while per procedure, Tallchief waited in the armored-car. But this time, when the two guards returned, both she and the truck were gone."

"Metro and the FBI immediately threw out a dragnet. Eventually the truck was located but she and the money had disappeared. The FBI later determined that she and Solis, the brains behind the heist, had fled to the Netherlands in a private jet they actually rented in cold, hard cash, out of the stolen truck."

"In 2005, Tallchief surrendered to authorities and received five years, out of a maximum possible 40-year sentence, for the crime. Solis, her partner, has yet to be captured."

"Okay, now back to May of this year," Bill noted. "The armored truck that was hijacked on May 3rd, had already made stops to service ATMs at the Candlelight Wedding Chapel on Riviera Blvd; Circus Circus on the Strip; the Las Vegas Hilton on Paradise Road, and the Sahara on the Strip."

"These Armored-car companies never seem to learn from their past mistakes. When they get hit, they tighten up security procedures and the hiring processes for a year or so. Then they assume that the threat is past, and gradually let everything slip back into its original rut. Nothing tells me this happened any differently."

Shifting gears slightly, he continued. "Now on May 3rd, as I said before, the armored-car had already made five deliveries."

"But it happened to be a convention weekend. The tourists and conventioneers were spending money, excuse me for not to being PC here, but like Ira Hayes, the Medal of Honor-winning Arizona Pima Indian from World War II."

He continued, "If you follow your history, you know that the Pima's had a very profitable agricultural economy going until the U.S. Government stole their water rights. That left the tribe destitute. Ira Hayes drowned in a five-inches-of-water in a ditch on the reservation while drunk, if you are interested. They even wrote a song for Willy Nelson about him."

When I gave Billy one of my patented get-back-on-the-subject glares, he blushed, and the returned to his report.

"The point being that the ATM's all around town were being bled of cash almost as soon as the armored-car people could refill them."

"For that reason, the Loomis/Fargo depot manager had authorized the driver and his crew to upload twice as much money to keep up with demand, a lot more than company procedure normally permitted."

"The armored-car's next scheduled stop was a ten-machine location at the Las Vegas Convention Center, over on East Desert Inn Road."

Expelling a sigh as if wondering how people could be so stupid, Frisbee continued. "Well, naturally, it happened again. It took the guards about forty-five minutes to replenish all the ATM's in the Convention Center and when they came out—surprise, surprise—no truck. They immediately contacted the depot manager via cell phone, and *again* Metro and the FBI put out a *bolo* for one of its trucks and drivers."

The young agent paused his recitation to take sip of cold coffee to wet his whistle, then continued. "In less than twelve hours, the police located the missing International Armored truck behind a local bank. Of course, it was empty."

"A couple of loose twenty-dollar-bills found underneath the truck gave speculation that the money had been transferred out of it, into a large SUV—it would require a large utility vehicle with heavy-duty shocks to carry approximately three-million-dollars in twenty-dollar bills—that's a lot of weight not to mention its cubic bulk."

"Loomis/Fargo company files revealed the missing driver's name to be a Maurice Jones. When the FBI pulled his fingerprint card, they found his prints were smudged. The FBI called in the Metro police I.D. officer who had fingerprinted the man earlier in the year in for a interview, and questioned him at length."

"The feebies wanted to know why had he done such a poor job of fingerprinting the applicant. The ID officer, despite the lousy fingerprints, had gone ahead anyway and issued the applicant a Nevada State armored-car driver's license."

Frisbee shifted around in his chair trying to get comfortable before carrying on. "But, here is the back-story. Turns out, the police officer had a perfectly valid answer to the fingerprint quality question. You see, Maurice's hands had been badly-burned in the past. The scar tissue made his fingers almost impossible to print. Said it was from helping a friend out of a burning car late one night."

"Here is where it gets interesting, Boss. After fingerprinting the guy, and getting the unacceptable prints, the I.D. officer had taken the matter to his supervisor, who in-turn checked the department manual. According the department's procedure manual, the ADA, the Americans with Disabilities Act, expressly prohibits denying an individual the right to seek gainful employment for any reason caused by having a disability, if he or she is otherwise qualified for the position."

"As Jones already had a commercial driver's license and had passed his DOT physical, the examiner had no choice other than to issue the applicant the permit he was requesting. True story, Boss. Check the ADA regulations."

At this point, Special Agent Frisbee asked for a brief break to enable him to get a soft drink out of the soda machine is the office's lunchroom. "Sure thing, Billy," I said, flipping him three one-dollar bills out of my wallet and asked, "bring me a Coca-Cola Zero, will you please?"

When we resumed our discussion ten minute later, Billy took up where he had left off with his report. "Now, while the FBI had finally accepted the ID Examiner's explanation, they decided to send the original print cards off to their crime lab in Virginia, flagged with a request for immediately handling."

"A couple days later, the FBI crime lab manager called the investigating agent and informed him that they had only been able to identify two points from the prints that had been sent to them and that two points or indices unfortunately doesn't meet the bureau's minimum criteria to qualify for the print be processed through AFIS."

I'd like to take the liberty of interjecting a little about fingerprint indices and AFIS here. It will serve to enhance the reader's understanding of the process, and hopefully increase his or her reading enjoyment.

Fingerprint indices are made up of loops, deltas, ridge count, bifurcations, islands, tented arches, ulnar loops. Prints actually have three basic fingerprint patterns: Whorl, loop, and arch. Whorls are concentric circles—like target with a bull's-eye at the center, or a cross section of a onion. A loop pattern is more complicated; the ridges come in from one side, make a U-turn, and go back out the same side. In an arch pattern, the ridges come in from one side, go up in the middle, and then go out the other side.

AFIS, or the Automated Fingerprint Identification System, is supervised and under the control of the Federal Bureau Of Investigation (FBI) or the National Crime Index Center (NCIC), depending on which organization you ask.

AFIS takes less than 2-hours to process a criminal fingerprint request, and 24-hours for a civil request like a background check.

The system was upgraded and its name changed to IAFIS (Integrated Automated Fingerprint Identification System) by the FBI in 1998. But you'll find most law enforcement personnel continue to refer to the process as AFIS.

IAFIS is superior to AFIS because it compares AFIS to other databases that contain TenPrint, Palm print, Latent and Partial print databases. IAFIS was developed by the FBI's Laboratories Division, Latent Print Unit, and put into operation in June 1999, fully operational in 2002. IAFIS can search and compare up to thousands of prints daily.

Many of smaller cop shops can't afford the cost, and with the trimming of the FBI's current budget, demanded by House Speaker Nancy Petosi (DCA), has forced the bureau to reduce even further the annual number of no-charge outside agency searches to a several hundred thousand.

Before AFIS, it took one FBI agent, eight-hours, to process one hundred print cards, looking to match a single fingerprint.

IAFIS has over 50-million fingerprints sets on-file, while AFIS only has about 10 million. Besides criminals, you have prints from cops, firemen, teachers, service personnel, social workers, and other individuals whose jobs require a criminal security check.

Billy returned to his report. "The FBI lab manager said that one of his people, a former soldier in Iraq, looked at the prints and suggested he run them through the Department of Defense. This former soldier had been exposed to a lot of combat and he thought he recognized the scar tissue as being similar to the injuries that soldiers often received in Iraq when IEDs, or Improvised Explosive Devices, are used by insurgents to ambush coalition convoys.

"The FBI lab manager sent prints over to a friend of his at DoD with a request to expedite the search. In less than two days, the DoD came back with a report positively identifying the print as belonging to Maurice Jones, a U.S. Marine Staff Sergeant, whose last billet was the 2/18 Military Police Battalion. At that time, the unit had been assigned to support a coalition Forward Operating base a few miles south of Fallujah, Iraq, a town known to be a hot-bed of insurgents."

The young GCB Agent continued, "According to Maurice Jones' service record, he had been seriously-wounded when on a convoy traveling a highway that ran past Fallujah, attempting to transport a high-value prisoner to CIA intelligence headquarters in the Green zone, when it was ambushed."

"Sergeant Jones' injures resulted in him initially spending a month at the U.S. Army 28th CSH. That is a portable Combat Support Hospital that operates out of one of Saddam's old palaces near Baghdad."

"But since it is designated and funded as an emergency medical unit only, the 28th CSH is not authorized to have any beds dedicated to long-term recovery. So Jones ended up being shipped to Ramstein Air Base hospital in Germany for further recuperative care and therapy."

"At the end of three months, Ramstein's physical therapy doctor informed Sergeant Jones that they could do nothing further for him. That he was being sent home and would receive an honorable discharge under the provisions of Medical Disability."

"Jones flew into a rage and demanded that he immediately be returned to his outfit in Iraq. When the Doctor informed Jones that he was sorry but that his decision was final, the Marine nearly beat the him to death with his bare hands."

"Jones fled the hospital and attempted to hide in a nearby German village. But Military police captured him, incarcerated him, then shipped him back under armed guard to the United States for an immediate Bad-Conduct discharge."

"That is all the information that we've been able track down on the fugitive to date. Of course, Metro has a Bolo out on him, but there has been no reported sighting that we know about."

I leaned back in my chair and gave what Billy had told me, a moment's thought. So Jones had been an experienced combat soldier. And the gang that hit the Riverboat Casino in Laughlin had been judged by experienced FBI agents to be using techniques typical to that of an elite military unit.

Billy apparently had been reading my mind, because he said, "What you are thinking could be true, Boss. Maybe the gang is made up of former members of a military combat unit. But what we have come up with from the BRINKS heist really gives that theory some legs."

"Evidence that Las Vegas' FBI/ERT team came up at the BRINKS depot included DNA obtained from hemorrhage residue on the concrete floor from the wounded woman the gang took with them."

"The Feds processed it to establish its DNA sequencing markers, then ran it through CODIS. No hits. So they hot-shot forwarded it to the DoD."

"The defense department keeps DNA samples in additional to fingerprints on all military personnel. Both are used to determine identity when the body is burned beyond recognition or badly traumatized."

For the knowledge of my readers: DNA tests establish a genetic fingerprint. DNA can be extracted from body tissue such as salvia, blood, hair, skin, semen, feces and urine. Taking a sample used to require a needle stick but now can be as simple as sliding a buchal swab along the inside of the cheek to collect a person's salvia.

DNA is found in the cells of almost all living things. DNA is considered the biological equivalent of a fingerprint, because every person has a different DNA structure. In big city, major high-profile crimes, it takes an average of seventeen hours for the most-basic preliminary DNA typing, unless it is a homicide. Then the acceptable margin-of-error decreases and it can take thirty or more days.

High-priority, mitochondarial DNA analysis, like for human hair and bones, can take thirty-to-ninety days. But as a rule of thumb, prosecutors usually plan on it taking at least sixteen weeks. Even then there is no certainty that the results they come up with will be worth the paper the report is printed on.

You see, no centralized and statistically significant DNA databases exist for highly-expensive and time-consuming tests of that type. And unlike the nuclear DNA of blood and tissue, the mitochondrial DNA of hair and bones isn't going to tattle on the perpetrator's gender. Any results the lab comes up with from mitochondarial testing may never matter. That is unless the police can identify a substantive suspect and that person agrees to supply a DNA sample to permit a direct comparison to be made.

Frisbee continued his report to me. "The FBI lab did the ballistics processing of the bullets from the bodies of the gate guard and the employee that the gang leader executed in the building. The results of the GSR, gunshot residue test, that the feds did on the hands of the employee who had been shot, came back positive."

"However, there were no hits on the slugs from the dead employee and the gate guard that were extracted during autopsy, even though they both were run through NIBIN, the National Integrated Ballistics Information Network."

NIBIN is to bullets, what AFIS (the Automatic Fingerprint Identification System) is to Fingerprints, and what CODIS is to DNA profiles.

However, the Ballistics guy did say to look for a shooter with access to military ammunition. And as usual, they signed off on the report with the traditional statement, *"Bring us the gun."*

"Statements were taken from the BRINKS employees that the gang tied up and left locked in a closet while the gang made their escape. The investigators felt they seemed to more-or-less match each other, at least as much as eye witness statements usually do."

Glancing at his notes, Billy went on. "Ownership of all the fingerprints that the techs raised in the cash room, no surprises there, belong to BRINKS employees."

"All the tape from the facility's security cameras jived with what the employees told us. No results back yet from FBI's tool mark identification lab to positively identify what was used to crash through the main gate. But everyone is pretty certain it was the Dodge Power Wagon."

"Last but not least," Frisbee said, "the DoD has come back with a tentative identification, obtained from DNA, that could identify the female employee who was shot. They won't put it into a written report yet, but they told both FBI Special Agent Gardner and myself that the woman was U.S. Marine Major, Mary Levinson. In 2006, her billet was the 2/18 Military Police Battalion Major attached to the Coalition's Forward Operating Base outside Fallujah."

"Major Levinson, coincidentally, was seriously wounded in the same convoy as U.S.M.C. Staff Sergeant Maurice Jones, when radical insurgents ambushed it with IEDs on September 10, 2006."

"As for the Dodge Power wagon that was used in the June 15th heist at BRINKS, the State of Nevada DMV reports that it had been reported as *parted out* more than a month before the robbery. The license plates found on the burned-out truck had been lifted off a truck of the same type and model from a Bullhead City junkyard in Arizona about that same time. Forensic hasn't been able to yet raise any prints from off the Power Wagon."

"Boss,' Billy continued, "moving on to the abandoned warehouse out at the speedway that you and Special Agent Dupont searched. The only thing that is proving probative from that location are the fingerprints that the FBI techs managed to raise off the MRE cartons that Senior Investigator DuPont recovered from under the furnace."

"Again AFIS and NCIC came up with nothing, but the owner of the prints did have had a drunk-driving arrest *under an alias* in New York State a couple of years ago. So again, on a hunch, the prints were couriered over to the Defense Department."

The young agent reminded me, "Those guys at DoD have been very helpful running these folks down for us. When you get a minute, perhaps you could drop a written 'Atta Boy' to the Commanding General over there."

I interrupted, "Will do, Billy. Now what did DoD find out about the print on the MRE that I know you are dying to tell me about?"

His face blushing once again, Billy spit it out. "Boss, the prints belong to Staff Sergeant Maurice Jones. They match the prints to the driver of the armored-car servicing ATMs that took the armored-car and vanished on May 3, 2008."

That was what I had been afraid of. All the information from the Laughlin robbery on April 10th, to the ATM truck hijacking on May 3rd, and now to the perpetrators of the BRINKS job only eight days ago, pointed to the fact that a military-trained unit had declared war on Las Vegas.

And it was my job to solve the crimes and arrest the gang members. This not being Hong Kong, we didn't have the option of finding some alternate method by which the people could be rendered to be no longer part of the problem.

I thought. *Why hadn't I steered clear of politics and remained in Hong Kong? At least there, the Chinese Peoples Liberation Army made certain that their former soldiers didn't use their military acumen to commit crimes that would embarrass the government.*

"Okay, Billy, let me take the night to think about how we are going to handle this. Get an all-states bolo out on Sergeant Maurice Jones. And tell the Defense Department that by noon tomorrow, I want all the personnel files on my desk covering anyone and everyone that survived the ambushed convoy outside Fallujah in 2006, or hung around with any of the major participants in the operation. Got it?"

Billy nodded and began to gather his notes together to return to his cubicle, before I remembered the two abandoned vans.

"Okay, you had something to tell me about what the technicians found in the two vans that the FBI suspects were used in the Brinks robbery. What was it?"

He paused before leaving the room and stammered, "Sorry Boss. And I also forgot to tell you what was found out in the desert yesterday. But as they drummed into us at the POST, Police Officer Standards and Training Academy, first things first."

"It isn't exactly small potatoes, but two sets of fingerprints and one sample of dried blood was found inside the cargo boxes of both vans."

Billy continued, "Two partial sets of fingerprints were in the rear cargo boxes of both vans, one of them also appeared on the van's rear door handles. One set of belonged to the speedway's rent-a-cop who originally reported finding the two vans to the Metro dispatcher. In his written statement that he wrote out for the responding Metro officers, he claimed he never left his vehicle."

"So this past Saturday, the FBI picked him up and brought him to their office to offer him an opportunity to clarify his statement. Eventually, the retired Metro cop admitted that because times were tight, and he had in fact left his patrol car and approached the vans. He'd even admitted that he had crawled into their cargo boxes, hoping to find some clue that could get his name in the paper and make his famous, if only for a day," Frisbee said.

"The security guard then admitted to agents that if he had found something of value, he would have taken it. He explained that the reason he would taken it was that times are tough for an old retired cop living on a pension, when he is unable to afford the medicine for his terminally-ill wife."

"She apparently needs some very expensive pain medication to ease her final days, at least according to her doctor. Anyway, to prove once again that no good deed goes unpunished, as soon as the guard admitted to lying, the agents notified his boss. Who subsequently fired the old man without any severance pay."

Frisbee took a deep breath before continuing, "The other partial print we are pretty certain belongs to the woman who was shot during the BRINKS dustup. The techs also recovered a sample of dried blood off the floor of one of the abandoned vans. Even though no body was found in the van, the forensic techs think it could belong to the woman."

"Boss, that assumption became even more plausible on Saturday, when a buried body was found in the desert, northwest of town. The victim's hands and head had been removed and taken with, obviously to prevent easy identification of the body. The corpse had evidence of a gunshot wound in the left groin areas similar to that suffered by the woman who was shot by a co-worker during the BRINKS job."

Billy went on, "The Clark County coroner asked the FBI to bring in one of the male employees from the robbery to view the body. They also asked him whether the wound in the corpse was generally in the same area as the woman who had been shot during the theft. The witness was able to concur that it was."

"The corpse was of the same general coloring, sex, height and weight as the woman from the BRINKS scene. Whoever buried her had attempted to excise a small tattoo off the dead woman's breast. Again we think it was to further delay identification of the body, rather than intentional desecration of the body."

"One of the woman's female coworkers claimed to have seen the tattoo in the locker room one day when they both had been changing from their uniforms into street clothes. The woman employee said she'd seen the tattoo on her co-worker's breast, explaining that the woman had been proud of her figure and never wore a bra on-duty."

"Preliminary indications are that the dead body discovered in Red Rock canyon on Saturday belongs to Marine Major Mary Levinson," Billy Frisbee concluded, with a deep sigh.

I took a minute to absorb everything Billy had just reported to me. It was obvious that this was an organized gang of ex-Marines working hand-in-hand with some other military-trained malcontents to take their frustration out on Las Vegas, while fattening their retirement portfolios at the same time.

These renegade Marines had to be rolled up. And law enforcement arm of Nevada's Gaming Control Board didn't have the manpower or the training to be able to accomplish that. We are a small, lean and mean organization, and as such are incapable of heading up an assault on a highly-trained ex-military rogue combat unit.

FBI analysts who had compared the Laughlin, Armored Car, and BRINKS jobs, told us that taking into consideration the planning, execution, back-up, Logistics, financial needs, and communications, it appeared there were no less than eight, nor more twelve specialists in the gang.

These combatants had to come from somewhere and I damn well was to going to find out where. The Department of Defense was our only source of that information. A State Agency like the GCB didn't have the weight to get the DoD off their butts.

But the Homeland Security Office in Washington D.C. certainly did. I grabbed a yellow legal pad and jotted down the names of the ex-Marines we had come across so far in our investigation—Major Mary Levinson, USMCR, and Staff Sergeant Maurice Jones, USMC.

To that list, I added the military unit designator we learned those two individuals had been assigned to in September of 2006—the USMC 2/18th Military Police Battalion stationed at the Coalition Forward Operating Base, the FBO, outside Fallujah, Iraq.

To reduce the extent of the file search task the DoD would have to process in order to provide us the information we needed, I added the known fact that on September 10, 2006, both of these Marines had been assigned to a sling-shot convoy that had been ambushed in Iraq's An-Bar province.

The convoy routing, according to our local intelligence, formed up at the coalition's FBO. It had proceeded roughly northbound, its intended destination being the CIA intelligence section located in the Green zone in Baghdad. Their convoy's mission had been to safely transport a single high-level Iraq insurgent to the agency so he could be interrogated, and the location that the kidnapped Blackwater contractors were being held obtained so that they could be rescued by a extraction team that was on 15-minute recall, standing by.

The convoy commander, a decorated Marine light-colonel named Jeffrey Johnson, apparently decided to disregard his boss's recommendation that the convoy hook-up with heavy firepower, namely Abrams tanks, that higher-authority felt would be necessary to provide enough fire support to protect the convoy along its planned route.

The Lt. Colonel, an respected officer but who was also known to be an renegade egotist, had the reputation of looking at orders from his superiors as mere suggestions, had opted instead to slim down the convoy and make a run for it. He elected to use the slingshot convoy concept developed decades before, when Americans had to run supply and munitions replenishment convoys on the most dangerous highway in Vietnam, the north-south running Highway One.

Politically, the convoy commander had placed himself at-risk of being censured for making that decision. Should the Lt. Colonel fail to get their prisoner to the CIA, he likely would be courts-martialed by the U.S. Marine Corps for not following orders.

Feeling that I had given the DoD plenty to work with, I placed a call to Homeland Security and got them to order the DoD to pull all personnel files. The file was to include fingerprints, DNA markers, and photographs of the Marines that had been part of the failed convoy mission. Particularly anyone who had subsequently been disciplined because the insurgents had ambushed the slimmed-down convoy and assassinated the prisoner to prevent him from telling the CIA anything when he was certain to be subjected to the interrogation technique called *waterboarding*.

To secure the Homeland Security's complete cooperation, I was only forced to invoke the names of *two* high-ranking FBI administrators, known for being on a crusade to get the President to downsize the new upstart agency.

The suddenly enthusiastic HLS officer assured me that not only would he commit that the DoD would provide all the information I was requesting, but he would also arrange to have it flown by military C-20 executive jet from the military records depository, direct to McCarran. The agents of the DIA, the Defenses Intelligence Agency, would ensure that all the data reached my desk no later that 9:00 a.m. the following morning. *Absolutely, positively overnight, right?*

We were getting closer to a confrontation with this dangerous unit of former Marines, all hardened by combat. Someone was going to end up dead when we came together for a final accounting. And the GCB wasn't going to be able to take on that on alone.

I must have had a premonition when I prayed that the confrontation wouldn't be at the cost of the lives of any of my people.

EIGHTEEN

June 24, 2008, Tuesday, 9:00 a.m.
Regional Gaming Control Board Office
555 E. Washington Blvd
Las Vegas, Nevada

When I arrived at the office at 9:00 a.m. on Tuesday, I first checked my office and found there were no files sitting there awaiting my perusal as promised me last night by the bureaucrat from Homeland Security.

I'm certain that my blood pressure was beginning to skyrocket, flushing my face to a bright shade of red, when I thought of one more place to check before I had a coronary. That was Agent Billy Frisbee's cubicle.

I removed my suit jacket and tossed it towards the coat rack—missed again—picked it up again, again hung it on the coat rack, before fast-walking down the hallway to Billy's domain. Peering over the wall of his cube, I saw the young agent had one of the DoD personnel files on the desk in front of him, with about nine more neatly stacked to his right on his small government issue gray metal desk. Dozens more lay discarded on the carpet.

Billy looked haggard. I wondered what time he had gotten to the office this morning. Well before me, that was obvious. His office attire for today consisted of a UNLV basketball sweat suit and a pair of grubby old athletic shoes that he wore without socks.

Billy looked up at me though his red eyes after he noticed that the personnel files that adorned the floor of his cube caught my attention.

He said, "Dead, all dead." Which I assume he meant that the Marines whose personnel files now graced his floor, had died since 2006, and therefore weren't viable candidates for the gang of ex-Marines who were raining hell down on Las Vegas. Causing pressure to be put on me, Billy, the GCB, and whoever else was a victim of the reality of Shit-Running-Downhill.

"What time did you get to work this morning, Billy," I asked?

Billy rubbed his eyes before answering, "I was having a wonderful dream about being on a deserted island with Ann Curry who does the news on NBC's *Today Show*. That is until the *probie* agent who had the duty last night at the front desk here, called me at home about 4:00 a.m."

"He seemed to be all shook up." Frisbee said. "Claimed that two *suits*, backup by a couple of Air Policemen with M4 carbines, were demanding that he open the office's front door which is kept locked after-hours."

Continuing, Billy explained. "The kid said the two suits were pulling a flight attendant's two-wheeled cart overloaded with military personnel files. On top of the case were stacks of brown paper personnel files. From his vantage point, the probie said he could see the top one had military characters stamped all over it."

"When I woke up enough to get my feet on the floor," Frisbee said, "I thought about what I would do in the same situation. I decided to tell the kid to check the emergency procedures manual and do what it told him."

"Long story short, Boss, is that the kid ended up calling Metro and asked them to send a two-man car around to the office to check the dudes out."

"While the kid waited for the cops to arrive to check out the guys, I threw on some clothes, left my apartment, and ran the mustang Code Three down to the office in case the kid was drunk or was being scammed."

"By the time I rolled into the parking lot here, the cops had relieved the airmen of their weapons, shook the suits down, who also were found to be carrying weapons, and put everybody on their faces in front of the elevator."

"The kid wasn't of much use for anything about then. He had convinced himself that some rogue military unit was attempting to force their way into our office and kidnap him for interrogation."

Sighing, he continued. "I checked all the guys ID's. The suits were two very pissed-off DIA agents. Homeland Security had dispatched them and the armed airmen from Nellis AFB to McCarran to meet the early morning arriving DoD jet carrying the personnel files you requested."

"By the time the armed escort left grumbling, freeing up the cops to return to patrol, it was nearly 6:00 a.m. So I decided to stick around and get a head-start on vetting the DoD personnel files before you arrived this morning."

Pointing at the files littering the floor, Billy continued, "Last time I looked, you can't arrest someone who is already dead. Except in Las Angeles where it is procedure."

Author's note: By coincidence, I happened to know claim is true concerning the LAPD's archaic crime scene procedures.

"Billy, grab yourself a cup of Joe." I said. "I'll carry the files of living people down to my office and we'll go from there."

By 11:00 a.m., we had narrowed our selection to what we called the *basic six*. Plus another six who hadn't been in the same outfit, or been serving in Iraq in 2006, or at the same FOB, but they could be Marines that had received Bad Conduct or Dishonorable discharges and although now civilians, could have decided to throw their lot in with that of the basic six.

Because of the their lousy Discharges and DD-214's, they no doubt were pissed-off at the U.S. military, and likely would have been ripe candidates for the gang, if the basic six managed to convince them that they could make some quick money by tying their wagon to the hijack gang.

Each of the basic six had been assigned to the Fallujah FBO in September of 2006. Each of them had been on the slingshot convoy that got ambushed. They all were members of the USMC 2/18th Military Police Battalion. And all six had been mustered out of the service for various disciplinary reasons, within six-months of their company commander being courts-martialed for not following orders.

The first two Marines we identified, were a no-brainer. Major Mary Levinson, now deceased, and Sergeant Maurice Jones, currently wanted and in the wind for both the May 3, 2008, armored car hijacking and for being a confirmed participant in the June 15th, 2008, BRINKS robbery.

The next three were known to be tight with convoy's commander, Lt. Colonel Jeffrey Johnson. Staff Sergeant Leigh Copperfled; Staff Sergeant David Shapiro, and staff Sergeant Robert Jackson.

Since we had already made the previous identifications, the last of the six wasn't much of a surprise to Frisbee and myself. Lt. Colonel Jeffrey "Kick Ass" Johnson was a highly-decorated, if contentious, combat officer.

Everything but one item in his personnel file pointed to the fact that higher-authority had intended to promote Johnson early, on the basis of merit, to bull-colonel at the time of the convoy incident.

That one negative item in his personnel file that could explain his motivation to throw away a promising military career to turn to a life of crime, was a copy of an unendorsed draft citation. It recommended that Lt. Colonel Johnson be awarded the Navy Cross for courage above and beyond the call of duty.

Draft:

The President of the United States takes pride in presenting the NAVY CROSS to:

Lt. Colonel Jeffrey Johnson
United States Marine Corps
For service as set forth in the following:

CITATION

For extraordinary heroism on 10 September 2006 while Commander of the 2/18 Military Police Battalion, in connection with combat operations against enemy forces in An Bar Province in the Republic of Iraq. After leading his Marines on a mission to deliver a high-ranking insurgent leader to CIA intelligence officers though a high-risk area known to be populated by radical Muslim insurgents, he commanded a slingshot convoy that was ambushed through use of Improvised Explosive Devices planted by insurgents. Lt. Colonel led his unit through concentrated enemy mortar and automatic weapons fire. Ten of his men were wounded or killed by hostile machine guns. With enemy soldiers firing directly at him, he first threw three grenades into the on-coming enemy, and then returned along the blazing line that was all that was left of his destroyed convoy of vehicles. At great personal risk to himself, Lt. Colonel Johnson continued to administer first-aid to his men until a rapid response force from the coalition's forward operating base could be summoned to suppress the enemy and permit emergency medical personnel to land and treat the wounded.

However before a coalition rapid response team arrived on-site, fire from another enemy position pinned him down. Then an enemy grenade landed near he and his fallen men. Lt. Colonel Johnson kicked the grenade aside and threw himself between it and the casualties to protect them from the explosion. Still under fire, and even though fragments from the grenade had caused a painful wound to his left leg, he rallied his Marines, grabbed the radio from his critically wounded radio operator, and restored communications. After radioing his unit's location, he used his hands and a small machete to slash a path through the brush to establish a helicopter landing zone. Then, he returned to the casualties and carried three of his men, one after another, back to the LZ for evacuation by air. He continued to direct the operation until his own blood loss made it impossible for him to continue and he was also evacuated to a medical facility. By his indomitable courage, determined fighting spirit, and selfless devotion to duty, Lt. Colonel Johnson was directly instrumental in saving the lives of several of his fellow Marines, thereby upholding the highest traditions of the Marine Corps and the United States Naval Force.

For the President
The Secretary of the Navy

Well, I could see that higher-ups certainly had made Colonel Johnson pay for not following orders. Their refusal to endorse the citation effectively killed it. I could see how a proud Marine like Johnson would of taken the rejection personally, and forced by his pride to resign his commission. That was the end of his meritorious career.

Billy and I used PhotoShop to copy the file photos all the twelve Marines. We copied their fingerprints and enough of the DD-214 in the personnel files, to give the various law enforcement agencies a well-rounded background of the individuals for use in justifying the bolos that would be issued this afternoon.

As time was of the essence, our front desk called and requested that the security chiefs of all the Las Vegas casinos to send a runner over to GCB to pick up the packet we had prepared for them. They would use the photos and fingerprint records to begin combing the work cards photos they kept on-file for all their gaming employees. Nevada law is very strict that employees working in gaming must have an official State gaming work card in their possession at all times. After all, those individuals were employed in Nevada's largest tax revenue producing industry.

What the general public didn't know was that the larger casinos would take that one step further. Modern casinos are equipped with no less than 500 security cameras. The public calls it Eyes-in-the-Sky; professional security and surveillance managers who work in the high-stakes world of gaming, refer to it as Facile Identification Technology.

Larger casinos use anthropometric comparison, or AC, to identify any person who attempts to access their gaming floor after being previously banned and listed in the Nevada GCB Black Book. Supposedly, the technology was so good that it even could catch someone using a disguise.

AC is a technique by which the computer compares images metrically, one of a known subject from the Black Book, or in this case, the photos we were providing them, and any other individual that appears on-camera. A computer takes measurements between the individual's anatomical landmarks, ratios are calculated, and the computer's statistical program determines whether the individual's image that has been captured on tape, and the banned individual, are the same person.

That technology can also be bastardized (this ability is a closely-guarded secret that casinos and law enforcement keep from the general public) to seek out a known individual who is a fugitive and being sought by authorities. We hope the latter use would be employed by the casinos to assist us in identifying the rogue Marines. And that the casinos would subsequently give GCB and the FBI a headsup, if the individuals were seen in and around the City of Las Vegas.

While the casinos did their thing, Billy took copies of the Marine's personnel files over to Metro Police headquarters and requested their assistance in issuing bolos on each of the suspect individuals.

I took an identical pile of files and drove down the street to see FBI Special Agent Steffy Gardner who was heading up the local FBI's response to the crime spree.

If my past experience working with local offices of the FBI was a rule to go by, I knew that Gardner would feign any interest in the priceless gift I was bringing her. However, I've always been a guy who believes that more crooks get caught when law enforcement works as a team to achieve common goals.

Now I know that your relatives or friends who work in law enforcement will be quick inform you that my having even the smallest positive expectation relative to my dealings with the egocentric FBI, will question whether I wear rose-colored glasses and live in the world of OZ.

Admittedly, some are known to crudely claim that when it comes to sharing information on an open case with the FBI, the FBI eats like an elephant but shits like a mouse.

June 24, 2008, Tuesday, 9:00 a.m.
The search continues
Las Vegas, Nevada

Yesterday, we had dialed-in the security chiefs in those casinos whose play volume put them at the highest risk of attracting the gang's attention.

The cops were doing their part, issuing bolos for the remaining eleven Marines we had identified. In an unusual move for Metro, the powers-that-be in the Ivory Tower at the department's 400 Steward Street headquarters, decided to bite-the-bullet. They decided that the threat from the hijack gang was such that it necessitated canceling the planned vacations of over one-hundred of their officers. The freed-up officers would be assigned as a ride-along officer in police cars that normally are manned by a single patrolperson. The police brass told Union president that their move was a protection-of-the-force issue, and therefore nonnegotiable.

The local FBI office followed suit. They also cancelled some vacations and ordered that the agents lean on all the confidential informants, or CI's, they had in their snitch stables.

The case team leader, Supervising Special Agent Gardner, also requested that FBI Headquarters in Washington D.C. loan a dozen more agents to her taskforce. It was my understanding that her temporarily-assigned agents would be on-the-ground in Las Vegas by mid-afternoon, today.

Gardner had also decided to not stonewall the Media. Which I thought was a prudent decision. Considering the fact that I was certain their crime beat reporters had already gotten wind of the unusual issuance of eleven bolos. The Media probably knew all about it, even before the word flowed down the police department grapevine.

Before I left the office that day, I sent Maggie DuPont an email giving her a status update on the hijacking gang case on which she had been the initial investigator. We hadn't been in touch by phone or email since Maggie had been ordered to return to Carson City, and work on her own caseload.

It seemed odd to me at the time that Maggie hadn't at least called, but then I assumed the powers-that-be were keeping her nose to the proverbial grindstone.

During the next ten days, or through coming Friday, on which July 4th happened to fall on this year, Media interest and police pressure was producing results, some good, others bad.

On the good side of the equation, on Wednesday, June 25, 2008, one of the security guards at the Bellagio Casino and Hotel phoned the FBI's hot line to report that he had gotten his regular haircut last week at the barbershop located in the Bellagio mall.

What made that notable was that the military-type wearing a buzz cut that had cut his hair was, in the security guard's opinion, either one of our fugitives or an exact twin of him.

On a separate line, a FBI agent had called the unlisted cell phone line of the Bellagio security chief to inquire into the employment background of the guard they had holding on the other line.

The chief testily assured the agent that the security guard was a retired Navy Chief and not given to making things up. To lend more credence to what the guard was reporting, the security chief followed up by informing the agent that once the guard had told him his story, he'd left his office and walked with the reporting guard down to the hotel's barber shop.

When they two men walked into the hotel's barbershop, the guard told his boss that the barber they wanted wasn't at his assigned chair in the shop. When they asked the shop manager where the man had gone, she reported that the man had reported for work as scheduled that morning.

Then, having no customers waiting, the man had sat down in his chair to read the morning papers. But when he saw the first page, above-the-fold, story the *Las Vegas Review-Journal* ran about the dragnet, the man bolted from his chair, told the manager that he was ill and had to go home, and fast-walked from the shop.

The shop manager thought the barber's actions had be a little unusual but reconciled her concern with the fact that he was just a piece-work casual employee, not one of her regular staff.

As background, the woman explained to the hotel's security chief that casual barbers for-hire in Las Vegas were a dime-a-dozen. They got paid in cash at the end of every shift so the man they were interested in didn't leave being owed any wages.

The security chief waited while the guard walked back to their office to retrieve the photos of the eleven wanted Marines that his office had received from the GCB.

When the guard returned he was bearing two *six-packs,* which he laid out on the shop's blue Formica counter.

Six-pack is the term cops use when they arrange six photos of individuals on a single piece of white hardboard. The intent is to present the photos in a non-biased manner to prevent witnesses from making their identification from a single photo. The other faces could well be those of cops that had been available when the six-pack was prepared.

Almost immediately the shop manager printed out one of the men and without any hesitation, said, "That's your guy."

The casino security chief stayed behind to take a statement from the shop manager as the guard returned to the main security office to a call in his tip into the FBI hotline.

The security chief had no expectations that the missing barber had used his correct name, had given the shop manager his real social security number, or even his actual home address and phone number.

Therefore the man in-charge of the Bellagio's security department wasn't disappointed to find out that the barber that was now in the wind had made up every bit of information he either had given his boss, or shared with his co-workers, during his brief two-week stint of employment in the shop.

What the Security Chief came away from the hotel's barber shop knowing is that the man the shop manager had picked out without hesitation, was none other than Staff Sergeant Leigh Copperfeld, U. S. Marine Corps-Retired.

June 26, 2008, Thursday, 11:15 a.m.
The FOOD-4-Less Market
North Las Vegas, Nevada

Another stroke of luck for the taskforce came on Thursday, June 26, 2008. About 11:15 a.m., a woman called the FBI hotline to report that she was currently shopping her weekly grocery list at FOOD-4 LESS Market in North Las Vegas.

The shopper said she had been going about her business when two men, recklessly pushing grocery carts, nearly ran over her to get to the Canned Food aisle. She told the hotline operator that they looked like military guys, short hair, white sidewalls, shined boots, starched and ironed clothing—the works.

She said that she almost had decided to ignore the slight because North Las Vegas is a high-crime area. Its residents therefore tend to look the other way when little confrontations like what had just happened her, occur.

But then the shopper noticed that when the two men would bend over to retrieve a case of canned food off the bottom shelf, the shirts they were wearing outside their trousers would hike up, revealing the butts of handguns.

As she thought over what she had just seen, she suddenly remembered that the headlines in yesterday's newspaper had reported a dragnet by cops and federal agents looking for a gang of rogue Marines that had been robbing, hijacking, and even killing citizens, in the vicinity of Las Vegas.

She had abandoned her cart and went into the store's ladies room. She got out her cell out of her purse and dialed 911. She was transferred to the North Las Vegas police dispatcher to whom she told her story, describing the two men, their suspicious mannerisms, explained where the grocery store was located, and about the handguns.

The dispatcher had to go off-line for about five seconds to dispatch two sectors cars to the location. Then he came back on the line and instructed the woman to lock herself inside the ladies room and not come out until the cops arrived. Once they determined what the situation was, they would knock on the door, identify themselves, and tell her that it was okay for her to come out. Because the woman sounded terrified, the Police dispatcher made the decision to stay on the phone with her until the threat was past.

In the meantime the two men had filled their carts with cases of canned goods and had checked-out without incident. They'd pushed their carts out through the store's automatic doors and out into the busy parking lot towards a Ford gray van that had seen better days.

Unknown to the men, two North Las Vegas 2-man black-and-white police cars had taken up blocking positions in the parking lot, using other parked cars to conceal their presence.

One of the men had unlocked the rear door to the van as the other began to pass the cases to him to place inside. They emptied both carts and then shoved the carts off into the lot where they had collided with the cars of other shoppers.

As the two men opened the doors of the van to get in, they were confronted by four armed police officers, two on either side of their vehicle.

The cops first identified themselves. Then they told the men to get their hands in the air, lie down on their faces, cross their legs, and not to move a freaking inch thereafter.

The men had looked across the van's front seat at one another then went for their weapons.

In summary, once the men went for their guns, the cops separated themselves slightly to avoid any possibility of being shot by friendly crossfire, and then pumped bullet after bullet into the men as they seemed to dance like a martinet puppets when the cop's bullets found their marks.

Soon after, a search of the bodies of the men revealed they were carrying several thousand dollars each in cash. But no pocket trash or identification.

The van had been stolen from a parking lot out near the Las Vegas Speedway after 9:00 a.m. that morning. Probably the vehicle's owner worked the day shift and hadn't yet discovered that his van was missing.

Fingerprints and photos from their military service records would later identify one of the men as Staff Sergeant David Shapiro. The other was one the potential malcontents the DoD had reported as being known to keep the company of the Marines we had already put a name to.

June 28, 2008, Saturday, 9:30 a.m.
Northeast Area Command
Las Vegas, Nevada

A third incident tied to the dragnet for the gang occurred on Saturday morning, June 28th, in Las Vegas' Northeast Area Command, which is known to cops and citizens alike as the *Big Dogs*.

Two cops, Corporal Bethany Jones, Senior Training Officer, and her rookie, Probationary Patrol trainee, Linda La'Sard, were on-patrol in their marked patrol car, designated Six-Adam-Fourteen.

Both officers had been out late the previous night celebrating the recent award that Las Vegas Mayor Oscar Goodman had bestowed on them for providing emergency assistance to an elderly citizen. The citizen had the misfortune to have been bitten by a venomous rattlesnake, and they had transported him to a hospital and he was expected to live.

Both the women had hangovers and were regularly making stops at coffee kiosks to get their caffeine quotient boosted.

It was at one of their periodic survival stops for a fresh injection of caffeine that the rookie office, La'Sard, observed a late-model, green Chevy sedan with two, white middle-age males in the front seat commit a serious traffic violation. The car had blown through a red stoplight and almost collided with a responding ambulance, running Code Three.

Anytime a couple of white guys choose to disrespect a couple of hungover female cops of color, they are just asking for trouble. Their actions might even be considered by some to be self-destructive.

Both the cops chugged down their lattes and tossed their empty cups into the back seat. Corporal Jones stomped down on the Crown Victoria's accelerator sending the car fishtailing out of the parking lot and onto the tail of the green Chevy.

As Jones concentrated on her driving, La'Sard pulled out her ticket book and started adding up all the citations these white boys were going to receive for interrupting the two cop's coffee break.

Once Corporal Jones had managed to pull her marked cruiser up on the bumper of the speeding car, the rookie flipped on the patrol car's emergency roof lights as Jones activated the siren.

Apparently amused by the patrol car on their ass, that was now using its external speaker to direct the driver of the Chevy to pull over to the shoulder, he showed his disrespect for the two cops once again by sticking his arm out the window and giving them the finger.

This only made the two hungover women all the more intent on stopping the fleeing car, and transporting its sorry-ass occupants to jail. When the chevy didn't make any indication that it was stopping, La'Sard activated the MDT laptop computer attached to the dash and electronically transmitted the car's license number to dispatch inquiring as to whether the chevy had been was reported stolen.

It really invigorated the two cops when their inquiry came back promptly and the message was displayed on the MST's eight-inch monitor, informing them that the car had been reported stolen after being taken without the owner's permission off a used car lot in North Las Vegas, two days before. Now the cop's adrenaline was really beginning to flow.

La'Sard again queried the MDT requesting immediate backup to assist them in safely taking the two fleeing subjects into custody. The dispatcher would decide which currently unassigned patrol unit was closest to assist Six-Adam-Fourteen, and dispatched that unit to assist the primary in terminating the pursuit.

In less than three minutes, a back-up unit, coincidentally assigned to two other female officers, pulled up on the primary unit's rear bumper.

The senior officer in the backup unit radioed the senior officer in Six-Adam-Fourteen, asking for instructions.

Jones in the meantime had already come to the conclusion that the two mutts fleeing in the stolen car didn't have any intention of stopping. What increased the severity of the situation exponentially was that the chevy was drawing the chase into the downtown area of Las Vegas, an area heavily-populated by tourists out for a morning stroll and window shopping.

Jones told La'Sard to message the dispatcher explaining that the situation was getting more critical by the second. Officer La'Sard followed her electronic transmission with a request for approval to use a PIT maneuver, or Pursuit Interruption Technique, to stop the fleeing chevy before it plowed into a crowed sidewalk and killed innocent civilians.

To the two cops in the primary unit, it probably seemed like the patrol sergeant took an hour to respond to her request. But, actually, in less than ten seconds, the magic approval appeared on their MDT monitor.

Magic, because such a request was rarely granted and even less frequently was it authorized in a pursuit by a couple of relatively low-time patrol cops.

Jones took a deep breath then used her personal communicator to inform the senior officer in the backup car behind them what she intended to so.

After the backup unit acknowledged Jones' transmission, the officers in both units yanked their seatbelts and shoulder harnesses even tighter. Then, just as the primary black-and-white passed by the Elks Lodge at

902 Owen Avenue, near Martin Luther King Blvd, Jones began to ease the Crown Victoria up alongside the rear bumper of the fleeing Chevy.

When their patrol unit had pulled up until its front bumper was even with the Chevrolet's rear bumper, Jones yelled, "Hold, on Linda!" as she violently twisted the steering wheel briefly to the left, causing their patrol car's front bumper to impact the right corner of the Chevy's rear bumper.

As soon as the car's bumpers made contact, Jones yanked the steering wheel back to the right and began to fight the skid that she'd been taught in the academy to expect. The Crown Victoria fishtailed down the street seemingly for hours until it came to a shuttering stop against the right curb, brakes and radiator smoking.

The driver of the fleeing Chevy obviously had not been trained how to respond to the PIT maneuver. He over-corrected one direction, then back to the other, until the sedan just flipped, came down on its roof, and in that position, and in a shower of sparks, slid down the avenue until the hulk finally came to a stop. Smoke bellowed from the Chevy's engine compartment and flames began to shoot out from underneath the wrecked vehicle.

Gasoline from the Chevy's gas tank immediate began to pool on the ground under the overturned top of the vehicle.

Jones first checked her partner and found La'Sard be dazed but okay. The rookie, however, had suffered a small cut over her left eye. As with most facial lacerations, even though it was a very minor injury, it was beginning hemorrhage profusely.

Jones hopped out of the car, as did the other two cops out of the backup unit. All knew that their responsibility now to rescue the two men from their burning car before its gas tank exploded.

Regrettably, continuing to maintain their vigilance against an attack by others as they all had been constantly lectured about at the Academy couldn't have been further from the cop's minds. Thinking as one, they *assumed* that their primary responsibility was to do whatever it took to get the men out of the burning car.

Because of that inattention to the lessons they had been taught, all of the women were unprepared when the two men somehow managed escape the inferno by kicking out the windshield of the car. And they came out shooting.

As ex-Marines, the two shooters knew their weapons. They had rolled out of the void that the missing windshield had created with blazing

M4s, Colt's controversial shorter, lighter, replacement for the M16A assault rifle.

The expert marksmen's headshots took out the cops who never even managed to pull their service pistols from their holsters.

Then, realizing the Chevy was going no longer of any use to them in making their getaway, the Marines limped across the street to the police primary chase unit that was still parked against the far curb, its engine ticking over and radiator steaming.

But, unknown to the adrenaline-driven mutts, Probationary Officer Linda La'Sard, who Jones had elected to leave in their slightly-damaged patrol car while she assisted the other cops in rescuing the two men that they all had assumed were trapped in the wreckage of the burning Chevy, had gathered her wits and bit her tongue to control her fear when she saw her partner and the other officers shot down without warning like rabid dogs.

Because Corporal Jones always preferred to start their patrol with the prisoner restraint cage down, Officer La'Sard was able to crawl into the patrol car's backseat when she saw the two men from the Chevy hobbling over to her vehicle. She could only assume that the men intended to finish the job of killing all the cops on the scene, and hijacking her vehicle.

As the killers yanked open the front doors of still-idling patrol car, and jumped into the front seat, Officer La'Sard calmly shot them both in the back of their skulls, which totally obscured the inside of the car's front windshield with blood and gray brain matter.

―――

When Metro supervisors arrived on-scene, they found the three dead cops who had died where they had fallen, a pair of nearly headless former Marines, and a female cop, who, although she had emptied every bullet in her weapon into the two killers, her eyes still burned bright with the fire of hatred.

When members of the FBI taskforce arrived at the scene, they brought with them copies of the photos and dental work x-rays from personnel files that the Department of Defense had provided. That permitted the agents to identify the dead men as former Marines Staff Sergeant Maurice Jones and Staff Sergeant Robert Jackson.

―――

When I leaned of the terrible incident that Saturday afternoon, I'd placed a call to Maggie's condo in Carson City figuring she'd better hear about the cop killings from me before she heard it from the Media.

However, and unusual I thought for a Saturday, there was no answer. Her answering machine informed me she was out and to leave a message.

Feeling it to be totally inadequate to describe to an answering machine what had just happened, ending the lives of three brave police officers, I hung up without leaving a message.

NINETEEN

July 4, 2008, Friday, 11:15 p.m.
The Bellagio Casino and Hotel
3600 Las Vegas Blvd S., Center Strip
Las Vegas, Nevada

It was a gala Friday evening at the Bellagio Casino and Hotel. The hotel was fully-booked for the entire July 4th, 2008 weekend. Most of the hotel's guests had checked in earlier in the week to ensure they had a room over the busy 3-day weekend. Over-booking is not an unknown practice in Las Vegas.

Another drawing card for the holiday weekend was at the Bellagio *Bank*, a lounge-cum-showroom, which was featuring *Dancing With The Stars*, with the show's stars Kristi Yamaguchi, Mark Ballas and Derek Hough, the last two who were celebrating their birthdays that weekend.

The early check-in was especially necessary for those families with children, because no one under 18 is allowed on the Bellagio property unless they are staying at the hotel. In fact, few of the hotel amenities are geared towards kids.

But people of all ages from around the World had come to the Bellagio to see tonight's extra-special fountain show.

The $40 million dollar, 8.5-acre, man-made Bellagio Lake has 1,000 fountains and a total of 1,214 water emitters. Some of them can spout water several-hundred-feet in the air.

A total of 5,000 surface lights compliment the fountain performance, which is choreographed to music. However, tonight, the Hotel's famous annual July 4th fireworks show will also be choreographed into the performance.

The fountain show requires a staff of 37 who work behind the scenes, seven days a week, 365 days a year. Normally a performance is scheduled every 30 minutes between 3 and 7 p.m., and every 15 minutes until midnight on weekend evenings.

To maintain the fountains, the crew works with several different types of blasters, compressors, purification equipment and a fog system said to be so intense it could literally blanket Las Vegas Boulevard and turn Paris (the hotel across the street) into London, in less than five minutes.

Scott O'Connor, the hotel's technical engineer, frequently tells reporters and tourists that, "Maintenance, and Research and Development on the pool, can only be performed by scuba divers."

The hotel's gaming floor, underneath the floral mural painting on the ceiling, done by artist Dale Chihuty ten years previously, was empty of everyone but the serious gamblers who had grown immune to the anything but putting their financial welfare at risk at the tables.

Tourists and hotel guests had gathered outside, on the eastside of the hotel complex on the Strip, at the Flamingo road intersection, to view the tonight's extravaganza that is famous the World over.

Despite the July 4th hoop-ala that attracted most of visitors out onto what locals refer to as the *Center Strip* to watch the midnight performance, two men had stayed behind in their guest suite to prepare for a different type of adventure.

Nine days previously, early the morning of June 25th, a Wednesday, the two men had been forced to drop what they had been doing and rush to claim their guaranteed early-arrival room reservation at the Bellagio that had been pre-paid by postal money order a month earlier.

The reason behind the men's sudden deviation from plans, was the fact that a story concerning of the police dragnet, including pictures, had made that morning's early edition of the *Las Vegas Review-Journal newspaper*, in large headlines on the first page, above the fold.

Former Marine Lt. Colonel Jeffrey Johnson was fully versed in the modern day capabilities of the biometric and anthropometric identification systems that major Las Vegas and Atlantic City Casinos have installed in the past 12-months.

He knew it would take less than a day for Vegas' casinos to program-in all the biometric, visual markers and photos of each member of his team, once they received it from authorities. He had no doubt that the FBI and the local Nevada Gaming Commission cops had already obtained this information from their DoD service records.

Therefore, as soon as they had been forewarned by an ex-Marine that the newspaper would be carrying a story on the hijack gang, the men had checked into their over-priced view suite at the Bellagio before 8:00 a.m., just before the dragnet story was due to hit the newsstands.

Less than an hour after checking in, the colonel and Staff Sgt. Copperfeld were in their suite unpacking the suitcases they had checked-in with. A pair of battered hard-side Samsonite suitcases filled with their equipment and the canned food they would need to survive for the nine days until the night of the 4th.

Because of the Bellagio's biometric and anthropometric recognition system, neither man could show his face anywhere on the hotel grounds for the duration of their stay. They both would be *eating in*.

To make the Bellagio's front desk was aware that the two men demanded absolute privacy; the leader had buried his pride when he concocted a story that the two men were at the hotel for a homosexual tryst. And as such, they didn't want to be bothered for anything, unless than the hotel was fully-engulfed in flames.

Back to present day, July 4th, Johnson and Sgt. Copperfeld had been figuratively driven out of their minds by inactivity since they had checked-in.

They'd read every piece of paper in the suite at least twice. They could review their plans for the night of July 4th only so many times, before the risk of the excessive concentration began giving rise to doubts and second-guessing about the mission's success.

The men hadn't called on room service for *anything*, and that included newspapers. There was too much chance that the FBI had placed agents in all the hotels room service staffs on the Strip.

When Friday night, July 4th, finally rolled around, both men were relieved. Zero hour was 11:15 p.m. and when the clock finally crept around to that time, both men were pumped to begin executing their plan.

The first thing the two men did was to one again employ a special tool they had purchased off a down-and-out master burglar, to open one of the suite's two, triple-pane 'non-opening' windows.

Both men were certified Rappelling masters. Slipping into their tactical harnesses, they adjusted their carabineers to chest level, as they'd be taught in Marine Ranger School five-years previously.

To rig the line, the men took lengths of 11 mm line and a pair of steel figure-eights. They pulled a bight of the rope through the larger of the figure-eight's two holes, and looped it around the stem. Then they clipped the small hole to the harness, using a locking carabineer. Then tugged vigorously on the line to ensure it would hold.

They had already secured rappel bases and petzl stops to the engineered masonry wall outside their "non-opening" room windows the night before, on the moonless night, dark as the ace of spades, in the early morning hours.

Their room was on what is referred to as the backside of the hotel, which compared to the front side where the pool is located, is dark after midnight.

They would rappel down the exterior wall to a little-known cash room on the casino's second-floor. This special accommodation room was the only one located on the second floor. The others were below on the main gaming floor.

The renovated room had been created a couple years earlier by the former casino manager, to ensure that impatient high rollers, or '*whales*' as they are called, wouldn't have to wait in line to cash in their winnings, or to purchase more chips, or to extend their line of credit. The private gaming rooms that catering to whales and their guests are all located on the second floor, in close proximity to the accommodation room.

The second-floor accommodation room was located seven floors beneath the two ex-Marine's guest suite, and one floor above the perimeter-wall 'change' cages located the casino's main gaming floor.

The amount of money that the second-floor accommodation room kept on hand at any one time was unknown to anyone but the casino's shift bosses. But it was never more than thirty or less than ten, million dollars. The casino's Manager either increased or decreased the 'load' depending on the high-stakes table's volume of play during that timeframe, when reviewing the room's maximum cash levels monthly.

Before the accommodation room had been created, the space had been intended as a perimeter guest room.

While reinforcement had been added to the converted room's walls and a metal frame and face door added, the fact that was located on the second floor of the hotel was considered to be low-risk. Therefore, the room still had windows like those in the other guest rooms. For budgetary reasons, management had never seen fit to go to the added expense of replacing them with truly immovable, tamper-proof, bullet-resistant, glass.

Rappelling is a technique that permits a vertical assault down a building face. Tonight's descent would be made in seven stages, or drops with the men braking their descent by extending their roped hands outward. That action increased the friction on the double-loop through the steel figure-eights that were hooked to their harnesses. When they arrived outside the accommodation room's window, they would use the special access tool once more time to quietly open it.

At this point, things could go slightly crazy as the room's electronic sensors were linked to Metro that was capable of rolling patrol cars towards the Bellagio in under five minutes, and alerting Casino Security instantly.

That security feature had to be eliminated or its response delayed, before the men could gain entry to the room.

Therefore the gang had hired an ex-con who was an out-of-work electronics security specialist. He had visited the second floor twice during the early morning hours, wearing a uniform and I.D. Badge identical to those worn by the hotel's electricians. The first visit was to determine what equipment he would need, and on the second, he had installed what is called a loop wire to every sensor on the 2nd floor to prevent the alert from being broadcast.

The temporary circuit around the second floor's alarm systems was only intended to buy time for the two men who would be robbing the accommodation room.

Once the gang was inside the room, the three cash room employees would be tied up and gagged, then put to sleep with a moderate but safe subdural dose of medical twilight medication.

Then the colonel would do one last inspection of the alarm system, looking for a secondary alarm circuit that may have had been added but didn't show on the building's electrical plans.

The men wouldn't take any further action until the leader punched in the test code, got a green light, and beeped the rest of the team over a secure radio frequency indicating a figurative thumbs up, indicating the alarm systems were down and the heist could progress according to plan.

The two men knew how responsive the casino's guard staff could be if the alarm sounded anyway. Most of the guards were ex-cops, who believed in the old adage, *Kill them all, and let God sort them out*.

So, to be prepared for that possibility, in addition to Glock .45-caliber handguns worn in shoulder holsters, both men also carried Remington model 870 shotguns with extended tubes and poly-choke barrels, slung upside-down over their shoulders. The guns held eight-rounds of double-ought buckshot with twelve more in a butt cuff. The weapons were loaded with Hornady tactical shells with a shot pattern that expands to eight-inches at fifteen-yards. Real man-killers.

They also had acquired an expensive, one-of-a-kind, lock-picking gun, made for them by a another master burglar who had be forced to retire due to poor health from lack of exercise during his last prison term, that had resulted in him becoming too feeble to work at his trade.

The Sergeant operating the lock-picking gun and turned the adjustment wheel on the device's right frame, selecting full engagement. Then he inserted the pick into the lock of the accommodation room's safe and flexed the gun's mechanical triggers. That action elevated the probe less than five centimeters, which engaged the tumbler, before he returned it to the horizontal, and sought out the next detent, until all of the tumblers had been engaged. Then with an almost invisible motion of the man's wrist, the lock had opened.

When they didn't locate a secondary alarm inside the safe, they hurriedly began stack the high-denomination currency they found in shoulder-high cages around the steel box into two collapsible laundry carts they had piggy-backed into the room on their backs, that had been painstakingly designed and manufactured to exacting specifications to appear identical to the hotel's regular carts, except their material-handling frame was ten times stronger than the hotel's unit.

Once the carts had been filled about three-quarters full, as much as the men felt the cart could hold and still be moved along on its rollers without drawing suspicion, they covered the greenbacks with an armful of very soiled linen. Soiled linen in hopes that any hotel personnel they met in the hallway, once they exited the accommodation room, and were on their way down to the first floor's rear entrance, would be put off by the smell and sight of baby feces and what appeared to be menstrual blood.

Before exiting the accommodation room where the room's three employees continued to sleep the dreamless sleep of babes, the former Marines quickly and expertly applied stage makeup to each other's face and hands to make task of identifying them later that much harder.

Both were already wearing a laundry vendor's bright white, heavily-starched uniforms. When they cautiously let themselves out of the room, the colonel pulled the self-locking door shut behind them. Then pushing the carts they headed for the freight elevator down to the hotel's first floor non-public areas, and out the rear doors onto the loading dock.

Outside the Bellagio's loading dock door sat a dinged-up laundry truck with the vendor's name affixed to both sides, waiting for them. The driver had stolen the truck two hours earlier from the rear lot of a closed body shop.

An laundry vender employee, indebted to a loan shark, had been bribed a princely sum of $500 to first get the rig involved in a traffic accident, resulting in minor damage, then tell the driver where his employer had parked the van, while it waited for the body shop to get around to repairing the front-end damage.

The gang member who had stolen the truck was parked in the Bellagio's loading dock area, acting as if he was not-too-patiently waiting for a couple of under-performing employees to bring the final two carts of dirty laundry out of the hotel, which then would be loaded onto the lift gate and hoisted up into the truck's cargo box.

Of course this subterfuge would not have been possible except that the hotel guard, assigned to protect the Bellagio's loading dock from incursions such as this, had fallen into debt to a couple of loan sharks who were threatening to break his legs with baseball bats.

The guard owed nearly $34,000 in gambling markers. He had traded assignments with co-workers so he would be able to work the graveyard shift at the rear exit guard station that morning.

The gang had bribed him the full amount of money he owed the loan sharks, to fake having to take an urgent call of nature, necessitating that he desert his duty station for the five-minutes the gang needed to get the carts aboard the stolen laundry truck.

Of course the guard would be fired once the robbery became known, for deserting his duty station regardless of the justification. However, the man rationalized his firing would be more than offset by the fact that he would pay off the loan sharks, and still be able to get around without the need for a wheelchair.

The crooked guard returned to his duty station at the rear vendor's door just as the laundry truck drove out of the hotel parking lot, and turned left to head north on Las Vegas Blvd South.

Almost immediately a large black Ford 'dully' pickup and two smaller blue Nissan Pathfinder Sports Utility Vehicles, joined up to from a tight convoy.

The three vehicles would serve to protect the battered laundry truck, now hauling over ten million dollars in cold cash, by sacrificing themselves in the role of 'crash cars' if necessary should anyone attempt to stop the convoy.

All four vehicles, with the Ford and one of the Nissans ahead of stolen laundry truck, and the remaining Nissan behind it, proceeded at the speed limit, obeying all Las Vegas traffic laws to the letter.

July 5, 2008, Saturday, 12:45 a.m.
The Bellagio Hotel and Casino
3600 Las Vegas Blvd, Center Strip
Las Vegas, Nevada.

Law enforcement, the FBI, Las Vegas Metro, and Nevada Gaming Control Board agents were notified the instant the hotel began to suspect that it had been robbed.

Hotel security had promptly sounded the alarm when it was reported that the money cart from the first-floor cash room, had been unable to gain access or raise any response from the second floor *Whale* accommodation cash room.

While senior FBI, GCB, Metro, and IRS agents responded to the hotel, the authorities' backup game plan was activated.

The traffic cameras at every intersection around town had been programmed to accept alternate operating instructions from a Metro police electronics expert assigned to Metro's traffic management command post.

The special signal ordered the cameras to stop taking photos of license plates of Las Vegas' habitual red-light runners. And instead, begin steaming video of the vehicles passing through that particular intersection back to the command center.

Traffic officers sat transfixed in front of the command post's two-hundred or so colored monitors, intently looking for a damaged laundry truck, accompanied front and rear by several dark-colored trucks, which appeared to be running interference for the box truck.

Another part of the task force's plan, called for every law enforcement helicopter in the county to get airborne and to respond to any sightings of a convoy matching that description. The search grid coordinates were fed to the pilots by the traffic cops watching the streaming video from the Command Post.

Never to be left out of any potential for publicity, the FBI had leased two jet-turbine helicopters to augment those of Metro Police.

The Air Force out at Nellis, wanting to get into the action, had offered up the use of a pair of unarmed cobras with long-range fuel tanks, should the chase become extended. They were on the ground at Nellis waiting for orders from the command post.

On the other side of that coin, the Media had gotten wind of all the chopper launches and had responded by launching their news helicopters to find out if they were missing out on a major news story.

Of course, all that did was reduce what little air space was available for each of the helicopters, making a very bad situation inherently more dangerous.

The Executive Director of the Gaming Control Board in Carson City had called me at home a little after 12:20 a.m. this morning, now July 5th, to order me down to the Bellagio. I was instructed to let the long arms of the law attempt to run the miscreants down.

Meanwhile, I was told I would spend my next few hours or so working with FBI Special Agent Gardner, Mayor Oscar Goodman, Sheriff Gillespie, and what we all figured must be a particularly ambitious Clark County Commissioner to have gotten out of bed so early on a Saturday morning, in a full-court attempt to smooth the ruffled feathers of the Bellagio shareholders.

The Bellagio's wealthy stockholders that lived in and around Las Vegas had flocked to the hotel within thirty minutes of the early morning news media coverage of the robbery hitting the streets.

I would much rather have been out on the streets chasing down these *alpha hotels* in that convoy.

FBI Supervising Special Agent Garner had bitten the proverbial bullet and admitted to Bellagio's management that the FBI task force and the rest of us who had an oar in this mess, had made a mistake in assuming that the gang would employ the same *smash and awe* method they had used to knock over the Riverboat in Laughlin on April 10th, of this year. We had all been badly mistaken.

Instead, according to early reports, the gang had employed skill, stealth, technology, and unbelievable daring to pull off the job.

I still had my ear to the ground monitoring the progress of the chase, because before leaving home I had called Billy Frisbee and told him to get down to the City's command post as fast as he could drive without killing anyone. He would be my eyes and ears for the next few hours and keep me advised of any progress or problems via cell phone, while I played nice with the biggies at the Bellagio.

It was getting close to 1:45 a.m. when my cell phone trilled. I searched for an vacant corner, and checked Caller ID to make certain the caller was Billy, not a member of the Media which alleged had bribed the former FBI office's front desk receptionist for all our personal cell phone numbers.

I answered with my customary greeting, "Speak."

It was Billy, all right. I knew that the young agent always prepared a list before he reported to me, and figured that despite the hour, this report would be choreographed in the same manner. So I kept my pie hole shut and let him talk.

"Boss," he began, "things are going nuts down here. Apparently the gang has figured out that we have linked the traffic cameras throughout the city to stream video back to the command post."

"The last six video streams have shown that the gang is still running in-convoy. The Big Dodge pickup is now out in front, one of the small utility vehicles is running in the second spot, then the dinged-up laundry truck, with the other small rig in the tail-end Charley position. The Metro sergeants here tell me it is textbook military convoy philosophy. Sacrifice the lesser value units of the convoy to protect the mission."

"So far they have continued to head northbound. The weird thing is that occasionally the convoy will disappear from camera view for up to twenty minutes. The Command Post commander thinks that the gang has figured out that we are tracking them through the traffic cameras. Or they heard the racket from all the law enforcement choppers, and those damn media helicopters, that have so far have refused police orders to break off from following the pursuit."

"Billy," I interrupted, "you have the Marine's personnel folders there, correct?"

"Yes, Boss, I do."

"Okay," I continued, "page back through them to the DD-214 section and tell me how many of them are helicopter pilots."

There was a momentary pause as Billy set down his cell phone to leaf through the personnel files. In a couple minutes the young agent came back up on his phone.

Frisbee reported, "The two surviving Ranger-certified Marines, Colonel Johnson and Staff Sgt. Cooperfeld, were both helicopter-rated when they left the Corps."

"Okay, Billy," I said. "Now this is what I want you to tell Metro's Command Post commander. If he or she gives you any guff, tell him to call me because I am currently standing right alongside his boss even as we speak. Okay?"

I thought about what I was going to say, and began. "Billy, the first thing any student learns in flight school is that all helicopters, especially the civilian models, have very, very short legs. As a rule, the bird can't stay aloft without returning to base for refueling every 90-minutes, which includes a safety factor."

"The reason the gang leader is making his little convoy disappear from time-to-time is because he knows the police and FBI choppers, and even the birds from the news stations for that manner, are very close to their low-fuel points."

"A few of them may have already reached their bingo-fuel state and been forced to head back to the McClellan for re-fueling. When they all reach a bingo fuel state and have to return to base, the convoy will be free to continue the direction they are going, or deviate from it, because they will then be free of any surveillance."

"I also think the gang leader is a smart guy and is monitoring the police radios and the frequencies that the command post and helicopters are using to communicate with each other."

"Billy, here is what I want you to suggest to the boss over there. Tell him diplomatically that I suggest that he been prepared to launch the two Cobra gunships with extended tanks that Nellis Field has sitting on the tarmac. Not launch, just be prepared to launch, at a moment's notice."

"Once the law enforcement helicopters reach their bingo-fuel states, tell the commander to let them RTB, return to base. I personally don't care what the news helicopters do. They are just getting in our way and making the pursuit more dangerous, anyway."

"As soon as the law enforcement helicopters are five minutes away from having to declare bingo-fuel and return to base for refueling, I suggest that the Command Post request the immediate launch of the Cobra's and have them orbit two miles north of the convoy's last known position."

"Have Nellis order the cobra pilots to pick up the tail of the convoy and follow it until they either go bingo-fuel and have to RTB, or something else prevents them from continuing the surveillance," I said.

"If the Command Post commander there doesn't want to follow my suggestion, please call me right back so I can get his boss involved, Okay?"

Billy replied, "Sure, Boss. I'll talk with him right now. And if there is a problem, I'll get back to you. Now go hold the hands of all those big shots and make Nice," Billy chucked as he terminated our connection.

Even though I wanted to be in on the action, I decided to leave the chase after the gang in the Metro command post's able hands, and as Billy suggested, return to my hand-holding assignment.

TWENTY

July 5, 2008, Saturday, 9:00 a.m.
FBI Office—Main Conference room
700 E. Charleston blvd
Las Vegas, Nevada 89104-1509

Billy Frisbee and I were among the first into the room that morning because we wanted to get a good seat up in front of, not under, the overhead screen. Not to mention the opportunity to be at the head of the line to take advantage of the FBI's nationwide reputation of being totally incapable of having a meeting without sporting a generous layout of finger food, I.E. Krispy Kreme donuts.

The brave soul whose inauspicious job it was to start this morning's meeting off with bad news was Air Force Major General, Harry Lewis. The officer had been a mover and a shaker back in the days of B-52 bombers during the Cold War, more commonly referred to as the days of Dr. Strangelove.

Nellis Air Force Base has a vibrant mission and an exceptional group of men and women committed to implementing it. But like all large military bases, it is also somewhere that the Pentagon uses as a parking place to send their worn-out generals to hang out, until their retirement date rolls around. Sort of like a graveyard for old dinosaurs.

These old warriors roam to and fro about the base, often sticking their noses into places the Air Force rather they didn't. However, General Lewis was respected at Nellis because he had sucked up his ego and agreed to act as a base spokesman whenever there was unpleasant news to report.

The job, which is often incorrectly referred to as Public Affairs, was normally slotted for an officer 6, if not 7, pay grades lower that a Air Force Major General with 30-years of command experience under his belt.

Today's grim report informed the attendees that an in-flight maintenance emergency had forced the initial flight of Cobras to RTB, return-to-base, and abandon the surveillance of the gang convoy. The convoy had been heading northeast on State Route 95, just before the Village of Indian Springs, when the cobras had to abandon the chase to RTB.

The flight leader had reported a bad vibration that only could be explained as an impending main rotor malfunction. That is about as bad, no, it is the worst thing that can ever happened for a helicopter pilot and his crew. The flight commander immediately aborted the mission, even before he notified Nellis of his problem.

As Air Force policy never permits one of their multi-million-dollar combat airships, armed or not, to operate solo during peacetime, the wingman had to follow his flight leader back to Nellis.

While the helicopters were RTB, they had reported over the cobra's encrypted radio frequency, that they had been forced by a level-5 mechanical malfunction to abandon the mission. So Nellis launched a second pair of Cobras to take over the surveillance, at the coordinates where the first flight of assault helicopters had been forced to abort their mission.

It had taken the second flight of cobras ten minutes to arrive on-station. After a thorough search of all roads within those grid coordinates, they had reported back to base that the convoy was nowhere to be seen.

The convoy had been heading in the general direction of the Nellis Air Force Firing Range, which was just past the turnoff of the State Route 156 access to the Red Rock Canyon recreation area. Apparently it had been beamed-up by alien spacecraft.

The possible coincidence of the buried body of Marine Major Mary Levinson that had been discovered by a couple off-roaders in the Red Rock recreation area wasn't lost on any of us who had been summoned to the LAS/FBI impromptu meeting at 0900 hours on July 5, 2008.

The General retook his seat as the room erupted and less-than-complimentary opinions began to fly. The inferences centered mostly uninformed speculation that the Air Force's lack-of-attention to their aircraft's preventive maintenance needs had indirectly been the cause that the Cobras had been unable to complete their mission.

Naturally, as those familiar with the high-level of aircraft readiness in our military services know, those accusations were nothing but what Brahma bulls leave on the trail.

Finally, after about five minutes of the unfair accusations, FBI Special Agent Gardner got to her feet and yelled, "Shut Up! If you overrated, overpaid, egocentric law enforcement types can't say something constructive, please permit a mere woman to make a couple observations."

She began to tick her thoughts-points off on the fingers of her ringless left hand.

"First, where in the hell can a convoy of four good-sized vehicles each weighing over 3,000 pounds disappear to, in that section of the county. To the right is nothing but the desert that the Air force uses as a firing range."

"To the left, is nothing but Humboldt Toiyabe National Forest, where the gang would find it impossible to conceal the convoy, inasmuch as it is possibly the densest area of free-growing brush, shrubs, and thin-trunk, old-growth trees in the county."

"Second, anyone have any thoughts on where in the hell the mokes are hiding all that money? Is anyone willing to venture a guess as to the amount of the gang's total take, since they hit the Riverboat casino back in April?"

When no one spoke up, a short, middle-aged, balding, bespectacled man timidly stood up and raised his hand. Gardner appeared taken back by the man who politely stood there as if asking permission to speak. Gardner had posed the question as a hypothetical, and hadn't been expecting an answer.

"And you are?" she asked.

"Miss, I am Special Agent Gerald S. Rotweiller with the Internal Revenue Service. My boss sent me over her to represent the Service on your taskforce." Then Rotweiller continued to stand there, waiting for Gardner to ask him another question.

"Okay," Gardner said, ignoring the chuckles from the peanut gallery of agents who also had been forced to *volunteer* for taskforce duty.

"First, Agent Rotweiller, am I pronouncing your name correctly?"

"Yes, Miss, you are," the unremarkable man confirmed.

"Okay, Rotweiller, first, *don't call me Miss*. You can call me Special Agent. You can call me Gardner. You can even call me 'Hey, You.' Anything but *Miss,* understand?"

He replied, "Absolutely, Miss. You don't want me to call you Miss, is that correct?"

Gardner briefly shook her head, as if thinking, "*Why Me,*" before continuing to address the IRS agent.

"Okay, Special Agent Rotweiller. You *did* have a purpose when you stood up, didn't you?"

Agent Rotweiller took in a deep breath to inflate his meager chest before he began speaking. "Well, yes, Miss, I did. You asked if anyone knew how much *loot,*" smiling inwardly at himself for using the police term, "that the gang has *heisted.*" Another good cop term stolen from his weekly viewing of NBC's long-running Law And Order series.

He continued, "You did ask how much money the gang has stolen since they *hit* the Riverboat, isn't that right, Miss?"

By this point, even I was having trouble not laughing out loud. As for Frisbee, he was close to rolling in the aisles.

A smile was even beginning to tug the corners of Gardner's lips when she said, "Well, damn it, Rotweiller, how much *loot* have they *heisted* as you so succinctly put it?"

"About $30.5 million dollars, Miss," he answered proudly.

"No way, Rotweiller. They couldn't have taken that much. Where do you get that figure?"

"Audits, Miss," he answered. "Audit, you know. Like those the IRS does every year to catch tax cheats. And I know you'll be shocked to learn we catch a disproportionate number of police officers and FBI agents in our net."

By now, everybody in the conference room but the IRA agent was hysterically in stitches. It had gotten so loud that one of the FBI's civilian security guards stuck her head into the room to see if everything under control. Gardner stopped laughing long enough to tell the guard "It's Okay. Really, its okay," and waved the guard back out of the room.

Through all of the hilarity at his expense, Rotweiller had continued to stand stoically as if he encountered unbalanced local cops and federal agents acting like they breathed in nitrous oxide, everyday of the week.

When the laugher had finally died down, Gardner bit her lip and asked, "Can you break that total down for us, Agent Rotweiller? You know how it is. For us poor federal agents who occasionally cheat on our taxes, $30 million and some odd change, is a bit too large a number to get our felonious minds around."

Gardner waved down the reemerging laughter, as it was obvious that the self-important IRS agent was ready to walk from the room in disgust.

"Yes," he replied, pulling a small notebook out of his 3-piece suit's vest pocket. "Of course, we haven't finished our final audits yet, and you know how these casinos are. They always add a few extra million on top of their loss claim to rip-off their insurance companies."

The IRS agent continued to speak, completely oblivious to the fact that the President of the Nevada Casino Owners Association, as well as the State Attorney General of Nevada, first cousins, were attending the meeting together. Both men, after turning a nice shade of beet red upon hearing Rotweiller's disparaging remarks, left their seats and headed for the door.

"Our preliminary audit indicates that $3.5 million was taken at the Laughlin Riverboat; $3.0 million in the May 3rd armored-car hijacking; $14.5 million from BRINKS on June 15th, and based on the Bellagio's cash room count after the robbery this morning, which, as I mentioned, could be inflated by ten million dollars."

The silence in the room was so thick you could cut it with a knife. The sheer size of the sum shocked everyone. But as they say, a million here and a million there, and pretty soon you are talking real money.

Frisbee stood up and asked, "Agent Rotweiller, how much would that amount of money weigh? And what would be the minimal amount of cubic feet of space required to store it?"

Agent Rotweiller turned to Frisbee and asked, "Young man, who might you be?"

After Billy apologized for not introducing himself, he asked Rotweiller the question once again.

The IRS agent made a few quick calculations in his notebook, before he looked up and said, "Well, I can't answer that question, Agent Frisbee."

Billy persisted, "What do you mean, you can't? You have been disparaging some good people here. You ran off a couple of others who no doubt will one day make you eat your comments. If you are the monetary expert you claim to be, why can't you answer my question?"

"For one very simple reason, young man." the IRA agent responded. "The weight of the currency and cubic feet required to store it would depend on the denominations of the bills. Can you tell me exactly how many bills of each denomination were stolen?"

"No, Agent Rotweiller, I cannot," Billy responded, "I assumed that since the IRS has audited the losses at the all four locations, that the IRS could give an accounting as to how many bills of each denomination were taken."

"There your assumption is wrong, Agent Frisbee. The IRS in only is interested in the total of the sums stolen, as that determines the tax liability. Understand?"

"Well, Agent Rotweiller, will you take an educated guess at it? Weight and cubic footage?"

The IRS drone made more notations on his notebook. Five minutes later, he looked up, and condescendingly stared out at the room of cops and agents, before he said, "Assuming the bills are mostly of the $100 denomination, I think you could go with a hypothetical weight of ten-tons which would require a 20-by-15-foot room with stacking limited to no more than six-feet off the floor, for floor-loading restrictions you know. That is just a shotgun estimate, but it would be in the ballpark."

Rotweiller glanced at a battered old 1950's style Timex, and said, "Now if you don't have anything further for me, I have to get back to the office. This is the time of year that our post-audits catch most of the tax cheats, you know."

When no one spoke up to stop him, the little man snapped his well-worn Samsonite briefcase shut, carefully adjusted his gun-metal-gray fedora on his head, and fast-walked from the room.

As everyone broke for a quick break and rest room call, Frisbee leaned over me and asked if I would mind if he continued to address the group? I knew he was ambitious, but then young agents almost always are. The good ones, that is.

Billy said he had some ideas he wanted to toss around the group for comment. He had spent an hour this morning printing out some maps that he thought were germane to the meeting. When I told him "Sure," he handed me a handful of stickpins, and asked me to help him stick the maps up onto the bulletin board before everyone returned to their seats.

By the time everyone had returned from the break, Billy and I had plastered the corkboard with large-resolution Goggle maps of the Nellis Air Force Range. The scale of each was such that it covered a number of miles. Yet each was detailed well enough to show dwellings, major physical features, and all paved and unpaved desert roads.

When everyone had retaken their seats, following another raid on the seemingly endless supply of Krispy Kreme donuts, Billy began.

He started off by again introducing himself. Then he began with his presentation.

"I don't think there is anywhere that a convoy of four trucks could have gone in such a short time, other than out into the desert. Into the Firing Range. So I've printed out these Google maps to show us what exactly what is out in that area."

"After studying at each of the maps, there was one that seemed to jump out at me. Someplace that was conceivably large enough to store the money, and protect it against the desert's harsh environment. Somewhere base security wouldn't bother to check because it is protected from trespassers and precious metal scavengers by a razor-wire-topped, chain-link fence."

"Somewhere that has access to a paved road. That has outbuildings that could be used to conceal up to ten vehicles."

At this moment, Major General Harry Lewis, using the seat back in front of him to pull himself to his feet, interrupted Billy.

The old man took in a deep breath before excitedly saying, "By jove, Boy. You are talking about the old Intercontinental ballistic missile silo next to Dry Lake, aren't you? Christ, that would meet all their needs. Plenty of metal sheds with pull-up doors to hide their vehicles from the eyes of base security and satellites."

"The Base facilities department doesn't keep the utilities connected out there. So, the lights, air-conditioning, dehumidifiers, electrified security fence, the elevator down to the control center, the toilets, sinks, and showers in the heads wouldn't be operational. Of course, a pair of hefty portable generators could provide enough electricity for the complex in the short-term."

The General continued, "Some of the younger officers claim to have taken a female airman or two out to the silo for some sexual fraternization. Of course, there is no truth in that. They'd be courts-martialed out of the Air Force. Stuff like that can ruin an officer's career."

"And it might explain something else," the old man remarked.

By now, every set of ears in the room had perked up and Agent Frisbee was being looked at with renewed respect.

Billy, oblivious to what was going on around him, asked, "General, would you expand on your last comment, Sir?"

The old man started to grin, then shrugged the shoulders that in their time had borne the weight of the World.

"Yes, Agent, I guess I can suffer through a few minutes of embarrassment to help you out in this matter."

"When the public learns about these bastards, it will degrade the average American's view of the fighting man. Bad enough we go into the war in Iraq and over 4,000 of our troops lose their lives. Then we learn that the reason our leaders claimed as the justification reason for us going into that fight in the first place, supposedly, weapons of mass destruction, didn't even exist. 4,000 plus lives lost, and that is just the American troops. Hell yes, I'll tell you, boy."

The general continued, "I imagine most of you know that old dinosaurs like me get assigned to bases like Nellis to bide our time until we have our thirty-years in, and can retire with something approximately an reasonable pension and life-long health insurance benefits."

"All the Air Force asks of us is to stay out of the way of people who are running the base. Well, sometimes keeping your nose out of Air Force business gets a little dull. Hell, *a lot* dull."

"So I began to occasionally sneak the intelligence reports, which are based on the daily satellite observations, out of the office in my briefcase at night."

He continued, "Oh, I'd be certain to be the first one into the Pubic Affairs office the next morning to put them back, of course. But the reports started to form a pattern. The intelligence interpretation of the satellite film stated that headlights were seen on paved roads where no one was authorized to be. The satellites heat sensors occasionally identified heat signatures of human-size being emitted from inside the grounds of the fenced-in old silo location where no one is authorized to be. The Satellites didn't detect any movement during daytime hours, but it did suggest that humans could be moving around inside the old silo facility wearing the new high-tech 'chill jackets' that had been designed by technicians at Elmendorf Air Base in Alaska."

The general explained, "Now, I couldn't go to base security and tell them what I had deduced. Hell, I'd violated almost every regulation in the book by sneaking the damn satellite intelligence reports out. If anyone found out, I could lose my pension. So against my better judgment and obligation to my country, I selfishly kept my mouth shut. And I'd appreciate it if you all here would do the same. No one needs to know where you got this information, do they?" the old man asked with a strange combination of dignity and self-pity.

July 7, 2008, Monday, 9:00 a.m.
Nellis AFB—Convert Operations Building
Location: Restricted
Las Vegas, Nevada

Frisbee and I cleared the main security gate and reported to the clandestine U. S. Air Force Special Operation hanger on Monday morning. The hanger is guarded around-the-clock by a small base operations contingent made up of a Bradley Fighting Vehicle; two Humvees sporting .50 caliber machine guns in their cupolas; a couple goggled men on olive-drab ATV's circling the hanger, and grizzled-looking Air Force guards wearing cammies and carrying M4s, stationed at every entrance of the Restricted special ops hanger.

FBI Special Agent Steffy Gardner greeted us. She didn't waste anytime with any niceties such as, "Good Morning, Agent Fox, how in the hell are you?" before she dropped the bad news on our heads. "Higher-authority at FBI Headquarters has made some decisions since this past Saturday's action meeting."

Please note that my input as the State's Gaming Control Board's designated supervising agent in-charge of the casino heist case had neither been requested nor considered before the FBI made their decisions.

Gardner made a half-hearted attempt to explain. Well, not so much explain, as cryptically inform me that the Feds were assuming total control over all facets of the multi-incident case.

Including the Riverboat heist in April; the hijacked armored-car on May 3rd; the BRINKS heist in June; and now the Bellagio caper a few days previously on July 4th.

Oh, I can hear my valued readers now. "*Where does the Federal Bureau of Idiots get off strong-arming case control away from local authorities . . . .*"

Well, friends, a specific piece of Federal Law exists that determines when the FBI can and cannot take over an investigation from local and

State law enforcement. It is Title 18, of the U.S. Code of Crimes and Procedures.

Some high-level FBI gofer obviously ran around Washington D.C. on Sunday with one of the FBI's famous PowerPoint Presentations in-pocket until he or she found a tame Federal Judge willing to agree with the bureau in this matter.

The linch pin in the FBI's argument I'm certain revolved around May 3rd Armored-car hijacking and the BRINKS, June 15th robbery. Both involved the transport of money to or from the Federal Reserve Bank. Anything to do with banks has always been the Bureau's bailiwick since the days of J. Edgar Hoover.

Since the Bureau was taking this investigation away from the Nevada state law enforcement authorities, they also would be heading up the assault on the old decommissioned ICBM Missile silo out by Dry Lake. That being something I agreed with. Except for the military, who are currently occupied elsewhere, only the FBI has the money and resources to mount an assault of the magnitude required, for what we were facing.

One of the FBI's stealthy NIGHT STALKER aircraft, a Mitsubishi twin-engined props jet, equipped with advanced surveillance electronics and FLIR, forward-looking infrared radar, had already made a couple of high-altitude runs over the silo, pre-dawn.

The purpose of the over-flights, that had required approval of the Commanding General of Nellis Air Force Base, was to second-source the old Major General's claim that the satellite's FLIR had detected the presence of unauthorized, unknown individuals trespassing inside the decommissioned missile silo compound.

The NIGHT STALKER touched down at Nellis at daybreak, and had been directed by the Base's ground controller, using an encrypted frequency, to taxi to, and into the special operations hanger where Billy and I currently stood, thrilled to be playing with the big boys.

The aircraft's Intelligence Suite agent had passed the report to the FBI that the Mitsubishi had detected the presence of at least seven *unsubs*, FBI-speak for unknown subjects, and several hot spots that the FLIR-surveillance equipment had identified as highly-muffled, high-output, gasoline-powered, mobile generators.

So with the General's information second-sourced, the assault would proceed as scheduled, early Wednesday morning, July 9, at 0300 hours, FBI speak for 3:00 a.m. Tuesday evening was forecasted to be a moonless night.

As to who would physically make the assault, take the ex-Marines into custody, hopefully recover what was left of the over $30.5 million in-cash the gang had stolen over the past four months, the egocentric FBI never relied on local police departments when they knew someone who had the juice to get approval to use HRT.

HRT, or the Hostage Rescue Team, is the FBI's elite counter-terrorism team, and charged with being air-mobile within four-hours. They move in two mission-dedicated Air force C-17's that are capable of flying at 500 MPH.

Each C-17 is capable of carrying a MD-530 McDonald Douglas helicopter which is designated to fulfill the Command and Control function.

The first part of any mobilization is the mount-out, or the uploading the gear needed for the mission, and to support the team's presence for several days on-site.

What turns on a HRT movement? The FBI strategic Operators and Information Center (SOIC) plans the response and whether it is to be classified as a counter-intelligence action. Then they notify the Assistant Director (ADIC) of the Investigative Support Division (ISD) who in turns calls the Special Agent in-charge (SAC) of the Critical Incident Response Group (CIRG) who mobilizes HRT.

It may appear to the reader to be an excessive amount of bureaucracy, however it serves to ensure HRT is only activated when there is no other appropriate course of action available. HRT is unbelievably expensive to deploy. Each HRT activation sucks a significant portion of the underfunded bureau's operating funds into the black hole necessary to ensure the semi-covert unit's missions are successful.

Often airlifted in for a HRT mission when appropriate are two Bell Twin 412 Jet turbine helicopters, each of which can airlift fourteen operators, which when the hyper-muffled helicopter is over the designated assault site, or in its general vicinity, the operators of HRT belay or fast-rope down to the ground.

Keeping in mind that the *unsubs* were ex-Marines, highly-trained in the use of explosives, traditional weaponry, and chemical and biological warfare, I assumed that the HRT would be utilizing one of their Air Force C-17s to bring the CIRG's, Critical Incident Response Group's, CIVs, or Critical Incident Van, to Nellis for deployment with the assault team.

HRT operatives and their team leaders are like everyone else. They want to do their job and safety return home to their families at night. The FBI is very cognizant of that fact and willingly spends a lot of money to ensure that happens.

So if it takes the aerial transport of a CIV into the location, although expensive as hell as it requires its own C-17 just to transport it, the FBI bites the bullet and orders it flown in to protect the HRT employees, who are often called-on to operate in high-risk, live-threatening situations.

But fortunately for the bean counters in this case, the FBI already had a CIV in storage in Las Vegas. The equipment had recently finished up its last assignment and was now waiting to be redeployed to another assignment.

The CIV had been airlifted-in earlier in the year as a command post for investigators who were checking out a HAZMAT incident at *Extended Stays of America*, located at 4270 Valley View Blvd in Las Vegas.

A guest had been found unconscious in his room, which later was found to contain the deadly poison, Ricin. It wasn't until the week of April 19, 2008, that the man responsible was finally charged with various major felonies for possessing the deadly poison, let alone manufacturing it.

The CIV is slightly larger than most motor homes. Its MSR, or Mobile Squad Room, contains a cornucopia of police equipment.

Inside, on the left, is a compact communications center that occupies a full third of the wall. On it, are lots and lots of pretty pulsating multicolored light-emitting diodes, or LEDS. Then in stacks under the layout, is most every kind of radio and telephone known to mankind.

Across the aisle, a dozen orange biohazard suits hang from a steel bar. Black neoprene HEPA breathing devices are neatly arranged on a narrow shelf above.

On the remainder of the left wall are a series of shelves and bins bursting with god-only-knows-what. On the right are four downtime rooms only slightly larger than an airplane bathroom. The rear of the coach consists of four holding cells, each with its own little seat that permits the occupant to spend his or her his episodic confinement in relative comfort.

HRT operatives seem to have been all hatched from the same mold. Buzz-cut haircuts, black-tactical fatigues, black-jump boots, a black pistol in a shoulder holster slung under the 'weak' arm, wearing level-four, black body-armor vests with snap-on FBI logos emblazoned in vivid yellow on the back. Snap-on thigh guards, 185-Dba flash-bang grenades, and black composite helmets.

Each man carries a black-knit ski-type mask. The mask is folded twice and tucked under the left shoulder epaulet where the operative can easily get to it when needed. HRT operatives clip flash-bang grenades to their black Alice combat harnesses and stow their composite helmets under the seats of the black lightly-armored black Suburban SUVs that the C-17's have delivered to carry them into battle.

The operatives carry MP-5s, M4s, CAR-15s, and so many extra magazines that it seems impossible to accommodate them all in their multi-pocketed black fatigues.

For the assault on the silo they would use their *Gillie,* or camouflage, suits they each had brought with them. Ghillie suits are self-built using an infrared camouflage smock, a veil of unbraided hemp, and lumps of cordova and burlap, topped off by a banged-up pair of suede ranger boots.

A gillie suit must appear to be equal parts of shadow and flora material. Snipers and operators move ahead on their bellies, either pushing their equipment ahead of them, or behind them in a drag bag.

In 2008 the FBI is funded for eight, seven-man HRT teams. FBI Supervising Special Agent Gardner informed me that the ADIC has deployed two of those teams, a total of fourteen multi-specialty operators, to lead the assault on the silo.

In an attempt take a little of the sting out of having my case taken away from me, Gardner had received approval from higher-authority permitting me to go along on the assault as long as I agreed to obey the HRT team leader's orders immediately and without question.

Gardner said that FBI headquarters had not been in-favor of my going along on the raid until she had briefed them that I was a FBI National Academy Graduate, and had worked with HRT before when I had been on the NYPD. I didn't know she was aware of those facts, so it showed like any good cop, she had requested a background check on me, as I had on her.

As a final comment before returning to the mission planning that was in-progress on any flat surface available all over the hanger, she grinned, as like she'd just had an afterthought, and said, "Oh, Fox, I forgot to tell you that since you are 47-years-of-age, the Bureau requires that Billy here accompany you to make sure you don't get into trouble."

Having once again gotten the last word in, she spun on the sole of her low-heeled sensible flats like a ballerina and walked towards one of the chart covered work tables, making sure her swinging ass captured my and Billy's attention.

Following Agent Gardner's flamboyant exit, Billy and I joined a group of FBI/HRT team members and listened with rapt attention to a gray-haired man tell them everything they never wanted to know about this particular missile silo.

The team leader, Special Agent Freddie "Fireball" Jefferson, was speaking in a manner that gave his listeners the mistaken impression that he knew everything. Actually, I was certain that the tall FBI agent must have stayed up half the night memorizing all of the pertinent details that even remotely applied to the impending mission.

The men listening, and the speaker, were clustered around a flat work surface, which was covered with Air Force charts stamped with the foreboding legend of TOP SECRET.

Jefferson glanced at Billy and I when we joined his audience, then without skipping a beat, returning to his briefing.

"As you can see from studying the charts, Gentlemen, our objective for Wednesday, at O'-dark-forty, lies less than three miles up a poorly-maintained macadam road, north of Nevada state route 95."

"Now if this was the good-old-days, and I say that with tongue-in-cheek obviously, and the silo was still hot, one of the three Air Force officers down in the Launch Center 180-feet below the ground, would be watching us via video camera as we approached and attempted to enter through the security gate."

"In addition to the silo's domed-shaped access portal, you'd see a total of four, twenty-by-forty-foot, butler-building-type structures inside the compound's security fence."

The Team Leader continued, "Now, if your arrival here was expected, and you had all the necessary passwords and counter passwords, you'd be permitted to enter the access portal. Its walls are at least ten-feet thick and entry is restricted by a massive three-foot-thick, bank-type, blast door."

"If on the other hand, you weren't expected, you can make book that a dozen buzz-headed Air Force guards, madder than pissed-off rattlesnakes, would suddenly pop up from concealment and proceed to totally ruin your day."

"But let's say you were expected. And possessed the necessary clearances to go down to the Control Center. To go there, bet on them not permitting you to use the facility's only elevator. You'd face a disquieting descent down a flight of 163 steep concrete stairs."

"Everything echoes down there, footsteps boom ominously, and the metal security doors clank into metal latches. It is somewhat like a crypt, I suppose."

"When you reached the bottom of the stairwell you would be met by a very unfriendly man who has you in the sights of his .45-caliber Colt Commander semi-automatic pistol. As the silo's launch consoles were manned by two officers at all times, you only would have to convince the one individual who was holding a gun on you of your good intentions."

Shifting his weight, the lecturer continued, "Of course, this silo isn't active. The missile is long gone. The actual silo long-ago was filled with concrete. And it is likely that the silo's original security monitors have been replaced by the silo's current occupants."

"We've been told that there are at least seven, perhaps more, well-trained ex-Marines down in that silo. Well, I really don't think all of them will be under-ground. My reason for saying that is the structures above-ground will provide excellent concealment for observation posts and snipers."

He proceeded, "At the most, perhaps only one guy, or perhaps two, will remain down in Launch Control. The rest will have set-up sniping locations throughout the above ground portion of the complex."

"As with most of these old ICBM silos, the above-ground portion of this one faces west. And consequently, most of the silo's surveillance monitors, cameras, and visual view ports also face that direction. I assume that the reason for that is they expected either the primary rocket attack, or counterstrikes by the Soviet Union, to arrive at their front door from that direction."

"This HRT assault force consists of two, seven-man HRT teams, or fourteen shooters. Plus a couple of civilians from the Nevada Gaming Control Agency that you see standing at the back of this group, say hello to Special Agents Fox and Frisbee."

"Now, this is how this turkey shoot is going to go. At exactly 3:00 a.m., Wednesday morning, Nellis base security is going to stage-manage the apparent crash landing of a helicopter five miles west of the silo, out on Dry Lake's bed. The aircraft will catch fire and burn like hell for about thirteen minutes. The airwaves will be filled with bogus calls for help from the crew requesting medical and fire suppression assistance."

Agent Jefferson briefly paused for emphasis, "Of course this elaborate deception has been sited to provide the gyrene malcontents with ringside seats."

"While those above ground are being entertained, we hope that the guard or guards stationed down below in the launch center, watching over their ill-gotten gains, will become curious. Curious enough that they will use the elevator, or the concrete spiral stairwell, to hoof it up to the surface to catch the phony action scenes that base security is producing off to their *west*."

Checking his notes, the first time I'd seen him do *that* since he had started speaking nearly twenty-minutes earlier, the agent went on. "However, Gentlemen, just like the Romans back in the days of when there was no television, our assault will be from the *east*, timed to coincide with the explosion of the fake helicopter out to the west, the action of which will hopefully to hold the gyrenes attention until we are able to establish control over the bad guys."

"We'll be using the 300-foot-high hill immediately to the east of the silo site for cover."

"At 1300 hours, 1:00 a.m., all fourteen of us including the two state agents will be trucked into position in a deep wash, 1,000-yards east of the silo. We'll be staging from the desert road which is two miles to the east."

"The Air Force has graciously agreed to provide us with two super-silent battery-powered 10-man off-road lorries so we don't have to walk the two miles of rugged terrain in from the road, humping our equipment."

"At first, we had intended to use the CIV for transport, to prevent the possibility that any spotter the gang may had deployed close to the highway 95, from seeing a gaggle of black suburbans turn onto, and head north up the old desert trail."

He continued, "That was until someone remembered that the CIV is diesel-powered and noisy as hell. As night-time desert air transmits sound only slightly less effectively than over water, use of CIV was ruled out."

"But the plan is to still hold it close. It will be parked off Highway 95 in a rest area, in the sorry event that the gyrenes have obtained access to biological or radioactive weapons."

"First out of the box about 0130 hours will be the bomb guys. We must never forget that these unsubs are highly-decorated Marines, despite their current status with the military. They are combat-tested and trained and know more about explosives and ABC warfare than most of us."

"The bomb squad will PACKBOT friend in with them, and unload him from his carrying case when they feel it is appropriate. I want everyone to monitor the bomb squad's encrypted radio frequency so everyone is immediately aware of any surprises that the bomb squad discovers that the gyrenes have thoughtfully left for us."

PACKBOT is a robotic warrior that is remotely-controlled by the operator. It has been deployed to Iraq for R & D purposes, and so far, has acquitted itself well. The robot has tank-like tracks that can propel it over almost any obstacle.

Its surveillance capabilities, depending on load-out, are a zoom camera, night vision, a biological sensor, laser rangefinder, heat sensor, and a detachable communications device, called a throw phone, designed for use in hostage situations.

Jefferson continued, "The remainder of both teams will follow the bomb squad at a minimal interval of 150-feet. Close enough that we can provide them fire support if they run into an ambush, and but far enough back to protect the bulk of the force if they run into booby traps. Questions?"

When no one spoke up, he gave the men his final instruction. "Check and recheck your gear. Get some sleep. The Air Force is delivering cots, fresh uniforms, hot meals, cold drinks, and even a couple flat-screen televisions. I had the base security officer activate the parental control feature to prevent you morally-above-board, high-minded, Christian young men from watching *tittie shows* on FBI time."

"The Base commander assures me that the showers here have unlimited hot water. You can call your loved ones, but per usual, you are not to tell anyone where we are or what our mission is. The Media will do that soon enough once they learn once this turkey shoot—poor choice of words—is over."

"The base is sending over a non-denominal Chaplin for those that want one, and a doctor to treat any ills you have. I'll be back in the building as soon as I pay my respects to the base's commanding general. When I get back, and if you have any questions, don't hesitate to come over and ask me."

"We'll have three live ammo practice drills tomorrow; one immediately after breakfast, and two after lunch. Snooze time for the operation commences at 6:00 p.m. tomorrow, no exceptions.

We'll be rolling out of here a little after midnight, about 0030 hours, early Wednesday morning. Good hunting. Let's show those damn renegade Marines and our hosts, the Air Force, how HRT does its job."

Jefferson shook hands with everyone. Then climbed in the Humvee which would transport him to Base Headquarters to meet the CO, and back.

Frisbee and I had no intention of staying overnight in the hanger so we slipped out a side door and claimed into our rigs, and headed back to our respective homes in Sin City. We'd returned before breakfast the next morning to participate in the live-fire exercises.

As I cleared the base gate, I made a mental note to try to contact Maggie DuPont once again when I got home to fill her in on what was going down. I know I had just received explicit orders not to, but if I couldn't trust the woman who had saved my life a couple of weeks before, who could I trust?

TWENTY-ONE

July 9, 2008, Wednesday, 3:00 a.m.
1000-yards east of the decommissioned ICBM Missile Silo
Nellis AFB Firing Range, Dry Lake
Northwest of Las Vegas, Nevada.

The four bomb guys had slipped out of the wash lugging the Halliburton-type aluminum case containing the PACKBOT and headed for the silo about five minutes earlier.

The Gillie suits that the agents on the HRT assault force were wearing made them appear to be large tumbleweeds.

Then the *Word* came down telling us to move out. Noise discipline was in-effect as the silo was just over a small hill less than 3,000-feet away. In the desert's night air, noise travels far.

The morning was blacker than a whore's heart. Each of us had a glow-stick taped to the rear of our helmets so the good guys wouldn't shot another good guy during our morning adventure. Everyone on the assault wore NVGs, night-vision goggles, which I kind of thought defeated the whole purpose of the glow-sticks, but then no one had asked me.

We could talk with one another and the taskforce commander over our encrypted personal communicators.

Frisbee and I were being babysat by a large 50-ish African-American FBI agent named Scrubs who I could tell was thrilled to have the responsibility. He was curt, and only spoke when absolutely necessary. We'd only gone a little over 500-yards before we began to approach the base of our side of the hill. I had some questions and decided to push my luck and ask them.

Keying the sound-absorbing microphone attached to the left breast pocket of my black coveralls, I switched over to the individual frequency assigned to Scrubs, and broke squelch. Nothing ventured, nothing gained, I thought.

Scrubs immediately came up on the frequency, and barked, "What's wrong, Agent? Tired out already? Want to take your buddy and go home?"

Speaking to the bush that was floating along in a graceful crotch ten feet in front of Billy and myself, I asked, "What is their security going to be like, Agent Scrubs?"

"Normally, and if I were them," the agent replied to me through the fob that was inserted in my ear, "I'd have put a lot of motion detectors on the fence, big locks on all the doors, and place about five of them in the outbuildings with sniper rifles. Course, this here confrontation isn't going to be *that* easy."

"Why not?" I asked.

"Because these guys have nothing to lose, that's why. Put yourself in their boots. They're responsible for killing at least four civilians, maybe more. We are assuming they have more money than god stashed in the launch control room 160-feet below-ground. And, no matter what Jefferson is telling the younger agents, they *know* we are coming. Have to. It is just default thinking on their part. Because that is exactly what they would be doing if they were the assault team and we were the bad guys."

"You think?" I asked. "How many of the rogue combatants does Jefferson think will be facing us? Seven?"

"If we are lucky. But it could be more. 30.5 million dollars in cash can buy a lot of idiots willing to risk their lives and future freedom to get a shot at some of that money. Now you and Frisbee check your equipment one more time. If I was planning an ambush, I'd place it just past the brow of this hill."

Scrubs continued, "If things start going bang, keep your head down but keep pressing on to the objective. If we get separated, just head for the large bush alongside the fence perimeter. Hopefully that will be me. When the shooting starts, remember you are responsible for Frisbee. If I take a round, just keep going. I'm a big boy and knew the risks when I signed on. Now stow the talk!" he said, as he broke the connection.

Ten minutes later, an excited voice came through our ear fobs. "Shit, Teams A and B. Be advised that the bang boys are at the crest of the hill, and have deployed PACKBOT. The robot has positively identified three Claymore booby mines, placed so they would take out anyone not wearing NVGs."

"You need to bypass us so we can disarm these things. And keep your NVGs on. The infrared goggles will pickup the coolness of a bomb casing better than your naked eyes ever could."

What I had just heard over the command net made my blood run cold. Even sarcastic agent Scrubs had no comment. Finding the Claymore ambush reminded all of us that we were dealing with highly-trained, experienced combat warriors. Who, even two years after their discharge, still had access to one of the U. S. military's most-feared individual weapons.

———

Claymores are generally placed in a daisy chain. In this type of configuration, each device must come with a minimum of 100-feet of detonation cord—and two timers—one for backup.

The Claymore is a weapon with a storied history. The device is made up of 650 grams of explosive and 700 small steel balls. The steel balls, when the mine is detonated, fly in a 60-degree arc covering up to 2-meters in height. For maximum affectivity claymores are placed on 25-meter centers to ensure overlap. Which guarantees a kill-zone of up to 50-meters.

The bowed casing surface of the device is embossed, "FRONT toward enemy." Cautions printed on each of the cardboard container states: *Fire only through the use of a hand 'clacker' or trip wire placed by a certified demolitions expert. Make certain to read all instructions before using. This blast from this personnel mine is highly-directional."*

The Claymore mine is an old but still awesome weapon when used as intended. A German named Schardin, working in concert with a Hungarian named Misznay, invented it during WWII. Both men loved the thought of blowing things up. The U.S. Army was prompt to adopt the weapon when the PRC began to send droves of Chinese over the North Korean Border into South Korea during the Korean 'Police Action' or Conflict.

The U.S. Military is not above stealing the original inventor's ideas, and upgrading them a bit to make it even more deadly to provide even greater protection for our troops.

The weapon propels metal balls in an arc, rather that a 360-degree circle, as a hand grenade is designed to do. The fact alone increases friendly-forces safety, avoiding blue-on-blue incidents. A blue-on-blue type incident, also called friendly forces incidents, killed former NFL great, Pat Tillman, in Iraq a couple of years ago.

By the time Vietnam rolled around, the redesigned Claymore was packed with 700 steel ball bearings that could make quick work of an enemy patrol attempting to overrun an American position, or approach their hidey-hole using a jungle trail.

It doesn't take a rocket scientist to set one up, just so he or she is bright enough to know what the inscription, "Front Towards Enemy," clearly stamped into the device, means.

You see, the device is contoured with the business end *towards* the enemy. But if the contour faces towards the soldier, he is in deep kimchi, which will be immediately rectified when the weapon detonates.

American soldiers are repeatedly lectured in basic training that if the contour of the weapon fits the contour of your forehead when you are facing in the direction the enemy is expected to come from, and then the device has been correctly placed. Wounds caused by Claymores are not pretty, but they are effective and likely to be terminal.

Claymores come to the battlefield in a claymore kit bandoleer. It contains a powerful M18A1 mine, the M57 firing device, the M40 test set, the spool with a 100 feet of firing wire, a electronic blasting cap, insulation tape, and two wooden stakes.

Some Special Forces troops refer the neat little kit as '*a package of death in a convenient carrying case.*'

The Germans in WWII had investigated the concept of a mine with a concave surface that would be capable of propelling a wall of steel projectiles through the armor of an enemy tank. By Vietnam, all most every infantryman carried a modern lightweight version of the Claymore, which had 700 steel balls that could devastate enemy personnel and take out thin-skinned vehicles. It was considered by modern field commanders to be the perfect ambush and perimeter defense tool. Again, the trick is to remember how to place it.

It had been named the Claymore, because like its namesake, the ancient Scottish broadsword, it could cut both ways.

The soldier uses its built-in spikes to solidly set the mine into the dirt. Then he stretches the trip wire low across the road, about four inches above the surface, and ties it to one of the wooden stakes provided. Then he runs a quick circuit test and stacks anything available, such as tumbleweeds, over the mine. It is generally placed during hours of darkness, which ensures that the hidey-hole of the placement team is less likely to be discovered.

The solder with the 'clacker'—the detonating device—has to be at least 20-yards behind it and under-cover because of the device's back blast.

Every member of the strike force was nervous, regardless of the fierce game faces they all wore. I thought, but wasn't asked, that leaving the HRT bomb squad, or the bang boys as they were called, behind to defuse the Claymores, only made sense if one knew for sure that the enemy didn't have a second emplacement of the explosive devices waiting ahead for us. But again, no one asked me.

Frisbee and I were following Scrubs down the front face of the small hill when firing began to come from inside the compound. Scrubs, was one of the four FBI agents that was hit immediately. He went down like a falling old-growth tree.

I yelled back at Frisbee to hold his position and crawled forward on my elbows and knees to render first-aid to the fallen agent as the intermittent firing from the compound continued.

I gagged and threw up when I reached the motionless man and saw the huge hole in his forehead. Wiping the vomit from my mouth with my hand, I looked away. Then grabbed my microphone and without taking time to clear the frequency, and said, "Jefferson, Scrubs is down. They're must be using a .50 caliber Barrett M82A1. I've practiced with that weapon at Quantico. No question. That's the only infantry weapon I know that can make a hole like this."

The Barrett is a light .50-caliber rifle, used for sniping and other uses, normally out-fitted with a Swarovsky ten-by-forty-two scope. The twenty-eight-pound rifle has a ten-round magazine loaded with Raufoss explosive armor-piecing rounds, and a muzzle brake, and is generally used as a sniper weapon, which requires a bipod to steady the weapon.

Jefferson's response nearly blew the fob out of my ear. "Fox, I can see that! I have two dead agents up here with me. You and Frisbee just keep pushing forward for the silo and met up at the fence as we planned. Don't stop to give aid to any of our guys who are down. I assume you have just observed firsthand that a .50-caliber full-metal-jacket shell doesn't leave any wounded. And keep your ass off the command frequency."

I rolled on my side and motioned for Billy to join me. When he didn't move, I tried his communicator. But he was in his own world, attempting to burrow himself under dirt to get away from the huge slugs that seemed to be whizzing like bees past our ears. So I broke the noise discipline rule, and yelled, "Billy, Get your ass up here."

While Billy reluctantly low-crawled up to my position, I did some mental arithmetic and came to the conclusion that counting the four bang boys that Jefferson had permitted to remain behind to defuse the claymores at the crest of the hill, and four agents already dead from sniping from inside the compound, our original force of sixteen shooters had been reduced to a group of eight. And we hadn't even reached our objective.

Glancing back every minute or so to make certain that Billy stayed directly in-trail behind me, I low-crawled the rest of the way down and off the west side of the hill.

I saw one of the agents ahead of us stand up and begin to 'bloop' high explosive rounds from a grenade launcher onto the silo's outbuildings. The buildings were constructed out of corrugated tin, deteriorated, and showed signs of eventual collapse.

Then once again, the sound of the easily-identifiable crack of a Barrett sniper rifle snapped through the air and the head was torn off the shoulders of the brave agent who had exposed himself to rain hellfire down on the outbuildings. But judging from the flames that were now raging through the outbuilding structures, I figured the agent had taken at least two of the snipers with him.

Then another agent crawled up to take the grenade launcher from the lifeless hands of his combat partner. As he raised it to his shoulder to continue the dead man's fusillade on the outbuilding, a lucky shot from a sniper, who had immediately then taken off running for the control bunker, unceremoniously blew the head of the second agent backward into the shrub grass.

At that point, Frisbee and I hopped to our feet, slung our M-16a's upside down over our shoulders, and ran hell-for-leather for the silo's perimeter fence. As I ran, I dragged my arm down enough low to permit me to snatch up the grenade launcher and a bandoleer of high-explosive rounds off the dead bodies as we sprinted for the fence.

I could see that Jefferson and three of our survivors were on the ground alongside the chainlink fence, and were attempting to cut their way through it using wire cutters.

Figuring I had a better wire cutter in my hands, I waved Frisbee ahead as I took a knee, loaded the single-shot blooper, and blew an eight-foot hole in the brittle chain-link fabric.

Then I remained where I was, and attempted to provide cover as Jefferson, Frisbee, and the remaining three agents jumped to their feet, dove through the smoking gap in the fenceline, and raced for the bunker firing their weapons on the go.

Then, out of the flaming embers of one of the smoking outbuildings, a sniper who had remained in-place to foil just this type of adrenaline-driven assault head-on, began to pick off the runners.

The first agent to be hit by the Barrett .50 caliber round was Jefferson. In no more than a microsecond from the team leader being shot, another round followed with Billy Frisbee's name on it.

A third and fourth shot tore off the arm and leg respectively off two more agents. I could do nothing as they lay silently on the ragged concrete. Only one was moving, and he was talking to himself has he attempted to field-dress a terrible wound.

I stayed on my knee, turned to the direction that the shots were coming from, and blooped round-after-round of H.E. into the burning building, as fast as I could fire and reload the weapon.

I began to wonder when the four bomb squad guys would arrive on-scene to provide cover fire for us. But then I decided that if I waited, we'd lose the momentum that had cost so many lives already. So I decided to throw the dice and just hope for the best.

Running out of HE, or high explosive, rounds for the blooper, I tossed it aside and ran up to the only remaining FBI agent still standing and dragged him along with me towards the door of the control bunker.

Noting that the that the young man was carrying a munitions bag, that told me he was one of the strike force's explosive experts referred to as a *powder monkey*, I shook him until he came out of his daze and gave me his full attention.

"Blow the door," I yelled in his face. "*Blow the goddamn door!*"

Suddenly, he mentally shrugged off his shock and returned to the present day. He acknowledged my command to blow the heavy door with a nod. Then dug around in his padded munitions backpack until he selected a device.

He waved me out of his way as he slapped a ring of thermal entry plastic onto the steel door, and then slapped a second breaching charge against the weathered steel surface, just to be certain he got the desired results.

He mimicked turning to his side and covering his eyes to me, and then did the same himself, as the plastic ignited with a sound that reminded me of the slow-burning explosion that launches the space shuttle into orbit.

I partially uncovered my eyes enough to see a searing white light and hear a pronounced 'crack' and 'clang' as the explosive first burned its way through the thick metal, then slammed the heavy door backwards into the entry foyer, as if it was weightless.

The explosion triggered an alarm that began to shatter the dark night. The sound was so loud, it reminded me that we had been provided with a pair of yellow-colored foam FBI shooting range ear plugs, that hopefully still were in a pocket under my bullet-resistant vest. Digging them out, I pinched them into a tight roll and jammed them into my aching ears.

The young explosives expert and I inched ourselves along the smoke-filled hallway, and over to the elevator that provided access down to the launch center 160-feet below.

We attempted to pry the elevator doors open with our bare hands, but for all our effort all we managed to accomplish was a six-inch-wide opening between the opposing steel doors. Unthinking the kid tried to maintain the gap we had fought for by inserting his munitions backpack into the opening. That move would soon return to haunt me.

August 23, 2008, Sunday, 2:00 p.m.
Nellis Air Force Base
Nellis Combat Support Hospital-Critical Care Ward
Las Vegas, Nevada

I would learn six weeks later while occupying a bed in Nellis' combat support hospital that among the munitions in that bag we had used as a doorstop was an experimental explosive known as a thermobaric device. The shock of the blocked door halves slamming back and forth against the bag had caused it to fall through the door opening and down the elevator shaft where the device had detonated.

The high-tech explosive was a device that our Marines in Iraq had begun using against insurgents only a couple years previously. Of course, the Marines never disclosed that it was one of the devices that our CIA stole from the Soviets who had been using it as far back as their war with Afghanistan.

The device utilized two principles: Thermobaric and overpressure. It created a humongous explosion that just kept on exploding, as long as any oxygen remained to feed its combustion. The device exploded, which carried molecules of the explosive along with its blast, which in turn, exploded.

Bottom line, it created a massive overpressure condition instantly killing everyone present, blasted away even massively-reinforced airlocks, and tossed heavy objects weighing tons through the air as if they were mere confetti.

One day I was surprised to receive a visitor. It was the young FBI explosives expert, now wearing an arm sling and a patch over one eye, who had been with me during the last moments of the strike on the silo. He introduced himself as David Chin.

He explained that the FBI had already taken his statement for the after-action-inquiry but were anxiously waiting until they received my doctor's okay before getting my statement. There would be an incident inquiry held at FBI headquarters. Nine FBI agents out of the fourteen who staffed the strike force had been killed during the raid.

Chin explained that the powers-that-be in Washington wanted to find out why the HRT team leader permitted the bomb squad to remain behind to defuse the Claymores. That decision in itself reduced the possibility of the mission's success as it reduced FBI manpower on the sharp point of the assault by a shocking 29%.

Chin told me he had avoided major injury when he suddenly had realized what was going to happen, and had subconsciously had thrown himself back out of harm's way. Otherwise he would of lost more than an eye and the hopefully temporary use of his arm

He told me what had happened, and that the Air Force was tending to my recovery in their base hospital, attempting to keep the Media away from me.

The thermobaric explosion had killed the renegade Marines who had sought safety in the below-ground launch center. The gang had chosen to hide the money, except for thirty thousand in cash they'd apparently used for expenses, in a small space left in the adjacent missile launch silo, which the Air Force had previously mostly filled with concrete. The heavy blast doors between the silo and the launch control room had protected the money from the thermobaric explosion.

The bodies of the dead Marines had been turned over to the Department of Defense for burial. Because some of the dead had been decorated Marines, those particular bodies would likely end up being interred in the national cemetery at Arlington. The other men's remains would be offered to their families. If they failed to claim them, then the remains would be buried in a pauper's grave.

As soon as the Las Vegas coroner had finished with the post-mortems, the FBI, with permission from their families, had loaded all the FBI agent's bodies onto an Air Force C-17 and flew them directly to Manassas Airport. That is the airport that HRT uses for its deployments.

———

To get to the airport, you exit from Quantico's rear gate then go northwest along State Route 234 like you were headed towards Dulles International. When your odometer indicates that you have driven thirty miles, you'll see Manassas airport on the right.

———

After Special Agent Billy Frisbee's autopsy, his girlfriend had claimed the body, and understandably, refused to permit any of the man's co-workers to attend his funeral.

Doctors told me that I would be discharged from Nellis in a couple weeks. As I still had to walk without a cane, and my burns hadn't yet healed fully, an Air Force ambulance would be provided to transport me home to my condo in Henderson when I was discharged.

As soon as I felt able, the FBI and the director of Nevada's Gaming Control Board had requested a common interview, with me to decide the time, and they, the place of the meeting.

Four citizens, twelve ex-Marines, nine FBI agents, and my partner had been killed. I knew some would wonder how someone who had less than four months on the job as a Nevada State Gaming Control Board Special Agent, could have survived the slaughter. That was a question I was asking myself everyday, of every week, of every month, and would continue to do so throughout my life.

TWENTY-TWO

September 15, 2008, Monday, 11:00 a.m.
Maggie DuPont's family home
1700 Lazy Robin Blvd
Carson City, Nevada

 Towards the end of my disability leave, I had received an unexpected call at my home from Maggie DuPont's mother. She asked if it would be possible for me to visit and have lunch with an old lady when I next found myself in Carson City?
 I'd decided not to tell the woman that I was disappointed that Maggie hadn't called or visited during my hospitalization and recovery period. In fact, she hadn't answered any of my calls for the two-weeks prior to the raid either.
 But I had to admit I was dying of boredom sitting around the condo. I tried to stay busy watching sports on my big screen, but you only can watch so much sports before you go nuts.
 Since I had to fly to Carson City on Monday anyway to get a GCB physical, permitting me to return to work full-time, I agreed to stop by and have lunch with the woman.
 I figure I'd have time to have lunch with Maggie's mom in the morning, then stop at the Nevada Medical Center for my physical, and if there was still time before my flight back to Las Vegas late that afternoon, perhaps swing by the GCB office and find out what was keeping Maggie so busy that she couldn't find time to return my phone messages.

Monday morning, September 1st, I was following through on that promise when I knocked on the front door of well-maintained two-story white house with green trim at 11:00 a. m.

Mrs. DuPont answered the door in a wheelchair. She appeared weak, drawn, and tired, and was wearing a clear plastic nasal cannula, which hung back over her shoulders to connect to an oxygen bottle.

Waiting until after I introduced myself, she waved me in, told me to lay my coat anywhere, and took me into the dining room where place settings for two had been set next to one another at the end of the a large walnut table.

She waved me to my seat, and asked me what I preferred to drink? I told her "Ice tea, if you have it," and offered to help the woman serve. She refused saying she was used to getting around in the wheelchair and *didn't need assistance from anyone.*

She was balancing our beverages on a tray when she returned from the kitchen. Once she had placed those on the table, she spun her chair around and returned to the kitchen.

In a couple minutes she reappeared balancing chilled watercress salads on her tray. She carefully set those on the table before setting the tray on the floor alongside where she was sitting.

I decided to open the conversation. "Mrs. DuPont, I couldn't help but notice the table is set for two. I hoped that Maggie would be joining us for lunch. I haven't seen or heard from her since she returned home to GCB Headquarters after saving my life."

The woman hesitated for a minute, and then her eyes flooded with tears.

"No, Mr. Fox, Maggie won't be joining us. You see she died last week from colon cancer. She must have not shared her disease with you."

I was so shocked and unprepared by what I had just heard, I dropped the glass of ice tea I had been sipping, which fell hitting the table, and glass and tea went everywhere.

I hurried into the kitchen to grab a couple dishtowels, returned to the table, and blotted up the spilled tea, carefully picked up the broken shards of glass before carrying it all outside and putting it into one of her clamp-lid-garbage cans.

I returned to the table and took my seat.

Mrs. DuPont began speaking. "As my mother would have said, Maggie thought you were the cat's meow, Agent Fox. She spoke about you constantly, how good-looking you were, what personal tribulations you had faced in your own life, and how she had harassed you about her pet peeve."

When I found my voice, I asked, "And what was her pet peeve? I know she seemed a little obsessed in wanting to know how my dead wife and I coped in her final days before she died of cancer. How I had later dealt with her death, which wasn't very admirable."

I continued, "Then I again lost a loved one when I was with the police in Hong Kong. My girl friend was tortured and murdered by a rogue police officer in a misguided attempt to stop my investigation into police corruption."

"And I was living in China with my son's mother who is a Medical Doctor. I was forced to leave the country because I refused to become an agent for their secret police and spy on American tourists during the upcoming Summer Olympics in Beijing. My son's mother apparently decided a life among the new China elite would be far superior than tying her skirt to a worse-for-wear middle-aged Caucasian cop who wasn't even gainfully employed at the time. So she elected to remain in China with our son."

"Mr. Fox," the woman interrupted, "Maggie wanted to die with dignity. She kept the knowledge of her fatal disease from you and her other co-workers because she didn't want to burden you. Didn't want to be treated like she was anything but what she was, an agent able to do her job. And, I don't think she knew what to do when she first realized that she had fallen in love with you."

I stood and moved over to the grieving old woman and wrapped her in my arms. Before I knew it, my tears had joined hers in memory of a brave woman who just wanted to go out with dignity. Without becoming a burden to anyone. And all this without me ever suspecting the love that burned in her breast.

GLOSSARY

ALLAHU AKBER: God is Great

ASR: The call to Muslim prayers.

AUTOTRAK: A private service that a police department can contract with to locate individuals. Some government databases are often out of date (IE Drivers licenses renewed only every number of years). The service searches all public records including DMV, public utilities, the Courts, Labor and Industries, cable service and credit agencies to determine individual's present and past addresses.

BALISONG: Filipino flip knife.

BEIJING: China's capital city. Formerly, and sometimes still, referred to as Pēking.

BOA: Bank of China.

BOLO: International police procedural for, be-on-the-lookout.

BOOC: Beijing Olympic Organizing Committee.

CARS: Collision Analysis Reconstruction Section.

COD: Cause of Death.

CODIS: Computerized method of comparing known DNA files. The combined DNA Index System. Renamed National DNA Index System by FBI in 1988.

CRUSADER: An uncomplimentary Muslim term for any foreigner that is in their country, especially Americans.

CYANOACRYLATE: Superglue fumes in an enclosed container that can reveal fingerprints that are nearly invisible to the naked eye.

DATA BASES, FINGERPRINT: Ten-Print, Palm-Print, Latent and Partial Print.

ERT: FBI Evidence Response Team

EXEMPLAR: In Forensics, an exact copy, such as a *positive* casting of a shoe tread; fingerprint cards; a *positive* impression of the bite from a set of teeth.

FLIGHT-OR-FIGHT: When confronted by a dangerous situation, you get sweaty palms and your body introduces more adrenaline into your blood stream. Your breathing and heart rates increase and your muscles get ready to either run away or face the danger.

FOB: Forward operating base.

GUTRA: Arab headdress.

IAFIS: FBI's Integrated Automatic Fingerprint Identification System.

IED: Improvised explosive device.

IMAN: Muslim cleric.

INDICES, FINGERPRINT: Loops, ridge counts, islands, ulnar loops, deltas, bifurcations, whorls, and tented arches.

INSTANT INMATE SINCERITY: Defined as a means by which to identify an ex-con.

ME: Medical Examiner.

MITOCHONDRIAL DNA: An involved, costly process used mostly on bones, hair shafts, and highly-degraded DNA samples of all types. Process can take thirty-to-ninety-days to complete. A preliminary

DNA profile of blood or tissue by a cheaper, if less exacting, method can be accomplished in seven-to—seventeen days.

MO: Modus Operandi.

MOOK: A scumbag, criminal, degenerate, military deserter.

NCIC: National Crime Index computer. Television almost has convinced most civilians that NCIC stands for National Crime Identification Center.

OCKHAM'S RAZOR: A principle stated by William of Ockham in the mid-1200's, that loosely translated from the Latin (*Pluralitas Non Est Ponenda Sine Necessitate*) is 'Do not make things unnecessarily complicated without necessity.'

OPEN CITY: Mob-speak for a city not under the control of any one gang.

PCR: Polymerase Chain Reaction. The latest in DNA profiling. It is further enhanced by STR—Short Tandem Repeats. Which can be used on bloodstain samples as small as a dot on this typed page.

PERP: Perpetrator.

PM: Post-mortem. A forensic autopsy.

POPULATION: Las Vegas' population is roughly 1.8 million residents.

PROBATIVE: Qualifying as evidence. Serving to test or prove. Furnished as proof.

RAPID START: A management tool adopted by the Federal Bureau Of Investigation that permits interchanging of personnel assigned to a particular case, without the necessity of the individual having to go through a learning curve to acquire the history of the case. *Rapid Start* lays out the pertinent facts on a case, graphically, and only requires that the primary agent on a case, or his or her designee, maintain and update the *Rapid Start* graphic file every twenty-four hours, or less, if appropriate. A newly-assigned agent need only pull up the case file on his secure laptop computer to familiarize himself on the sequence of events and facts, from case inception to current day, which permits the agent to be productive from day one, if not hour one.

RPG: Rifle or rocket propelled grenade.

SALAAM ALEIKUM: Peace be with you.

SALAT: The required intonation of Muslim prayer five-times-a-day.

STR: Short Tandem Repeat. DNA Method that along with PCR, replaced RFLP.

TOD: Forensic and police procedural term for Time of Death.

TRAVELING ROAD SHOW: A term for the FBI's invaluable program of providing training to local police departments across the country. Typically, the FBI's training agents go to a central point in the jurisdiction, and the police officers from the local departments travel to that location on a daily basis, saving their departments the attending student's travel and lodging expenses.

TRANNY: A transvestite.

TROBE: An Arabic robe.

UNSUB: FBI-speak for an unknown subject.

ABOUT THE AUTHOR

The Author's diverse career history includes military service, teaching college-level martial arts, instructing Scuba diving, technical engineering on the Boeing Supersonic Jet Transport program and in the commercial aircraft manufacturing and aerospace industries. His career continued in administrative law enforcement, and as a pilot in aviation. Mr. Stollwerck recently retired after a career with a major international airline. He remains active in physical fitness training and writing. This is his eighth novel.

Mr. Stollwerck holds a FAA Commercial Pilot's license for the operation of fixed-wing, high-performance, multi-engine aircraft; as well as turbine-powered rotorcraft (jet-turbine helicopters). The author is U.S. Coast Guard-certified in Advanced Coastal/Celestial navigation and Command/Operation of high-powered boats such as multi-engine offshore racers.

The Federal Bureau of Investigation has certificated the author as a Combat Firearms instructor. He also holds certification in a course on Advanced Law Enforcement taught by the FBI and Washington State Criminal Justice Commission.

Mr. Stollwerck spends his time between residences in Washington State and Lake Havasu City on the Colorado River, and currently is working on his ninth novel.

Email: Ghstoll@NPGCABLE.COM

Made in the USA
Middletown, DE
07 May 2022